IMPOSSIBLE

'Holy s***. This book. I loved everything about it. The zingy dialogue, the romance, the suspense . . . It's a love story of the greatest kind' GILLIAN MCALLISTER

'What an absolute joy of a book. I completely fell in love with Bee and Nick and their impossible situation. Witty, engaging and so emotionally resonant, *Impossible* is the book we all need right now' SARAH PINBOROUGH

'It's warm, funny, clever, creative, thrilling. I feel the same way as when I first read *One Day*. It's going to be a classic' EMMA GANNON

'I was utterly hooked from the start . . . Full of twists that made it genuinely unputdownable' JENNIFER SAINT

'It blew my mind. Some books become cultural touchstones that people bond over for years, like *One Day* or *The Time Traveler's Wife*. *Impossible* is one of those books' LAURA PEARSON

'Amazing, an actual masterpiece. There will not be a book I love more in 2022' ANSTEY HARRIS

'Indeed amazing. It has twisted my brain – in a good way – and made me wonder how much of it could be true. Ingenious and beautifully executed' JILL MANSELL

‘I blinked and I was fifty pages in. It’s breathtakingly good, it has blockbuster movie written all over it’ JOSIE SILVER

‘I have devoured *Impossible* . . . It’s so funny, so original – I am seething with envy that I didn’t write it myself’ SOPHIE COUSENS

‘Such a clever, hilarious read with characters so real, I’ll never forget them. One of the best, most original love stories I’ve ever read’

JESSICA RYN

‘Heart-warming, compelling and intoxicating, a very modern love story about a tale as old as time: how far would you go for true love?’ ARAMINTA HALL

‘Really memorable and special. A work of total genius’

SARAH J HARRIS

‘The book I never knew I was desperate to read. Characters who felt real from the first line, pacy, realistic drama and an absolutely mind-bending early twist. I *loved* it’ EMILY ELGAR

IMPOSSIBLE

Sarah Lotz

HarperCollins*Publishers*

HarperCollins*Publishers* Ltd
1 London Bridge Street,
London SE1 9GF
www.harpercollins.co.uk

HarperCollins*Publishers*
1st Floor, Watermarque Building, Ringsend Road
Dublin 4, Ireland

First published by HarperCollins*Publishers* 2022
1

A catalogue record for this book is available from the British Library

ISBN: 978-0-00-846400-4 (HB)
ISBN: 978-0-00-846401-1 (TPB)

Typeset in Sabon LT Std by Palimpsest Book Production Ltd, Falkirk, Stirlingshire

Printed and bound in the UK using 100% renewable electricity
by CPI Group (UK) Ltd

MIX
Paper from
responsible sources
FSC C007454

This book is produced from independently certified FSC™ paper
to ensure responsible forest management.

For more information visit: www.harpercollins.co.uk/green

For my sister-elves Paige Nick and Helen Moffett,
whose love and support makes the
impossible seem possible

PART ONE

YOU GOT MAIL

From: NB26@zone.com
To: Bee1984@gmail.com
Subject: What the HELL is wrong with you?

Listen you tight-fisted pea-brained grouse-shooting tweedy twat, you may own half the fucking countryside but you don't own me. You think I *like* hounding you? You think this is *fun* for me? But if you think I'm just going to lie back and let you screw me over like you no doubt screw over everyone who comes into your entitled orbit of damp lolling spaniels, vintage Land Rovers and Eton-induced PTSD then you've got another think coming.

DO THE RIGHT THING FOR ONCE IN YOUR BADGER-BAITING FOX-SLAUGHTERING LIFE.

From: Bee1984@gmail.com
To: NB26@zone.com
Subject: What the HELL is wrong with you?

Hi.

You might want to double-check the recipient address. Far as I know, I've never owned a Land Rover & have definitely never been to Eton (don't have the right equipment). Or is this a fiendishly creative scam & you're using my response to embed malware? If so, you got me. Enjoy!

From: NB26@zone.com
To: Bee1984@gmail.com
Subject: What the HELL is wrong with you?

Gawd. I'm so bloody sorry. Using a new account and mis-copied the address. Angry fingers. Thanks for replying and letting me know. Sorry you had to read that, whoever you are.

From: Bee1984@gmail.com
To: NB26@zone.com
Subject: What the HELL is wrong with you?

TBH almost didn't reply, but that was some impressive Malcolm Tucker-grade cursing you did there, & I was intrigued. Did the intended recipient kill your cat or something?

From: NB26@zone.com
To: Bee1984@gmail.com
Subject: What the HELL is wrong with you?

Worse. Didn't pay me for work owed. That's the toned-down version believe it or not. Took out all the 'C' words at the last minute. There were a lot of those.

From: Bee1984@gmail.com
To: NB26@zone.com
Subject: What the HELL is wrong with you?

What kind of work? You don't have to answer obvs, I'm killing time. Don't usually strike up conversations with complete strangers I swear!

From: NB26@zone.com
To: Bee1984@gmail.com
Subject: What the HELL is wrong with you?

You deserve an answer – I did unintentionally call you a twat. I'm a freelance editor and my tweedy arse of a client commissioned me to edit his novel. Ended up rewriting the thing, pretty much from scratch. Sent it to him 2 months ago. No feedback. No payment. Nada.

From: Bee1984@gmail.com
To: NB26@zone.com
Subject: What the HELL is wrong with you?

Very sorry to hear that. What was the novel about? The Girl in the Grouse Shoot?

From: NB26@zone.com
To: Bee1984@gmail.com
Subject: What the HELL is wrong with you?

HA! Close! You really want to know?

From: Bee1984@gmail.com
To: NB26@zone.com
Subject: What the HELL is wrong with you?

Sure. You'll be saving me from the perils of online shopping. I've already bought a duvet cover with David Bowie's face on it that I don't need.

From: NB26@zone.com
To: Bee1984@gmail.com
Subject: What the HELL is wrong with you?

You can never have too much Bowie. I'd sleep under him and I'm as straight as they come. Crime novel. Not a bad plot. The remains of a body are unearthed on a country estate. Turns out to be a violent hunt saboteur who went missing in the 80s. Narrated by a landowner who may or may not have killed him . . .

From: Bee1984@gmail.com
To: NB26@zone.com
Subject: What the HELL is wrong with you?

Well don't keep me in suspense. DID he kill him?

From: NB26@zone.com
To: Bee1984@gmail.com
Subject: What the HELL is wrong with you?

Yeah. Accidentally on purpose. Like you do when you have guns to hand and the underclass try to mess with your blood sports. Supposed to be morally ambiguous but not sure I pulled that off. Hard to get a reader to root for a main character whose idea of a good time is killing baby animals.

From: Bee1984@gmail.com
To: NB26@zone.com
Subject: What the HELL is wrong with you?

Is it autobiographical? If so, you might want to tone down that message . . .

From: NB26@zone.com
To: Bee1984@gmail.com
Subject: What the HELL is wrong with you?

Wouldn't put it past him. Nah. That's not fair. Said he didn't do that kind of thing anymore.

From: Bee1984@gmail.com
To: NB26@zone.com
Subject: What the HELL is wrong with you?

What kind of thing? Hunting or murder?

From: NB26@zone.com
To: Bee1984@gmail.com
Subject: What the HELL is wrong with you?

Both (I hope). Thing is, despite the tweedy twatness, I quite liked him when we met. Old bugger, generous with the booze, lives in one of those crumbling stately homes straight out of a period drama about emotionally stunted aristocrats. Said he wanted to write a novel before he died but 'didn't have the time'. They always say that. Worked my arse off on his manuscript, sent it to him and apart from a 'thanks, will read asap' haven't heard a word.

But you don't want to hear all this.

From: Bee1984@gmail.com
To: NB26@zone.com
Subject: What the HELL is wrong with you?

I share your pain. Non-Paying Clients from Hell are the freelancers' curse.

From: NB26@zone.com
To: Bee1984@gmail.com
Subject: What the HELL is wrong with you?

Spoken like a fellow sufferer. What field are you in?

From: Bee1984@gmail.com
To: NB26@zone.com
Subject: What the HELL is wrong with you?

If I told you that, I'd have to kill you.

From: NB26@zone.com
To: Bee1984@gmail.com
Subject: What the HELL is wrong with you?

You'd be doing me a favour the way things are going. If you're an assassin I might commission you. Only . . . can I pay you in instalments?

From: Bee1984@gmail.com
To: NB26@zone.com
Subject: What the HELL is wrong with you?

Ha ha. Nothing that exciting. I'm in fashion. Kind of.

From: NB26@zone.com
To: Bee1984@gmail.com
Subject: What the HELL is wrong with you?

Kind of? Tell me more. Just so you know, my idea of fashion is trousers that aren't covered in dog hair.

From: Bee1984@gmail.com
To: NB26@zone.com
Subject: What the HELL is wrong with you?

I'm more of a glorified seamstress. Have a small business repurposing wedding dresses.

From: NB26@zone.com
To: Bee1984@gmail.com
Subject: What the HELL is wrong with you?

What do you repurpose them into? Shrouds? Doilies?

From: NB26@zone.com
To: Bee1984@gmail.com
Subject: What the HELL is wrong with you?

Sorry. That was rude. I'm a dick. It sounds cool. And e-friendly.

From: Bee1984@gmail.com
To: NB26@zone.com
Subject: What the HELL is wrong with you?

Feel free to take the piss! I do it all the time. Hmm. Shrouds. Hadn't thought of that. Could start a new line: 'Till death us do part'.

I repurpose them into whatever the client wants. 'Give the most expensive dress you ever bought a new lease of life' kind of thing. Get a lot of divorcees actually.

From: NB26@zone.com
To: Bee1984@gmail.com
Subject: What the HELL is wrong with you?

Aha. A 'fuck you ex-husband/wife' dress?

From: Bee1984@gmail.com
To: NB26@zone.com
Subject: What the HELL is wrong with you?

Exactly. Waiting for a client to pitch for a fitting right now. She's a bit of a pain in the arse TBH, which is why I was self-medicating with Bowie merchandise.

From: NB26@zone.com
To: Bee1984@gmail.com
Subject: What the HELL is wrong with you?

Tell me more. Misery loves company.

From: Bee1984@gmail.com
To: NB26@zone.com
Subject: What the HELL is wrong with you?

She can't make up her mind. Been back 3 times. 'I've been thinking, can it be asymmetrical? With a peplum? With a jacket maybe? Can we do it in black? No, scratch that, peach?'

Listen to me, whingeing to a stranger. I sound like a total cow. She's got every right to be fussy. She's the one paying.

From: NB26@zone.com
To: Bee1984@gmail.com
Subject: What the HELL is wrong with you?

It's easier to whinge to a stranger and you've already listened to me going on about my own shitty client. Hold on. BRB.

From: NB26@zone.com
To: Bee1984@gmail.com
Subject: What the HELL is wrong with you?

Sorry had to let the dog out. When she needs to go she needs to go.

From: Bee1984@gmail.com
To: NB26@zone.com
Subject: What the HELL is wrong with you?

What type?

From: NB26@zone.com
To: Bee1984@gmail.com
Subject: What the HELL is wrong with you?

A shit I think.

From: Bee1984@gmail.com
To: NB26@zone.com
Subject: What the HELL is wrong with you?

V funny. What type of dog!!!

From: NB26@zone.com
To: Bee1984@gmail.com
Subject: What the HELL is wrong with you?

Mongrel. Like her owner. Let me know if you need me to write Ms Peach a strongly worded e-mail. I'll even throw in a few 'C' words for free.

From: Bee1984@gmail.com
To: NB26@zone.com
Subject: What the HELL is wrong with you?

And I can help you out by badly altering your client's tweedy suits.

We could be a low-rent version of Strangers on a Train!

From: NB26@zone.com
To: Bee1984@gmail.com
Subject: What the HELL is wrong with you?

Strangers on a Train?

From: Bee1984@gmail.com
To: NB26@zone.com
Subject: What the HELL is wrong with you?

The novel? You MUST know it! Movie as well. 2 strangers meet & then decide to kill each other's enemies or whatever. Patricia Highsmith.

From: NB26@zone.com
To: Bee1984@gmail.com
Subject: What the HELL is wrong with you?

AH – I know it as Crossed Lines. Must have read the US version. Sometimes they change the titles.

From: Bee1984@gmail.com
To: NB26@zone.com
Subject: What the HELL is wrong with you?

You're in the US?

From: NB26@zone.com
To: Bee1984@gmail.com
Subject: What the HELL is wrong with you?

Nah. Way more glamorous. Leeds.

From: Bee1984@gmail.com
To: NB26@zone.com
Subject: What the HELL is wrong with you?

OK the client's just texted & is on her way. Let me know how it goes with Tweedy Twat, stranger. I have to know how it ends. Also, not for me to say but might be best if you did tone down that message. Never show them that they've got to you.

From: NB26@zone.com
To: Bee1984@gmail.com
Subject: What the HELL is wrong with you?

You're right. You did me a favour by intercepting it. And let me know how it goes with Ms Peach.

Shouldn't we introduce ourselves?

From: Bee1984@gmail.com
To: NB26@zone.com
Subject: What the HELL is wrong with you?

I'm Bee. You're NB.

Strangers on the Interwebs. That way if we ever need each other we'll have plausible deniability ☺

She's here! Wish me luck.

From: NB26@zone.com
To: Bee1984@gmail.com
Subject: What the HELL is wrong with you?

Ok Bee. And thank you. You pulled me out of a dark place today. You really did.

BEE

It's astounding how many red flags there were, right from the start. *Strangers on a Train* was just the first of many. Would things have been different if we'd been less complacent and picked up on them? Maybe. Maybe that would have simply fast-tracked us into the craziness to come. Maybe one of us would have assumed the other was delusional and walked away. Then there's this: I still don't know what made me check that old Gmail account that day. I hadn't used it for weeks. And who answers random e-mails from strangers? (Idiots, that's who.)

NB was the one who got back in touch first (<how did it go with Ms Peach? She asked you to make her a leopard-print cat suit yet? Please say yes>), but I was the one who instigated the next step, nudging us from being little more than strangers swapping silly banter into something deeper. It wasn't intentional. At that stage, I wasn't daydreaming about moving to Leeds, reading the Sunday papers in bed and going for long walks on the moors (or wherever people walk in Leeds). But right from the start, there was no doubt that NB and I had a good thing going: an instant ease between us, a lack of judgement that was both fun and freeing, and an unspoken pact to avoid thorny topics or anything too personal – no relationship or sex stuff. Which I suppose makes it ironic that the seeds of the next step were planted while I was on a date with another virtual stranger. I did a fair bit of that back then, rarely going further than a one-night hook-up. My best mate Leila said I was addicted to the roulette wheel of the dating app, the thrill of discovering if it would land on Oh Hell No, Maybe, or Shag. 'Classic commitment-phobic behaviour,' she'd say whenever she found out that I'd swiped right again. 'Using mindless sex with strangers to fill a hole' (Leila never missed an opportunity for a double entendre. She was also right about me).

The date ('Matt 36') had suggested we meet in one of those new hedge-funded bistros in White City, a choice of venue that should have set alarm bells ringing the second the text came through. Faux animal heads on the walls, vintage oils customised with spray paint, leather-clad booths designed with Instagram rather than comfort in mind, and staff dripping with ironic tattoos and smugness. We hadn't texted much beforehand – I'd been swamped with work; he said he hated online correspondence – so apart from the fact that he had crap taste in restaurants, I knew little about him. His profile pics had all the hallmarks of being professionally shot, and his three-line bio was as non-committal as they get: *Strong. Silent. Secure in myself*. Not that I was anyone to judge. My profile – *Funked up. Have soul. Bring snacks* – was both shite and trite, and I only used it because it made Leila crack up.

I'd arrived early, hair still damp from the shower, and picked out a booth that gave me a clear view of the entrance. Despite the nervousness I always felt whenever I dipped a toe in Tinder's foetid waters, I was in an upbeat mood that evening. I'd delivered Ms Peach's dress the day before (yes, in peach, and yes, asymmetrical, a nightmare to seam), and she'd shared pics of her wearing it on a girls' night out (#transformation). She looked happy – triumphant, almost. For her the dress was a symbol that she'd left behind a marriage that had run its course, and it made all the hoops I'd jumped through worth it (and yes, I did feel guilty for whingeing about her). I considered forwarding the link to NB, but as she'd name-checked me, it would be the work of seconds for him to find out exactly who I was, and I was reluctant to mess with our Strangers on the Internet shtick.

Matt 36 was only five minutes late, arriving as I was midway through my second 'chocalottini'. On first impression, he was a definite Maybe: a faint trace of a Geordie accent; resembled his profile pics to a surprising degree, ordered a JD on the rocks so wasn't a health freak. It went downhill from there. After a polite laugh when I joked about the grimacing elephant head stuck above the bar, he launched into a monologue about the drop in London's property prices; kept ricocheting back to the subject. Rationalising that the babble was a sign that he was as nervous as I was didn't help – that would mean two-thirds of his bio was bullshit.

My phone buzzed in my pocket, and I laughed as I sneaked a glimpse at it under the table. Another e-mail from NB: <SO. Would you rather be a reverse centaur or a reverse mermaid?> We'd been trading childish 'would you rather' silliness all day.

Matt 36 paused, mid-stream. 'Did I say something funny?'

'No. I'm sorry. Just nervous. I don't do this very often.'

He let the lie pass, smiled and slung an arm across the back of the booth's slippery skin. 'Me neither. You said you're a designer?' I'd downplayed the success of my business to NB – no one likes a show-off – and to be fair, I still couldn't believe how well it was doing. 'For Frock's Sake' (a drunkenly conceived name) had started when I'd revamped Leila's wedding dress as a birthday gift, more for a laugh than anything else. She'd splashed it all over Instagram, and almost overnight, requests and commissions had flooded in. It had grown to the point where I had a six-month waiting list, allowing me to quit my soul-destroying gig designing sportswear for a fast-fashion outlet. To his credit, Matt 36 listened to this potted history without letting his eyes glaze over, and then asked about my clients.

'I think my favourite were the couple who wanted their wedding suits turned into cushions.' I'd thought that commission was charming and witty, and when I'd told NB about it, he had too (<but hope you took the pins out>).

Matt 36 just looked confused. 'Cushions? *Seriously*?'

And with that, he went from a weak Maybe to a Hell No. If the waiter hadn't chosen that moment to glide up, brandishing menus, I would have called it a night right then. But there was nothing back at the flat: I'd forgotten to put the Tesco order in again, and the delicious odours wafting out of the kitchen almost made up for the crap décor. I went for the poutine, and Matt 36 chose the same. When the waiter was out of earshot he leaned across the table and admitted that he didn't actually know what poutine was, which made me soften a little towards him.

'It's basically a big pile of chips, gravy and cheese. All the good things.' I only knew what it was because I'd seen it on *MasterChef*.

He laughed, genuinely this time.

My phone trembled again, and I excused myself and made for the ladies' room. The mirrors were shaped like eyes and the poor lighting made it impossible to tell if I'd reached the part of the evening where my mascara would defect to my cheeks.

<Sorry NB. Can't really talk> I thought for a second, then added: <On a date> It was crossing the 'nothing personal' line we'd adopted, but hey-ho, blame it on the booze.

For once he didn't respond immediately. A minute passed. Then another. I was considering sending another message, something jokey this time, when in came: <Ok. Catch you later maybe. Have fun!>

I was reluctant to let him go, especially considering what was waiting for me back in the restaurant. <Actually do have a few minutes to chat if you like?>

<Won't your date mind?>

<I'm in the toilets>

<Hiding out? Or doing coke?>

<Coke with a capital 'C' is more my style. Just taking a break>

<Doesn't sound promising . . .>

<Had worse>

<Got his own teeth?>

<Think so. Well, he paid for them anyway>

<What does he do?>

Mr Secure-ish had told me, but I couldn't remember. <Dunno. Something corporate maybe? Wears a suit, has a fancy satchel-type bag ☺>

<A fancy satchel, eh? Maybe he's a very old-looking schoolboy. Or a postman. Or both>

<Ha ha. A very stylish schoolboy/postman>

<Not your type?>

<Don't have one>

<Everyone has a type>

<I don't. I'm an equal opportunities dater>

<Ah. Broadminded>

I tapped in: <That's a nice way of saying desperate> then deleted it. <Let's just say I'm not that picky>

<Really? So there's hope for all the single neo-Nazis who run puppy mills then?>

<Depends. Do I get a free puppy?>

<No, but think of the perks. Rallies, marches, Macklemore haircuts, hanging around with large groups of bare-chested men, nights in police cells . . .>

<Mmm sexy. OK, so: no Nazis, neo or otherwise, property developers, vivisectionists, homeopaths, cult members, Tories, SUV owners, climate-change deniers, golfers, swingers, hedge fund managers> And then I added: <And no married men>

That was his opening to write back: 'That counts me out then!', but all I received was: <good call>. It would have been the easiest thing in the world to ask him if he was married, engaged, seeing someone, but something held me back. Honestly? At that stage, I didn't want to know. If he *were* in a relationship, he'd recently spent far too much time bantering with a strange woman, which, while not cheating exactly, wouldn't have sat right with me.

<How did you and Satchel Man meet?>

I considered fudging the truth, but why should I? It wasn't as if I was doing anything shameful. <Tinder>

<?????>

<The dating app?>

<Never heard of it. Sad old git out of the loop>

Another red flag: who hasn't heard of Tinder? But I let it go.

Like I let all of them go until it was too late. <how old of a git? You don't have to tell me of course. I'm prying . . .>

<Approx 315 in dog years. On the cusp of a mid-life crisis. Or euthanasia>

<Dog years. Divide by 7, right?> I did the maths – of course I did. If he was being truthful, he was mid-forties or thereabouts. Acceptable.

<Not always. It can vary if you've been neutered or have a pedigree. You?>

<273 years young. No pedigree though. Better get back. He'll think I've done a runner>

<Good luck. Keep me posted>

Back in the restaurant, my food was waiting for me. Satchel Man hadn't started eating, seemingly disturbed by the tower of carbs on his plate. I dug in, too hungry to be self-conscious.

He eyed me patronisingly. 'I like a woman who eats.'

'Everyone eats.'

'My ex didn't.'

I sighed inwardly. Still, a bad relationship story was more exciting than the property market, safer than religion or politics, and he didn't need any encouragement to spill the details, which came out with a hefty side order of bitterness. A six-year relationship, no kids, drifted apart, issues with trust, ended badly. They were selling the flat in Brixton, which explained his obsession with property prices.

As I ate and he talked, I kept being drawn to my phone like the worst kind of social media addict. *Keep me posted*. 'What did you say you do again?' I asked, when he paused for breath.

'Actuary.'

I stealthily tapped in: <Found out what he does. He's in MI5. Black ops>

<Licensed to carry a ridiculous bag?>

If Satchel Man noticed I was cheating on him with my phone, he didn't seem to care. He pushed his plate away and waved for the bill. 'Are we going to split this, or . . .?'

'Or what? Course we're going to split this.'

He shrugged. 'I don't mind paying if we're going to fuck.'

I laughed, assuming he was joking. 'Deal. As long as you throw in dessert.'

'Really?'

'No. We're not going to do that.'

He leaned in close, invading my space. His breath was sour. 'Should have known you'd be a time-wasting bitch. And some advice for you. If you're going to keep doing this, best get down to hunting weight, yeah?'

He hadn't raised his voice, but the vicious undercurrent stole my breath as effectively as if he'd punched me in the gut. With a smirk, he got up and left, leaving me with the bill. My hands shook as I swiped the card, so much so that even the self-involved waiter asked if I was okay. Was I? Nowhere close. So far, I'd managed to avoid the usual dating horror stories, stupidly thought I had it taped.

On the way home I took a medicinal detour into a Tesco Metro for Pringles, and by the time I reached my street, my tongue was burning from too much salt. I'd left a light on, but not even Clarice's silhouette at the front window comforted me. I showered, then made for the kitchen table, the nucleus of my makeshift studio, where my latest commission, a nineties number, was waiting to be French seamed. Work was my go-to – you can't wallow when you're in workaholism mode – but my heart wasn't in it. The terraces opposite, most of which were unloved Airbnb lets or investment properties, were uniformly dark as usual, and the abandoned, apocalyptic feel didn't help my mood.

I edged my chair closer to Clarice, who stood out stolidly next to her more practical, adjustable dress-form sisters. When Nate lived here, he'd insisted I relegate her to the basement storage unit ('she creeps me out'), and the first thing I did when he left was wheel her into the front room. Once upon a time, Clarice had belonged to my mum, and she'd been in my life for as long as I could remember – a headless muse made of wood and plastic.

It was too late to message NB, but I did it anyway, thinking he'd see it in the morning. <sorry I disappeared>

He responded immediately, making me jump. <No problem. How did it go?>

Just been verbally abused by an arsehole, how's you? <Non-starter. He was a dick>

<Sorry to hear that. You ok?>

No. To nix the threat of tears, I changed the subject. <Can't sleep?>

<Insomnia>

<Me too>

<Why does time move slower this late at night?>

It's impossible to accurately gauge someone's tone from a one-line message, but I sensed we were creeping into more serious territory than our usual flippancy. Now could be an opening to dig a little. *Where is this going? Why are you talking to a strange woman at this time of night?* Instead, I wrote: <Do you ever get lonely?> Thought for a second, then pressed send.

<Yes> No hesitation, no 'that's a strange question'. <You?>

By anyone's standards I was fortunate and privileged: a career I loved, no health issues, no serious addictions (unless you count takeaway tandoori and Tinder), a best friend who loved and supported me. But. *But*. No matter how many times I told myself I didn't want or need anything more serious than an occasional shag, the spectre of growing old alone, dying alone (eaten by cats, maybe – or worse) grew closer every year. I'd tried to articulate this fear to Leila, but she didn't fully get it. How could she? Leila had two-year-old twins, envied my freedom, and while her husband Lev could be a pain in the arse at times, he was always *there*. As if to stick the knife in, a thunk came from the flat above, followed by the faint sounds of piano music. My landlords, Magda and Jonas, up late again.

I saw them every morning, walking arm in arm past the window, en route to the shop. Jonas had early-onset Alzheimer's, and I sat with him whenever Magda had to run an errand. Jonas was no trouble, mainly stayed put in his armchair, humming to himself.

Their flat was stuffed with musical instruments, old books, art and photographs: the detritus of a rich, shared life. Sure, occasionally the sound of raised voices and odd noises would float down from their flat (most notably on Thursday nights, for some reason), but despite the strain, Magda's devotion to him had never dimmed; you could see it in her eyes. Deep down, that's what I secretly wanted: a Magda. Someone who'd stand by me when my mind and body crumbled. A *soulmate*, although that wasn't a concept I bought into (or I told myself I didn't).

The phone trembled: <You still there?>

<Yes> *And by the way, what's your real name? Who are you, really? What do you want out of life? What do you want from me?* And then there was the biggest, dumbest question of all, which I tapped in and sent because I was still half-pissed and pissed off with myself for being so pathetic: <Are you happy?>

A minute went by, then another. Then: <My life's fucked. I feel like I'm living with a stranger. I'm looking down the barrel of another 30 years of penury. Does that answer your question?>

No throwaway humour. No self-deprecating jibes. No sarcasm. A rush of exhilaration – *now we're getting somewhere!* – swiftly sobered by dismay: *He's married?*

NICK

Are you happy?

It didn't occur to me to lie or respond with the kind of nothing answer we all trot out when we're asked this sort of inane question, knowing deep down that the other person doesn't give a shit. They don't really want to hear about your bursitis, your elderly parents who are losing it, or that your dog is on its last legs. And I didn't come clean because I'd been nipping at the booze that night and my guard was down. Nope, I *wanted* to confess, wanted to lance the boil of self-disgust. *The boil of self-disgust.* Christ. And that, if further proof were needed, is why I won't be winning any book awards any time soon.

The morning after I lanced the boil, spilled my guts or whatever shitty metaphor suits, I woke stiff-necked on the couch, feeling both lighter and heavier: lighter because I'd finally admitted to myself (and someone else) that I was a failure. Heavier because I'd finally admitted to myself (and someone else) that I was a failure. Poll had draped a blanket over me, presumably when she got up for work, and there was something both caring and passive-aggressive about the gesture. Rosie white-eyed me from her basket, furious that my selfishness had thrown her morning routine out of whack. In the usual course of events, she and I stuck to a schedule honed for maximum time-filling:

1) 6.30 a.m.: Get up. Make Poll a cup of tea. Let Rosie out. Pretend to be awake and chirpy.

2) 7.30 a.m.: Back to bed for a sneaky hour after Poll leaves for work.
3) 8.30 a.m.: Up. Caffeine injection. 45 mins of morning telly. (You know you're in trouble when you find yourself watching *Baby Animal Rescue Squad* in your pants and having a little weep.)
4) Washing on. Quick hoover if necessary.
5) Empty the dishwasher, sound-tracked by Radio 1, just to feel young again.
6) Make the day's roll-ups, sound-tracked by the World Service, just to feel smarter.
7) Out with Rosie for her morning walk/ablution.

As it was past eleven, I decided to skip steps 1–6 and go straight to the dog ablution chore. As I dragged on the closest jacket to hand, the phone on the coffee table seemed to eye me as balefully as the dog. Remorse flooded in, extinguishing the confessional lightness. *What have you done, Nick?* Thankfully, the battery had run down, saving me from the horror of revisiting the self-pitying shite I'd bored Bee with during the wee hours. What had started as a game, a challenge to see if I could make a stranger laugh, had taken over to the extent that I spent hours crafting 'witty' things to say to her. Bee saw something in me. She got my sense of humour. Didn't mind – liked, in fact – when it got too dark. I couldn't lose that on top of everything else.

Leaving the phone attached to its umbilical cord, I clipped on Rosie's lead and headed out. The sky was the colour of sludge, but even that was enough to spike my hungover eyes. We took the usual route: through the new estate at the end of our street (orange fake-brick insulation, leased electric cars attached to their own – mostly illegal – umbilicals); around the balding park (aptly nicknamed 'Dog Shit Meadow'), past the Stop n Shop and a circle back to Dreadnought Street. Rosie wasn't ready to let me off the hook. While I followed in her wake like a servile shite collector, she toyed with me, sniffing the kerb, acting as if she was just about to go, then slyly trotting on. It was pointless getting impatient. Rosie was a dog pensioner and knew her own mind. Bought as a puppy from a rescue organisation for Dylan, just after Poll asked me to move in, she was supposed to be my way into his affections: *The bad news is that Mummy has a new boyfriend. The good news is: we got you a dog*. Only the dog had glommed onto me for some reason. Over the years – 'The Dreadnought Years', I'd call them if I ever wrote a memoir (which I won't, don't worry) – we'd become allies of sorts.

As we shuffled along, I composed missives to Bee in my head. Sorry for being such a self-indulgent loser arsehole. You didn't need to hear all of that. *Sorry, sorry, sorry*. At least I was good at failing. At that I excelled:

1) Failed writer: one published novel, what they used to call dick-lit back in the day. Written in my twenties, it was your typical semi-autobiographical, trying-too-hard-to-be-amusing load of wank. One reviewer summed it up as 'smug, self-important and swarming with smarm'. Those words are branded on whatever part of the brain makes you wake up at one a.m. going '*fuuuuuuck*,' and punched the ambition, the desire to write, right out of me. Years back, in my second year of teaching English at an A Level college, I'd spied a couple of kids sniggering over it, reading the sex scenes aloud. There were a lot of those. Poll read it of course ('it's diverting' was the best she could manage), but I'd kept it away from Dylan. Didn't want him to judge me any more than he already did.
2) Failed teacher: I was all right with the kids – knew how to keep their attention, make them laugh, even enjoyed the job – but didn't have the patience to deal with the bureaucracy. That career ended when I told a school inspector to get fucked during assessment week.
3) Failed breadwinner: the odd bit of tutoring that drove me to drink. A stint as an assistant manager at a Blue Bay Coffee

franchise (a *short* stint – I let the staff get away with murder). And now a sinking freelance career editing self-published novels. In the last month, I'd brought in the grand sum of four hundred smackers.

4) Failed husband. Nuff said.
5) Okay-ish stepdad, but that wasn't my call to make. Dylan would have his own views on that.
6) Good dog owner. But that wasn't much of an achievement, was it? All you have to do is not kick the buggers.

All of that should have chased Bee away. Maybe it had. Who wants a middle-aged loser? Fifty waved at me with its age-spotted hands, inviting me to join it in another decade of being sub-par. Which was why Tweedy Twat's silence burned, as for some reason his project had reignited a spark doused by my early failure. Shamefully, a part of me, a small part of me, had wanted to please the posh bastard. Doffing my cap, impressed, yeah, bloody impressed, by the miasma of old money. I'd asked Poll to read it, but she was too knackered to do anything except flump in front of a mindless cooking show after a day of teaching stroppy teens. I'd slaved over it, weeding out mistakes, rewriting the sentences that went on forever, turning that mess – that piece of garbage, which, admittedly, had a good spine – into something readable. And the formatting. The bloody formatting . . . When I'd pressed 'Send', I'd cried. Fucking cried. I hadn't told Bee that part.

Nor, thank Christ, had I given into the temptation of going into too much detail about my failing marriage. I had enough loyalty to Poll to refrain from doing that. Except, of course, for the 'living with a stranger' shocker. And really, was that even true? She was still the same Poll. I was the stranger. A stranger on the brink of an emotional affair. Which didn't elicit the level of guilt it deserved, pathetically because the novelty of anyone, even a stranger, enjoying my company trumped everything else. Early on, Poll and I had had the cheating conversation, smugly curled in bed, knowing it would never happen: *If you ever want to do it, Nick, I don't want to know*.

I crossed the road to avoid a woman who was being dragged along by an overenthusiastic Staffordshire terrier, and tried to shut out the black thoughts. Rosie finally deposited her prize, naturally choosing someone's pristine driveway. Bend, knee pop, scoop. Sometimes I found myself swinging the poop bag like it was a Prada handbag: *look everyone! That dog shite you see peppering the pavement? It's not me. I'm a* responsible *dog owner.*

On to the home stretch. The second we reached her gate, my neighbour Lily darted out of her front door, proffering a custard cream. Rosie knew the drill: a tail-wag, a lifting of a paw, the gentle taking of the biscuit.

'I suppose you'll be wanting tea,' Lily said to me grudgingly, like I was doing her a favour. Which we both knew I was. Sometimes I doubled-back to avoid her, but apart from the health visitor and me and Rosie, Lily didn't have anyone else. I did her shopping for her too, which makes me sound like a saint, but really, it was just another excuse to kill time. Lily's tastes ran to the food of her childhood – wet walnuts, tinned red salmon and puddings in tins – and I enjoyed the hunt for vintage food. For once I was glad to see her.

Her terrace was a mirror image of ours, except while Poll had gone all out with the bling, Lily's was an overheated cave stuck in a nineteen-eighties time warp. Rosie loved it: it smelled of decades of roasting meat and every surface was covered with some sort of cloth. Lily's eyes were failing her and while she made the tea, I cleaned up a little, scraping off the greasy crust around the counter edges and eco-Jiffing the tea stain in the sink.

As the tea bags stewed into Lily's preferred industrial strength, she eyed me suspiciously. 'You're late today.'

'Been up all night.'

'Something on your mind, lad?'

'Nah. All good.'

'You look different.'

'Haven't shaved.'

'Not just that.'

'Might be coming down with something. Anyway, how's you?' It was easy to deflect her – she could be a selfish old cow, which partly stemmed from loneliness. She launched into a tirade about her new health visitor, who had committed the unforgiveable sin of buying almond instead of cow milk when she popped to the shop to replenish Lily's supplies ('do I look like the sort of person who drinks that muck? I know my own mind, me.') As I'd learned the hard way that defending whichever poor sod was Lily's victim *de jour* would only result in her doubling down, I let her rant on and tuned out, the tea taking the edge off the hangover.

I escaped Lily's clutches, deposited Rosie on the couch for her post-walk snooze, then headed out to my writing shed, which sagged at the end of the garden, garlanded by stinging nettles. If I close my eyes, I can bring up every detail. The rickety ethanol heater, the skull-shaped ashtray Dylan bought me for Christmas when he was going through his 'alternative' phase, the long defunct lawnmower, the sagging pile of books, enough spiders to populate Mars, my desk, a chip-board cast-off, rescued from a skip, wobbly-legged and shedding cheap screws, and the emphysema huff of my elderly laptop's fan, a machine which bravely clung to life with the tenacity of a Russian miner despite the amount of fag smoke and dust it was forced to inhale. Too cold in winter, too hot in summer, and all year round, the hum of Lily's telly in the background, which was always up too loud. Poll never crossed the shed's threshold; couldn't understand why I hadn't co-opted Dylan's room when he left for college. The reason was simple: the shed was *mine*.

I sat and smoked another rollie before I opened the laptop and mustered up the courage to check the i-mails. What was it that connected Bee and me? I pictured it as an invisible strand twanging through cyberspace from my heart to hers. Fanciful as fuck, sure, but it seemed to fit. I'd been jealous when she'd revealed she was on a date (I'm not above hypocrisy), which was why I couldn't sleep. Which was why I'd stayed up with the dog watching back-to-back episodes of *Bailiff Bail-Outs*, and drinking the gin that Poll kept for when her mum visited.

I manned up, logged on and jumped to our thread, hoping against hope that while I'd been out Rosie-ing and Lily-ing Bee had been messaging. But the thread was as we'd left it last night – hanging in the wind so to speak – so instead of the dopamine rush that accompanied every new Bee missive came the heavy thud of deflation. Seemed I had chased her away with my self-pitying shite after all. *So, what are you going to do about it? Mope, or be proactive?* For once, being proactive won, and after allowing myself five minutes to obsess over word choice (okay – ten), I fired off: <Hey! Sorry for getting all heavy last night. Last thing you needed to hear. I'd blame it on the gin but that wouldn't be true (or fair on the gin, even if it was the nasty cheap kind). Anyway, totally understand if you'd rather back away slowly (or run)>

I slumped back in the chair and began rolling another ciggie for something to do, telling myself not to get my hopes up, but unable to resist keeping half an eye on the thread. When Bee's response came in a minute later, I sat up so abruptly that I sent half a packet of loose tobacco confetti-ing over the keyboard.

<You should probably know that I'm crap at running so that isn't an option ☺ Also, if anyone should apologise it's me as I started it & you weren't the only one who got heavy . . . Catch up later? Back-to-back fittings all day 😫 Free from around 8-ish>

I punched the air like a twelve-year-old. <It's a date! Meet you back here at 8.30 p.m.? I'll put the coffee on. You don't need boozy me again. Good luck with the fittings> It would do. My brain was too sluggish to come up with anything sharper. The relief that I hadn't chased her away made me feel a little horny if I'm honest, but what could be more of a cliché than a sad old loser wanking in a shed? *You are not that guy. You can be a better person.*

Pepped up by Bee's message, I salvaged the spilt tobacco and scrolled through the rest of my mails. Nestled within the junk was a missive from Tweedy Twat. I'd taken Bee's advice and hadn't sent the abusive i-mail, just another copy of the invoice:

Dear Nicolas,

First please accept my fulsome apologies for such a long silence. I had a rather nasty fall and broke my hip and fell behind on dealing with my correspondence. I am now on my way to recovery!!! You have done a marvellous job on the book, above and beyond in fact. I have transferred the payment along with a bonus as it is clear to me how much extra work you have put in. Thank you for your patience. I so enjoyed the process and seeing how wonderfully you have brought my ideas to life. My granddaughter Poppy has promised to put the book up for sale on one of those sites popular with readers of electronic literature.

Yours truly

Bernard Eldridge Esq.

I re-read it, then checked my bank balance. Five grand (minus the overdraft that my UBI never seemed to dent). He wasn't kidding about the bonus. That was double what I'd quoted.

It wasn't Poll I wanted to tell first, but Bee. Went so far as to type in: <HOLY TWEEDY SHITBALLS, BEE YOU'LL NEVER GUESS WHAT>, then deposited it in drafts. She was working – it could wait until later. Instead, I wrote Bernie a *fulsome* reply thanking him for the payment and sending my best wishes for a speedy recovery. A bit grovelly, but sod it.

The rest of the afternoon passed in a kind of anticipatory, joyful haze. I paced, bunged on the Bowie – the *Silent* album, my favourite – and had a little victory dance to that. I was itching to get out, even thought about going for a run of all things. The cash injection symbolised a new chapter. *A new hope*. I could *breathe*. Holding back from mailing Bee was killing me, made worse by Poll's reaction to the news: a lacklustre <Great> followed by, <Play rehearsal tonight back late>). This rote response stung more than it should. God knows why – I should have counted myself lucky I'd received a reply at all seeing as

a) Poll usually kept her phone switched off when she was a work; b) our non-verbal communication tended to be terse and impersonal, as if we were hiding behind a veneer of cordiality; c) I was fairly sure that for Poll, this smidgeon of good fortune, however unusual, wasn't enough to make up for the years of watching me spiral down the greasy plughole of failure, and on towards a future where the best I could hope for was the metaphorical equivalent of being lodged in a fatberg. And seeing as Poll preferred things (and people) to be orderly and predictable, it was no wonder that she'd backed away from the sink and diverted her energies into the areas of her life that weren't as messy.

In the end I called Jez, an old mate from my teacher training days. 'Pub?'

'No one goes to the pub these days, Nick.'

'Got the cash I owe you.'

'Don't worry about it. I'd written it off, if I'm honest.'

'C'mon. Let me treat you. You got me out of a hole.'

'I dunno, mate. I've got marking. And an assessment.'

'All the more reason to have a cheeky few. It'll make the pain more bearable.' I didn't care that I was coming across as desperate.

I took Rosie along for the outing. The conversation between Jez and I was unusually stilted, but I was too buoyed up to think this was significant at the time. Jez had never been the life of the party, and I suppose I put his reticence down to the fact that I hadn't contacted him since he'd loaned me money. Three pints in, Jez excused himself for a slash. Alcohol's supposed to be a depressive, but that evening it gave me the illusion that anything was possible. Even the long-buried itch to write – for myself, and not as someone's bargain basement proxy – was resurfacing.

In her spot beneath the table, Rosie sighed and farted gently, as if she were not only scoffing at my uncharacteristic optimism but foreshadowing the shit storm about to hit. Jez's phone parped out the theme tune to *Frey Fights Fear*, and I glanced at it, bemused to see a snapshot of Poll pulsating on its screen. I hadn't told her

I was popping out for a drink or three with Jez, but I checked my phone all the same in case she'd tried ringing me and hadn't been able to get through. Nothing. Jez's rang again, dovetailing with his return. I didn't need to ask him why my fucking wife was calling him. The answer was all over his face.

*

From: NB26@zone.com
To: Bee1984@gmail.com

You know that thing where hours later you can't stop thinking, why didn't I say that? The French have a phrase for it. *L'esprit de l'escalier* (just looked that up). See? Even when I'm at my lowest I can be an annoying bastard.

From: Bee1984@gmail.com
To: NB26@zone.com

Again, I'm SO SORRY NB. What did you say to him?

From: NB26@zone.com
To: Bee1984@gmail.com

Nowt. I got up and left. Forgot the dog, so had to go back. I should have punched him or something. And I feel shite unloading this on you. It's just . . . I don't know how to feel about this.

From: Bee1984@gmail.com
To: NB26@zone.com

Hey, easier to tell a stranger, right? And please don't feel shite/guilty about unloading. I can take it. You're hurting. And you're entitled to hurt. Betrayal is the worst.

From: NB26@zone.com
To: Bee1984@gmail.com

You've been through this?

From: Bee1984@gmail.com
To: NB26@zone.com

I have.

From: NB26@zone.com
To: Bee1984@gmail.com

You want to talk about it?

From: Bee1984@gmail.com
To: NB26@zone.com

No! You're the one with the crisis.

From: NB26@zone.com
To: Bee1984@gmail.com

Speaking of crises – her ride-share's just pulled up. Wish me luck.

From: Bee1984@gmail.com
To: NB26@zone.com

I'm here if you need me. Any time. Midnight. 3a.m. Whatever.

From: NB26@zone.com
To: Bee1984@gmail.com

Thanks. Christ. You're going to make me cry.

From: NB26@zone.com
To: Bee1984@gmail.com

She's just left. She told me everything. Been going on for a year, after they ran into each other at a training course. I feel so fucking stupid. Said she's been putting off coming clean as I was going through a rough time and she didn't want to 'totally crush me'.

From: Bee1984@gmail.com
To: NB26@zone.com

Do you want to talk? In person I mean.

From: NB26@zone.com
To: Bee1984@gmail.com

As tempting as that is, best we stay like we are. You really don't need to hear me blubbering uncontrollably . . .

Thing is, I'm angrier at myself than I am at Poll. Should have thrown in the towel years ago.

From: Bee1984@gmail.com
To: NB26@zone.com

Why didn't you?

From: NB26@zone.com
To: Bee1984@gmail.com

Lots of reasons. Inertia. My stepson, Dylan.

From: Bee1984@gmail.com
To: NB26@zone.com

You have a stepson?? How old is he? Why didn't you tell me about him before?

From: NB26@zone.com
To: Bee1984@gmail.com

Perhaps because my life is messy enough and didn't want you to go, 'Bloody hell, is there no end to this man's drama?' He's 24. 12 when me and Poll got together. He was a bit fragile when I came onto the scene. Felt wrong to implode his life when he was younger. Still stayed after he left home though, didn't I? Like I said. Inertia.

From: Bee1984@gmail.com
To: NB26@zone.com

We all do that. I'm still living in the flat I shared with my ex. When did it all start going wrong?

From: NB26@zone.com
To: Bee1984@gmail.com

Good question. Not sure there was an exact moment. We just drifted there. Things were good at the start. Then I suppose we started taking each other for granted. Stopped having a laugh. Didn't talk about that. Stopped having sex. Didn't talk about that either. Fell into a routine of arse on the couch, telly on, one holiday a year in Tenby, Christmas with her family of tossers, marking time. We were seeing life as something to be gotten over and done with, not something to be . . . I dunno . . . lived.

From: NB26@zone.com
To: Bee1984@gmail.com

Ok I've just read that back. Pretentious, moi?

From: Bee1984@gmail.com
To: NB26@zone.com

I get what you're saying.

From: NB26@zone.com
To: Bee1984@gmail.com

I think if you met Poll you'd really like her. Probably take her side. Not that there should be any sides.

From: Bee1984@gmail.com
To: NB26@zone.com

There are always sides.

From: NB26@zone.com
To: Bee1984@gmail.com

I know. I'm trying to say I'm not a saint, Bee. Trust me on that. Anyway, I'm sick of myself. I don't ever want you to feel like you're my therapist.

Tell me about your heartbreak.

From: Bee1984@gmail.com
To: NB26@zone.com

Ugh. It's a sorry tale.

From: NB26@zone.com
To: Bee1984@gmail.com

Were you married to him?

From: Bee1984@gmail.com
To: NB26@zone.com

No. Almost. Engaged.

He was a buyer for M&S and I was a lowly designer. It happened really quickly. Within 2 weeks of meeting, we were living together.

From: NB26@zone.com
To: Bee1984@gmail.com

2 weeks. Wow. Love at first sight?

From: Bee1984@gmail.com
To: NB26@zone.com

I suppose.

From: NB26@zone.com
To: Bee1984@gmail.com

Here's a question: how do you know that you're in love? Not the boring scientific version that everyone knows – dopamine, serotonin etc. The other, less tangible stuff.

From: Bee1984@gmail.com
To: NB26@zone.com

You can't stop thinking about the other person. You want to be around them all the time.

From: NB26@zone.com
To: Bee1984@gmail.com

They stop you feeling lonely.

From: Bee1984@gmail.com
To: NB26@zone.com

They have your back.

From: NB26@zone.com
To: Bee1984@gmail.com

They complete you.

From: Bee1984@gmail.com
To: NB26@zone.com

OK, I've got one. It feels like coming home.

From: NB26@zone.com
To: Bee1984@gmail.com

Ha! Ok, you win in the cynicism stakes. Now, ON with the story. Why did you break up and what's his name?

From: Bee1984@gmail.com
To: NB26@zone.com

Nate.

From: NB26@zone.com
To: Bee1984@gmail.com

Nate. I can picture him now. Facial hair? Tall? Tattoos? Hates footie but likes rugby? Speaks posh? Parents in the entertainment industry?

From: Bee1984@gmail.com
To: NB26@zone.com

Ha ha! No. Short. 5 7. Same height as me. Grew a beard once, but it made him look like he was hiding something (spoiler – he was). Posh yes. Parents both civil servants!

From: NB26@zone.com
To: Bee1984@gmail.com

And the break up? Cheating?

From: Bee1984@gmail.com
To: NB26@zone.com

Yes. Just once he said, but who knows?

From: NB26@zone.com
To: Bee1984@gmail.com

How did you find out?

From: Bee1984@gmail.com
To: NB26@zone.com

Same as you. The phone.

From: NB26@zone.com
To: Bee1984@gmail.com

Bloody phones.

From: Bee1984@gmail.com
To: NB26@zone.com

I was snooping. I knew something was going on. Just knew it. Sensed it. He'd been texting someone. Read the texts. They were . . . explicit. I didn't think anything could hurt as bad as that. I was off work for a week. Spent most of the time curled in a ball sobbing and watching Dancing on Ice on a loop. I wanted to die. So dramatic! If it wasn't for my friend Leila I don't know what I would have done. Then, he wanted to come back & I almost said yes. Thing is, he knew how much cheating would hurt me.

I'm old-fashioned. Boring. Believe in monogamy. Well I did believe in it. After that, I decided love, relationships, the whole caboodle wasn't for me.

From: NB26@zone.com
To: Bee1984@gmail.com

Do you still think like that?

From: Bee1984@gmail.com
To: NB26@zone.com

I'm not sure.

From: NB26@zone.com
To: Bee1984@gmail.com

But you go on dates. You can't have given up entirely.

From: Bee1984@gmail.com
To: NB26@zone.com

Just one-night things mostly. Feel free to judge me on that. And after Satchel Man, I'm changing my policy on that.

From: NB26@zone.com
To: Bee1984@gmail.com

Hey – no judgement here. And who could forget Satchel Man and his burgeoning MI5 career?

From: Bee1984@gmail.com
To: NB26@zone.com

You know, you should use what you're feeling now. Write it. Turn it into a book.

From: NB26@zone.com
To: Bee1984@gmail.com

CHRIST! With all the drama I completely forgot: I have some good news. Tweedy Twat paid!

From: Bee1984@gmail.com
To: NB26@zone.com

NO WAY!!!!!! AND??? Did he love it?

From: NB26@zone.com
To: Bee1984@gmail.com

Yeah.

From: Bee1984@gmail.com
To: NB26@zone.com

I knew he would. So write another one. You have to get something good out of this, don't you?

From: NB26@zone.com
To: Bee1984@gmail.com

You're right. Thank you for being there. I don't know what I would have done otherwise.

From: Bee1984@gmail.com
To: NB26@zone.com

I feel the same. Do you think now we should at least swap first names?

From: NB26@zone.com
To: Bee1984@gmail.com

I'm Nicolas. Nick if you like.

From: Bee1984@gmail.com
To: NB26@zone.com

I'm Rebecca. Or stick with Bee if you prefer. My best mate calls me Bee.

From: NB26@zone.com
To: Bee1984@gmail.com

Because you're always busy?

From: Bee1984@gmail.com
To: NB26@zone.com

Maybe. Or it could be because if I'm forced to sting you, I'll die.

BEE

The fact that Nick chose to confide in me about the affair stripped away another layer of our protective 'strangers on the interwebs' insulation. *Now we're* really *getting somewhere . . .* And our growing trust and intimacy flowed both ways (<You lance my inner emotional boils, Bee, and I'll do yours> <Ew. You sure? Mine are pretty hard to reach. And gross> <Go for it. Scalpel (and bucket) at the ready>). As well as airing the Nate-Gate saga, I found myself telling him about my parents, a subject I rarely discussed, even with Leila. How I'd spent my childhood watching my dad betraying my mum again and again. How each time Dad was caught out, he'd grovel his way back into our lives, whining excuses. ('I'm a sick man, Lisbeth.' 'It's the last time, I swear.') How I'd watched Mum's self-esteem slowly erode, worn down by the hope that this time, he really would change his ways. When he finally left, buggering off to Australia with a thirty-year-old barista (<Knowing him, he probably meant to hook up with a barrister, but his spelling's always been rubbish> <10/10 for black humour there, Bee>), I felt like I could breathe again, but it almost broke my mum. I hated him for what he'd put her through, and a nasty part of me resented her for putting up with it for so long. Cue years of guilt for that, because just as she was getting her spark back, pancreatic cancer came knocking.

<No reason to feel guilty, Bee. You were always there for her, weren't you? And it's natural to judge our parents, saves us making the same mistakes they did. Gawd, listen to me being all grown-up and sensible. Next stop, a cardigan and a Volvo-lec>

<And golf. Don't forget golf>

<Who could forget drinks at the nineteenth hole with the chaps? Seriously though, your mum wouldn't want you agonising over this. Shelve the guilt>

Selfishly, Poll's betrayal also allowed me to shelve the guilt I'd been harbouring about our growing connection, and I yo-yoed between feeling angry at her and grateful, which made for a distasteful mental mix. <I can't help but think of Poll as a Nate, or like my dad>

<She's not, Bee. I'm not saying that what she did wasn't completely shit, but she's a good'un at heart. Crap taste in men, mind, but you can't have everything>

The fact that he defended her, and meant it, did him credit. As did the easy way he could bounce from heaviness into silliness. <If you think about it, we're both orphans. Like in a Dickens novel. If all else fails, we can sell matches on the streets, 'Awright guvnor? Spare us a shilling?'>

<Well, I'm not strictly an orphan. Does that mean I'll have to go up the chimneys?>

<Emotional orphans then?>

<That'll do>

Other similarities surfaced. We both had a shameful predilection for letting friendships slide (<Basically my only mate is the dog, and she only stays because she likes the food>), which reminded me that I was long overdue a catchup with Leila. *That* was a relationship I couldn't risk letting slide. We'd been inseparable since school, immediately bonding over our outsider statuses (she was Acne Face, I was Fatty Boom-Boom). She'd been there through all the shitty times: Mum's illness; Nate's bullshit. I was there for her during three rounds of IVF, her ups and downs with Lev, and the regret and guilt she felt for quitting her accountancy practice after the twins were born. And although our lives had diverged, hers to the suburbs and parent and baby mornings, and mine to workaholism with a side order of Tinder, we still made an effort to see each other. Just as I was about to text her to suggest we meet, she called to request an emergency gin-walk.

<What's a gin-walk when it's at home, Bee? Or does it do what it says on the tin?>

<We both need to exercise but would rather be drinking & because we don't have the time to do either properly, we combine them>

<Multitasking for functioning alcoholics?>

<Exactly!>

<In solidarity I will have a gin-sit>

After a brief bout of soul-searching, I left the phone on the work-table when I set out to meet her, because Leila was sharper than your average bear, and I wasn't quite ready to spill the beans about Nick yet. Not until I knew for sure what Nick and I *were*. We usually shared everything, but she had enough on her plate without worrying that I was diving head-first into a relationship with a random, soon-to-be-divorced stranger who I'd randomly met online. If a message came in while we were gin-walking, I wouldn't be able to resist looking at it, and Leila would see on my face that something was up.

She hustled her way through the skiving schoolkids and greeted me with a hug. 'God, I need this. I know I'm in a bad way because going on the Tube felt like a holiday.'

'How long have you got?'

'Forty-seven minutes. Lev's mum is twin-wrangling and she'll lose her shit if she's not home in time for *Pointless*.' She stood back and gave me the once-over. 'Hmm. You're looking *good*. Glowy.'

'Glowy? Like I've been exfoliating too much or like I've been too close to a nuclear reactor?'

'Both. What's up?'

I shrugged. 'Well, against all the odds I did find the time to shower today.' (This was both true and an evasion.)

'Lucky you. I haven't, so don't get too close.'

Leila always came to me for gin-walks because my area of West London was within striking distance of Holland Park, and we both liked having a good old nose around what Leila called 'dodgy rich people's real estate'. (<Are you saying you're posh, Bee?> <Fraid

not. Told you, moved here with Nate & never left #inertia>). We rambled past the takeaways and my beloved fabric shops, cut down into Hammersmith Grove and (semi) power-walked towards the Holy Grail of gentrification and property flipping. We'd given names to several of the more ostentatious houses. The sash-windowed Victorian with the enormous chandelier was Bling Palace, the one with no curtains and a giant abstract painting on the wall was Exhibitionist's Alley, and our favourite, a double-fronted terrace, was the Gnome Home, named after the cheeky garden ornament that took pride of place among the planters and birdfeeders that were artfully arranged in front of the steps. We were always chuffed to see it, partly because a cheap and cheerful garden gnome wasn't something you expected to see in this regularly-featured-in-*Tatler* postcode, partly because it was a miracle no one had nicked it. The house itself was an outlier too. It had defiantly resisted the trend for concreting over the front garden, and in summer, it was shaggy with ivy and wisteria, as if it had an identity crisis and secretly longed to be a country cottage. Leila handed me a tin of ready-mixed gin fizz, and we leaned against its wall, cracked our cans, and drank.

She gestured at the house's frontage. 'What do you call the one that goes purple in spring again?'

'Wisteria.'

'I know I'm getting old because I've started appreciating plants. And not just the type you smoke.'

'Uh-oh. Next you'll be visiting garden centres and then it's a slippery slope to living in the shires and voting Tory.'

The front door opened and an ancient woman in an obvious but rather jaunty auburn wig peered out at us. Leila gave her a wave. 'Don't worry, we're not casing the joint. Just admiring your wisteria.'

The woman shook her head and retreated.

'God, I miss London,' Leila sighed. 'The distrust. The surliness.'

'Bromley *is* London.'

'And when I'm old, I'm going to wear a mad wig like the Gnome Home woman and embrace my wrinkles.'

'You are old, remember?'

'Properly old. Like ninety. No plastic surgery or Botox for me.'

'Didn't you have Botox three years ago?'

'Fuck yeah. I did. Forgot. See? My brain is crumbling.'

'Or maybe your tiny can of gin has gone right to your head.'

We wandered on, Leila filling me in on the twins and airing her worries that her brain really was stultifying from lack of use. 'I could take on a couple of clients, but you know me, if I dropped the ball, I'd go crazy. Lev says I should volunteer for something, but can you imagine me sorting handbags and old men's pants in a charity shop? I'd drive the other volunteers round the bend with my control-freakish ways. Anyway, that's enough whingeing from me. Tell me some exciting single life news.'

Nick was out of bounds – for now – so I told her about the disastrous Satchel Man date, trying to turn it into an amusing anecdote. Not the best idea, because it sent Leila into a state of apoplexy. She stalked on, raging about entitled arseholes and threatening to dox him and worse. 'You should have called me right away. You shouldn't have to deal with this kind of thing alone.'

I didn't say what I was thinking, which was, I *wasn't* alone. 'It was the middle of the night.'

'I would have been up. The kids have decided sleep can wait until I'm dead. Are you *sure* you're okay?'

'I really am. No bad date PTSD, I promise.'

We circled back to the Grove, crossing to inspect a neglected but elegant Georgian lady, recently sold and no doubt destined for the house equivalent of Botox and major plastic surgery. Leila couldn't resist rooting in the skip outside it, unearthing a broken wicker chair with a triumphant: 'I can do something with this.'

I gave her a look. 'Seriously? Do you even need another chair?' We both knew it would end up in the shed along with the other skip finds that she would never get around to repurposing.

'Someone's got to save the poor old thing from rotting to death in a landfill site.'

As we wove our way back to the world of buses and chicken shops and normal people who didn't have squillions to invest in property, she carried the seat, and I carried its skeleton.

'Dinner. Soon. Promise? Come over and I'll microwave us something. Lev can watch the twins and we can get pissed and plot our revenge on that abusive arsehole.'

'I promise.'

'You know, you really are looking good, Bee.'

I watched her wrangling the rescued chair through the turnstile at the Tube station, then made my way back to Clarice and my empty flat. But when I retrieved the phone from the worktable and opened our thread, it didn't feel so empty anymore.

*

From: Bee1984@gmail.com
To: NB26@zone.com

Other than that, no news. Oh – apart from a low-rent influencer who keeps nudging me for a freebie.

From: NB26@zone.com
To: Bee1984@gmail.com

Apart from a what?

From: Bee1984@gmail.com
To: NB26@zone.com

I forget sometimes that you're a dinosaur ☺ Your turn. Have you told Dylan yet?

From: NB26@zone.com
To: Bee1984@gmail.com

Poll still wants to wait for the right time. *Is* there a right time? He's sensitive, sure, but it's not as if he's a five-year-old who'll blame himself for mummy and daddy splitting up. Hopefully.

From: Bee1984@gmail.com
To: NB26@zone.com

His main concern will be that you and his mum are OK. Long as you can reassure him of that, he'll cope.

From: NB26@zone.com
To: Bee1984@gmail.com

I AM ok.

From: Bee1984@gmail.com
To: NB26@zone.com

You're not, and you won't be for a while, but you will be.

From: NB26@zone.com
To: Bee1984@gmail.com

Wise words as per. But that's enough of me heavying things up again. It's cheer-up time, and it's your turn to think of a stupid question.

From: Bee1984@gmail.com
To: NB26@zone.com

OK. How's this: Would you rather eat a whole dog or a single human foot?

From: NB26@zone.com
To: Bee1984@gmail.com

Wow, Bee, that's *monumentally* stupid. Well done! Animal abuse AND cannibalism. Can I cook them?

From: Bee1984@gmail.com
To: NB26@zone.com

No. And no sauce.

From: NB26@zone.com
To: Bee1984@gmail.com

Foot then. Not that I'm a fan of feet (too many bones), but after seeing what Rosie eats on her walks, I'll give the dog carpaccio a miss. Ask me another.

From: Bee1984@gmail.com
To: NB26@zone.com

Here's a less stupid one: Who would you invite to your dream dinner party?

From: NB26@zone.com
To: Bee1984@gmail.com

Dinner party?? I KNEW you were posh.

From: Bee1984@gmail.com
To: NB26@zone.com

Dream takeaway party then.

From: NB26@zone.com
To: Bee1984@gmail.com

That's easy. Rosie. And you.

From: Bee1984@gmail.com
To: NB26@zone.com

But that would mean we'd have to meet . . .

From: NB26@zone.com
To: Bee1984@gmail.com

I suppose it would.

From: Bee1984@gmail.com
To: NB26@zone.com

Which we're not going to do. Because we have rules.

From: NB26@zone.com
To: Bee1984@gmail.com

And although rules are made to be broken, this is working. For now. Unless you want to break them?

From: Bee1984@gmail.com
To: NB26@zone.com

No. I like this. There's something old-fashioned about it. Like in the olden days when people used to send each other letters and they had to wait for ages for a reply, not knowing if the other person was dead or whatever.

From: Bee1984@gmail.com
To: NB26@zone.com

Nick? You still there?

From: Bee1984@gmail.com
To: NB26@zone.com

Oh I get it. Very funny.

From: NB26@zone.com
To: Bee1984@gmail.com

I would never have cut it back then. I got bored after a minute of not replying.

I like it too. Means I don't have to worry about brushing my hair or teeth or even getting dressed. Just so you know, I am wearing clothes, otherwise that could have come across as creepy. I'm just not wearing clothes very well.

From: Bee1984@gmail.com
To: NB26@zone.com

Is it weird that I almost don't want to know what you look like? Like I do, obviously. Just not yet.

From: NB26@zone.com
To: Bee1984@gmail.com

Don't blame you. We'll have to build up to it. There's a reason they call me the Quasimodo of Leeds, and it's not because I'm into bells.

From: Bee1984@gmail.com
To: NB26@zone.com

I'm not doing hunch puns. Too easy.

Maybe we should have a code word. For when one of us decides it's time to break the rules and swap pics or meet etc.

From: NB26@zone.com
To: Bee1984@gmail.com

Nice. Like the safe words sadomasochists use (apparently . . .) Any ideas?

From: Bee1984@gmail.com
To: NB26@zone.com

Um. Tweedy Twat's Opus? Ms Peach's Dress? Old Man's Foot?

From: NB26@zone.com
To: Bee1984@gmail.com

So it was an old man's foot was it? No wonder it was so chewy.

You know what, Bee, we won't need a code word. When the time is right, I think we'll just know.

NICK

I wasn't okay. Bee was right, again, about that. I *wanted* to be okay, but you don't just scrub twelve years of marriage off the slate without there being some emotional fallout. But thanks to Bee, who had a sixth sense for whenever the black dog was creeping in (and I don't mean Rosie – although she does like a good creep), the fallout was less toxic than it might have been. A minor environmental disaster, instead of a full-on scorched-earth apocalypse.

Boringly, I discovered that the hoary old cliché, 'time heals all wounds' had some truth to it. I did my best to stick to my time-filling routine, skipping the early morning faux-sprightliness and tea-making for obvious reasons (bringing Poll her morning cuppa was now Jez's job), but keeping to the crappy morning telly, Rosie ablution-walk, and Lily-visiting chores. I even wrote to Tweedy and asked him if I could do another pass over the manuscript as a way of keeping myself busy while Bee was working (I'd decided to drop the 'Twat' descriptor: not only was it gender abusive – Dylan would have disowned me for even using it once – I no longer thought of Tweedy that way).

It took a week for Lily's blunted empathy radar to pick up that something was off. 'Haven't seen that mardy cow of yours around for a while. Something going on, lad?' (Poll had earned her 'mardy cow' moniker after she'd politely asked Lily to turn down the volume on her TV. For Lily, this had been akin to a declaration of war.)

'We're taking a break.'

'Are you now. Good thing too. You can do better than her.'

As I genuinely wasn't sure that was true, I deflected her with the Tweedy news. She even managed to put a damp spin on that. 'That's typical of them with money, that is. Can't be arsed to write his own book, so he pays some poor penniless bugger to do it for him.'

The cantankerous old cow had a point. Bee had suggested I write – for myself, for once – what I was feeling, but how exactly *was* I feeling?

The ego-bruise was ever present (*you honestly left me for* Jez, *Poll*? JEZ?), but I could also bounce from righteous anger to relief at the slightest provocation. Relief that what had been a long time coming was finally here; relief that I wasn't the bad guy for once. Relief that Poll's extra-curricular activities allowed me to feel zero guilt about my own emotional entanglement with Bee. And lurking in the background were the Miserable Bastard stalwarts: misery, loneliness, and regret.

It didn't help that with Poll gone, the house felt emptier, less substantial, as if she'd been the only thing holding its bricks and mortar together. Then there was the daily jolt of missing the tiny things you took for granted when you lived with someone – however dysfunctional the relationship. I did the main bulk of the shopping, but Poll had always picked up the toothpaste tab for some reason. Waking up to find that the empty canister hadn't been magically refilled left me in a foul-breathed funk for hours.

Poll had asked me to message her whenever I was going out so that she could dart in to collect her belongings ('without bringing you down, Nick'), and on more than one occasion it had taken me far too long to figure out which part of our life together she'd hustled into Jez's van while I was sloping around Dog Shit Meadow. (<It sounds like that kids' memory game, Nick. You know, where someone removes a painting or an ornament from a room and you have to recall what's missing> <I'd be crap at that. Yesterday it took me four hours to realise that the kitchen clock was gone>)

Gradually, Poll's side of the wardrobe became a wasteland of skeletal coat hangers. Her half of the bed seemed to double in size (until Rosie and her chew toys claimed it for themselves). The place smelled different (<Different how?> <I dunno. Less perfumey, maybe. Although that could be because the bedroom now pongs of eau de Rosie>) The upsides of having the house to myself, watching B-grade action movies at three a.m. or playing my music as loud as I fancied, didn't balance out the emptiness.

And it wouldn't be my home for much longer. We hadn't yet discussed the details, but how could I stay? I might have injected cash into the mortgage (back when I could), but it was her home – I'd moved in with her. Had it ever been mine? I had my shed, my corner of the bedroom, a small glass shelf in the bathroom, a place on the couch, where a million years ago Poll used to lie with her feet up on my lap – but that was it.

Poll. When we'd first met, was there an instant 'this feels right' connection like I'd experienced with Bee? The short answer was no. There was no discernible click, no fanciful thread linking us together. We were colleagues, then friends, before the inevitable drunken hook-up. Sure, we had a good laugh every so often, there was rarely any conflict, and we balanced each other out (she dealt with the life admin; I was the entertainment). The early days were comfortable, not thrilling, although I have a clear memory of being accosted in the Co-operative's parking lot by Saul, her ex. As we loaded the boot with brown bags – this was back in the days when we shopped and cooked together – he came thundering towards us. I'd steeled myself for a physical confrontation, but he ran out of steam once he was within striking distance: 'It won't last. You'll see. It won't fucking last.' And maybe that was another reason why I'd held on for so long. I didn't want Saul to be right. Mine and Poll's relationship had started as a slow burn, but it had stayed that way until the end. It hadn't ignited. It had died out, a bit like this torturous metaphor, because no one had bothered to feed it. But me and Bee . . . Where would that go? I no longer had to worry that Bee and I were embroiled in an emotional affair. I just had to worry about not fucking *that* up, too.

Then there was Dylan. If there was a thread linking Poll and I, it would be him. He would have to be told soon. How *would* he take it?

One evening, when the black dog was being particularly tenacious, instead of flumping on the couch I detoured up to his old room, sat on the bed, and stared at the posters that were still tacked on the walls. Britney, Team Zho, the impossibly good-looking lead actor in *Senses*. I'd told Bee a fair whack about Dylan, but I hadn't told her *everything* about him. There were some things that were out of bounds, even to her.

As I sat there, indulging in my usual one-man pity party, in came, <You OK?>

I wasn't okay. But I would be. Bee was right about that too.

BEE

I was the one, yet again, who pushed us towards the next, ultimately fateful, stage. Three consecutive incidents – *bam, bam, bam* – got me there. I've never been into the woo stuff, but who would blame me for believing an external force was interceding?

The first involved a client, Gemma, who travelled all the way up from Bristol for the fitting, accompanied by her mother. I usually consulted with my out-of-town clients via Skype, showing them how to take their measurements via webcam (and not always successfully – especially when they confused metric with the imperial), but Gemma had insisted on doing it in person. When I let them in, the mother greeted me with chilly civility – it was clear she had doubts about her daughter's choice to do this – then fussed around Gemma as if she were a child or an invalid, asking her if she needed to use the bathroom, or wanted anything to drink. Gemma smiled at me apologetically, but I didn't blame her mum for being overprotective. She was so slender that every vein popped beneath her skin – I desperately wanted to give her a chip butty and a hug – and there was something in her eyes that spoke of an inner fragility, too. Her dress was carefully packed in an opaque plastic sleeve, and even before the mother unzipped it halfway, I could tell it was something special. A Vera Wang, boned, and a beautiful shade of cream. Couture: the kind of dress that should become an heirloom. Most of the gowns I did over were store-bought or mass-produced designer knockoffs and taking my shears to this piece would be sacrilege. Even on eBay it would fetch thousands. When I said this to them, the mother replied, snottily: 'I know that. This is her choice, not mine.'

I looked to Gemma for confirmation. She nodded, glassy-eyed. There was a story there, but I wasn't about to pry. Most of my clients talked eventually, saw me as part tailor, part therapist. After months of doing this, I thought I'd heard all the sob stories about disappointing partners: the cheaters, the gaslighters, the ones who didn't want sex, the ones who wanted too much sex. Others were sick of looking at the dress in the closet, but couldn't bear to donate it to charity or sell it on eBay. The happier ones – like the fabulous couple who commissioned me to turn their suits into cushions – wanted a memento. This was different; the backstory hummed ominously in the air. As I took Gemma's measurements, tears crept down her cheeks. Silent tears that she didn't seem to be aware of. I asked if she wanted to stop, but then out it came, the words tumbling over each other, her mother letting her talk.

Gemma had met her husband in her early twenties, said they 'just knew' they were meant for each other 'the instant' they met. They'd moved in together within a week; simultaneously proposed to each other a month after that ('which sounds unbelievable, but we were so in tune it just felt . . . natural.') Her husband hadn't run off. He hadn't cheated or dumped her at the altar. He'd died: a bike accident on their honeymoon in Tuscany.

The dress was a cruel reminder of everything she'd lost, but she couldn't bear to part with it entirely. Nor did she have any thoughts on how it should be repurposed. I suggested using the underskirt to line a classic, timeless jacket that she could wear all year round (I'd regret that later – my tailoring skills were rusty). It would mean that the dress's integrity would remain (partly) intact, and she could have him with her whenever she needed it. 'Close to your heart, love,' the mother said, finally softening towards me. As they left, her mother whispered, 'They didn't have enough time. Doesn't seem right, does it?'

*

The second shove came when I was round at Leila's, taking her up on the promised microwave meal and booze combo. Thinking it made for an interesting story, I told her about Gemma, totally underestimating the effect it had had on me. It came out on a tide of tears, startling both of us. 'Jesus,' Leila said, handing me a piece of kitchen roll. 'It's like the ending of a Nicholas Sparks movie.' Lev had made himself scarce, choosing to run the nightmare gauntlet of bathing and putting the twins to bed rather than help his wife mop me up. I didn't blame him.

'Okay,' Leila said. 'What's really going on here?'

And then I told her about Nick. He was becoming such an integral part of my life, it didn't feel right keeping it from her any longer.

'How long has this been going on?'

'A while.'

'I *knew* there was a reason why you were looking all glowy. Why didn't you tell me about him before?'

'Because I knew what you'd say. "Don't overshare with strangers online, Bee. He could be a scammer, etc., etc." And then . . . when I found out he was married, I knew you'd think that was dodgy. I mean, *I* thought it was dodgy.'

'It *is* dodgy. And he *could* be a scammer.'

'He hasn't hit me up for cash.'

'*Yet*. You haven't even seen a pic of him or checked him out online. He could be an octogenarian serial killer for all you know.'

'So could I for all he knows.'

'But why didn't he want to FaceTime? He must be hiding something.'

'I told you. We have rules. We like it this way.'

'And these rules would be extremely convenient if you happened to be a scammer.'

'You see? This is why I didn't tell you. I knew I'd get the third degree.' We were creeping dangerously close to a fight, a rarity for us.

'I just don't want you to get hurt again.'

'I know you don't. But you have to trust me on this. We've got a connection.'

She wasn't buying it. I could see her thinking, *You can't form a connection that strong with someone online*. Which was bollocks. It happened to thousands of people every day. If she was going to support me in this, Leila would need proof. I brought up our e-mail thread, ridiculously long by now, and passed the phone to her. 'Here.'

I watched her carefully as she scrolled through it, and there was a second, an instant, where I caught a flicker of something I'd never seen on her face before. Envy? She handed back the phone, and after a weighty pause, said: 'Okay. I get it.'

'You do?'

'Yeah. The way you bounce off each other . . . I can see why you're into him. And you've been honest with him. About everything. About Nate.'

That wasn't entirely true. I hadn't told Nick everything about Nate. I hadn't told *Leila* everything. I hadn't told her that a week after Nate did the dirty on me, I'd discovered I was pregnant. Leila was going through IVF at the time, and while I knew she would have supported my decision to end the pregnancy, it didn't seem right to burden her. It wasn't a hard decision. If anything, all I felt was relief. Dealing with it gave me a sense of control over my life, which at that point had felt like it was spiralling into a shit-show.

'You know, if he is a scammer, he's an incredibly creative one. They usually say they're soldiers trapped in a war zone with no access to funds or some other heroic shit. I'm not sure what angle he's going for saying he's a failed writer in a failing marriage – pity, maybe?'

'Nice, Leila. What happened to "I get it"?'

'Okay, okay. Look, if you're going to go any further with this guy, let me at least check him out.'

'How are you going to do that? I don't even know his full name.'

She huffed. 'There's more than one way to skin a catfish.' She unearthed her Mac from beneath a pile of teething toys and got to work. '"Nick freelance editor". There can't be that many.'

'Leila . . . can't you just trust me on this?'

'Weird. Zone.com isn't coming up. Nor is the IP. Must use blockers.'

Lev returned from bedtime duty with the air of a soldier who'd just survived a particularly bloody skirmish and grabbed a beer from the fridge. 'You're not talking about The Fucker again, are you?' The Fucker. Our name for Nate.

'God, no,' Leila said. 'Bee's got herself a new one. Only we don't actually know who he is.'

'Riiiight.' Lev crept towards the door. 'If you need me, I'll be in bed with Netflix and some tranquilisers.'

'Don't you dare finish watching *BoJack* without me,' Leila called after him. She shut the laptop and gave me one of her hard Paddington Bear stares. 'If he's on the level about his marriage ending, that means he's free. That means he could end up being more than a one-night thing – unless he's a catfishing serial killer. How do you feel about that?'

'About him being a catfishing serial killer?'

Another Paddington stare.

How *did* I feel now that he was free, other than less guilty about what we were doing? On the upside, there was no doubt we had a connection, he made me laugh, seemed to be honest, and while he could be scathing, he was also kind. He didn't bore me. On the downside, he was messy. A wobbly career and nursing the fresh wound of a break up. Who wants mess? And he didn't live anywhere near London. But he was a writer, a reckless voice in my head whispered: *He could move anywhere.*

'He isn't even divorced yet.'

'So? He says the marriage has been dead for a while. You should meet him. Know one way or another. If he is a scam merchant, he'll make an excuse and won't pitch up, but if he isn't, this could be something that's worth taking further.'

'I don't want to spoil it.'

'I get it. This is safer for you.'

She was right. This was intimacy without the fear of disappointment. Taking things further might warp what we had and – yes – destroy the fantasy. This was cowardice.

*

Leila's words ghosted me home. As I turned into Goldhawk Road, everything seemed to have a sinister cast to it; even the windows of my beloved fabric stores appeared to eye me malevolently. Criss-crossing to my street, the darkened buildings were more foreboding than ever, and I kept hearing footsteps behind me. Which was why, when I entered the communal hallway and saw the figure standing on the stairs, I overreacted and screamed. Jonas, in nothing but a pair of ratty pyjama bottoms, his ribs and sternum visible beneath a wrinkled sleeve of yellowing skin, said something to me in Russian, and then darted for the door. I slammed it behind me, leaned my back against it, and he loomed in closer, not threatening exactly, but with purpose. A thunder of footsteps and then Magda appeared, her hair a thin, grey cloud. I barely recognised her without the makeup mask and headscarf she habitually wore.

'I am sorry, Rebecca,' she said. 'All of today he has been different.'

I helped Magda corral him upstairs and offered to make tea while she gently led him into the bedroom.

'No, no. We will have whisky.' She flapped a hand at a decanter on the drinks trolley.

I sat in Jonas's armchair – permanently imprinted with his shape – downed a double, and listened to Magda singing softly to him in the background. She returned ten minutes later, lipsticked and headscarfed. Without a word, she refilled my glass and poured herself a healthy slug. Then she sat opposite me.

'How do you do it, Magda?'

'Do what?'

'Cope?' *How do you cope watching someone you love drift away from you? Or is it better than being alone?*

'Sometimes I wish he were dead.' Deadpan. 'But do I regret the time we have had? No. I would do it again, even with this outcome.' We sat in silence and finished our drinks. As I left, she gripped my wrist and said, softly – so softly I couldn't be sure I hadn't misheard – 'Don't wait.'

From: Bee1984@gmail.com
To: NB26@zone.com

Shall we meet?

NICK

Shall we meet?

Yes. No. OF COURSE WE SHOULD MEET. Delete, delete.

I could sense the thread between us twanging. It had taken bravery to suggest that. I couldn't keep her hanging for an answer, but I needed to think. Seconds turned into minutes as I sat in the kitchen, the wooden chair numbing my arse, fighting the temptation to dig into the gin again.

Shall we meet?

Bee was all I had that was good in the world. Well, her and Rosie (there was no question about who'd get custody of the dog). Did I want to fuck with that? Here's where I should say, *if only I'd known how it would all turn out* . . . but despite foreshadowing being a cheap trick, I've never been any good at it (and I'm nothing if not cheap – ask Tweedy).

Lost in this back-and-forth, I barely registered the front door slamming open. 'Anyone home?' Dylan called, before appearing, holdall in hand. He looked me over. 'There you are.'

'Here I am.'

'Mum asked me to get some stuff for her.'

'You came all the way from Brum for that at this time of night?'

'Nah. Wanted to see how you were doing.'

I loved him for that. 'She's finally told you then.'

'Course.'

'Beer?'

'Nah.' He dug in his backpack and proffered a joint. 'Don't tell

Mum.' He sat at the kitchen table and lit up without bothering to open the back door. 'You and Mum . . . was it something I did?'

'Of course it wasn't. You . . .' Then it dawned that he was messing with me. 'Very funny.'

'Sorry. Couldn't resist.' He squinted at me through the smoke and passed the joint.

'How are you really feeling about this, Dylan?'

'About you and Mum? I'm twenty-four. I *think* I can handle my parents getting divorced.'

Parents. A flush of warmth. So he did see me as a father figure. *Not a total failure*. 'We'll always be friends, your mum and me. You know that, right?' Would we? A shuddery thought of Christmases at Poll and Jez's – Poll and Jez, who, come to think of it, sounded like characters out of a toddlers' show.

'Yeah.'

'And I'll always be there for you, too.'

He didn't give me a rev for this sappy cliché. He knew I meant it. And I did, although it had been a long haul to get there. I'd been completely at sea with him at first. In retrospect, aping my mum and dad's practical, gruffly affectionate Northern style of parenting, which was light on the hugs and the 'I love you's and heavy on the 'get outside and play, bit of sleet won't kill you,' wasn't the best approach. He was smart, nerdy, intense, serious, nothing like I was at that age. I was the loudmouth class clown, swearing and shagging my way into puberty and beyond. Thanks to my name, Nicolas Belcher, I'd had to learn survival skills fast, and apart from the occasional jibe, I'd avoided being targeted by the bully brigade.

Dylan, sensitive Dylan, wasn't so lucky. They'd hit him hard, both physically and psychologically, and for years he'd hidden the trauma from Poll. Then it all came to a horrible head, on the night before his fifteenth birthday. Poll and I were supposed to be helping her parents move into their new flat that evening, but I'd come down with a stomach bug. I returned home unexpectedly, and knew something was wrong the instant I opened the front door. Dylan's musical taste was typically vanilla in the extreme, but The Innocence Project was thumping angry bass throughout the house. But it wasn't just that. The atmosphere felt *off*, somehow. Up the stairs, a knock on Dylan's door, the cold wash of panic when he didn't respond, then opening up to see him, plastic bag in hand, attempting to loop the noose over the faux Tuscan beam in his room. A freeze-frame second, and then we both said the same thing: 'Shit.'

He'd begged me not to tell Poll. Not the sort of secret you should keep from anyone's mum, but I did it all the same – with the caveat that we took steps to sort out what had driven him to consider such drastic action. A quiet, but insistent word to his teachers, undercut with the threat of a lawsuit. Hours spent sitting outside counsellors' offices straining to hear the murmured voices inside; taking his side when he dropped out of university and transferred to design school, which created another rift between Poll and me. It had taken a matter of life and death for us to connect – an incident that neither of us ever explicitly referenced, but which was never wholly out of my mind. We'd gone through a lot, him and me. Now an art gallery curator, there was a contentment about him these days that seemed genuine, and he was earning double what I'd made at the height of my teaching career, so it had all worked out in the end. For him, at least.

I was hogging the joint, and he motioned for it. 'You look . . . younger, Nick.'

'Don't talk shite.'

'No, you do. Less stressed. More *here*.'

'Well, I am on my way to being stoned.'

'Maybe it's the relief that it's finally over.'

'What do you mean by that?'

'You and Mum were just going through the motions. You weren't happy, you were bored.'

'Was it that obvious?'

'Yeah. At least now you can move on and not pretend anymore.'

I needed to tell someone about Bee. It shouldn't have been Dylan, but out it came anyway. 'I've met someone. Not like that,'

I clarified hastily. 'I haven't been cheating on your mum. That's her department.' *Smooth, Nick*. 'Sorry.'

"S'all right. She did cheat. And with him as well. Jeremy. Ugh.'

'Thought you liked him.'

'He's as boring as shite.'

He *was* as boring as shite. The insult made me feel warm inside. Yes, I am that petty.

'Who is this person, then?'

'Met her accidentally online. We've been talking – *just* talking – for a bit.' My tongue was woolly from the joint. 'But there's . . . something good there. And she wants to meet.'

'So do it.'

What was making me hesitate? Fear, of course. What if I didn't measure up? And, on the flip side – shallowness. I'd been harvesting personal info scraps in order to build up an image of what Bee might look like, and if she turned out to be less than attractive, would I care? Yes. A bit. Why lie? 'Worried I'll fuck it up. Worried there won't be a physical attraction.' There. I'd said it.

He gave me an eye-roll, a throwback gesture to his pre-teen self. 'You can always go back to how you were.' *Duh, old-timer*. 'Do you love her?'

'I told you, I don't even know what she looks like.'

'Do you, though?'

'You know what? I think I *could*.'

*

From: NB26@zone.com
To: Bee1984@gmail.com

Let's do it!

From: Bee1984@gmail.com
To: NB26@zone.com

Really?

From: NB26@zone.com
To: Bee1984@gmail.com

Of course. When? You decide. As you know, my social calendar is flexible.

From: Bee1984@gmail.com
To: NB26@zone.com

Tues/Wed? No fittings on those days. Are you sure? Don't want you to feel pressured. I get that what we have right now works. Understand if you don't want to mess with it.

From: NB26@zone.com
To: Bee1984@gmail.com

I'm sure. Don't get cold feet on me now . . .

Either is fine for me. Where? Happy to come to you. Make it a day trip. Would be an excuse to get out of this dump.

From: Bee1984@gmail.com
To: NB26@zone.com

Um . . . Under the clock at Euston Station? Or wherever you fancy.

From: NB26@zone.com
To: Bee1984@gmail.com

Under the clock it is. How will I know you?

From: Bee1984@gmail.com
To: NB26@zone.com

I'll wear a red coat. Obviously I'll know you because of the hunch and enormous bell.

From: NB26@zone.com
To: Bee1984@gmail.com

A red coat? That's all I'm getting?

From: Bee1984@gmail.com
To: NB26@zone.com

I'm not a supermodel if that's what you're asking. Is that a problem?

From: NB26@zone.com
To: Bee1984@gmail.com

If you *were* a supermodel it would be a problem. I may not be Quasimodo, but I'm not exactly Jason Frey either.

From: Bee1984@gmail.com
To: NB26@zone.com

Who's that?

From: NB26@zone.com
To: Bee1984@gmail.com

Movie star? Ex-wrestler?

From: Bee1984@gmail.com
To: NB26@zone.com

Oh right. Seriously though, If you want to swap pics/call/switch to WhatsApp etc beforehand, we can.

From: NB26@zone.com
To: Bee1984@gmail.com

Nah. Let's leave it. We've gone this far, why chicken out at the last hurdle?

From: Bee1984@gmail.com
To: NB26@zone.com

Hey! Wear tweed. I dare you . . .

From: NB26@zone.com
To: Bee1984@gmail.com

Dare accepted. I'm already nervous. But in a good way.

xx

BEE

The big day . . . Oh God. Where to start with that?

Leila came over that morning for moral support, leaving the twins with her mum for a couple of hours. While she sat on the bed, I must have tried on six or seven different outfits. Above us, Magda was playing the piano softly, something she hadn't done for a while. It needed tuning, and the off-key tone made it sound portentous, like the soundtrack to a low-budget drama.

'Hair up or down?'

'Down. Obviously.'

I hated my curls; Leila loved them. She'd been furious when I'd chopped them off a few years ago (so had Nate, the controlling bastard). My armpits stung from that morning's shave; and the rest of me was as freshly plucked and waxed as a supermarket chicken – the kind of crap I thought I was done with when I'd deleted Tinder. I'd been up most of the night tidying the flat and packing away anything potentially embarrassing (a joke vibrator, the worst of the self-help books, the piles of dusty out-of-date makeup in the bathroom) in case Nick came back here. Without the fabric swatches and works in progress, the faux mid-century furniture (Nate's choice) looked stark and unwelcoming. The David Bowie duvet cover was the only splash of colour left, and Ziggy Stardust pierced me with his zingy, screen-printed eyes. I didn't have enough books. Would he judge me for that? He was a writer, after all. In the days before the meeting, he'd shared the titles of his favourite novels: one I'd read (*Catcher in the Rye*); another I'd ordered from Amazon (*Things*

Fall Apart), and one I was still trying to track down (*Zanzibar*, by Juliet Boyd). I couldn't find it anywhere online – RED FLAG – and naively assumed it was out of print.

Clarice was going to stay where she was next to the window. I would never consign her to the box room again – *that* was non-negotiable.

I'd steam-cleaned my good red coat, bought a pair of black ankle boots off eBay, and invested in new underwear – agonising over bras in M&S, nothing too sexy, nothing too safe. Leila and I finally settled on a little black dress I'd made in college, which used to be form-fitting but now hung slightly loose. I'd been so swept up in everything that, without even being aware of it, I'd lost a few pounds.

'You look stunning, Bee.'

'I'm never going to be stunning.'

'Well, you look it to me. If it doesn't work out, don't be too disappointed, right?'

'I won't.' *Liar*.

'Be safe. Stay in a public place if you pick up any dodgy vibes. Call me as soon as you can, and if he's a dick and you need rescuing, just text, and me and the devil children will come and fetch you.' She hugged me. 'I love you.'

I saw her out and watched as she walked to the end of my road and disappeared around the corner. A forensics van was parked diagonally across the street, which sounds more ominous than it was. The two women inside it were laughing and smoking. I killed time by straightening my hair, singeing lock after lock for no other reason than it was something to keep me occupied. As I left, I glanced up at Magda's window. Jonas was staring down at me, fingers splayed against the glass like a child, or a prisoner.

The trip to Euston Square usually took twenty-five minutes, but I'd given myself an hour to be safe. Little by little the carriage filled up, every passenger, regardless of age, attached to their phones. I kept catching strangers' eyes, couldn't help but wonder if any of them were also en route to a potentially life-changing encounter.

Antsy, I joined the gang and put in my earphones, listened to 'Life on Mars?' on a loop. Bowie may have been one of our touchstones, but if anything, the soundtrack heightened the jitters. The rain greeted me as I was funnelled out onto Euston Road, and I paused to drop some change into a panhandler's cup. Just for luck. *Karma*. With fifteen minutes to go, I made for the loos to double-check my makeup. The lighting made my skin appear sallow; the rain had undone an hour's worth of hair straightening.

Okay. Deep breath. Here goes.

I stood directly under the digital clock, self-conscious, trying not to sweat, watching as the numbers clicked over. Every time an announcement came, the crowd staring up at the boards reconfigured around me as pockets of people swarmed off to the various platforms. The scent of fast food and cigarette smoke wafted through the concourse doors; every sense felt heightened. *This is it. The moment that could change the rest of your life.* Tick. Tock. The digital clock tipped into 12.00.

NICK

I didn't feel like myself that day. Which wasn't a bad thing, necessarily. In the days preceding, Dylan had taken me in hand, generously using up his precious holiday time: 'She's a designer, right? You can't pitch up in your usual gear, she'll run a mile.'

'Cheers for that. She dared me to wear tweed. An in-joke.'

It was a challenge for him, and he loved every second of it. *Stepdad Makeover*. Off we went to trawl the charity shops, where I yawned and watched posses of elderly women professionally swiping through racks of cardigans, while he made a beeline for the far smaller menswear sections. We found the suit, a three-piece, nineteen-fifties-style tweedy number in the Cancer Society shop. There were gasps from the other shoppers when I emerged from the cramped fitting room. 'That's champion, love,' a cardigan browser proclaimed. It fit perfectly, 'like it was meant to be,' Dylan said, before wafting away to search for a shirt to go underneath it.

It was a tad itchy, but it didn't smell of must like the stuff I used to pick up from jumble sales during my teenage grunge years, and although it was older than I was, I sensed it had more integrity. *Clothes maketh the man.* I could almost imagine myself fwah-fwah-fwah-fwahing with the old-school Bullingdon boys, taunting 'plebs', trashing restaurants, or whatever those privileged pricks used to do for fun. *If only Bernard the Tweedy ex-Twat could see me now.*

Next, Dylan swept me into an upscale salon, fussing around me like a personal stylist and barking orders at the surly barber. And to top it off, he insisted I splurge forty euros on teeth whitening. Strapped to what felt like an electric chair, gums stinging, and drooling over a paper bib, I bid farewell to thirty years of cigarette and coffee stains.

I'd become a new man. A new man dressed in a dead man's clothes (I've still got that suit).

I barely slept the night before. Gave up and rose at five, showered until my fingertips puckered, shaved (cutting myself twice), and slid on my tweedy skin. I lumped gel on the new hair (long fringe, short back and sides, in keeping with my new vintage aesthetic), then took Rosie next door. Lily had offered to watch her for me, giving me a knowing wink when I'd asked if she could stay over the night. The old bag cackled at my get-up, but didn't ask who I was going to meet, merely saw me off with a muttered, 'Hope she's less of a mardy cow than the other one.' I splurged on a first-class ticket for the first time ever, which added to my sense of fraudulence. There was a smug matiness between the passengers as they ignored the harassed worker bee parcelling out the 'free' breakfast sandwiches.

I'd brought along a book, but I couldn't concentrate. Would Bee and I look into each other's eyes and just know? Why not? After all, we already had a solid 'how we met story' that we could one day reminisce about in a care home while a nurse wiped our arses. I hadn't had that before (a *coup de foudre*, not arse-wiping, obviously). Lust, yes, who hasn't? But love at first sight? Real love? No.

The other passengers were cracking cans of G&T and mini bottles of red wine with the greed and enthusiasm of people determined to get their money's worth, but I resisted the temptation. I didn't want to show up stinking of booze. Instead, I sipped at a can of no-brand cola. Bad idea. The caffeine exacerbated the nerves.

Bing bong, then: 'We are now approaching Euston Station.' Bee seemed to think there wasn't a direct line to Euston from Leeds, but here I was, minutes away.

The worker bee hustled up the aisle, sweeping the detritus off the tables in preparation for the next influx of privileged arseholes.

When I thanked her, she blinked in surprise, then gave me a collusive grin. 'Nice suit.'

'Cheers. Bought it especially.'

'Somewhere nice?'

'Someone nice.' *Hopefully*.

*

From: NB26@zone.com
To: Bee1984@gmail.com

Running late?

From: Bee1984@gmail.com
To: NB26@zone.com

About to ask you the same question!! I'm here. Under the clock?

From: NB26@zone.com
To: Bee1984@gmail.com

Me too.

From: Bee1984@gmail.com
To: NB26@zone.com

OK are you the tall guy with the hat?

From: NB26@zone.com
To: Bee1984@gmail.com

No hat. Tall though. Wearing a three-piece tweed suit as instructed. It's as itchy as fuck.

From: Bee1984@gmail.com
To: NB26@zone.com

Can't see you. Are you sure you're at Euston?

From: NB26@zone.com
To: Bee1984@gmail.com

Of course. There are bloody great big signs everywhere.

What are you wearing?

From: Bee1984@gmail.com
To: NB26@zone.com

Red coat. Told you. Can't miss it. Green scarf. Boots. Messy black hair.

From: NB26@zone.com
To: Bee1984@gmail.com

Hang on . . . nope, not you.

From: Bee1984@gmail.com
To: NB26@zone.com

I'm right under the clock!! Opposite the Pret.

From: NB26@zone.com
To: Bee1984@gmall.com

Opposite the what?

From: Bee1984@gmail.com
To: NB26@zone.com

The Pret stand. Pret a Manger?

From: NB26@zone.com
To: Bee1984@gmail.com

Can't see that. FFS! I'll go over to the information counter.

From: NB26@zone.com
To: Bee1984@gmail.com

Can you see me now? I'm waving.

From: Bee1984@gmail.com
To: NB26@zone.com

Nope. Send me your number. I'll call you. This is crazy!

From: NB26@zone.com
To: Bee1984@gmail.com

90897886544

From: Bee1984@gmail.com
To: NB26@zone.com

Shouldn't it start with a zero?

From: NB26@zone.com
To: Bee1984@gmail.com

? That's always been my number.

From: Bee1984@gmail.com
To: NB26@zone.com

Won't connect.

Try mine. 0876567553

From: NB26@zone.com
To: Bee1984@gmail.com

On it.

From: Bee1984@gmail.com
To: NB26@zone.com

You call yet?

From: NB26@zone.com
To: Bee1984@gmail.com

3 times. Bad signal??

From: Bee1984@gmail.com
To: NB26@zone.com

This is freaking me out. Take a pic of where you're standing & send it to me.

From: NB26@zone.com
To: Bee1984@gmail.com

Got it?

From: Bee1984@gmail.com
To: NB26@zone.com

Nothing's come through.

From: NB26@zone.com
To: Bee1984@gmail.com

Says it's sent. I'm going to shout BEE really really loudly. In 3, 2, 1

From: NB26@zone.com
To: Bee1984@gmail.com

You hear that?

From: Bee1984@gmail.com
To: NB26@zone.com

No.

From: NB26@zone.com
To: Bee1984@gmail.com

You must have. People are staring at me like I've lost it.

How can we both be here and not see each other?

From: Bee1984@gmail.com
To: NB26@zone.com

We can't.

From: NB26@zone.com
To: Bee1984@gmail.com

Go to platform 22. Stand under the info screen.

From: Bee1984@gmail.com
To: NB26@zone.com

There IS no platform 22.

I know what this is.

From: NB26@zone.com
To: Bee1984@gmail.com

?

From: Bee1984@gmail.com
To: NB26@zone.com

You've been messing with me the whole time, right? Some big joke. Fuck you. FUCK YOU. Go and fuck yourself.

From: NB26@zone.com
To: Bee1984@gmail.com

Bee? I'M HERE AT EUSTON STATION. I am not fucking with you.

From: NB26@zone.com
To: Bee1984@gmail.com

Bee?

From: NB26@zone.com
To: Bee1984@gmail.com

[You have been blocked by this recipient]

PART TWO

NOTTING HELL

Transcript of the minutes of the Berenstain Society, Livestock Road, Manchester, 15/04/2019

Secretary: Kelvin Oduah.
Chairperson: Henrietta Mueck.
Also present: Geoffrey Gleeson, Debbie Gough and Isaac French.
Absent (with apologies): Adil Singh.

The meeting opened with the recap of last month's minutes, followed by Debbie Gough's reading of our Mission Statement.

I (Kelvin Oduah) then brought up the main order of business. I relayed that on 01/04/2019 Nicolas Belcher, a male of forty-five years, currently unemployed, contacted the society [see addendum 1a], requesting 'help with an unusual dilemma'. Taking the precautions we voted into practice at the 13/06/2017 meeting [see addendum 1b/17], I entered into i-mail and telephonic correspondence with him.

Mr Belcher related to me that he had 'accidentally' formed a connection with a woman he had met via a misdirected i-mail, and, after corresponding daily for an unspecified period, they formed a strong attachment. When they finally decided to meet in person at Euston Station, she had not been present, 'although she swore she was there, and I believed her'. He said that the woman, known to him as Bee or Rebecca, 'repurposed wedding dresses' and lived in West London. He had searched for businesses of this type and under this name but had found no corresponding evidence. He had explored the possibility that she was lying to him but knew 'in his gut' that she was a genuine person.

Confused, Mr Belcher had re-read their correspondence and discovered several discrepancies which he 'had found weird at the time but hadn't taken seriously'. These included the following:

She used a dating 'app' called 'Tinder'.

She referenced a (frankly bizarre) television show called *Love Island*.

She continually got the titles of books 'a bit wrong'.

She professed no knowledge of the well-known actor Jason Frey.

She believed there was no direct train line to Euston from Leeds.

She cited 'pounds' as currency instead of euros.

Most notably, she mentioned that Donald Trump, the American mogul who was recently (and unsuccessfully) prosecuted for ecocide, was the American President.

(At this, Geoffrey Gleeson expostulated, 'You've got to be [expletive] joking.' I responded that Mr Belcher had indeed related to me that he'd assumed she was joking.)

Mr Belcher said that he had 'fallen into an Arpanet hole' in an attempt to make sense of these discrepancies, which had eventually led him to us. He said that while he did believe there could be a 'multitude of universes or timelines out there, the whole thing is [expletive] mad, isn't it?'

Isaac French took umbrage at this, but Henrietta Mueck reminded Isaac that he too had once been in denial until he'd accepted the truth.

I remarked that if Mr Belcher's assertions were correct, this could be the first recorded instance of technological communication occurring across the mesh. Isaac French countered that 'we know from past experience' that the chances that Mr Belcher was 'on the level' were slim.

Henrietta Mueck suggested that she meet with Mr Belcher 'on neutral ground' to assess his claims in person. Geoffrey Gleeson and I volunteered to accompany her. In addition, Geoffrey volunteered to embark on further surveillance of Mr Belcher, to ensure that he is not 'another [expletive] time-waster'.

NICK

Desperation. Hope. In the weeks following what would eventually become known as Euston-Gate, I became overly familiar with those two words. I now understand why desperate people find religion or end up believing in aliens or conspiracy theories. Because sometimes the rational answer doesn't cut it. Sometimes you have to look outside the box. And my hope-desperation twofer had led me *way* outside the box, all the way to a Willow Green allotment in fact, where, God help me, I was waiting to meet a bunch of people who even the most charitable among us would label, 'raging nutjob weirdos'.

But first, rewind.

As far as soul-crushing experiences go, hanging around a train station in a stupid suit and staring stupidly at your phone's screen while pieces of you break off and shatter is right up there with the worst of them. Along with catching the next train home because a security guard is eyeing you with increasing suspicion, and you don't know what the fuck else to do. Then there's fielding the pitying 'didn't work out, huh?' smiles from the mildly flirty worker bee you bantered with on the journey in; creeping past your neighbour's house like a dirty stop-out because you can't face the belligerent old bag; letting yourself into your empty soulless house that isn't really yours, and lying to your stepson when he messages you to see how it went (<Great! She seems nice>). And who could forget the profound ignominy of sitting at the kitchen table drinking the last bottle of cheap Christmas gin when your soon-to-be ex-wife walks in because you'd forgotten you'd messaged her to say you'd be out. (At least she hadn't brought Jez along.)

Poll jumped when she saw me.

'I thought you were supposed to be out till late?'

'I was. Came back.'

'Why?'

'Came down with something.' *I believe the medical term is a broken heart.*

'You don't look ill.'

'Thanks. I think.'

'What the hell are you wearing?'

'What's it look like?'

'It looks like you're about to take part in a nineteen-fifties' tea dance. Where's Rosie?'

'Lily's watching her.'

A frown. 'Is that the shitty gin we keep for Mam?'

'It is.'

She assessed me with her teacher radar. 'What's going on, Nick?'

'Nothing. Can't a cuckolded man get pissed on bad gin in a bad suit without an interrogation these days?'

She sniffed. 'Cuckolded. What a word. Haven't heard that for years.'

'Yeah well. Old suit. Old word.' (I was slurring only slightly at this point.) 'Do you want me to go out into the shed so you can sort out your stuff in peace?'

'You're all right. I was only coming for my ID card.'

'Tea?'

'Is there milk?'

'Course not.'

She took out a glass, sat opposite me and poured herself an inch. When she'd first walked in (shock aside), part of my brain had picked up that there was something subtly different about her. She hadn't changed her outward appearance (Poll knew what suited her and she'd resisted the temptation of the post-break-up makeover), and it had taken me a while to figure out what it was. Her body language was looser, more relaxed. As if I were the equivalent of an overloaded rucksack she'd been lugging around for years, and now that I was off her back, she could move with more ease and lightness. Dylan had picked up a similar internal change in me during our tête-à-tête in the kitchen pre-makeover, and I was grateful he couldn't see me now – I felt like I'd aged forty years in the last four hours.

She sipped and grimaced. 'How does Mam drink this stuff?'

'You know her. She'd drink sewerage if it was thirty per cent proof.'

'She asked after you the other day, you know.'

'She must be delighted you've finally given the miserable bastard the boot.'

'Give over, Nick.' We shared a smile.

'Dylan's taken it well.'

'He has, hasn't he? I was worried he'd be furious at me. I wouldn't have been surprised if he'd disowned me and taken your side.'

'There are no sides in this, Poll.' An inner wince – hadn't I said this exact thing to Bee? 'I think he's relieved. He said that at least we can stop pretending now.'

'Wise words.'

'Wise kid. Not kid. Adult. Christ, we're old.'

'We are at that.' She pushed the glass away. 'I know you. I can see something's going on. You really can talk to me about it, Nick.'

It was certainly tempting to spill the rancid beans. Whatever had happened to our relationship, we were friends once. It wasn't as if I had anyone else to confide in. Lily wasn't an option. Dylan didn't need more stepdad bullshit complicating his life, my parents were in the lower-middle-class suburb in the sky, and thanks to a combination of depression, self-loathing and rampant money borrowing, I'd burned bridges with my other friends. After a few seconds of indecision, I babbled something about 'being caught up in work'. It would have been gratifying on an ego level to tell her about connecting with Bee: *you're not the only one who's wanted*, but the soul-crushing ignominy of 'she didn't pitch' would have cancelled that out – and then some. And I didn't have the words to adequately describe how profoundly the subsequent message blocking had affected me. I hadn't fully realised how deep Bee had crawled under my skin until she was no longer there.

'I'm worried about you, Nick.'

'Don't be. I'll be fine. Really, Poll. You know me, I like a good wallow.'

'We really do need to sort out the other stuff at some stage. The practicalities. Will you let me know when you're ready to do that?'

'I will.'

With a sisterly pat on the arm, Poll left. I hadn't given into the temptation of telling her about Bee, but I did the next best thing. I asked myself, if I *had* told her, what would Poll, practical Poll, have said?

There must be an explanation, Nick.

I'd pitched up, I knew that for sure, unless my life was one giant plot twist and I was massively, insanely deluded. There was only one Euston Station in the world, so a miscommunication was out. And there was no way Bee *couldn't* have seen and heard me yelling my head off on the station forecourt. That left the ego-annihilating possibility that she'd been there, spotted me and my tweed suit, and done a runner. Unlikely – because the Bee I knew (or thought I knew) wasn't cruel, and she wasn't a coward. If she had found me physically repulsive, she would have been more likely to let me down gently with 'I think we should just be friends, Nick.' Not leave me stranded next to a Frites outlet looking like a plonker while pretending I was the one in the wrong. I was there. And unless *she* was a scammer or psychopath who got her kicks from messing with emotionally fragile losers – and I really didn't think she was – she was there, too.

Then there was this: *There is no platform 22.*

I could let it go, or I could attempt to find out what that explanation could possibly be. (Incidentally, I didn't do this immediately – I was too drunk. I slept off the gin, collected Rosie the following morning, deflected Lily with some rubbish about needing to re-edit Tweedy's book, and drank an ocean of coffee first.)

In the shed, with the spiders and Rosie for company (until she got bored and trundled back to the house), I began. When an extensive online search for any sign of Bee/Rebecca and her business came up empty, I dove into our i-mail thread. Re-visiting Past Nick and Bee's interactions made me laugh, cry, and cringe (mostly cringe). But I eventually homed in on a number of 'platform 22' style oddities and discrepancies – throwaway references to books, movies, politics, and tech. There were too many to discount – fifty-four to be precise – and while some could *just* about have been rationalised away as jokes (Trump as President, because *seriously*?), typos, or that thing we all do: pretending to have heard of a book or a movie so as not to seem ignorant, there were others where I wanted to slap Past Nick upside the head for not being sharper (for example, when Bee had mentioned Brexit, why didn't I follow up on it instead of stupidly assuming it was a typo and she'd meant to write 'Biscuit' or 'Breakfast'?). It was Patricia Highsmith who eventually pushed me into tin-foil millinery land. *Crossed Lines* versus *Strangers on a Train*. After searching in vain for Bee's version of the title, I took a punt on a sweep for 'Alternative book titles no explanation?' Buried in a slew of useless links was an article with the strapline: 'These People Think They're Living in an Alternative Universe Because of a Kids' Book!' An exposé, not kind, about a group known as The Berenstain Society. According to the article, their beliefs were based on the (bizarrely inconsequential) fact that they 'remembered' a childhood book entitled *The Berenstein Bears* being spelled as BerenSTAIN. Instead of just shrugging this off, they'd concluded that this was proof that they'd somehow slipped into a different reality and were 'displaced persons'. Thinking, *fuck it* (like I said, desperation), I tracked down the society's Arpanet page. There was nothing on it about their beliefs, just a copy of a digitally altered Berenstein Bear book cover, ominously titled *The Berenstain Bears and THE TRUTH*, and an i-mail link. Double-fuck it. I cobbled together an i-mail with the subject header, 'Need help with an unusual dilemma', and blasted it off into loon land.

After a surreally formal and unexpectedly sane i-mail exchange and a dry, halting phone chat with Kelvin Oduah, who said he was the group's secretary, he eventually invited me to meet with him and a couple of his fellow conspiracists in order 'to assess the viability of your claims'.

So here I was, sitting on a mildewing bench next to the allotment's rickety coffee kiosk, wondering what the hell I was hoping to achieve. To be fair, it would have been a pleasant place to while away the time, if it weren't for the fact that the kiosk was shut, there wasn't a soul around apart from me and some tenacious rooks, and the allotment was next to a funeral parlour. That seemed apt for some reason. You could watch Granny's remains being wheeled off to be broken down into fertiliser and then pop next door to dig up some (previously fertilised) veggies for the wake. The circle of life at work. I was musing on this, annoying myself with cod-philosophical meanderings, when I heard my name being called.

At first sight and despite the fact they were a spectacularly mismatched crew, the three people wending my way didn't fit the loon brigade stereotype I'd been expecting. (To be honest, I'm still not sure what that was: mad shiny hats, enormous beards and clown makeup, maybe?) It was obvious which of the two approaching men had to be Kelvin. His appearance mirrored his precise, buttoned-up way of speaking to the letter – neat, bespectacled, and with his shirt tucked neatly into sensible trousers, as if he'd been dressed by his mum. After a perfunctory handshake, he introduced me to his companions, Henrietta (age indeterminate, grey-haired, grey-suited, German, intimidating) and Geoffrey (fifties, bullet-headed, stocky and anoraked). Initially, Geoffrey was the only one who gave off obvious weirdo vibes. Neither Henrietta nor Kelvin were what you'd call friendly, but Geoffrey radiated hostility from the get-go.

After the introductions, we lapsed into silence, which no one but me seemed to find awkward. Unable to bear it any longer, I said, 'Nice place. Do you usually meet here? Your group, I mean?'

'Course we bloody don't,' Geoffrey scoffed. 'We'd be fucking stupid to show you our . . . show you our headquarters till we knew for sure you weren't a time-waster.'

'Right. Makes sense.' It actually did make sense in a weird way. That article had been brutal. And paranoia went hand in hand with anything conspiratorial, didn't it?

Then Henrietta, who I'd instantly pegged as the leader, got into it. 'To confirm, Mr Belcher, you have explored all other possibilities that may explain your situation?'

'Nick, please. Other than I'm delusional or she's a psychopath, there aren't any. Which is why I ended up here. With you.' I smiled. No one smiled back.

'Now please elaborate on what you term the "discrepancies" in your correspondence.'

'I listed them in the i-mails.' I glanced at Kelvin for confirmation, but he was studiously avoiding eye-contact. Perhaps he found Henrietta as intimidating as I did. She had the self-assurance of someone who should be running a bank or a country. Hardly the sort of person you'd expect to encounter in an allotment during a clandestine conspiracy group meet-up.

'I would like to hear them in your own words.'

I ran through them ineptly, Henrietta's piercing, interrogative gaze throwing me off my stride.

'And you do not have Rebecca's full name or address?'

'No. We had these rules about not exchanging personal info.' I chuckled. 'Stupid, right?'

'Yes.' *Okaaay*. She held out a hand. 'These i-mails? May I see them?'

'I'm not sure I'd be comfortable with that.'

'Then we have nothing more to say here.'

Fuck it. Henrietta didn't look like the sort of person who'd do a runner with the phone. Geoffrey did, but at some point during my dissertation, he'd wandered off to inspect a scarecrow in a neighbouring plot. 'Okay. Fine. But don't judge me.'

'I am not in the business of judging people, Nicolas.'

Henrietta smoothed her skirt and sat primly on the edge of the bench. Kelvin stayed where he was, stock-still yet somehow also managing to appear anxious. Geoffrey lit up a rollie and kicked at the dirt around his new scarecrow friend (who was arguably better turned-out). There can be few things more squirm-inducing than watching a stranger who believed she was from another world scrolling through your most private messages. Henrietta gave nothing away: she could have been reading the weather report rather than mine and Bee's often outlandish 'would you rather' banter. My only hope of distraction was to initiate a conversation with Kelvin – it was that or trade hostilities with mad-dog Geoffrey. But Kelvin was lost in whatever internal world he inhabited. Or *other* world, seeing as he believed he was a 'displaced person'. Might as well start with that. 'When did you first realise you were a displaced person, Kelvin?'

He jerked like a robot that had been kicked into life. 'In my late teens.'

'Because of that book's misspelled title?'

'That was one indication of my status, yes.'

'There are others?'

'Of course.'

I waited for more. None came. 'Right. And you didn't have any issues coming to terms with this . . . status?'

'Of course I did, Nicolas. Everyone doubts it at first.'

'I fucking didn't,' Geoffrey called. He must have ears like a bat. I didn't miss that Kelvin winced at Geoffrey's bad language.

'And what do you reckon the chances are that this is what's happening here? That me and Bee are in different timelines or realities or whatever and have somehow managed to communicate?'

'We will need time to consider if this is indeed an example of a glitch occurring.'

'A glitch?'

'In order for the mesh to be crossed, there must be a glitch.'

'And the mesh is . . .?'

'It is what we term the theoretical space, or lack thereof, between timelines.'

'Right. Of course.'

Henrietta stood and handed me my phone. 'Thank you. It is unfortunate that your correspondent broke off communication, as it would be useful if she could confirm this from her side. Is it possible she will reconnect?'

'Your guess is as good as mine, Henrietta. I bloody well hope so.'

'There is always hope, Nicolas.' The first hint of humanity. Henrietta didn't strike me as the hopeful or romantic type, but hey, I was at the stage where any port in a storm, however loopy, was welcome.

'So. What happens now?'

Henrietta drily informed me that they would need to confer before the group accepted me as one of its members. As I hadn't actually requested to join, I should have politely backed away right then. *Oh hindsight . . .*

I thanked them for whatever it was that had just happened, and watched them walking away, Geoffrey pausing to gift me with a parting glare and chuck his cigarette butt in a compost bin.

I sat on the bench for a while before I called for a ride-share. The meeting had been odd, to put it mildly, and while I hadn't managed to confirm anything of note, it helped to be doing *something*. And there was something credible about Henrietta, her aura of authority perhaps, that made me begin to take seriously that this *might* actually be the explanation. A bat-shit crazy explanation, sure, but curiously more palatable than the psycho/scammer/delusional options. But Henrietta was right. To be sure, Bee and I would need to compare notes. The gnawing desire to reconnect wasn't just because of my aching heart and the fact that I missed her every second of every day – I needed to know if I had joined the ranks of the conspiracy nutjob brigade or not.

And that thread between us . . . Could that be the 'glitch' Kelvin had mentioned? Was it still there? It felt like it was, so perhaps there was hope there, too.

BEE

After Nate-Gate, I'd developed a mild addiction to self-help guides (*Moving on: Breaking Up without Breaking Down*; *The Shattered Heart and Other Myths; The Grief Cycle and How to Break It*, etc., etc.), which meant I was more than familiar with the five stages of grief. And after I blocked Nick, I experienced them all in a matter of hours. It was as if my brain, heart, soul – whatever – had stamped its foot at the thought of going through this process again, and pressed fast-forward on my emotions in order to get it over and done with asap.

1) DENIAL: As I stood under the clock, this was the first to hit. *He's here. He* must *be here. You've got it wrong, you're just not seeing him. Unblock him. Unblock him* now. Instead, I headed up to the mezzanine seating area, bought a green tea from an outlet, laced it with sugar for the shock, then sat and stared down at the commuters below, heart cartwheeling whenever I spied anyone wearing tweed. Most were elderly women or one half of a couple, and I sat there until the drink went cold and the hope dribbled away.
2) ANGER: *Fuck Nick. Fuck him. Fuck him all the way to hell.* As I crossed the intersection to Euston Square Station, a cyclist – male, fifties, goggle-eyed, I can still picture him now – ran a red light, narrowly missing me and a couple of fellow pedestrians. I screamed at him with such force my vocal chords were bruised for days, which wasn't like me at all. Rage usually made

me introverted and weepy, so who was this articulate, foul-mouthed bad-ass? A taxi driver gave me the thumbs-up and a 'you tell him, gel,' which felt good. But that didn't last, because hot on its heels came:

3) BARGAINING: While I waited for the Tube to Hammersmith, delayed due to works on the line, I found myself making deals with a god I didn't believe in: *If you make this work out okay, I'll do better, help the homeless, donate more to charity.*
4) DEPRESSION: To the extent that I sobbed without caring what anyone else on the Tube thought about me, giving in to a full-on Ugly Cry (gasping, streaming snot, melting makeup – the works). In retrospect it gave me hope for humanity. An accordion-playing busker handed me a packet of tissues and wouldn't take payment; two girls dolled up to the nines and heading for the Westfield Shopping Centre shot me sympathetic looks and, as they left, whispered, 'It'll be all right, babe.'
5) ACCEPTANCE: This came when I reached the flat. *Well, what did you expect, idiot? You should have known this would happen. It was too good to be true.*

I sat next to Clarice, and let the numbness that had saved me after Nate-Gate creep in. My phone danced with texts and missed calls from Leila.

I considered lying to her, just in case I *had* got it wrong (*he had to postpone due to illness in the family, etc., etc.*). But there wasn't enough hope left for that. <He didn't show>

<SHIT. You at home? I'm coming over>

She wouldn't take no for an answer. I tried to squeeze out more tears before she arrived, but they wouldn't come.

A taxi pulled up – a black cab, which must have cost her a fortune – and I ran outside to help her unload the twins. They'd missed their nap and were grumpier than usual, which helped in a way. Dealing with a pair of hysterical two-year-olds meant that our conversation was scattershot, and didn't allow me to wallow in too much self-pity. We bribed them with a Hobnob each, which gave us a biscuit's worth of peace. 'A no-show is SOP for scammers, Bee. I should never have encouraged you to meet him. I'm so sorry.'

Oh, the temptation to lay the blame at her door . . . a moment of unreasonable anger – *yeah, it is your fault, we could have carried on forever like we were if you hadn't encouraged me* – then perspective rolled in. 'It was my choice. And it's no biggy, really. It's not as if we'd even seen each other, is it? I'll be okay.'

Bullshit.

In the days that followed, Leila was brilliant. So was Lev, in his own way. They insisted I come over every evening for supper – even asked me to move in for a while. 'I'm fine,' I kept telling them. More bullshit. I hadn't reached the acceptance part at all, of course. *Nice try, brain.* My emotions yo-yoed: running a gamut of pulsating fury that I'd been so cruelly tricked, to sorrow. The worst of it was the hole where Nick used to be, a hole I tried to fill with work and podcasts (most of which were true crime tales, almost all, ironically, featuring some kind of scammer or social media twist). Messaging him to share the minutiae of my day had become second nature. He was still the first person I wanted to tell when, the week after Euston, I snagged a minor celebrity client (big-haired, Botoxed, the whole reality TV cliché), or the shameful day when I was so busy I ate a can of cold baked beans straight out of the tin with a dirty fork. I couldn't allow myself to re-read our e-mails and pick over them for forensic evidence that I'd been duped, as that was a one-way ticket to Obsessional City.

The anger and sorrow turned into humiliation, bolstered by the three a.m. sneer of: *You're just not good enough. What if he* had *been there after all? What if he'd taken one look at you and went, bleugh, no thanks?* There was only one solution to a battered ego: Tinder. I fired it up again, recklessly swiping right on the most obnoxious profiles I could find to lessen the risk of rejection. I used to have rules about this: no bios with ab pics; no sunglasses or fancy cars; no group pics; no pics of dogs or food designed to lure in the emotionally damaged – but all those went out the window. It became a game. I swiped on bios containing the word 'playa';

the profiles of shirtless twenty-somethings leaning against Porsches; the moodily awful posed black-and-white pics, and one that was merely a photo of an ice-cream sundae from 'Sam 43', captioned: 'Let me feed you.' As bios went, it was up there with the creepiest, and reminded me of that German man who'd advertised for someone to eat him (literally eat him, I mean). The dopamine hit as each match came in did help a little, although ninety per cent of my picks' opening gambits were just emojis or the word, 'HEY'. Creepy Sam 43 only stood out because he'd bothered to type a semi-sentence: <I like you're bio Bee>

The grammar was off, but who cared? Not me. <Thanks. So. You want to feed me or what?>

<Are you hungry?>

<Always. Do you like a woman who eats?>

<Everyone eats!>

Hmmmm.

He sent through the address of a café in North London, which turned out to be less of a café and more of an ice cream shop. I wanted to hate it, but despite myself, I approved of the vintage vibe. Pink walls, a fifties-style glass cabinet displaying thirty types of gelato, and happy-looking staff in retro aprons. I rationalised that if I got a free dessert out of it along with an ego-salve, what was the worst that could happen?

I chose a table near the window, and a portly guy in an apron approached. I ordered a cappuccino.

'Bee? It's me. Sam.' The hint of a Scottish accent. Nice smile.

Blink. 'Is this your place?'

'Yep. I'll be right back.' He disappeared behind the counter and returned bearing a carbon copy of the sundae in his avatar pic. It even had sparklers on it.

He sat across from me. 'Go on. Try it.'

'Are you not having one?'

He tapped his gut. Kind eyes, thick, close-cropped black hair. 'I try and make them, not eat them.' I'd usually feel self-conscious stuffing my face in front of a non-eating stranger, but sod that. I dug in.

He leaned forward conspiratorially. 'You know, I've never done this before.'

'Yeah, right.'

'No. Really.'

And then I looked up and realised that the staff were watching us while pretending to do something else.

'They helped me pick you.'

'Pick me? Like I'm an item on a bloody menu?' He blanched, babbled an apology. He deserved to be called out for this borderline dodgy approach to dating, but he didn't deserve this level of snappishness. I was taking weeks of pain out on this pleasant stranger. 'Sorry. I've had a bad time recently. And this is delicious.' It was.

'Bad break up?'

'Terrible.'

'Me too.'

And cue the backstory . . . I waited, but it didn't come without a prompt. I glossed over mine; rehashing the old Nate debacle because that was less loser-ish than being scammed by a catfish. His was far worse: married for seventeen years, his wife had absconded with a twenty-year-old sous-chef who'd come third on *MasterChef: The Professionals*.

He made me laugh. There was a sparkle between us, and not just on the food. Sam pretty much ticked all of the 'Potential Relationship Material' boxes. I could picture myself spending downtime in the gelato shop, hanging out with the staff, having a laugh, possibly developing type two diabetes, but hey. Our lives would fit. He was a good'un, a real mensch, but he wasn't – wait for it – The One. I was being tested again, living out my own version of a romantic comedy twist, this particular storyline a mirror of the dating montage scene from *Notting Hill* (I even re-watched it to be sure). And that was exactly how I felt meeting Sam: *I thought I was over The One. But it would take a perfect match for me to realise I was WRONG.*

A bad date with Psycho Satchel Man had pushed me into taking things further with Nick. A good date with Genial Gelato Guy pushed me into reconnecting with him. Because of course I reconnected with him. You knew I would. I should have started with that.

From: Bee1984@gmail.com
To: NB26@zone.com

Hey.

NICK

Hey. How can one of the most annoying words in the English language sound so beautiful?

How do you say: *I think we might be living in different, parallel universes.*

How do you say: *I think I'm losing my mind.*

How do you say: *I think I love you.*

Quite simply, you just fucking say them. And I did.

Only not immediately because Bee's unexpected, life-changing 'hey' came through at the most inconvenient moment possible – while I was in the midst of negotiating with Poll and Jez. Unable to put it off any longer, I'd finally bitten the bullet. Poll had suggested we meet on neutral ground to discuss 'the practical details', but I'd insisted we meet at Jez's flat, partly because I was curious to see their set-up; mainly to make Jez feel as uncomfortable as possible. After our kitchen confidential, I'd forgiven Poll, but Jez was still fair game for a spot of righteous anger. On the walk there, I indulged in a series of ridiculous revenge fantasies: head-butting Jez the second he opened the door; self-righteously shouting, 'I'll see you in court!' before storming out, pausing to deliver a deathless 'It won't last' (the same words Saul, Poll's ex, had blustered at me all those years ago). But when I arrived, Poll hugged me and Jez stole my thunder with a mumbled, 'I'm so sorry, mate, punch me if you like, I wouldn't blame you,' so I had no choice but to behave like an adult.

To be fair, fantasies aside, my personal beef with Jez paled into insignificance next to the staggering realisation that I might be living in a real-life episode of *Mirror World*. Fighting for custody of the Billy bookcase no longer seemed so important. While Jez slunk off to make tea, I obediently followed Poll into the lounge. The décor was even more juvenile than I remembered, which cheered me up. She'd done her best to brighten it up with a throw rug, the ex-kitchen clock (which oddly looked more at home here), cushions and flowers, but these touches sat uneasily with the unframed posters, the jukebox, and the guitar and speakers propped against a wall (horribly, I couldn't stop picturing Jez serenading Poll with 'Stairway to Heaven').

Poll sat opposite me and gave me the once-over. 'You look tired. If you don't want to do this now, we can always postpone.'

'Nah. I've been putting it off for too long. Let's get it over and done with.'

'I meant what I said, you know. You really can talk to me about anything.'

Temptation beckoned again, but I knew Poll well enough to be certain that blurting out that I'd recently met up with a bunch of people who believed they came from another reality in the hopes of reconnecting with my dream woman (whom I'd never met) would result in a suggestion that I get myself sectioned.

Jez returned, slopping tea all over his shagpile rug. Mugs in hand, after a smattering of limp small talk (how's Rosie? Fine. How's Dylan? Fine. How's your mum, Jez? Fine), we launched into things. Poll was good at this kind of stuff, and had prepared a spreadsheet of expenses: what I'd put in, what bills she'd paid. It went back years: a sign that she'd always known this day would come? Their hands kept straying towards each other, and Jez gazed at her with a mix of desire and hero worship that I found both repulsive and yet – despite myself – endearing. God knows, Poll deserved more than the lacklustre affection she'd received from me for the last few years. The plan was that his flat and the house would be sold, Poll would pay me my share, and that would be that. Poll suggested I stay in the house until they found a buyer. 'So there's no rush for you to move out.'

Then my phone beeped.

<Hey>

I don't recall exactly how I reacted, but it must have been fairly extreme, as, when I came back to myself, Poll and Jez were staring at me as if I'd just defecated on the coffee table.

'What is it?' Poll asked.

'I've got to go.'

'But we haven't finished.'

'I trust you, Poll. I know you'll be fair. Do what you like.'

Adrenaline fuelled me back home. The gods were on my side with Lily, too, as she didn't waylay me as I blundered past her gate. Safely inside, it took me over an hour to craft a response to Bee. Out it all came in a stream-of-consciousness message, culminating with the meeting with the Berenstains. It ran to five thousand words, which (you'll be relieved) I won't bore you with here. I half-expected the word vomit to chase her away again, but all I received was: <We HAVE to talk. Try calling me again>

I did but, as expected, it was a non-starter. <Bee – how are you really feeling about all this? Take some time if you like. It took me ages to come to terms with it. Is there something in it? Should we compare notes?>

She didn't reply for what felt like decades. Then: <Yes>

We stayed up all night, and well into the next day, using the discrepancies (which Bee termed 'Red Flags') as our starting point, and moving on from there. She cancelled her fittings; I cancelled Rosie's walk. There was an eternity's worth of history to get through for a start, but broadly, our worlds seemed to diverge around the mid-eighties and early nineties. We'd both experienced the horrors of Chernobyl, for example, yet our realities' responses to it didn't gel. From this point, my world began to explore the benefits of green energy; hers continued to rely on a carbon-based economy. Nor did her world have the controversial Attenborough Accords. (<What's that?> <Legislation limiting population of course> <Worldwide??> <Yep – you mean you don't have the vasectomy subsidy?> <No, worst luck>). We both had years of Thatcherism and Blair (although in my world he only made it to one term before Brown took over). In the US we had Gore (two terms), followed by Obama (<you lucky, lucky bastards, Nick>); she had a bushel of Bushes, Obama, and then Trump. (<In my world he's a laughing-stock and was prosecuted for ecocide> <Ditto, except for the ecocide part unfortunately>)

<Did you have 9/11, Nick?>

<???>

<The Twin Towers blown up?>

<Fuck no. Bloody hell Bee>

<So no Iraq War, Afghanistan?? ISIS?>

<No>

<Brexit?>

<You mean Biscuit? ☺ No. We're fully in the Eurozone>

<I thought it was weird when you kept mentioning euros! DUH>

Both worlds had experienced pandemics – hers a fairly recent outbreak of Ebola – but nothing that matched the scale of the ninety-six avian flu epidemic.

To lighten things up (<I'm getting seriously depressed here, Nick>) we moved on to pop culture, which was surprisingly similar:

<The Twilight Zone? (because here we are) Star Trek? Star Wars?>

<Yes, yes and yes>

<The Star Wars prequels?>

<? No. Just 3>

<Lucky you. The Marvel Universe?>

<Yes. Senses?>

<No! What's that?>

<Biggest film franchise ever? Chinese–US collab?>

<No>

<Good. It's shit. And you really don't have Jason Frey?>

<No, but we have The Rock. Dwayne Johnson>

<We have him too. He's running for Senate>

<Now you're REALLY making me jealous>

On it went, as we ran through genocides, natural disasters, technology, and politics.

In short: her world was technologically more advanced; mine was greener (<You really banned ALL plastic?> <Yep. In 2001>). Both worlds were poisoned with racism, sexism, social and gender inequalities, and capitalism, albeit with subtle differences (due to the social stigma around being a sociopathic, greedy bastard, we had fewer billionaires). We had Universal Basic Income (<Wow!> <Yeah, not really – 300 euros doesn't go far>). (Bee would eventually sum up my reality as 'Quaker capitalism with a side order of socialism.') We both had Google and the net (obviously), but in Bee's world it wasn't subject to reams of privacy legislation. Nor did she have Elective Euthanasia (<Like Dignitas?> <Yep. One on every high street>)

<Can I come to your semi-utopian world, Nick? Wait, do you have Netflix?>

<Nope>

<Scratch that then>

*

From: Bee1984@gmail.com
To: NB26@zone.com

If this IS what's really happening, you know what this means for us, don't you?

From: NB26@zone.com
To: Bee1984@gmail.com

Yeah.

From: Bee1984@gmail.com
To: NB26@zone.com

You say it. I can't bear to.

From: NB26@zone.com
To: Bee1984@gmail.com

It means that meeting in person is literally impossible.

BEE

The whole thing was bonkers, with a capital WTF, but in a weird way it made sense. The Red Flags, his sincerity (which, deep down, I knew couldn't have been faked), the technical glitches that occurred whenever we tried to communicate via methods other than e-mail. Alternate reality and parallel universe theories were part of our DNA and pop culture, even I, a quantum physics ignoramus, was aware of them. But, bizarre as it all was, it took me a surprisingly short amount of time to stop using the stipulation 'if this IS what's actually happening'. Because, I suppose, adaption and acceptance were also hard-wired into our DNA. Nick was right: people needed answers. *We* needed answers, and this was the only one we had. And, as shallow as it sounds, the overriding emotion was relief at having him back. A missing piece restored in good order.

Nick was the one who brought up the question of whether we should tell 'someone in authority'.

<Like who?>

<Good question. Not sure the Home Office in either of our worlds has a Department of Quantum Anomalies>

<There's always a shady organisation that deals with this kind of thing in movies>

<Yeah. And there's always a concrete bunker lab where people like us are experimented on>

<HA!! Actually, that's not funny. A Guantanamo Bay for people suspected of contravening the space-time continuum. Although I'm assuming your world didn't experience the joys of Gitmo and the

US government's open-secret torture outposts created under the guise of keeping us all 'safe from terror'?>

<You'd be right. But lest you're feeling left out, let me assure you I'm not living in some sort of utopian paradise. We have our own share of human rights violations>

<So we keep it to ourselves?>

<Us and the Berenstains, yes. For now, anyway. Hey, is there a similar group in your world?>

<Okaaaaay. Just looked it up. No group, but there IS a book with that title. And guess what, it's spelled 'BerenSTAIN'. There's a whole series of them>

And that wasn't all. Nick had his Berenstains, I had my own rabbit holes: Reddit, 4chan, and countless forums devoted to conspiracies related to multiverse theory in all its multiple forms. But there was no mention, not even in the murkiest corners, of people communicating across timelines via e-mail.

<Is it possible that we're the only people this has happened to, Nick?>

<Maybe. Who knows for sure?>

My buzzer went. I glanced out of the window to see Leila waving at me, a 'WTF Bee??' expression her face. <Hold that thought. Have a visitor>

I let her in with some trepidation. It had been a good thirty-six hours since I'd slept, showered, or brushed my teeth.

'I've been messaging you for bloody hours. You lost your phone or something? I've been worried sick.'

'I'm so sorry, Leila. I got completely lost in work.'

She assessed me with her bullshit radar. 'You look like crap. But also . . .'

'Also what?'

'More like yourself. I dunno . . . happier. Why?'

'You know me and work. It always helps.'

She wasn't completely buying it. 'Hmmm. But don't you ever do that to me again. I was seriously worried.'

'I know. I'm a dick.'

She dumped her bag on the couch. 'Now get me a drink for the love of god. Lev's watching the twins and now I know you're okay I need to take advantage of the situation *stat*.'

I poured us both a glass of wine.

'What the hell's this?'

I turned to see her picking through the mound of half-unwrapped books that had arrived that morning. In the hours following Nick's revelation, I'd ordered pretty much everything I could find on multiverses, quantum physics, and parallel universes. (Not that they ever helped. I'd only just scraped through maths at school.) 'I'm broadening my horizons.'

She examined the back of a Jim Al-Khalili tome. 'No shit.'

'A client got me interested in it.' I hated lying to her, but it felt like the right decision at the time. It wasn't solely because I didn't want to risk that she'd think I was crazy; I was bone tired and I didn't have the energy to come clean.

She didn't pursue it, for which I had the twins to thank. She was as knackered I was. The wine hit me straightaway – I hadn't eaten for hours – and it seemed to be having the same effect on her.

She drained the glass. 'Can I crash on your bed? I just need half an hour where no one is yelling at me to wipe their arse or refill their Peppa Pig juice cup.'

'Of course.' I was tempted to join her. But Nick and I weren't finished yet. *You can sleep when you're dead*, Mum used to say whenever I asked her to take it easy – she was a workaholic too. Her way of coping.

Leila flumped on top of Ziggy Stardust. 'You know, this duvet cover is as cheesy as hell. But I kind of love it. What a man. What a career. We'll never see his like again, as everyone everywhere is always saying.'

And then – *bam* – the answer to my and Nick's dilemma hit, blasting away the exhaustion with the efficacy of a line of coke: Nick had mentioned that his favourite Bowie tracks came from the *Silent* album – which didn't exist in my world. Patricia Highsmith had led Nick to the Berenstains, the truth about our situation, and the devastating realisation that we'd never physically be together. It was Bowie – another of our touchstones – who gave me hope that we could.

From: Bee1984@gmail.com
To: NB26@zone.com

There may be a way we can be together . . .

NICK

It was obvious. So obvious, I couldn't believe I hadn't thought of it straightaway.

If there were alternative versions of Bowie, Trump, etc., it stood to reason there were alternative versions of *us* in each other's timelines. So *what if* we tracked down these versions? *What if* we engineered meetings with Nicolas 2 and Rebecca 2, and using our 'insider knowledge' took that even further? While we still couldn't be together in a literal sense, it was better than nothing. At the very least I'd get to see what she looked like (shallow, *moi*?). Frustratingly, we couldn't get cracking until Bee had seen Leila out – which was just as well because Rosie (now beyond furious) was desperate for an ablution break.

<Ok, partner. Let Operation Rebecca 2 and Nicolas 2 commence! Where shall we start?>

<Facebook. You have that, right, Nick? A social network run by sociopaths that only exists to farm your data?>

We did, but as data farming was strictly controlled here, it wasn't anywhere near as ubiquitous – or insidious – as it was in Bee's world, and thanks to the Right to Be Forgotten Movements and the Do Not Track Act, there would be roadblocks ahead – at least on my side. From the sounds of it, hers was a technological Wild West compared to mine.

We began by swapping the personal details we'd glossed over before in our Nothing Personal stage. Full name, age (not in dog years this time), current and former addresses and other surface info that might help with the search: schools, universities, work histories (sketchy in my case). I learned new things about her: she'd grown up in Croydon, won a scholarship to Goldsmiths to study design (<Go you!>); her business was called For Frock's Sake (<too cheesy do you think?> <I love it – you know me, a sucker for a pun>), and she'd been bullied at school. (<Not sure why I told you that. It's not as if it'll help the search> <We don't know what will help, so keep them coming. Also, sorry you went through that, Bee> <Thanks. Not saying it didn't suck, but it had a silver lining because it was thanks to the bully clique that Leila & I joined forces & became friends>) The bullying revelation immediately made me think of Dylan. It would have been a natural jumping-off point to confide in her about his suicide attempt, but I held back, and not only because it didn't feel like the right time to lance *that* emotional boil (I'd regret that later).

She learned new things about me, too. I wasn't chuffed about revealing my surname, but perhaps the Nick in her world had had the good sense to change it.

<I quite like it. There's a ring to it>

<Kind of you to say that, but you're a terrible liar>

<Hey, at least it's memorable (unlike mine) & considering what we're about to do, that's a major bonus. Speaking of which: Three. Two. One and GO!>

I typed in her full name and came up with . . . nada. <Nothing from my side>

<There must be! I'm on social media in this world. Well, the business is>

<Maybe you changed your name. Maybe you're married?> *Shudder*.

<I would never take a man's name>

<Fair enough>

<And there's nothing about the business?>

<Nope. Maybe here you called it something else?>

<It's possible I suppose. Leila & I ran through loads of options. I've found you, though. I know what you look like!>

Here we go . . . Excitement, dread, panic. <And? Am I as devastatingly handsome as I am in my world?>

<Ha! Nice try. You're all moody and sincere in your author pics>

Whoa there, Nelly . . . <Author PICS? As in plural?> There was one, and only one, in existence – on the back of my debut shitpile. Moody and sincere it was not. If anything, I looked slightly constipated.

<There's loads of them. You have your own website, a Wiki page and a FB fan page>

Jesus. <Hang on . . . are you saying I'm successful? A *successful* author?>

<Seems like it. Yes, definitely!>

Whoomf. *Double Jesus*. I was proud of myself and also . . . *not*. It would take a while to work through the conflicting feelings I had about my alter ego, most of which involved my ego, but the first question that popped up was: *Why was Nicolas successful and I wasn't?*

<You also write books under a different name>

<I even have a pseudonym?> What kind of a multitasking workaholic had Bee's world spawned?

<M. G. Sanger>

Shite name – seemed Nicolas hadn't learned his lesson after all.

Here's what I learned from Bee's first harried search:

I – aka Nicolas – had written and published three novels under my own name. The first one had a similar title to my terrible debut and seemed to have the same subject matter. It had bombed. But instead of drifting into decades of self-hatred and self-sabotage, for some reason Nicolas had carried on writing. He hadn't published a Nicolas Belcher novel since 2014, but a Sanger book had appeared every year after that – a series Bee said was categorised as 'cosy crime', featuring 'cranky retired police superintendent, Norman Kellerman' (oh come *on*, Nicolas).

<OK . . . so according to the reviews, your second book is 'a blisteringly funny, behind-the-scenes account of teaching on the front lines. The author shows promise and a uniquely insightful

voice.' And you have loads of good reviews for the Sanger series on Amazon. That's a website we have here that sells everything>

<We have it too>

She tried cutting and pasting the other book blurbs into an i-mail, but they came through as indecipherable jargon.

<Any awards?>

<No, but you've been longlisted for several. I've ordered all of your books!>

Please don't let them be crap . . . My writer's ego wanted more – more info, more details about the good reviews I'd received – but there were other issues to consider. <What else? Am I married?>

<Hold on . . .>

This was doubly important to me, because a nasty, shameful voice was whispering: *Maybe it was Poll that held you back. Maybe* she's *the reason your career crashed and burned.* Yes, I went there.

<I don't know for sure. Nothing personal on your Wiki page, and it'll take me a while to trawl through your Twitter & FB accounts>

<How am I coming across?>

<Give me a sec . . . Let's see . . . well, you're not following anyone dodgy and you have 23K followers. Not bad!>

<I'm like Jesus>

<Ha ha. Your Twitter bio is cool: 'Full-time Writer. Part-time Space Oddity'>

<So Nicolas is a Bowie fan as well then. That's a relief> Was it? Christ, I didn't know. <Let's shelve Nicolas for now, the successful, suave man that he is, and concentrate on you. Give me a list of alternative names for your business>

I tried all of them – zip. Bee suggested tracking down her father, but apart from a mention in an ancient article about a long-defunct bioengineering firm he'd once worked for, he was similarly AWOL.

<Try finding out if I'm still living in my flat>

<Way ahead of you. Tried that. Falls under the RTP legislation>

<But you have Yellow Pages or something like that, right? An online phone directory?>

<Checked. It's not listed>

<Ok. Bugger. Try my best mate Leila. Leila Khoury>

Bee sent through her address but, as expected, the info was shielded from public access. She was an accountant, so in went Leila Khoury + accountant + finance, and finally, I hit pay-dirt: listed on the page of an accountancy practice in Farringdon was a 'Leila L Khoury, Director'.

<Think I have a work number for her>

<Wow. She's still working in your world? In mine she quit after she had her kids. Call her!!>

<It's midnight!>

<Of course it is. I'm an idiot. Time flies when you're . . . what? What do we call what we're doing?>

<There's no phrase for what we're doing. Spying on ourselves?>

<Does it feel wrong to you?>

Did it? A bit. I was still reeling from the Nicolas alter-ego whammy. <We'll get over ourselves. And if the whole thing doesn't work out there's always sexting>

<!! Read my mind. Have you done that before?>

<Once, when Poll was away at a conference back in the sands of time>

<And?>

<Not great. Back then I was a two-finger typist. You?>

<Tried having Skype sex with a guy last year. Didn't work. I was paranoid he'd film it and splash it all over Pornhub. Ended up pretending my wifi died>

<Then we have no choice but to make this work>

<Looks that way>

I was too wired to sleep. Poll may have run off with her Boring as Shite fancy man, giving me the run of the house, but I still couldn't bring myself to smoke inside. The street was holding its breath, every window darkened. A pair of foxes trotted nonchalantly around the corner, sniffed disapprovingly at the waft of cigarette smoke, then padded off towards the estate and the rich pickings in the recycling bins. Which reminded me to wheel Lily's bins back inside the yard. I'd have to tell her the house was going on the market sooner or later. It wouldn't be fair if she saw the sign going up without any notice. And I'd have to set my mind to the task of thinking about where the hell Rosie and I were going to live. Who knows? In London, with Rebecca 2, if things worked out, although that was definitely jumping the gun. That was when I saw it – a shadowy figure slumped in a banged up Mini-Lec. I knew all the neighbours' cars – most of the street's residents had taken advantage of the No-Drive subsidy and didn't own or lease one – and this wasn't one of theirs. Leaving Rosie behind the gate, I approached. Leaning against the window was a distinctive, bullet-shaped head that really shouldn't have been subjected to a buzz cut: Geoffrey.

I tapped on the glass and he jerked awake, gazing at me blearily as his brain recalibrated.

'What the *fuck* are you doing here, Geoffrey?'

Instead of answering, he fired up the engine. It would be hard to imagine a less dramatic, more inept getaway. Hemmed in by a couple of charging Tesla-Lecs, he was forced to inch his way free. At one point, I even, for the love of Christ, found myself directing him out.

I thought about rousing Bee with this latest turn of events – hey, I have an inept stalker! – but decided to keep it to myself. We had enough to deal with without adding a rogue Berenstain into the mix.

*

From: Bee1984@gmail.com
To: NB26@zone.com

WELL??? Did you call Leila??

From: NB26@zone.com
To: Bee1984@gmail.com

2 secs ago. She's just hung up on me. Sorry, Bee – messed it up. I said I was an old friend trying to reconnect with you, but she saw straight through my story, asked me where I'd got her number

etc. Think she assumed I was some kind of creepy stalker nutter. Got nothing out of her we could use.

From: Bee1984@gmail.com
To: NB26@zone.com

Bugger. That is like her though – not your fault. She can be very protective.

From: NB26@zone.com
To: Bee1984@gmail.com

Sorry. Want me to try again? I could put on a Scottish accent or something this time.

From: Bee1984@gmail.com
To: NB26@zone.com

She's way too canny for that. Shit. Anything on my dad?

From: NB26@zone.com
To: Bee1984@gmail.com

Nope. I'll keep looking. The voters' log was privatised a few years ago. Like I said, hard to find people unless you have access.

From: Bee1984@gmail.com
To: NB26@zone.com

And my mum?

From: NB26@zone.com
To: Bee1984@gmail.com

I've put in a request with the birth and death registry like you asked.

From: Bee1984@gmail.com
To: NB26@zone.com

Thanks. Is it wrong to hope that she survived in your world? I mean, it's not as if I'll ever be able to see her again, but . . . GAH. You get it, right?

From: NB26@zone.com
To: Bee1984@gmail.com

I get it. Of course I do.

From: Bee1984@gmail.com
To: NB26@zone.com

Thanks. I'm getting a bit worried about myself . . . Wish you could hire a PI, track me down.

From: NB26@zone.com
To: Bee1984@gmail.com

On limited funds unfortunately. Unlike your Nick.

From: Bee1984@gmail.com
To: NB26@zone.com

He's not 'my Nick!' Although . . . he's doing an event in York on Friday. Crime fiction conference. Should I go? Could be a natural way to meet him?

From: Bee1984@gmail.com
To: NB26@zone.com

Nick? You there?

From: NB26@zone.com
To: Bee1984@gmail.com

I'm here. This whole thing feels so fucking weird. What if you meet him and he's a complete arse?

From: Bee1984@gmail.com
To: NB26@zone.com

He won't be. He's you – kind of. Isn't this what we planned?

From: NB26@zone.com
To: Bee1984@gmail.com

Yes. Yes it is. Ignore me. Go. And I've been thinking, I can't hire a PI, but I could be one. Head down to London, follow the leads? Check out your flat, try and speak to Leila in person without (hopefully) coming across like a psycho?

From: Bee1984@gmail.com
To: NB26@zone.com

I was hoping you'd say that! Maybe set up an appointment with her?

From: NB26@zone.com
To: Bee1984@gmail.com

I'll try. I only have 1500 euros in my account, but she doesn't need to know that. I'll say I'm a high-rolling investor or something who needs her financial advice on some kind of investor-y venture. Turn my bullshit levels up to high.

From: Bee1984@gmail.com
To: NB26@zone.com

Thanks. You know, I can't stop thinking about the fact that in my world Leila quit work after she had the twins. That bothered her a lot – she missed it. When you spoke to her, did she sound happy?

From: NB26@zone.com
To: Bee1984@gmail.com

Wish I could tell you that, Bee. She was too busy telling me to fuck off.

From: Bee1984@gmail.com
To: NB26@zone.com

I know. Wish talking to you was my job, but I have a backlog of work. Chat later?

From: NB26@zone.com
To: Bee1984@gmail.com

Good luck x

BEE

Where *was* I – aka Rebecca 2? Why couldn't Nick track me down? It was impossible not to obsess about it: What if for some unfathomable reason I'd emigrated to Australia with Dad? (No. I couldn't see that happening. We only spoke once a year at Christmas, and that was a study in awkwardness.) What if I'd gone into another field of work entirely? Also doubtful. Thanks to Mum, I'd been sewing my whole life, and since the age of ten I'd wanted to be a designer – hadn't ever considered another career. What if . . . I'd married Nate? What if I'd ditched my feminist credentials, and for some reason had not only taken him back, but taken his name? (I held my nose and asked Nick to check this. Another dead-end – thank God this time.)

Then there were the darker thoughts: what if Rebecca 2 had died in Nick's world? *Murder, an accident, a quirky time-bomb gene* . . . No – Nick would have unearthed some kind of obit, surely. Or: what if I hadn't been born? What if, in a *Back to the Future* style twist, my parents hadn't met? What if Dad had chosen to take that Attenborough Accords vasectomy subsidy? If there was no Bee in Nick's world, which sounded, on paper, like a less screwed-up version of mine, was the absence of my alternative self the reason why it was a better place? Perhaps I was the difference that had made the difference.

It's not always about you. But it was, and I couldn't help that.

Then, just as the paranoia was really starting to bite, in came confirmation I was alive – or at least had been born and grown up: <You went to Goldsmiths in this world, too. You're listed on the alumni. Tried calling the office, but they wouldn't give me your current contact deets>

<Well that's something!> But where the hell was I working now?

The relief that I wasn't a statistic or a nonentity was eclipsed when, very gently, he later broke the news that the death notice request he'd filed about Mum had come back confirming that she'd passed away a month before she had in my world. The hope I'd been harbouring that her illness wouldn't win in another life flickered out, and for hours afterwards, the pain of this loss was almost as intense as it had been just after she'd died. Mum had prepared me for it as best she could (including practically – putting all her affairs in order, so I wouldn't be left with the harrowing task of going through her belongings), but no one can prepare you for the many creative ways grief can ambush you: the doppelganger in the street wearing Mum's good M&S coat; the smell of mince pies; a Freddy Mercury song playing in a supermarket. No one can prepare you for how disorientating losing a parent can be, how *lonely* it is. Mum and I had spoken every day, and it had been months before I stopped reaching for my phone to call her whenever anything – big or small – happened in my life. Back then, Leila had helped steady the world. Nick filled that role now.

<And the worst of it Nick, I've never felt so lost. And I mean lost. Like she was my anchor, someone had cut the rope connecting us and I was suddenly floating away by myself. God. Sorry. That sounds cliched, weak & pathetic>

<It's none of those things, Bee. And don't ever apologise for being honest about how you feel. That's the opposite of weakness. You need to take your own advice on this>

<??>

<Just after I found out about Poll and Jez you told me I was entitled to hurt. Well you are too. Then and now>

<Thanks for saying that. You lost your parents at around the same age. Did you feel the same?>

<To a lesser degree, yes. But I still miss them if I'm honest. That's

the thing about unconditional love, you can't overestimate how grounding it is. And parents (the good ones I mean) are champions at that – that's their job. (Well, that and fucking you up, of course)>

Work and Project Nicolas also helped keep the sorrow and the confusion in check. I booked a ticket for Nicolas's talk, secured one of the last rooms in the hotel where the crime fiction conference was taking place, and cleared my work slate. I was desperate for Nick to head down to London to see what he could discover about the mysterious Rebecca 2, but he could only get an appointment with Leila on Friday. *Serendipitous synchronicity*. We'd be embarking on our respective recces on the same day.

I also continued to trawl through Nicolas's social media for nuggets about his personal life. There was no mention of marriages or offspring on his Wiki page, and his Facebook fan page didn't state his relationship status. Nicolas wasn't a prolific tweeter, but everything he posted, including the quips and one-liners, had the ring of being carefully curated. He spent more time promoting other writers' books and good causes than his own material, so he wasn't an egomaniac, and apart from a few retweets, steered clear of politics, which made him either cowardly or smart. Connecting with him online was a no-brainer – a possible way in to meeting him on Friday ('hey, don't I know you from Twitter?'). The company had Instagram and Twitter accounts, but I'd never bothered with a personal one. This was the ideal opportunity to use Nick's insider knowledge of himself.

<What name or avatar should I use that'll catch Nicolas's attention?>

<Shag69?>

<Ha ha. Also: gross>

<Sorry. I am gross. Um . . . Mouseyhairedgirl? Bowie ref?>

<Brilliant! Done!>

And it worked. Minutes after I tweeted <Off to see @ NicolasBBauthor at @krimifest on Fri! Can't wait> he was following me back.

<Any other tips?>

<Yeah, tell him he should have come up with a better pseudonym>

<Am I detecting some bitterness here Nick?>

<You are – just a little. Play it cool, Bee. I've never been one for pushy people>

The rest of the week was a blur of high-octane multitasking: messaging with Nick, fielding texts from Leila, client wrangling, catnapping, and working with Nicolas's audio books playing in the background. All except his debut, which wasn't on audio or Kindle, and which I'd sourced from an online secondhand seller. Nick begged me not to read it – it did, after all, sound very similar to his own first novel – but I couldn't resist giving it a skim. He was right: it was pretty awful. Nicolas's second book was heartbreaking and hilarious. The third, more po-faced (I gave up on it in the end in favour of the Sanger novels). I offered to give Nick a running commentary on the plot like a book blogger with ADHD, but he declined: <Not sure I'm ready for that yet>

<Am I being insensitive?>

<To be honest I'm conflicted. I want to know everything and yet I don't. I gave up and he didn't. Feels a bit like that missed potential is being rubbed in my face>

<I get it> Well, I got it to a certain extent. If Rebecca 2 had turned out to be an iconic designer with an atelier in Paris, would I have felt threatened? I'll never know.

I barely slept on Thursday night. I longed to tell Leila, pick her brain about what to wear (in the end I went with the same outfit I'd worn for the Euston meeting), but she'd only worry herself sick that I was barrelling my stupid way into another toxic relationship. I couldn't even tell her where I was going. She'd find it really suspicious that I'd suddenly fostered an interest in both quantum mechanics *and* crime fiction.

My anxiety levels weren't helped by the fact that the train was delayed, meaning I had to run to the venue, and didn't have time to freshen up in my hotel room first. I arrived sweaty and out of puff as they were about to start, forced to sit at the back of the hotel's small auditorium, which was a sea of grey hair. Two armchairs were placed on the raised stage at the front – my view was restricted to some extent, but not enough that I wouldn't get a fair idea of what Nicolas looked like in the flesh. We all like to think that personality matters more to us than looks, but everyone knows that's bollocks. From the pics, Nicolas certainly had something about him (okay, I'll admit it, I was relieved that he wasn't the Quasimodo of Leeds), but that attraction could change in a heartbeat when we met in person. I may have fallen for his alter ego's personality, but what if there was no chemistry? And what if he found *me* repulsive? (<Jesus woman. Now you're being ridiculous. Seriously, Bee, if he's anything like me, unless you have an extra eye in the middle of your forehead you'll be quids in. Even then you'd still be in with a fighting chance>)

A hush. And then onto the stage he came.

NICK

This time, the journey to Euston was both uncomfortable and depressing, and not only because I was in my rightful place in cattle class. It was a reminder of how badly the last trip had ended – another reminder, if one were needed, that there was no hope of Bee and me being together in a conventional sense. Despite my recent neglect of Lily, she'd agreed to watch Rosie, although I hadn't escaped unscathed: 'Only comes round here when he needs something, doesn't he, Rosie?' I still hadn't found the courage to break the news about the pending house sale to the old bat.

As the train grumbled on, update after update from Bee came in – a live report of Nicolas's talk.

<You're good. And funny. Self-deprecating. I wish I could record this for you!>

<Me too> *Liar.*

<He says his detective is partly based on his/your dad. Not one to suffer fools lightly. It's been optioned for TV. Says they're hoping Jim Broadbent might take the role. Dunno if he's in your world, but here he's a UK A-lister>

Oh goody.

I was almost grateful to the teen sitting next to me, tinny music leaking out of his headphones. It was irritating enough to distract me from obsessing too deeply about Nicolas and Bee. I still hadn't got my head around what I thought of as Operation Doppelganger. I both did and didn't want it to work out. Was my reticence because Bee was ahead of the game, just minutes away from meeting 'me', when I was no closer to even discovering what she looked like? Or was it because whenever I thought about Nicolas's success, it was like being punched in the balls over and over? (Both.) And I was dreading my meeting with Leila. I'd given her PA some bumf about being the CEO of a start-up that specialised in converting human waste into electricity (<It's a shit business, Nick> <A lucrative one as well according to the Net>) – praying that Leila wouldn't check me out on Companies House pre-meeting.

But my first stop would be Bee's flat. In her world she'd lived there with her ex – the infamous Nate – and I was curious. And who knew? She might still be there. *And if she is, Nick? What are you going to say to her?* Bee and I had discussed this at length, of course. The truth was out of the question, at least for a first encounter. (<Too risky. I mean, how would you react if a stranger knocked on your door and hit you up with *that* spiel>) In the end, Bee suggested I go with something innocuous, that I was moving to the area and a friend of a friend suggested I look her up.

The creep into Euston was made all the more depressing with each missive. (<Okay. I'm going to get my book signed. Wish me luck!>) The familiar bing-bong, the rush of passengers collecting belongings, the surge onto the platform. As I was jostled towards the exit, my eye glommed onto a familiar figure, his dome-shaped head poking out from behind the doorway of a Frites concession outlet.

Geoffrey. Bloody, bloody Geoffrey. He tried to scuttle off, but his getaway was as inept as his previous one. I grabbed the back of his jacket, and a couple of older women tutted as we tussled in the walkway. 'All right. All *right*,' he said, shaking me free.

'Did you follow me here from Leeds?'

'Yeah. So what?'

'Do Kelvin and the others know you're spying on me?'

A withering 'of course, you fucking *idiot*' look.

I'd called Kelvin the morning after I'd spied Geoffrey lurking outside my house, but it had gone straight to voice mail.

'I suppose I don't need to ask why you're doing this. It's pretty obvious that you and the other Berensteins—'

'Stains.'

'What?'

'It's *stains*.'

Jesus. 'Whatever. I picked up that you and the other loons' – oddly, he didn't take offence at this – 'are cagey and more than a little paranoid, but what are you hoping to achieve by spying on me? Badly, by the way, because you're spectacularly shite at it.'

His eyes seemed to get smaller and darker. 'You're a writer, aren't you? Need to make sure you're not some bastard trying to in . . . infil . . . infil . . . infilwotsit our group to make us look like we got . . . you know, issues.'

'You're doing that yourselves.' And now I was right up close to him, he *did* look like he had issues. All sorts of issues, and none of them good. 'And I'm not trying to infiltrate you.'

'What you doing in London then?'

'None of your fucking business.'

'See? That makes me think you *do* have something to hide.'

'I'm here to see my accountant, if you must know.'

'Yeah, right. Henrietta says you haven't got a pot to piss in.'

'How in the hell would she know that?'

A shrug. 'She's good at that stuff.'

'What stuff?'

'Looking into things.'

That brought me up short. I'd clocked her as formidable when we met – just what the hell had I got myself into? 'Is she now? Less obvious about it than you are. If I catch you following me again, I'll have you done for stalking.'

A crafty grin. 'So you *are* up to something.'

'Listen, Geoffrey. I swear on my dog's life that I have zero interest in infiltrating your stupid group and writing about you. Not only would no one give a shite, I'm not that kind of writer.'

'Not much of any kind from what I can gather.'

'Oh, fuck off, you ridiculous bastard.'

I stalked off, pausing to check that he wasn't following me. He wasn't – he remained where he was, gazing after me, a vacant half-smile on his face. As I headed towards the Tube, I stopped every so often to ensure he wasn't on my tail, which made me feel like I was playing a one-man version of Grandmother's footsteps. To make absolutely sure, at a random stop I jumped off the train at the last second, a move that was way harder than it looks in spy thrillers (I narrowly avoided catching the back of my jacket in the door). En route, I called Kelvin again, only to be met by another robotic voice mail message. 'Listen up, Kelvin. Call me back or I *will* bloody well write about you.'

I'd never been to Bee's area of London before, and I was seriously impressed. Like the majority of the city, it was mainly pedestrianised, with cycle lanes weaving through rows of ancient and newly planted trees. I passed street after street of townhouses, each fronted by gardens sprawling with colour, their windows revealing glimpses of uniformly arty, curated interiors. It was far quieter than my area, and yes, I did allow myself to fantasise about moving here with Rosie. She'd have a blast fouling the beautifully maintained front gardens and driveways.

The address Bee had given me matched a four-storey Georgian townhouse with the type of unobtrusive insulation cladding that only the mega-wealthy can afford, fronted by a row of cherry trees. She said she lived on the ground floor, and I stood there for a minute, imagining her sitting there at the window, sewing and pausing every so often to send me a message. As the curtains were half-drawn, I couldn't tell if anyone was home or not.

I rang the bell and waited. And now I was right outside her door, potentially just seconds away from coming face to face with *her*, with Rebecca, with Bee (in a sense), the reality of the situation hit home and my mind went blank – the conversational openings I'd been rehearsing on the journey deserting me. I needn't have worried as it turned out, because after a couple of minutes of mild panic, the door was opened by a shirtless man with muscles so ridiculously defined that I initially assumed he was wearing a bodybuilder parody suit. Dismay: he didn't resemble Bee's descriptions of Nate (or Jonas – her landlord's husband), but if this was Becca's partner, there was no way I could compete with that man muscle. He looked me over with a supreme lack of interest, yawned, then said: '*Ja*?'

'I'm looking for Becca? Rebecca Davies?'

'Who?'

'She used to live here. Or lives here. In one of the flats. Probably.'

He shrugged, then called: 'Mags? Honey? Can you come?'

To the door came a glamorous elderly woman clad in a red silk robe (I'd clearly interrupted something), who assessed me with sharp, quick eyes. I repeated my spiel about Rebecca, adding a lame line about being an old friend who was trying to track her down.

'This house is a house. Not flats. There is no Rebecca here.'

'Are you Magda?' *Of Magda and Jonas fame*, I almost added.

'How do you know my name?'

'I heard the . . . that guy saying it.'

She wasn't buying it. Another flash of distrust, then she slammed the door in my face.

Strike out. Leila it would have to be. I had an hour to get to her offices in Farringdon, so there was time for a coffee or something stronger. En route, I filled Bee in, but there was no response. Nor had there been any further updates since the last book-signing missive. Into my head slid an unwelcome showreel of Imaginary Bee shagging a version of myself in some cutesy Yorkshire B&B. It couldn't be termed a masturbatory fantasy – the Nicolas in my head didn't look anything like me. More like a suave Jason Frey figure, a paragon of outdated masculinity like Man Muscle back there.

Kelvin called back just as I arrived outside Leila's offices. 'Bloody finally. Did you ask Geoffrey to spy on me?'

A pause. 'It would be more accurate to say that he offered.'

'What the *fuck*, Kelvin?'

'I would appreciate it if you did not use that language.'

'And I would fucking appreciate it if you'd tell your nutjob of a spy to leave me the fuck alone.' Silence. 'What the hell is wrong with him, anyway?'

'Geoffrey was involved in a motor vehicle accident in which he suffered some frontal lobe damage. It is true that he can come across as . . . erratic.'

Hearing that, I did feel a touch guilty about calling him a loon, but not enough to fully dilute the anger. 'Tell him to stop stalking me or I'll get the police on him.'

Oh, the irony. I was about to con my way into Leila's office, which, while not stalking exactly, wasn't exactly kosher either.

'We have come to a decision about you. Meet with us on Monday night.'

And with that, he hung up. Great. More weirdness. Just what the day needed. Shelving my irritation at Kelvin, I composed myself (*remember you're obscenely rich and successful, rich and successful*), then pushed my way through the glass doors, attempting to affect an air of moneyed nonchalance. The ground floor paraded its passive design credentials, and sported an atrium and signs boasting: 'over 70% of our staff are home-based employees!' Slick and elegant, it was the kind of place that made me acutely aware of my inherent scruffiness. My hair was already growing out into its usual mop, and my only good shirt wasn't anywhere near good enough judging by the sniffy glance it received from the assistant sent to whisk me up into Leila's penthouse domain. And what a domain it was: a 180-degree view, ergonomic everything, and a desk the size of a double bed.

Leila, who was as elegantly attired as her office, exuded the kind of confidence that comes from years of discovering you're always the smartest person in the room. Within seconds of meeting her, I knew without a doubt that she'd see right through my bullshit again.

There was only one way to play this. Deep breath, then: 'Leila, I'm really sorry, but I'm here under false pretences because I'm really, really worried about Rebecca Davies. Before you inevitably tell me to fuck off, can you at least tell me that she's alive?'

From: NB26@zone.com
To: Bee1984@gmail.com

I've found you.

PART THREE

FORCES OF NURTURE

BEE

I – aka Rebecca – was married. With a kid.

Married.

With a *kid*.

A mum. I was a MUM.

Thankfully I was taking a breather in my hotel room when I received this bombshell, which meant I could let out a semi-hysterical 'WHAT THE ACTUAL BUGGERING FUCK?' without attracting an audience. I'd needed some alone time to decompress after meeting Nicolas in the flesh for the first time, plus my phone had died as I waited in the signing queue. Having discovered I'd stupidly left my charger at home, I was forced to make a harried trip to Boots for another, which meant that as it juiced up, two hours of updates from Nick – each more shocking than the last – pinged into my inbox. I might have considered the possibility that in an alternative life I was married, but had I considered I might be a mother? Nope. Not at all. I'd only felt mildly broody once, just before my thirtieth birthday. It hadn't lasted more than a few days, and I'd put it down to social conditioning and the fact that several of my co-workers at the time were due to go on maternity leave.

Is this what had happened to Rebecca? Had she fallen foul of a hormonal blip? Or had she decided to go through with the pregnancy I'd ended? Unlikely, because in came another shocker: Rebecca wasn't married to Nate, but to someone called Benedict (*Benedict*!). Not only that, she'd taken his last name (adios feminist credentials), which explained why Nick had battled to track her down.

After scoffing all the hotel-room biscuits and a squashed emergency Bounty Bar that I found at the bottom of my bag, I was calm enough to ask Nick to talk me through his meeting with Leila in detail.

<First off – how did you convince her to talk? Did you tell her the truth? About our situation, I mean?>

<Christ no. That would have taken hours even if she did believe me. After I begged her not to throw me out, I said I was at Goldsmiths with you, wanted to reconnect but couldn't track you down. Said I remembered you talking about her. Also, I *may* have given her the impression I'm SS>

<SS?? Eh??? Secret service? A Nazi?>

<Same-sexer!>

<You mean gay?>

<Yeah, but that's a pejorative here. Think that's what tipped the scales in my favour as she didn't see me as such a stalkerish threat to you>

<Good thinking. Right. Part of me is dreading this, but what else do we know about Benedict? The husband. God it feels weird typing that>

<Are you sitting down?>

<Uh-oh this doesn't sound promising. OK. GO>

<You – Rebecca – married a millionaire. Some kind of eco-fashion investor/pioneer. Comes from old money. Serious money. Makes Tweedy look like a pauper>

I don't know *what* I was expecting – a Nate clone perhaps? – but it wasn't that. <You're kidding>

<Wish I was>

<Surname?>

<Mercer>

Mercer, Mercer, Mercer. <Hang on. Is he connected to the Mercer Foundation?>

<??>

<It's a fund that's awarded here to up-and-coming designers. I applied for it years ago, but didn't get it. If he's part of the Mercer clan, he's beyond loaded>

I was hitting up Google to see if I could confirm this, when the full implication of what this meant for us struck me like a smack to the chops. Blindsided by the initial shock, I selfishly hadn't considered the obvious fact that Rebecca being married essentially kiboshed our plans. I knew myself well enough to be fairly sure an affair was unlikely. But then again, Rebecca had done the one thing I was certain I'd never do – breed – so who knew?

<Oh shit, Nick. Now what? You must have been gutted hearing that>

<Well it did occur to me that as a soon-to-be-homeless-failed-writer, I might not be much of a prospect compared to a millionaire philanthropist – even if Rebecca's marriage were on the rocks>

<Don't you dare run yourself down like that. And hang on, DID Leila say the marriage was in trouble?>

That was when he broke the news that Leila hadn't been in contact with Rebecca since the baby (Scarlett) was born. This intel shook me just as powerfully as the married-with-a-kid shocker.

<Why?>

<Wouldn't say explicitly>

<Something to do with Benedict?> Could it be that? Maybe. Then again, Leila had stuck by me during the Nate years, even though they'd loathed each other.

<Could be. Hard to tell. She chose her words carefully when she spoke about him, let's just say that>

<Is she married? Does she have kids?>

<Don't know. I didn't ask about her. I asked about you>

<Christ. What if she doesn't have the twins?> A topsy-turvy world where I had kids – or at least one child – and she had none. Something she'd told me when she was going through round after painful round of IVF came to mind: that she couldn't bear being around people with children – it hurt too much. Was that why she'd severed the friendship? <Did she look sad?>

<A bit when she spoke about you, otherwise no. She's quite something. Her office is the size of my house>

<Any pics of her kids in this house-sized office?>

<Didn't notice>

There was more. As far as Leila was aware, Rebecca hadn't started her own business – there was no 'For Frock's Sake'. How *could* there be without Leila? The business began after I'd redone Leila's dress – she was my first client.

<THANK YOU for doing all of this, Nick. It can't have been easy>

<I'll admit it's been a hell of a day. Now. Your turn. How did it go with Nicolas?>

<Let's see . . . I think the term I'm looking for is: absolutely shit>

Our meeting hadn't lasted more than two minutes. There were other people waiting to get their books signed behind me, and I could hardly hang around like a desperado while he finished. It went, at first, sort of how I'd imagined it. He signed my book 'To the Girl with the Mousy Hair', laughed, and asked if I was the one from Twitter. It was then that the full, surreal reality of what I was actually doing tipped the world on its axis. *It's him – but NOT him*. Suddenly queasy, I nodded stupidly, couldn't find my voice. <I freaked out, messed it up. Being that close to him, to *you*, in a sense, sort of melted my brain. As if I couldn't quite put the two pieces together. Him in the flesh and the YOU in my head. Does that make sense?>

<Yes. And no. But more importantly: Did you fancy me? ☺>

<Ha ha. It doesn't matter if I did or didn't now, does it?>

<???>

<You can't have a relationship with Rebecca. Doesn't seem right that I pursue one with Nicolas. Even if I could. Which I can't as I've already messed it up. It wouldn't be fair>

<That's not how this thing works, Bee. Fair doesn't come into it. And we don't need to make any decisions now, right?>

<Right>

Wrong.

I didn't sleep that night. The first thing I did when Nick and I said our goodbyes, was hop straight onto Google and tap in 'Benedict

Mercer/Mercer Foundation'. I took a deep breath, then pressed ENTER.

Top of the search page was a *Financial Times* piece about 'The Sustainable Fashion Pioneers Changing the Industry for Good'. Pulse racing, I scrolled through it, pausing on a captioned pic of a guy in his early fifties, slick, groomed, be-suited, corporate. Pretty much everything that wasn't my type. It couldn't be him – could it? I dug deeper – there were other Benedict Mercers (including one in the States who'd been arrested for a double murder) – but none that matched Nick's sketchy description with such accuracy. According to the Mercer Foundation's Wiki page, Benedict was its CFO, and was linked to various other charitable organisations promoting sustainability and ethical working conditions in the fashion industry. He'd been married once to Alina LaRusso, an American ex-model who'd died in 2014 after a tragic accident in their home in the Hamptons. Alina's death hadn't made the British tabloids, presumably because it had occurred in the States and the Mercer family had enough wealth and influence to keep their private lives private when it suited them. *The tragic widower*. Perhaps that was the attraction. Had my other self been seduced by Benedict's Max de Winter-style backstory, like the heroine in the aptly titled *Rebecca*? I hoped for my/her sake there wasn't a Mrs Danvers lurking in the background. And he might not even *be* a tragic sexy widower in Nick's world.

Married to a millionaire. Or in this world, a billionaire. And yeah, okay, a teeny part of my psyche was impressed. 'Girl done well,' I could imagine my dad crowing to his mates on the golf course. The thing was, men like Benedict didn't usually go for women like me. Which sounds like I'm running myself down, but I'm not. It's the truth. Looks-wise, 'fairly attractive' is probably the most accurate way of putting it. I certainly wasn't model material like his poor deceased wife Alina. And women like me didn't usually go for men like him. Tinder and Nate-Gate aside, my dating history was peppered with creative types, mostly penniless. As the old joke goes, 'What was it that first attracted you to the millionaire Benedict

Mercer, Rebecca?' Were we that different? Mum and I had struggled, so being financially stable was important to me, but I'd never yearned for what Leila called 'massive fucking yacht money'.

I stared and stared at his photograph. Nope. It wasn't coming together.

Then there was the age difference: was she looking for a father figure? *Bleugh, bleugh, don't go there*. And what about work? What was she doing? I couldn't imagine a life without my business. Which brought me back to Leila – who in my world had put her accountancy career on pause, and in Nick's world was out of Rebecca's life. And let's not forget the relative side-street issue of Magda, who was *sans* Jonas and shacked up with (in Nick's words) a 'Living Sex Doll from the Balkans'.

Around six a.m. the hunger pangs I'd been ignoring for hours upped their intensity, shoving everything else aside. Breakfast began at seven, and the staff had just finished setting up the buffet as I blundered my way in, the scent of bacon and sausage grease making me semi-delirious. I have a secret love for generic hotel breakfasts: they remind me of the time Mum managed to save up enough cash for us to have a holiday at a budget resort hotel in Wales. It had been years since I'd eaten pork, but I gave in to temptation and piled my plate with a full hog's worth of artery-clogging crap, reckoning that after last night's shockers I deserved it. Checking none of the staff were looking, I picked a rasher out of the tray with my fingers and shoved it straight into my gob. Which was when this happened:

'Hi again.'

I turned to see Nicolas, empty plate in hand, smiling expectantly. Mouth stuffed with pig, I couldn't reply until I'd inelegantly scarfed it down, almost choking in the process (which I suppose would have made for a good anecdote – a Heimlich manoeuvre meet-cute).

I coughed out a 'Hi.'

'Is the coffee any good?'

'Haven't tried it yet.'

'Well wish me luck, I'm going in.'

Mortified, I retreated to a table. *Nice work, Bee.* I was still in yesterday's clothes, hadn't showered, or even brushed my hair or teeth. I'd planned to eat and run, in order to catch an early train home; I hadn't planned on running into Nicolas and embarrassing myself again. I concentrated on my plate – couldn't bear to look at him. Couldn't resist *not* looking. Rougher around the edges than he'd been at the signing – morning stubble, mussed hair – which suited him. And oh God he was coming over. I'd forgotten to collect a napkin – I was pretty sure I (literally) had egg on my face now too.

'Can I join you? Or is that too forward?'

'Course you can.' His plate, like mine, was filled with all the Bad Things, which made me feel a little less like Miss Piggy. I tried to dredge up some small talk, fought the urge to say something pathetic (and untrue) like *I don't usually stuff my face like this*. It struck me then how many of my recent interactions with men had involved food. Satchel Man. Gelato Guy. And now Nicolas 2. I half expected him to say, 'I like a woman who eats.'

He took a sip of coffee.

'Well?'

'Bad. Really bad. But it's better than a kick up the arse. Which would also clear my head, I suppose. Do you usually get up this early on a Saturday?'

'No. Have to catch an early train home. You?'

'Nah. These publicity things always make me anxious. Drank too much nasty red wine after the event to unwind. Bad idea as it only kept me up.'

'Anxious? Really? You didn't show it. You were great.'

'You don't have to say that. Fact is, I forgot the name of the murderer at one point.'

'No one noticed. I didn't.'

'And I'm sure you didn't need to hear that. Red wine keeps me awake and coffee makes me confess all kinds of shite.'

'Let me get you a refill then.'

He laughed. I relaxed. That cognitive dissonance I'd felt at the signing began to fade. This was the *real* him, not the author-persona him. A peek at the man behind the curtain. 'What do I call you? Mouseyhairedgirl is a bit of a mouthful, especially for someone with a raging hangover. Mousey? Ms Girl?'

'Rebecca. Or Bee, if you like.'

'Bee. I like it. Is that what your friends call you?'

It's what the other *you calls me.*

*

From: NB26@zone.com
To: Bee1984@gmail.com

A bacon sandwich together, eh? Is that a euphemism?

From: Bee1984@gmail.com
To: NB26@zone.com

Ha! No. But I meant what I said Nick. We can give this up right now. Stay as we are.

From: NB26@zone.com
To: Bee1984@gmail.com

Is that what you want to do?

From: Bee1984@gmail.com
To: NB26@zone.com

Like I said, it doesn't seem fair.

From: NB26@zone.com
To: Bee1984@gmail.com

It's not fair for me to ask you to stop. Not now you've had *breakfast* together.

From: Bee1984@gmail.com
To: NB26@zone.com

Does red wine stop you sleeping?

From: NB26@zone.com
To: Bee1984@gmail.com

Yep. It that a Nicolas-ism too?

From: Bee1984@gmail.com
To: NB26@zone.com

He's not as funny as you. Just so you know.

From: NB26@zone.com
To: Bee1984@gmail.com

I bet you say that to all the guys who are stuck in an alternative universe due to a random quirk of . . . something.

From: Bee1984@gmail.com
To: NB26@zone.com

Ha ha. Also, BTW the most likely Benedict Mercer candidate I can find in this world doesn't look like someone I'd go for AT ALL. I can't stop thinking about Rebecca. It shouldn't matter to me so much, but it does. It's almost as if she IS me.

From: NB26@zone.com
To: Bee1984@gmail.com

She kind of is, Bee.

From: Bee1984@gmail.com
To: NB26@zone.com

You know what I mean! I need to know she's OK. Why Leila isn't close to her anymore. Why the versions of ourselves are so different. Why she's married to someone who may be loaded but looks like an actor out of an erectile dysfunction infomercial.

From: NB26@zone.com
To: Bee1984@gmail.com

!!!

I get it. I'm the same. Is it nature versus nurture or something else? Why did Nicolas carry on writing while I gave up?

From: Bee1984@gmail.com
To: NB26@zone.com

OK. How's this. How about we find the answers each of us needs, see how that goes, then reassess? Deal?

From: NB26@zone.com
To: Bee1984@gmail.com

Deal.

NICK

As far as Operation Doppelganger went, Bee was streets ahead of the game. She'd met Nicolas, and they were now in regular contact. I had to think long and hard about what to do next. According to Leila, the Mercers lived in one of those intimidatingly exclusive eco-estates, nestled on the outskirts of the Kent green belt. Close enough to London to boast carbon-neutral commuting, far enough away from Leeds to make any future Rebecca recces a practical nightmare. Unless I moved there for a while. Which was a crazy idea. Because say I did engineer a meeting with Rebecca and somehow managed to extract the details Bee was desperate to know, what did I hope to achieve after that? An affair? Breaking up a marriage, Jez-style? But if there was a chance – however slim – that Rebecca *wasn't* happy with her incredibly good-looking millionaire philanthropist, wasn't it worth pursuing? The least I could do was meet her. I still didn't know what she bloody well looked like. But Nicolas did, and clearly he found her attractive.

But before I made my next move, I had chores to undertake: breaking the news about the house sale to Lily, which I couldn't put off any longer, and then the meeting to which I'd been summoned by the Berenstains – *if* I chose to go to that. I couldn't decide which I was dreading the most.

For once Lily wasn't lurking at her door when I trundled past with Rosie. Nor could I hear the blare of TV voices – odd as it was usually on 24/7 ('Only company I got'). I knocked. Waited. Knocked again. You read all the time about lonely old folk left to rot in their favourite chair. Should I kick the door in? Call the police or Social Services? Then I remembered she'd mentioned she left a spare key under the mat for the health visitors: 'Saves me getting up to let the buggers in.' I was digging under it when the door creaked open.

'Oh. It's you.' A sniff of distaste, then a smile as Rosie snuffled her way in. 'That's my girl.'

'You almost gave me a heart attack. I was worried about you.'

'Could've fooled me, lad. Haven't seen hide nor hair of you for days.'

'I'll go then, shall I?'

'Oh, don't be daft.' She waved me inside and into the lounge for once. 'Telly's on the blink.'

It wasn't, she'd just managed to flick it onto a channel that didn't pick up the satellite signal. It took me thirty seconds to fix. Deep breath and GO: 'I've got something to tell you.'

'Well out with it, lad.'

She showed zero emotion as I broke the news, which came out in a guilty rush, as if I were confessing a minor infraction to a particularly strict head teacher, or a police officer. 'But I'll make sure I keep in touch, Lily. Do your shopping when I can.'

'Don't worry about me, lad. You've got your own life to live, I know that.' Whoa: who *was* this person? 'Besides. I'll get that new bint from the social to do it. She's got sod all else to do when she comes over.' So not completely changed then. 'I'll miss the dog.'

I'd considered asking Lily if she'd take Rosie on while I made my first forays into Operation Doppelganger, but the dog needed walking, and Lily wasn't up to that on a daily basis. 'I'll visit. We both will.'

A tut as if to say, 'Yeah right.' Then: 'Off to live with the other one, are you?'

'What other one?'

'The one you keep slinking off to see.'

'That's a non-starter. She's married.'

'Bit on the side, eh?'

'No. We haven't . . . I don't know what to do about that, if you must know.'

'Love her, do you?'

Haven't even met her. Oh, fuck it. 'Yes.'

'Then go and get her.'

'Told you. She's married. With a kid. I can't.'

'No such thing as "can't". You'll do what's right. You're a good lad.'

'I'm forty-five.'

'Still a lad to me.' She scratched Rosie's belly, then gave me a sly glance. 'I was like you once.'

'An arsehole?'

'No, lad. Fell for someone who wasn't . . . what's the word. Available.'

'And? What happened with him?'

'Never said it was a "him", did I? Marion was married when we met. It wasn't easy at first. But we had a good five years together before she went.'

'Went where?'

'Cancer.'

Jesus. 'I'm sorry.'

She rooted around in a drawer and took out a photograph: Lily in her nineteen-eighties glory days (she didn't look that different, to be honest – like those kids you sometimes see who already look middle-aged), on a couch and laughing with a portly woman with a corona of black hair. Marion looked like she'd been a right old bruiser, but they seemed to . . . fit. There was something about their body language that seemed *right*. I can't put it better than that.

'You never told me this before.'

'Never asked, did you?'

Back at home, preparing for the meeting I still wasn't sure I'd attend, I found myself having a good old cry in the shower. Who or what was I crying for? Lily? Me? Poll? Christ knows. But it helped a bit – as if I'd lanced yet another inner emotional boil.

*

God knows why the Berenstains had been so cagey about their HQ, because it turned out to be a saggy old Scout hall in the hinterlands outside Manchester. Fittingly, it began to rain as my ride-share dropped me off outside it, the tipper-tap of water on the tin roof sounding like sarcastic applause. I almost turned back then, but curiosity about the 'verdict' and my righteous anger at Geoffrey's actions won the day. At the last meeting they'd been guarded, distrustful and weird, and on the journey here I'd prepared myself for a similar reception. But when I walked through the door, Henrietta strode up to me, hand outstretched. 'Thank you for coming, Nicolas. And first of all, please accept our apologies for Geoffrey's overenthusiastic actions. Rest assured he has been spoken to most stringently.' Kelvin gave me his version of a smile and introduced me to the other members, none of whom fitted my loon stereotype either. There was Isaac, seventies, who tried to give off a wise old man vibe but came across as more of a frustrated golfer; Debbie, fifties, roly-poly in shape and sunny in demeanour, and Adil, thirties, who was dressed like a teenager in a Peace Out logo-ed hoodie and who gushed, 'I've heard such *wonderful* things about you, Nicolas.' In fact, everyone, with the exception of Geoffrey, who murmured a grudging 'sorry' like a child who'd been forced to apologise against his will, greeted me as if I were a long-lost pal. This unexpected and exaggerated charm offensive, as Bee reminded me later, was a textbook tactic used by cults. It worked, as within minutes I found myself dropping my guard.

Henrietta invited me to sit. The chairs were arranged in a circle, support-group style, and there were snacks, courtesy of Adil. ('No one makes a better samosa, Nicolas,' Isaac purred, 'Please dig in.' To be fair, he was right, they were bloody delicious.) Eschewing the circle, Geoffrey lurked in a corner sipping a can of Special Brew and glowering at everyone – the first time I've ever had cause to use that word.

After a smattering of small talk about the weather, and a peculiar anecdote from Debbie about a couple of women in her allotment cooperative who'd been caught 'pilfering the eggplants', Henrietta clapped her hands and asked Isaac to recite their mission statement. A hush fell, and everyone in the circle dropped their heads as if in prayer. I glanced at Geoffrey: he lifted his can in a mock salute.

'We pledge to protect those in our world and others to the best of our ability.' (<I KNOW, Bee. I should have done a runner right then>)

The atmosphere shifted, and I became the focus of their attention.

Henrietta began: 'We believe you are who you say you are, Nicolas. And we believe that you have, in fact, engaged in communication across the mesh.'

'Right. Good – I guess.'

'Tell me, since we last met, has your correspondent been back in contact with you?'

A sixth sense whispered, *lie*. But I ignored it. 'She has.'

A faint smile. 'I see. I am happy for you. And she has corroborated your discrepancies from her side?'

'She has.' I left it at that without elaborating further or mentioning Operation Doppelganger.

'To confirm: you can only communicate via i-mail, is this correct? And only via these particular addresses?'

'Yeah.'

'And other media? Photographs, videos, spreadsheets? Do these translate across the mesh?'

'*Spreadsheets*? Why would you ask about spreadsheets?'

'Do they?'

'Spreadsheets aside, no. We sort of rationalised that other tech wasn't compatible for some reason.'

Kelvin and Henrietta shared an unreadable glance. Adil and Debbie were now staring at me with the kind of unblinking intensity favoured by religious fanatics. Thankfully Isaac was trying, and failing, to eat a stuffed courgette, which took the edge off the now disturbing atmosphere. Time to go on the offensive. 'Do you have a theory as to how – or why – this might have happened?' Like Bee, I'd tried to get my head around the seemingly countless Multiverse/Shared Consciousness/Chaos/Quantum Immortality theories out there: even the 'quantum mechanics for dummies' articles were an exercise in mind-fuckery. Other explanations we'd considered, most of which we'd cherry-picked from sci-fi films – a glitch in the space-time continuum (whatever that actually meant), a black hole, an unreported screw-up with the Hadron Collider (which we had in both our worlds, although it was only in Bee's world that it had gone haywire after a passing bird dropped a bit of baguette in it) – were similarly beyond our limited comprehension.

Kelvin opened his mouth to say something, but Henrietta silenced him with a glance. *Interesting*. 'We do not.'

'So now what?'

Henrietta frowned. 'I am not understanding you.'

'Bee and I were discussing if we should tell someone about this.'

'Someone?'

'I don't know. The scientific community? The authorities?' *And not just a bunch of possible paranoid nuts like you lot.* 'What Bee and I are experiencing – I mean, it's pretty much a game-changer, isn't it?'

'How so?'

'How *so*? I'm communicating with a person who lives in a different world. Multiverse. Universe. Whatever.'

'That is not a good idea, Nick. First of all, the proof you have is in your correspondence, which could be easily fabricated – the likelihood is that you would not be believed. We have been there in the past. We know.'

A murmur of assent from the others.

'And secondly, let us say that they did believe you, we do not know how they might use this information.'

'You mean they'd try and weaponise it? Like in every shitty thriller ever?' It was supposed to sound facile, and it did.

Henrietta gave me a patronising smile. 'Do you have any other questions for us, Nicolas?'

I did. A monumentally stupid one as it happened, but I needed to ask it all the same: 'Is there any way that Bee and I could be together?'

Blank looks, including from Henrietta. 'Together how? *Physically*?'

'Well, yeah. As you're all . . . displaced people, how do you believe you travelled across the mesh? Via a wormhole or a portal or something?'

Geoffrey barked a sarcastic laugh. 'A portal. Fuck's sakes.'

Adil took pity on me. 'I am sorry to tell you this, Nicolas, but if we knew how to travel across the mesh, we wouldn't be displaced, would we?' Fair enough.

Henrietta took charge again. 'Nicolas, have you and Rebecca been tempted to swap details that could improve your personal fortunes?'

I hadn't. I actually hadn't. 'Like what?' But then it came in a rush: *the plots of Nicolas's novels*. I could get Bee to transcribe them and take them for my own. He was me, I was him, which meant it wasn't strictly plagiarism, right? Wrong. I'm not a bastion of morality, but I wasn't about to nick Nicolas's novels. Technology then. Those dating apps Bee had mentioned . . . if I played my cards right, I could be a trillionaire by next week. Give Benedict a run for his money. 'That honestly hadn't occurred to me. Until now. So thanks for that.'

Silence, then: 'We would prefer, of course, that you ceased all communication.'

'Wait – what? Why?'

'Because, Nicolas, to be quite frank, we cannot quantify the level of risk to both of our worlds if you continue.'

'Risk? What harm are we doing?'

'We do not know. Nor do you.'

Then I got it: 'You're talking about the butterfly effect?'

'That is one way of putting it. From what we can gather from your correspondence, her world does not have the . . .' – here Henrietta paused and waved a hand vaguely around her head, as if searching for the right word – 'the *balance* we have found in ours. The safest course of action is to cease and desist.'

Now I *really* regretted allowing her access to the i-mails. 'That's not going to happen.'

'We assumed you would say that. As it is very clear how important your connection is to you, we would like to offer you a deal.' The entire group – including Geoffrey – were now staring at me expectantly. 'If you promise that you will not attempt to use the knowledge you have of each other's worlds to influence structural, societal, or economic changes, then we will allow it.'

'Hang on – *allow* it?'

'Yes. We have taken a vote, and there are more romantics among us than you might expect.'

Isaac smiled as if I should find this charming.

'Right. Let's say I turn down this deal. What makes you think you have the power to stop me doing anything?'

Ve haff ways of making you stop.

'Oh, Nicolas. I do not need to tell you how very easy it would be for someone to infect your devices, perhaps freeze or delete your zone account and thus sever your connection.'

Whoa. 'You're *threatening* me?'

'Yes.' Matter-of-fact. 'But we would rather all be friends here. Come. Have another samosa.'

My instinct was to let out a stream of invective and storm out of there right then, but something held me back. Did I really want to make enemies of these people? Who knew what they were capable of? Why taunt a mad dog when you can just walk away, whistling? I took the samosa, and in an instant the atmosphere went from sub-zero to warm. The chairs were pushed back, and Adil and Debbie corralled me into a round of small talk as if nothing out of the ordinary had just occurred. 'We meet once a month,' Isaac said as he zipped up his coat. '*Please* say you'll join us again.'

As *if*.

When I finally escaped, the rain had stopped. Geoffrey was outside, having a smoke. 'Be seeing you, Nick,' he smirked as I passed. I bit back the obvious response to that – but unlike the others, at least he'd had the good grace to remain his consistently shitty self throughout the meeting.

Shaken and seething, it occurred to me that if I upped sticks and moved to Kent, fully committing to Operation Doppelganger, for one thing it would make it harder for the Berenstains and their pet dog Geoffrey to keep tabs on me. I had them to thank for that decision.

But was I really ready to relocate to a place I hardly knew, in order to spy on the facsimile of the woman I loved, in the faint hope of breaking up her marriage?

Yes.

*

From: Bee1984@gmail.com
To: NB26@zone.com

ALLOW It? They really said that?

From: NB26@zone.com
To: Bee1984@gmail.com

Yep.

From: Bee1984@gmail.com
To: NB26@zone.com

Could they do that? Wipe out your account I mean?

From: NB26@zone.com
To: Bee1984@gmail.com

God knows. I don't know for sure what they're capable of.

From: Bee1984@gmail.com
To: NB26@zone.com

Have you backed up to the Cloud just in case?

From: NB26@zone.com
To: Bee1984@gmail.com

Have I backed up to the what now?

From: Bee1984@gmail.com
To: NB26@zone.com

Never mind ☺ Crossed Lines.

BTW – HAVE you ever thought about using our connection to get rich/famous etc etc?

From: NB26@zone.com
To: Bee1984@gmail.com

Actually no. Not until they brought it up. All I've been thinking about is what it means for us. Have you?

From: Bee1984@gmail.com
To: NB26@zone.com

Not once. Isn't that weird? Does that make us chronic self-obsessives or pure romantics?

From: NB26@zone.com
To: Bee1984@gmail.com

Both, probably. Or maybe we're just really, really thick.

BEE

It felt like cheating. E-mailing Nick, while messaging Nicolas and trading quips with him on Twitter. After our buffet encounter, Nicolas had reached out first, sending through a DM when I was on the train back from the conference (<Thanks for letting me crash your breakfast. Is the bad coffee repeating on you too or is that just me?>) We'd been chatting sporadically ever since, but I hadn't yet found an elegant way of framing the questions to which Nick wanted answers – I was still at the rapport-building stage. Nicolas's online persona wasn't as sharp and wicked as Nick's, but on a couple of occasions I almost confused the two and very nearly replied to Nicolas's messages with the kind of rude, sarcastic banter Nick and I were in the habit of trading. And my work was suffering. I was late on two commissions (one of which, unforgivably, was Gemma's silk-lined jacket) and for the first time, a client had returned her revamped dress because the lining was coming loose. Inexcusable sloppiness.

Adding a seasoning of poison to this toxic mess was my increasing fascination (oh admit it, Bee), *obsession*, with Benedict Mercer. *Benedict*. How had they met? Winning a Mercer Award was a big deal, and while I hadn't made the grade, what if Rebecca had and their eyes had met over a wad of 'future star designer' cash and the prestige that went with it? Then there was Scarlett. Who'd picked the baby's name? (Scarlett had no personal resonance for me, although I rather liked it.) Was he a good father?

But it wasn't just the big picture stuff I found myself fixating on; I could spend hours obsessing over minutia. Like, did she call him by his full name? *Pass the baby wipes, won't you, Benedict?* Or perhaps to her he was Ben, or Benny (ugh). *Ben and Becca, sitting in a tree . . .* Benedict wasn't on social media, but Google Images was awash with pics of him swanning around charity auctions, tuxedoed, coiffed, rubbing shoulders with fashionistas, influencers, models, and the moneyed. I hated that type of event – it was a social anxiety attack waiting to happen. If this lifestyle was mirrored in Nick's world, how did Rebecca cope? The Mercers here had a property portfolio that would make Rupert Murdoch squirm with envy, including a mansion in the heart of prime gin-walk territory. Not so in Nick's semi-utopia, where, thanks to its cripplingly high inheritance tax and property and land levies, the one per cent were relatively shackled. According to the Leila 2 intel, Ben and Becca lived in Chislehurst of all places – ironically a short bus ride from Leila's suburb – in what Nick described as 'a zero-emissions rich people enclave', called, ominously, Wilderville. No such place existed here. I was in danger of driving myself crazy, but I wouldn't know more until my personal PI got to work.

Needing a distraction that wasn't just work and male doppel-gangers, I invited myself over to Leila's for dinner and, despite my crippling workload, took a couple of extra hours off to explore Chislehurst beforehand, trying to imagine myself inhabiting this alternative, kiddified life of swing sets, family gardens, and soft-focused suburbia.

The twins were still up when I arrived, and as I helped Leila put them to bed – a complex give and take of story-time, veiled threats and pleading, culminating in a spot of bribery ('if you go to sleep NOW then Mummy will take you to the park *tomorrow*') I once again I tried to slide into Rebecca's skin. Tried to imagine her/me running downstairs for cups of warm milk, at the beck and call of a little person. Admittedly, when one of the twins held out his arms to me for a goodnight kiss, I almost – *almost* – envied her.

Leila turned off the light and we crept down the stairs like cat burglars, aware that the slightest sound would result in an inevitable, plaintive 'Mummy!' and a replay of the above.

Safely in the kitchen, Leila poured us both a glass of wine. 'Thanks for helping with that.' She drained half of her glass in one go. 'You're good with them.'

'*Really*? You really think I am?'

'Course. They love their Auntie Bee. You should come over every night – in the usual course of events I'd still be up there. Re-reading the sodding *Gruffalo* for the thousandth time.' She raised her glass. 'Anyway, cheers!'

'What are we drinking to?'

'I've got a new client. Kind of.'

'You're going back to work?'

'No. Voluntary stuff. Fundraising. I joined XR. Extinction Rebellion?'

'You didn't!'

'I did.' She nodded to where Lev was slumped on the sofa, headphones on, mashing the Xbox controls. 'He doesn't approve. Says they're anarchists. Thinks I'm going overboard. But someone's got to do something, right?'

Leila and I had gone through the usual teenage activism phase – joining Greenpeace, Amnesty International, going on a couple of marches, mostly for the fun of it – but it hadn't lasted long. We both did what I thought of as 'our bit' (recycling, voting Labour, signing the odd online petition, your basic run-of-the-mill conscience-salving armchair activism), and while no one could say Leila wasn't socially conscious, I'd never pegged her as a hard-core eco-warrior. 'Why XR? Is it something to do with your new-found appreciation of plants?'

'Very funny. I've been thinking about it for a while. You know, worrying about what kind of future the kids will have to face if we don't pull our finger out. So, there's that. And actually, part of it was down to you.'

'Me? How?'

She gave me a wicked grin. 'Come on. I've got something to show you.'

Bemused, I followed her out into the back garden, where, taking pride of place among heaps of kids' toys and last year's rusting barbecue, was the wicker chair she'd fished out of the skip, its raggedy seat now repaired, and its peeling legs sanded down (admittedly a bit ineptly, but I wasn't going to say that to Leila). 'Wow. Nice one.'

'I could see on your face you didn't think I'd get round to it, so I took that as a challenge. And it felt good *doing* something. Something practical, I mean. I thought if I can find the time to do that, I can bloody well do more than just sling Greenpeace a tenner a month. But like I said, Lev doesn't get it.'

'I do.' Jumping straight from some mild furniture repurposing to full-on activism did actually make sense – Leila never did anything by halves. 'Makes me feel guilty for not doing more too.'

She play-punched me on the arm. 'Your whole business is ethical, Bee. You're basically a one-woman wedding dress recycling factory.'

As we wandered back inside, she said: 'But, if I'm honest, there's a selfish element to it too. Keeping my hand in before the Velociraptors start school and I get my life back.' A pause. 'I don't mean that.'

'You don't have to explain anything to me. Ever. I get it. I know how much you love them.' And I could see how much strain she was under. Unwashed hair, baggy sweats. This hadn't stopped her seeing me through my recent crises though, had it? Rebecca had lost Leila 2 – I couldn't risk our friendship sliding, becoming unbalanced. It was about bloody time I did more for her. 'How about I babysit sometime? Stay over. Give you and Lev a night alone.' I had no clue how I'd fit this in as well. Between working and e-mailing Nick and Nicolas, it was a wonder I wasn't getting carpal tunnel.

'Oh God, that would be amazing. You mean for the whole night?'

'Why not?'

'Are you sure?'

'Of course. I've been crap. Self-obsessed. I'm sorry.'

'Don't be silly.' She refilled our glasses. 'You've had a nightmare of a time lately. Then there's the business, which is a massive time-suck. About which, by the way, I'm due an update.'

I gave her a brief rundown about my latest clients (thanks to the minor celeb's commission, which she'd splashed all over Instagram, the waiting list was now in danger of running well into the next year), and had a good old cathartic vent about the dress the client had returned. 'I still can't believe I did that.'

'Don't beat yourself up about it. You can't be perfect all the time, can you? Isn't it about time you took someone else on? You can afford it.' I could. I probably should. Especially if my current distractions continued to affect the business.

The wine was taking effect, and I very nearly told her everything then. The whole truth. The whole mad story – the tale of two Nicolases – the real reason why I'd cocked up that commission. So why didn't I? It wasn't just cowardice – the fear that as a supreme rationalist she wouldn't believe me (in anyone's books it was a crazy story) – it just didn't feel like the right time. I'd need hours to relay it properly. And say she did believe me, what if she wanted to know about her other self? The Leila with the corner office and blistering career. The Leila who may or may not have a family. Plus, Leila was smarter and more principled than me. I could just imagine her response: *Hang on, Bee. So you've found yourself embroiled in a situation that could be termed an unprecedented scientific miracle, and you're using it JUST TO DATE A GUY?* Instead, I asked: 'What would make you stop seeing me?'

'Eh?'

'Like, we've been friends forever, right? What would be the thing that would make you stop being my friend?'

'Seriously? Why are you asking this?'

'Humour me.'

'Jesus. Um . . . If you killed a child?'

'If I killed a *child*? You mean one of the twins?'

'No, for that you'd get a medal. Of course not one of the twins! A random kid. I mean, not if you ran over it accidentally or whatever. If you killed a child on purpose, like you were a serial killer or something.'

'Wow. Okay.'

'Or slept with Lev. No. Scratch that. I'd probably forgive you for that. Or feel sorry for you. Kidding. Yeah, that would be shit, unless I gave you permission and it was a loan-out.'

Lev looked over and lifted one of his headphones. 'Did I hear my name?'

'I was just saying to Bee that she could only sleep with you if I loaned you out.'

A deadpan 'Oh right.' Then he went back to his game.

'What's brought this on?'

'I just can't imagine my life without you.'

'Aw. Me neither. Hang on. You're not dying or anything, are you?'

'No!'

'Because being this deep isn't like you.'

'Thanks.'

'You know I don't mean it like that. What's going on?'

'Nothing.'

'Bollocks.' Paddington stare time.

Idiot. I should have known she wouldn't let it go. The whole truth was out of the question, but I had to say something. 'I've met someone. Kind of.'

'In person, or online?'

'Both.'

'*Tell* me you haven't got back in touch with that catfishing arsehole.'

'No! Of course not.'

'So why the caginess?'

'After what happened with Nate and . . . the other one, it didn't seem fair to put you through another episode of the Shitty Bee Dating Show.'

'Too bad. Now spill. I want all the deets.'

Leila had read some of our e-mail exchanges, she knew Nick

was a writer/editor who lived in Leeds. Remarkably similar – too similar – to Nicolas, a writer, who lived in Leeds. A turning point: I had to come up with a story, or tell her the truth after all.

She was waiting. 'Well?'

Then, 'Mummy!' Saved by the twins.

'Shit. Be right back.'

I'm not proud of this, but I chose to lie. Used the time it took for Leila to tame the twins to come up with a reasonable story. How, after Nick hadn't shown up at Euston, I'd gone into a Google frenzy, looking for Nick + Writer + Leeds. This had led me to another, different Nicolas. Out of mild curiosity I'd read some of his novels, connected with him on Twitter. Decided to go to one of his events, where we met in person and hit it off. As I relayed this to Leila, hating myself, I searched her face for any sign that the jig was up. Perhaps it was the wine, perhaps it was the exhaustion, but she seemed to be buying it (there was, after all, a grain of truth to it).

'I can see why you didn't want to tell me.'

'I really didn't want you to worry about me, Leila. It didn't seem fair after you held my hand through that last shit-show.'

She was already Googling Nicolas. 'Not bad. Does he know that he's a rebound off a catfish?'

'Nope.'

'My lips are sealed. And promise me you'll take it slow.'

'I promise.'

And I meant to, I really did.

NICK

My side of Operation Doppelganger creaked underway. I've always been a homebody. Not one for moving out or moving on, perhaps because my parents had me very late and died within six months of each other during my second year of university. Boringly, I'd never really considered living anywhere else but my hometown. It didn't take long to discover that if you put your mind to it, changing your life (or blowing it up in my case) is remarkably easy.

First, I needed funds. Universal Basic Income only went so far, there were no new clients in the offing as per, and Tweedy wasn't quite ready for his sequel. Poll was my only option. After chain-smoking two roll-ups for courage and luck, I made the call. A sprinkling of emotional blackmail ('I need to get away for my well-being, Poll,'), a touch of bribery ('if you want a quick divorce, that's fine by me'), *et voila* – she agreed to front me a couple of grand on the house sale.

Next: secure a base as close to Rebecca as possible, which was a far trickier proposition. The Mercers lived in an upmarket area, way out of my limited budget, and then there was the dog. The only affordable place I could find that was willing to take Rosie, and within a five-minute bus ride of chez Mercer, was a lodging house in Orpington called 'The Bergs'. Its booking site was stuck in the Dark Ages, and its only review was a cryptic and anonymous 'Good luck!' but its owner, Erika Berg, came across as friendly and charmingly eccentric on the i-mail. ('So we will have a writer in residence! How good for us.') Erika offered me the attic 'studio space' on a month-to-month basis, which included a 'continental breakfast and optional evening meal for an extra charge', and said she had an elderly Alsatian named Sausage who would enjoy the canine company. Rosie wasn't a fan of her own species (like her owner, ba-doom-tish), but I decided to risk it. She'd mellowed in her old age; it had been a good few years since she'd actively tried to pick a fight.

Next: what the hell to do with my stuff? All I really owned were vinyl, books, my parents' wedding album, clothes, and a dog. I donated the books to the charity shop where I'd bought the suit and sold the vinyl to a stall holder, and, with the ruthlessness of an evangelical minimalist, chucked and recycled and dumped until my worldly possessions fitted into two large suitcases. Although I kept the tweed suit: it held too much emotional resonance to re-donate. It was both freeing and depressing – it wasn't much to show for forty-five years on the planet. I tried not to dwell on the equally depressing fact that after twelve years in the area, the only person who'd miss me was the old curmudgeon next door.

Next: a call to Dylan. His response to my news was an understandably incredulous, 'You're moving *where*?'

'Kent.'

'Why?'

Oh, you know, the usual: to embark on a spot of mild stalking sparked off by a quantum anomaly soulmate fuck-up. I couldn't tell Dylan the whole truth, but I tried to stay in its ballpark. 'You remember my i-mail friend?'

'It's that serious?'

'Well, not really, but I'm going to see if it could be.'

'Good for you.'

Was it? Time would tell.

And finally: how to get there? Lugging my luggage, Rosie and her basket and bowls on the train would be a challenge. But help came from a surprising quarter when Jez offered to drive us there.

Did I want to spend four hours in a car with the backstabbing bastard? No. But it was a win-win for both of us. It helped assuage his guilt, and I got a free ride. To avoid listening to several hours of *mea culpa*, I brought Bowie along and cranked him up high. Apart from a touching moment between us when Rosie got carsick and we had to scrabble around for water and ecowipes, we barely spoke.

'The Bergs', a sturdy, 1930s retro-insulated number, was nestled within a fairly pleasant estate and was larger than I expected. In a blatant disregard for the Greening Laws, and in contrast to its more law-abiding neighbours, the front garden was concreted over, but you can't have everything.

As Jez helped me unload Rosie's basket and the bags, he mumbled: 'I really am sorry about everything, mate.'

I took pity on him. What did it matter now? 'It's for the best. You'll look after her, won't you?' We both knew it would be the other way around. As it had been for me.

'I'm here if you need me. We're both here.'

That I didn't dignify with an answer.

Home sweet home. I rang the bell. From deep within came the muffled ruff of what sounded like a very large dog. No one came to the door for an age. When it was finally opened, the first thing to emerge was the Alsatian – pushing its way out in defiance of a screeched, Scandi-accented, 'Sausage! No!' and making a beeline for Rosie. I attempted to simultaneously lunge for Sausage's collar and yank Rosie to heel – a dual move way beyond my limited reflexes – but I needn't have bothered. After a tail wag and a bum sniff, it was love at first sight. Not so for Erika and me. That charming i-mail tone was just a front. The cuddly, mildly eccentric sixty-something I'd been picturing was a world away from the real-life version: early forties, sharp-edged and brittle, as if there were too many bones in her body, and an expression and demeanour that would have won her the part of a sadistic prison warden in a clichéd drama. Dignifying my 'It's great to finally meet you,' with a nod and a, 'yes, yes,' she ushered the dogs inside and waited impatiently as I clumsily hefted the bags and Rosie's belongings into the hallway.

With a rude, 'Come, now we do the tour,' she marched me through the house with brutal efficiency, instructing me to leave Rosie's bowls and basket in the kitchen. Rosie, the traitor, left me to it – smugly flumping next to Sausage in the Alsatian's basket. Like the concreted front yard, the interior was a triumph of practicality over comfort or aesthetics. Walls painted in glossy industrial magnolia, tiled floors, the furniture a study in flat-pack Scandinavian discomfort, and passive-aggressive laminated signs with odd misspellings: 'Mugs and Plats to be washed ONLY in here'; 'NO smirking' (smoking, I presumed, but I wouldn't have put either past her). Erika ran a tight ship. The air hummed with the scent of lavender detergent – a bottle of which always seemed to be glued to her hand. Her only blind spots were the clumps of Sausage's hair that drifted around the house, dust-bunnying themselves around furniture legs and breeding in corners.

'Now. The lounge you can use with prior arrangements. The kitchen also. But always clean up after yourself.' A pause for emphasis (and threat). '*Always*.'

The attic room though, was charming, as if the few surviving refugees of the house's original character had fled up here to escape Erika's wrath. A honey-coloured wooden floor, an old-fashioned wardrobe, and a brass bed draped with a cosy vintage quilt that Erika informed me had been left by the previous occupant ('a man with no taste, as you can see'). It was far larger than I expected, with a sloping roof and a Mary Poppins style view over the rooftops from the skylight. The corner bathroom was beyond bijou (it took me a couple of days to figure out the contortions necessary to sit on the lavatory without bashing my knees on the shower door), but at least it was private.

'You will eat with us tonight? Then you can meet your fellow guests.'

I was too intimidated to refuse.

A more awkward meal it would be hard to imagine. There were currently two other regular lodgers, which, in different circumstances, could have been an Ealing comedy waiting to happen.

Three male lodgers, an amorous landlady, hijinks ensue. Only the landlady was terrifying, and the lodgers were . . . odd. On the floor below mine was Jorge, a borderline skeletal lad who never raised his voice above a whisper, and Maurice, hugely overweight, who, when we were introduced, mumbled that he'd rather not shake hands 'for reasons I can't disclose'. (When I described them to Bee, she immediately dubbed them Laurel and Hardy – another shared world touchstone.) They were both monosyllabic, and I got the impression they were desperate to move out but were trapped, as if in a cult, or a hijacking (after several attempts I managed to glean that Laurel and Hardy were contractors for the same nuclear energy firm, although in the entire time they lived there, they never showed any signs of being friends or even colleagues).

On the bright side, the food was edible – a vegetarian lasagne that Erika insisted she'd made from scratch, but which had the look of a hastily microwaved Co-op meal. Erika, oblivious to the awkwardness, gifted me with a smile for the first time when I asked about the room's sole decorations – a series of photographs of a man dressed in various shades of camo. 'Ah. That is Petrus. My husband. He does very important work in security all over the world. One day, if you are lucky, you will meet him.' Maurice shot me a cryptic look. As Petrus wasn't smiling in any of the pics and resembled a large, dangerous potato, the inference was clear: I'd be lucky if I didn't meet him.

If it weren't for the room's charm and the fact that Rosie, against all expectations, had settled in as if she'd been living there her whole life, I would have left right then.

I didn't do much on my first evening there, other than endure the meal (never again), sneak into the back garden (also a concreted gulag) for a guilty smoke (or *smirk*), unpack, and fill Bee in. She found it hilarious that I was living in a lodging house – they'd died out years ago in her world.

<Not only that, but I'm also living in an attic like a nineteenth-century servant. Or a piece of old luggage that no one can bear to chuck out>

<Or a bat>

<Thanks for that Bee. I feel much better about my accommodation choices now that you've compared me to a flying rodent>

<Bats are wonderful. Anyway, aren't artists supposed to live in attics?>

<That's garrets>

<Same thing. Which I didn't at all have to check on Wiki. I think it sounds romantic. Speaking of which: How are you feeling about tomorrow?>

Tomorrow: My first recce. My first chance – possibly – of seeing Rebecca 2 in the flesh. <Nervous. Excited. Worried I'll mess it up. Worried she'll think I'm a creepy Geoffrey-style stalker>

Unlike Bee, who'd had a plausible reason for meeting Nicolas, I was a man with a spectacular lack of a plan. Leila 2 wasn't an option – she and Rebecca were estranged, and as far as she was concerned, I was Rebecca's long-lost same-sexer pal. I could hardly knock on Rebecca's door and say, 'Hi there! You don't know me, but thanks to a quantum anomaly, we're actually soulmates. Can you pop the kettle on?' I'd have to wing it.

After the 'continental breakfast' (basically just toast and more misery), I set off. It started well. Rosie and I managed to get on the right bus and find the address. And what an address it was. The Mercer residence was nestled in the heart of an architecturally designed zero emissions estate, a wide boulevard flanked by identical glass and cedarwood mansions, each one set apart from its neighbours and fronted with sprawling greenery for privacy. It seemed to inhabit its own eerily quiet universe, as if money and privilege were capable of rebuffing the everyday sounds of the proletariat. Great for its inhabitants, shit for anyone planning on scoping out the joint (as Geoffrey would probably have put it). It wasn't the sort of place someone could lurk, unnoticed, for too long. The only point in my favour was the fact that I had a dog. A man hanging around by himself: uh-oh. A man with a dog: everyone's friend.

I wandered up and down the boulevard until the novelty of the new smells and environment wore off and Rosie rebelled, refusing to retrace our steps in favour of the direction she knew meant home. We were diagonally opposite Rebecca's place when a woman pushing a child in a stroller emerged. She paused to put in a pair of earphones, and I waited, barely breathing, in case she glanced back and saw me. She was slender, long black hair pulled into a ponytail and dressed in expensive-looking running attire. I couldn't see much of her face from my vantage point, but she was attractive, certainly. What I expected? How I'd pictured her in my head? Yes – and no. Bee said she'd really struggled to correlate her imagined version with the real deal (<You mean you were disappointed, Bee. I told you I wasn't a matinee idol> <No not disappointed. More discombobulated – one of your words>). Now I understood.

She didn't look back and moved on at a fast clip. Keeping our distance, we managed to tail her out of the estate and along a pedestrianised zone lined with stalls selling fresh fruit and veg, Rosie panting with exertion, me fizzing with adrenaline: *This could be it!* But it wasn't to be. As she jogged across a main thoroughfare, heading for the ornate gates of a park, Rosie dug in her heels and no amount of cajoling and pleading could entice her to move. All I could do was watch impotently as the woman, who might or might not be Rebecca, slipped out of sight. With no other option but to give up the chase before it had barely begun, I retraced my steps to the bus stop, burdened not only by the weight of failure and disappointment, but by the weight of the dog, as Rosie insisted on being carried. Neither of us was in a great mood when we made it back to The Bergs.

The second we walked in, Erika accosted me – she must have been lurking in the hallway, waiting for us to appear. 'Nick, may I say, that was most unfair of you.'

What had I done? I'd been in the house for less than twenty-four hours. Rosie left me to it, dumping me in favour of Sausage and her basket.

'If you are taking your dog out for a walk, you must please take Sausage too.'

'Oh right. No problem.'

'Good. And also, I notice that you indulge in smoking. Please do not do this near the windows.'

'Of course. Sorry.' I moved towards the stairs, but she blocked my way. 'Is there something else, Erika?'

'I have put something for you in your room. Come, I will show you.'

I followed her up with some apprehension. I liked the room as it was.

'There. For you to write.' I'd been expecting a new laminated sign, or for the quilt to have been replaced with a wipe-clean duvet cover, but set against the wall was a small, rather beautiful Victorian desk and a padded captain's chair. 'They are ugly, I know. They were discarded by the neighbour. I asked the boys to bring them up for you.'

'That's very kind.'

'You are welcome. I look after all my guests. This is your home now.' Said with such lack of warmth so that it sounded almost sinister.

Once she'd left the room, I placed the laptop on top of the desk. Sat. Stared at the screen: *Enter my world of pain, Nick*.

Write. Write something. Write anything. If Nicolas could do it, so could I.

But what? I was living in the plot of a novel, so why not exploit that? If anything, it might help me get perspective on the madness. And who knew, perhaps I could out-write my alter ego. According to Bee, it had been five years since Nicolas had published a novel under his own name: it was what she called the 'Sanger books' that were his main focus.

Deep breath and . . . GO.

Within seconds I was procrastinating. Bee would be working, so I wrote my update (<I know what you look like!>) and bunged it in drafts. Two i-mails – one from Kelvin reminding me in his dry way of the date of the next Berenstain meeting (delete – the only thing I'd regret foregoing would be Adil's snacks), and a rambling message from Tweedy saying that his granddaughter had put *A*

Shot in the Dark (my title) up on BookPost. I tapped the link he'd included, not expecting much. But whoever Tweedy had commissioned to design the cover hadn't done a bad job (a moody silhouette of a country house, fringed by dense ominous woodland), and there were a number of reviews under it already. Did I, with my history of bad-review PTSD dare read them? I reckoned I could handle it. I might have written ninety per cent of the novel, but it didn't feel like it was truly mine. Quickly, keeping my finger on the escape key just in case, I scanned the top one: 'Bought this on a whim. Glad I did. Read it in one sitting. Ended up rooting for the killer in the end, which I didn't expect. Will read more by this author.'

Wow. Okay . . .

The others were variations on the same theme (although I did report one for including a spoiler – so sue me).

I wished I could send them verbatim to Bee. The world was looking a little brighter already.

BEE

Skinny: that word. The word Nick had used to describe Rebecca. For me, it had connotations that went deeper than the impossible to achieve 'beauty' standards that had been drummed into the subconscious of pretty much everyone on the planet. Thin to me = unhappiness. The thinnest I'd ever been was when Nate and I were together. He'd never said something as explicitly cruel as Satchel Man's 'better get down to hunting weight' jab, but there are only so many 'been at the Magnums, Bex?' or 'are you sure you should have dessert?' comments that you can take before they start to grind you down – physically and mentally.

A red flag? I wouldn't know for sure until Nick knew more. For all we knew, the woman he'd seen might not have been Rebecca at all, but the nanny. They were rich enough to afford one.

<I'll get back on the case in the morning, Bee. How's it going on your side? How's Leeds's answer to Raymond Chandler today?>

<You tell me. You're the one racking up the glowing reviews. So happy for you, Nick. I wish I could read them>

<Wish you could too. So? What news?>

I was typing a response (<nothing new to report>) when a text pinged in: <In London to see my publishers. Dinner? Drinks? Short notice, I know>

I don't know why I suggested we meet in the dire restaurant where I'd experienced my worst date ever. To exorcise the lingering, nasty connotations? To see how he reacted to it? To see how *I* reacted to it?

I hadn't had time to obsess about what to wear and, in any case, I was meeting him primarily for Nick's sake – *wasn't* I? – in order to root out the answers he so badly needed. Nicolas would have to take me as I was – mascara smears and all – and let's face it, he'd seen me at my worst during our breakfast run-in. He was already there when I arrived, sitting in the same booth I'd chosen, staring bemusedly at the menu and sipping a pint of lager. I hesitated before I approached. Although I'd gradually felt more at ease with Nicolas as we chatted about Bowie and his books and my work over breakfast, seeing him again, how did I feel? *Was* there a spark there? Using the tics and idiosyncrasies I'd picked up from Nick's messages as inspiration, I'd built an imaginary collage of his mannerisms and quirks, and that picture kept superimposing itself over the flesh-and-blood person. To put it another way, it was as if he and Nick were two halves of a broken plate that mentally, I couldn't manage to glue together without the cracks showing. (<Is that a stupid analogy, Nick?> <No. It works. I might actually steal it>)

You always read about people 'lighting up', but when he saw me, as banal as it sounds, that's how I'd describe it. I wasn't sure how to greet him: a handshake? A hug? A double kiss? Thankfully the waiter (and also thankfully not the one who'd witnessed the Satchel Man fiasco) rushed over to take my drinks order, diffusing any potential awkwardness.

Not wanting to dither, I blurted: 'I'll have what he's having.' With a nod, the waiter drifted away. We sat. 'I've always wanted to say that. It's not something gross, is it? Or non-alcoholic?'

'Heineken. Boring, I know.'

'Well, you do hate real ale.'

'Who told you that? Did I put it on Twitter?'

Oops. 'Must have.' *Careful, Bee*. That was a Nick-ism, swiped from the thread: (<When my dad found out I preferred lager to ale, I reckon he would have been less horrified if he'd discovered I was a murderer>).

The waiter brought my pint. 'Cheers.'

We drank. He eyed the décor. 'This place is . . .'

'It's terrible, isn't it?'

'Well . . . yeah. Why did you pick it?'

Oh, the temptation to lie . . . But there was enough of that going around. I told him the whole sorry Satchel Man story. Minus the Nick messaging parts, obviously.

'What. A. Prick. I'm sorry that happened to you, Bee.'

'Comes with the territory.'

'Well, it shouldn't. And I get why you needed to come back here. In a way that means he didn't win, right?'

I hadn't considered that as a possible motivation. Smart. 'Right. And the food is good, I promise. What's your worst date story?'

'I don't really go on dates. I'm a serial monogamist.'

'You're in a relationship now?'

'No! I wouldn't be here if I were, would I?' An internal, not unpleasant shiver at the confirmation that to him, this *was* a date.

'Bad break up?'

'No. We sort of just . . . stalled.' Similar to how Nick had described the ending of his relationship with Poll. A fizzling out.

'Ever been married?'

'What is this, the Spanish Inquisition?'

'Sorry. God.'

'Nah, you're all right. I'm kidding. No. Had a couple of long-term relationships, but never took that step. Never felt right. Any more questions before I turn the Inquisition tables on you?'

'Just one.'

'Sounds ominous. Will I need another drink first?'

'Maybe.'

'Okay. Go for it.'

'Would you rather be a reverse centaur or a reverse mermaid?'

A blink. Then he laughed. '*Is* there a right answer to that?'

On the table, my phone buzzed. I hadn't told Nick I was meeting him, given how he was struggling to come to terms with his alter ego. Rather than let him stew for hours, I'd decided to see how it went, then report back.

'You can get it. I don't mind.'

I considered slipping to that terrible ladies' room, then decided, no. Not this time. 'My phone can wait.'

I've thought and thought how to describe the rest of that evening. There were parts of it that were almost too effortless. Too easy. Parts where (probably helped by the booze) that the Nick/Nicolas dichotomy faded and the easy familiarity I'd built up with his other self took over. Even extracting the answers Nick was after felt natural, unforced. Then, I'd glance at the phone, which sat on the table like a disapproving chaperone, trembling every so often as another ignored message hit the inbox, and the thought would come: *it's him but not him* again. The core was there, that same easy sense of humour, but Nicolas took himself a little more seriously, didn't have the same sardonic edge. I had to stop myself from watching him too closely: did Nick also tug on his ear when he was thinking hard about something? Eat the same way (far slower than I did, and almost thoughtfully)? If I'd met Nicolas without knowing him from the inside first, how would I feel about him? Impossible to answer.

We were the last to leave. I stood outside with him, waiting for his Uber to arrive. We stood in silence for a couple of minutes. There's always a sense of anticipation when a successful first date nears its end, but this was more than a sense – it was palpable. He spoke first: 'In case it isn't obvious, I really like you, Bee. I'd like to do this again. It's just, I've never dated a fan before.'

Wow. Had he actually just said that? Conceited, much? 'Is that how you see me? As a *fan*?'

'Christ. I've just fucked this up, haven't I?'

'Yes. Because I'm actually not *that* much of a fan.' It was true. I was still only on book two of the Sanger series.

He laughed.

'Are you worried you're heading for a *Misery*-style situation?'

'No. God no. But it could turn into some kind of situation, right? One without bloodshed. Or stalking.'

'Well, it could . . .'

And then he took my hand, pulled me to him and kissed me. I'm not going to go all Mills & Boon here (I couldn't if I tried), but something inside me *shifted*. Responded. No, clicked into place, as if my body had bypassed the mental doubts and decided to go for it.

The Uber pulled up. 'Be seeing you, Bee.'

*

From: Bee1984@gmail.com
To: NB26@zone.com

It wasn't exactly a date. OK, maybe it was. But not a date-date.

From: NB26@zone.com
To: Bee1984@gmail.com

Bee, you don't have to explain yourself to me. We've been through this. This was the whole plan, remember?

From: Bee1984@gmail.com
To: NB26@zone.com

I know. It still feels like I'm doing something wrong. Something disloyal. Unfair. I should have told you. I'm sorry.

From: NB26@zone.com
To: Bee1984@gmail.com

For the hundredth time. You're not doing anything wrong. And we have to be honest with each other, especially as there's no one else. We'll go crazy otherwise. It's not as if we've found ourselves in a situation anyone could term normal. Or rational.

From: Bee1984@gmail.com
To: NB26@zone.com

You're right. I'm shelving the guilt. For now.

OK. So. He's definitely never been married. No mention of Poll, but he did bring up a Jodie. Think that was his last big relationship. Does that ring a bell?

From: NB26@zone.com
To: Bee1984@gmail.com

Nope. Never met a Jodie. Doesn't sound like my kind of name.

From: Bee1984@gmail.com
To: NB26@zone.com

You can't judge someone by a name! And there are loads of cool Jodies out there. Jodie Foster, Jodie Kidd. If they exist in your world.

From: NB26@zone.com
To: Bee1984@gmail.com

Yeah, I know. Ignore me. Christ, he really didn't marry Poll?

From: Bee1984@gmail.com
To: NB26@zone.com

Doesn't sound like it. That must be weird for you.

From: NB26@zone.com
To: Bee1984@gmail.com

It is. Means he missed out on the thrill of spending years clinging to a stale relationship and the excitement of being betrayed by his best mate.

From: Bee1984@gmail.com
To: NB26@zone.com

It also means he wouldn't have had a relationship with Dylan, so if you think about it, he's the real loser here.

From: NB26@zone.com
To: Bee1984@gmail.com

Whoa, Bee. Way to stop Mr Miserable Bastard in his tracks. But yeah, you're right about that. Thanks.

Okay. Give me more. I can take it.

From: Bee1984@gmail.com
To: NB26@zone.com

He told me why he kept on writing after the first novel didn't succeed. How much do you want to know? Or is it too raw?

From: NB26@zone.com
To: Bee1984@gmail.com

When the first novel bombed, you mean. And I want to hear all of it.

From: Bee1984@gmail.com
To: NB26@zone.com

Boy was it a tricky question to frame without sounding like a psycho weirdo! He really didn't want to talk about that book. Anyway, he said a friend of his gave him a right talking to, even wrote him a list of famous authors whose first novels had been critically trashed. Told him that he owed it to himself to try again. And if he didn't, he'd regret it.

From: NB26@zone.com
To: Bee1984@gmail.com

Which friend?

From: Bee1984@gmail.com
To: NB26@zone.com

He didn't mention a name. Sorry, by that stage I'd had four pints of lager. So had he.

From: NB26@zone.com
To: Bee1984@gmail.com

Lager?

From: Bee1984@gmail.com
To: NB26@zone.com

Yes. You have the same drinking habits.

From: NB26@zone.com
To: Bee1984@gmail.com

My poor dad. Turning over in his grave in both worlds. Anything else I should know? Did he show me up? Do anything embarrassing?

From: Bee1984@gmail.com
To: NB26@zone.com

Like what? Do you usually embarrass yourself on dates?

From: NB26@zone.com
To: Bee1984@gmail.com

Probably. Although haven't had one for 13 years. Can't remember that far back.

From: Bee1984@gmail.com
To: NB26@zone.com

Oh! He said he was a serial monogamist too. Nature versus nurture do you think or genetic?

From: NB26@zone.com
To: Bee1984@gmail.com

Probably just desperation. Fear of rejection. Love the one you're with kind of thing.

Sounds like you're being lined up to be the next prospective item on the Belcher relationship menu.

From: Bee1984@gmail.com
To: NB26@zone.com

I wouldn't go that far. He said it would be weird dating a fan.

From: NB26@zone.com
To: Bee1984@gmail.com

He didn't! What an arrogant dick!

From: Bee1984@gmail.com
To: NB26@zone.com

Don't be so hard on yourself. Himself. You know what I mean. He is YOU, you know.

And he's not arrogant. He was nice to the waiter, insisted on paying. Left a huge tip.

From: NB26@zone.com
To: Bee1984@gmail.com

Oh well that's ok then.

From: Bee1984@gmail.com
To: NB26@zone.com

Go on. Ask it.

From: NB26@zone.com
To: Bee1984@gmail.com

Ask what?

From: Bee1984@gmail.com
To: NB26@zone.com

You know what. But no we didn't. Shag I mean.

NICK

I gave breakfast a miss and went out into the gulag for a smoke and a think instead.

Less of a think. More of a mope. Jez. It *had* to be Jez. Well, it didn't *have* to be, but considering the nasty tricks the universe had been playing on me lately, I would have bet all Tweedy's cash that Nicolas's career-saving lifebelt was thrown by the pal who, in this world, had run off with my wife. I picked and picked at the info Bee had given me as if it were a scab. Dug under the crust, rooted around in the fleshy memory bank beneath. Jez and I had been close back then, fresh out of uni and teacher training. I vaguely recalled us getting stinking drunk after the review appeared in the *Sunday Herald*, but that was it. There definitely wasn't a list.

There was more to that date that wasn't a date than Bee was letting on. I should have been happy that she was forging a connection with this other man, who really wasn't another man, but *me*. Happy that she found him attractive, even if he did sound like an arrogant arsehole.

I showered, shaved, sulked, scrolled through the i-mails. With excellent timing, Poll had sent through a short and sweet message, subject line: Divorce. She suggested a DIY affair, no lawyers involved, which suited me. And, like the i-mail equivalent of sprinkling icing sugar on a turd, she'd signed off with the news that there was a buyer interested in the house. Which reminded me I should really call Lily, something I'd been putting off for obvious reasons. Apart from an awkward moment when I had to remind her who I was

– 'Nick? I don't know a Nick' (to her I was always 'lad') – it wasn't as painful as I'd anticipated. She asked about Rosie, laughed when I told her about the dog's new love affair ('I knew she was a goer'), and then said: 'How's your married woman?'

'Still married.'

I diverted her away from the subject and let her have a good ten-minute vent about her latest long-suffering health visitors.

To cheer myself up, I went to the BookPost site to re-read the good reviews for Tweedy's book. There were more. A lot more. People were actually reading this thing. And all, except for one, which had taken offence at the 'inference of cruelty to animals', were glowing. *Swings and roundabouts*, as Mum would have said. I was re-reading them for the third time, having a good old self-indulgent bask, when Rosie came to fetch me for the morning walk, Sausage in tow. It was nearing the time I'd spotted Rebecca (if she *was* Rebecca) heading to the park – hopefully she had some kind of a routine. Either way it could be ages before I managed to finagle some kind of interaction.

I'd been apprehensive about taking Sausage along. She was a pussycat at home, but for all I knew she could be a pitbull in an elderly German Shepherd's clothing. Fortunately, if anything she was easier to walk than Rosie, obediently sitting on the floor of the bus (instead of attempting to jump onto an elderly man's lap, like Rosie), and padding along at my side without yanking at the lead or lunging at passing dogs.

We made our way to the park, which made Dog Shit Meadow look like . . . dog shit meadow. Carefully maintained pathways swirled through rewilded and wooded areas, flanked by carved benches and water bowls for dogs. There was a neatly fenced-off community coop allotment that was at least three times the size of the one where I'd first met the Berenstain trio, a duck pond fringed by reeds, and a bandstand. It was peaceful, the sort of place in which you could spend hours rambling and relaxing and clearing your mind. Sadly, it would take more than the glories of nature to clear *my* mind. God, I could be a miserable bastard when I wanted to be. No wonder Poll had left me. (And now I had time to contemplate, the number of times she'd said, 'God, you can be a miserable bastard, Nick,' should have been a clue she was reaching the end of her tether.) Jez was as boring as shite, but he was rarely miserable.

Oh, sod it. I had to know. Like a dog returning to its vomit, or a murderer to the scene of a crime, I couldn't help myself. It was a school day, but I got lucky and caught him during a free period. He sounded both wary and pleased that I'd called.

'Is it about the divorce, Nick? Because I can talk to Poll and—'

'It's not about that. Jez, years back, when I wrote my first book and it got trashed, did you give me a pep talk?'

'You what? What's brought this on?'

'Humour me.'

'Well . . . yeah. You were really cut up about it, so we went out for a few pints, more than a few, and I told you not to take it to heart.'

'Did you write me a list of famous authors whose first books had also been trashed to cheer me up?'

Silence, then: 'You know that's really weird, because I remember thinking about doing that. But you seemed to brush it off and said you'd get over it, so I didn't bother in the end. Seriously, mate. Are you all right?'

'I'm good. Working on another book.'

'That's brilliant. Because you're really, really good.'

I almost liked him again. 'Thanks.'

Was it this simple? *Could* life turn on a butterfly's wing like that? Seemed so. No wonder the Berenstains were so paranoid. My career had derailed because Jez couldn't be arsed to write me a list. *Nope. No. Not fair, Nick*. That was on me. And neither could I blame Poll for my lack of ambition. If I *had* got my act together and found it in me to quit the wallowing and write another book, it was possible that the two of us would have ended the relationship sooner. Part of the reason we'd limped on for as long as we had was because she didn't have the heart to kick a dog when he was down.

I wandered along the path that led to the pond, pausing at a particularly attractive spot next to a willow tree. Sausage and Rosie took the opportunity to foul the grass – they were now so in tune with each other that they even shat in tandem. I was midway through clearing up when Rosie yipped, and I turned to see a little girl toddling towards Sausage, who, after I'd dropped the lead to pick up the double load, had wandered off to sniff at the base of the tree.

'Scarlett! Wait! They may not be friendly.' Coming round the corner, slowed somewhat by her bag and the pushchair, was the woman I'd tailed from the Mercer residence.

Sausage seemed to be as soft as shite, but I'd never seen her interact with a child before, and she certainly had the potential to take off an arm. *The good news is the local park is glorious, Bee. The bad news is my landlady's dog ate your kid.* Scarlett would reach her before I could, but I gave it my best shot anyway, lunging for the lead and smushing the poop bags in the process. Fortunately, Sausage flopped on her back and lay with her paws in the air, then let out a soft sigh as the child gently rubbed her belly.

The woman finally caught up to us. 'Scarlett! You mustn't run off like that.' She turned to me. 'I'm so sorry. *Is* it okay if she strokes them?'

'Sure.' Rosie had never nipped anyone before, but I remained tense all the same while the little girl stroked her head. The dog, thank fuck, merely looked bored.

'Look, Mumma, the doggy likes me!'

Mumma. Fuck me. So not the nanny, then. The stress of imminent potential toddler-mauling now over, I allowed myself to breathe; allowed myself to take in the full import of what was actually happening. That here was Rebecca. In the flesh. Right in front of me.

'Thanks. She loves dogs.'

'I can see that,' thinking, *it's you. It's finally you.* Dark eyes, dark hair, strong nose, angular cheekbones. Lithe. A little more uptight than I'd imagined, but that could be down to the fact that her kid had just accosted an Alsatian. Otherwise, if anything, more attractive than the Bee in my head.

She wrinkled her nose. I'd been too distracted to give it much consideration, but a foul smell was coming from somewhere. Not somewhere, me. *Shit.* The poop bag had burst and leaked over my hand.

'Here.' Rebecca dug in her prepper-sized bag and handed me a packet of ecowipes.

'Thanks.'

'You're welcome. It was my fault in any case.'

'It's a good job you didn't offer to shake hands.'

A tight smile.

Say something else. Extend the conversation. Suddenly tongue-tied, I let the moment pass: mirroring, exactly, how Bee said she'd felt when she'd first met Nicolas.

'Well, thanks again. Come on, Scarlett. Home time.'

'Bye, doggies. Bye, man.' Undoubtedly cute, although I was certain Bee wouldn't approve of her 'Daddy's Little Girl' T-shirt.

'Bye.'

On they went. *Great work, Nick.* Rosie, Sausage and I trundled off. Preoccupied with mentally beating myself up, I barely managed to whip Rosie out of the path of a marauding red setter before she launched herself at it.

*

From: Bee1984@gmail.com
To: NB26@zone.com

So more of a meet shit than a meet cute then.

From: NB26@zone.com
To: Bee1984@gmail.com

Yes very funny.

From: Bee1984@gmail.com
To: NB26@zone.com

But you've met at least, that's something, right?

Did I, I mean, Rebecca, look happy?

From: NB26@zone.com
To: Bee1984@gmail.com

I only met you for five minutes, Bee. Your kid is really cute though.

From: Bee1984@gmail.com
To: NB26@zone.com

Thinking about that still tips me off balance. TBH I try NOT to think about it. SO? Do you fancy me/her? ☺

From: NB26@zone.com
To: Bee1984@gmail.com

Obviously. Nicolas clearly has the hots for you and I'm assuming we have the same taste in women.

From: Bee1984@gmail.com
To: NB26@zone.com

I've been thinking. What we're doing. Should we tell them? Before things go too far? Otherwise whatever kind of relationship we have with them, it's beginning on a lie. It feels so manipulative.

From: NB26@zone.com
To: Bee1984@gmail.com

Honesty is always the best policy. But how would we go about doing that? If I'd just met someone and they said I was their soulmate from another reality I'd probably run screaming. Not probably – I would. Would you want to know? They are *us* as you keep reminding me.

From: Bee1984@gmail.com
To: NB26@zone.com

Yes. No. Maybe. I suppose we'll have to play it by ear. See how it goes. Why is this so hard?

BEE

That kiss. It played on my mind. Must have played on Nicolas's mind, too, because the following Monday, in came: <Come to Leeds for the weekend>

We both knew what that meant: accelerating from zero to a hundred miles an hour. My body reacted first, a warm shiver of *hell, yes*. Then my head took over. When I didn't respond in my usual give-or-take-a-few-minutes timeframe, he sent through: <Forget I said that. Too much, too soon. I get it>

<It's not that. I'm snowed under with work> This was true – I'd been forced to put in some seriously late nights. I could hardly tell him my real motivation for stalling: concern about how his alternate world self would feel if I did go. How *I'd* feel if I did go. I'd barely slept the night after our date. Sitting at my kitchen table, messaging Nick just hours after being with Nicolas – *touching* Nicolas, kissing Nicolas – had shaken me up to such an extent I was still feeling the aftershocks, and not just physically. Being so close to Nicolas had added an extra dimension to my communication with Nick: because now I could clearly picture how he might smile whenever I said something ridiculous, hear his laugh, how he wouldn't be able to keep his hands still if he were revealing something personal. I'd felt a shadow of this after the breakfast encounter, but I'd been too self-conscious for it take root. <Can I get back to you?>

<Sure> By now I could read Nick's e-mail tone at a hundred paces. Nicolas's, not so much: I couldn't tell if that 'sure' was just a reasonable response or held a petulant undertone.

Either way, both he and Nick had to be put on hold. Finishing Gemma's jacket had to take precedence, and that evening I was babysitting the twins. Leila had called my bluff on that (fair play to her) and she and Lev had booked themselves into a hotel for the night: 'Which sounds romantic, but actually, we're just going to sleep.'

As the hand finishing for Gemma's piece was intricate and would take all of my concentration, I decided to work without my usual audio distraction. An hour into it, the sound of piano music floated down from above. It had been a while since I'd heard Magda play, and today, instead of the mournful classical pieces she favoured, Gershwin's *Porgy and Bess* kept me company, dosing me with nostalgia. Mum had loved musicals; they'd been the soundtrack to my early childhood. I hadn't run into Magda and Jonas for a while. The truth was, after Nick had described Magda's alternative life, the complex implications of which I tried to block out, I'd been avoiding them. Couldn't face seeing them together, to the extent that when I heard the click of the front door, signalling they were leaving for their daily walk, I'd dart away from the window. I hoped the music was a sign that they were doing well.

The music trailed away as I tied off the last thread. I placed it over Clarice's shoulders, and sat looking at it for a while. Mum would have been proud of me; it was the best work I'd ever done. You can't beat that feeling.

The twins were in bed when I arrived, curled like commas in their toddler cots. While Lev waited downstairs with the panicked air of someone who'd been told they were about to be let out of prison but didn't quite believe it, Leila gave me a crash-course in toddler night care.

'The emergency numbers are on the fridge, and don't panic if they want to go potty. Their pull-ups are on the changing table, so use those if you like. Jack is almost there, but Stevie still finds the toilet terrifying.'

'Right.' The shame of it . . . I could hardly tell Leila that despite being the kids' unofficial godmother, I still couldn't tell them apart. 'I'll be fine. Now go. See you in the morning.'

On their way out, Lev paused to give me a rare hug and a heartfelt, 'Thank you.' Leila play-punched me on the arm and said, 'Good luck, and don't fuck it up.'

The crying started ten minutes after they left. *Don't panic.* I ran upstairs. One of the twins was standing up in his cot, snotty-faced, tear-streaked. A hitched-breath pause as he took me in – *you're not my mother* – then the wailing intensified.

'It's okay, it's okay. I'm here.' He turned the volume up a notch, no doubt picking up that he'd been left in the care of an idiot with zero maternal instincts. Only, that wasn't true, was it? Rebecca must have gone through this a hundred times. *Help me out here, Rebecca.* The knowledge that I did have it in me (somewhere) helped. It wasn't rocket science. It was wiping an arse, for God's sake.

'Do you want to go potty?'

A snuffle and a nod. This had to be Jack, then. I lifted him down from his cot, and holding his little hand, we toddled to the bathroom. The potty's lid was decal-ed, rather sinisterly in my opinion, with a pair of eyes and a grinning mouth. I didn't blame Stevie for his toilet terror.

'You're a good boy, aren't you, Jack?'

'Yes. A *big* boy.'

That's when Stevie started whining. He didn't want 'potty', but nor could he articulate exactly what he did want. 'Juice?' A nod. A run downstairs for juice cups, and sod it – a couple of Hobnobs – then back up. They were both now wide awake.

'Do you want a story?'

Jack shook his head. 'Play time.'

What would Rebecca do? Probably not what I did, which was to capitulate immediately. Within seconds, the bedroom floor was a Duplo- and Lego-block apocalypse. I quite enjoyed it. They took charge as if I were some kind of idiot savant, patiently showing me how to click the pieces into place. When they were babies, I hadn't seen them as individuals ('squalling luggage basically' is how Leila put it), but now I'd actually bothered to spend some alone time with them, their personalities were emerging. Jack was the leader of the pair, and endearingly protective of his brother. Stevie was more affectionate, at one point wrapping his arms around me and giving me a chocolate Hobnob-smeared kiss. Jack yawned first, and I checked the time. It was going on for ten p.m.

'Now. How about sleepy time?'

'Mummy's bed,' Jack said.

Was that allowed? It bloody well was tonight. I checked Stevie's pull-up (damp, but I managed to change it with his help), then, a twin on either side of me, the three of us settled into Leila and Lev's enormous bed.

''Toons,' Jack said, pointing at the flatscreen at the base of the bed.

'It's a bit late for that, isn't it?'

''Toons.'

With a silent apology to Lev, Leila and Rebecca, I gave in to that demand, too. It was already on the Cartoon Network channel, which lessened the Bad Parenting guilt – I wasn't the only one who opted for bribery over discipline. Within minutes they were both asleep, Stevie's head resting against my shoulder, Jack with his thumb in his mouth.

Success. With a little help from Rebecca. And, in a sense, Scarlett. I'd be lying if I said I wasn't curious about her. Part of me did want to know the details: did she have my eyes, my hair, my mannerisms, my quirks? Who was she more like: me/Rebecca or her father? But what would this achieve? I would never meet her, and it was safer to ring-fence these gnarly, emotionally confusing thoughts until I had the space to work through them. I still couldn't see myself kiddie-wrangling on a daily basis, nor had Rebecca's choice to have a child ignited any subconscious maternal yearnings. But enlisting her imaginary help while I wrangled my unofficial godchildren made me feel a little more *connected* to her.

Now. To business.
I couldn't put it off any longer.

*

From: NB26@zone.com
To: Bee1984@gmail.com

I knew it! Fast work there, Nicolas. Least he knows a good thing when he sees it. Watch yourself there, Bee or you'll be married by Christmas.

From: Bee1984@gmail.com
To: NB26@zone.com

I'm not going to go obviously.

From: NB26@zone.com
To: Bee1984@gmail.com

Why not?

From: Bee1984@gmail.com
To: NB26@zone.com

You know why not. We agreed that we wouldn't throw ourselves into this until we knew more about Rebecca's situation. It's not sitting right with me. And I can tell it's not sitting right with you either.

It's not fair.

From: NB26@zone.com
To: Bee1984@gmail.com

If you don't want to go because you find him/me physically repulsive (which by the way, I WILL take personally) then don't. But that isn't the case. Come on, Bee. Be honest, please.

From: Bee1984@gmail.com
To: NB26@zone.com

If I do go you know what it means.

From: NB26@zone.com
To: Bee1984@gmail.com

Of course I know what it means. But I can't be there for you in that way, Bee. As much as I'd like to. And if you think about it, it'll be almost like a threesome. A quantum anomaly thruple. There must be a word for that. A quansome? A quaple? A threetum?

From: Bee1984@gmail.com
To: NB26@zone.com

I can't believe you're actually joking about this.

From: NB26@zone.com
To: Bee1984@gmail.com

Yes you can. It's how I roll. It's usually how *you* roll.

From: Bee1984@gmail.com
To: NB26@zone.com

I'll stall him. Wait until we know more about Rebecca. This is happening so fast. Too fast.

From: NB26@zone.com
To: Bee1984@gmail.com

Don't wait. Go. I know you want to. And I want you to. If only to see how the other half lives. If you turn him down, he'll take it personally.

I know myself. Us Belchers are sensitive souls. Sort of.

From: Bee1984@gmail.com
To: NB26@zone.com

If our situations were reversed, what would you do?

From: NB26@zone.com
To: Bee1984@gmail.com

I'd go and get laid. It's been a while. Seriously, GO. You have my blessing, Bee, not that you should need it. But don't ask me for any insider sex tips. I'm not prepared to go THAT far.

NICK

As weekends went, it was up there with the worst of them: reading that excoriating review for the first time; Dad calling my uni houseshare, his voice barely recognisable, and breaking the news that Mum had had a stroke; the aftermath of Dylan's suicide attempt. I was in such a state of Miserable Bastard-hood on Saturday morning that even Laurel and Hardy asked if I was feeling okay.

'No I'm not, as it happens.' I picked at a piece of toast; ignored the rubbery Emmental cheese slices Erika occasionally left out for us as a dubious treat.

That being the extent of their interest, the gauntlet was picked up by Erika. 'You are sick?'

'Yeah.' *Sick to death of myself.* The last time I'd felt like this – in the good old self-disgust boil-lancing days – Bee was the one I'd turned to. There was no one else. And Erika was the last person I'd dream of confiding in, even if, for the sake of argument, I managed to convince her of the truth of my unique situation. She was the type of no-nonsense practical person who'd tell me to get over it or say something facile about there being 'more herring in the sea'. Not what you want to hear when you're in full Miserable Bastard mode. I avoided them all for the rest of the weekend. Subsisted on ready-made meals that I covertly pinged in the kitchen like a secret eater while everyone was sleeping. Crept out to smoke at odd hours. At least the dogs benefitted. I spent hours rambling around the park, keeping half an eye open for Rebecca. She didn't show.

You convinced her to go, you daft apeth.

I'd never thought of myself as a jealous person. But clearly I bloody well was. Which again made me question if I'd ever truly been in love before. The hurt I'd felt when I learned about Poll and Jez's affair was nothing compared to the near physical pain whenever I thought about Nicolas and Bee being together that weekend. Having sex. MAKING LOVE, or however you want to put it. Intoning, *He's YOU, he's YOU, he's YOU*, didn't soothe it. Nor did: *You wanted her to be happy. This was the plan.* It wasn't as if there was anything I could do about it. It wasn't as if there was a magical portal that would zap me through into her world ('surprise!'). We'd decided not to contact each other until she got home, which made it worse. It was the longest period of time we'd spent apart (so to speak) since we'd reconnected after Euston-Gate. It didn't stop me checking my phone every five minutes on the off-chance there was an update. In the end I had to lock it in the desk drawer.

I wanted it to be wonderful for Bee. I wanted it to be an abject failure. I wanted him to give her the best weekend of her life. The best sex of her life. But I also didn't.

That's all I have to say about that.

BEE

Oh what a tangled web we weave . . .

Five minutes into my train journey home, Nicolas messaged me: <Missing you already XX>

Would Nick have written something like that after the two days we'd just shared? No. He would have penned something funny and borderline rude. An in-joke.

Stop it. I was being unfair. I responded: <Me too xx>

It was true. True-*ish*.

Christ, Bee, what exactly have you got yourself into here?

I opened the Gmail account I now used exclusively for my interactions with Nick. Except for a sneak peek while Nicolas was showering on Saturday morning, I'd resisted checking the thread. We'd agreed, for both our sakes, not to contact each other that weekend. A pact of sorts. It wouldn't have worked otherwise; I wouldn't have gone at all. Almost *didn't* go. But. *But.* Nick was right. There was no way we could ever be together. Wasn't it worth exploring if this could be an option? And I'd been the one, after all, who'd come up with this plan in the first place. *There might be a way we can be together.*

Nick had kept his side of the bargain. Nothing since his last message, sent on Friday as I boarded the train to Leeds: <Oh bugger it: My lower belly is an erogenous zone. Don't ask me why. And don't bother talking dirty. I always find it unintentionally hilarious. That's all you're getting, but if he doesn't last more than 7 minutes, judge him not me. Be safe. Over and out x>

He'd be waiting. It was up to me to write something first. But what?

We'd sworn to be honest with each other, so outright lying was out, but nor did I want to wound him with the truth. Attempting to put myself in his shoes only went so far: the way in which we perceived our other selves was so different. He saw Nicolas almost as a rival, as a threat. How would I feel if the roles were reversed? If he were the one spending a weekend with Rebecca while I languished at home? *Come on, Bee, be honest.* Yes, I would, I think, envy her a little. But she didn't threaten me; I wanted – no, needed – to know that she was happy, just like I wanted Nick to be happy. Perhaps it was a male/female thing. Perhaps it was because to me, Rebecca wasn't the embodiment of what Nick perceived to be his failure to launch.

SO: I could tell him that Nicolas wasn't the super-confident success story he perceived him to be. That he had the same doubts and insecurities and – if anything – a deeper seam of vulnerability. I could tell him that Nick wasn't as sardonic, as sharp-witted, as silly or as unselfconscious.

All of that was true.

But it was also true that it had gone better than I had any right to expect. Better than I deserved, in retrospect. On every level. And that, I was certain, was something Nick would rather not know. Something I'd play down.

On the train ride there, I'd given myself a good talking-to: *Don't get your hopes up*. That kiss, and my instinctive physical response – that 'click' – could have been a fluke, a one-off. And my body had betrayed me before: most notably with Nate. When we'd first met, we couldn't keep our hands off each other. Falling into the flat, barely making it to the bedroom, and once, slipping off to the disabled toilets mid-meal ('low-budget B-movie sex', Leila called it). And look where that had got me: a battered ego and a near-pathological aversion to relationships.

Nicolas was waiting for me on the concourse and, once again, I saw him before he saw me: hands in his pockets, rocking on his heels. A dreaminess to him that I hadn't picked up from Nick. The nervousness and doubt vanished as he gave me a hug hello. *Click*. I breathed him in. Was this Nick's smell? (Probably not, as he smoked.)

There was an immediate ease between us that I tried very hard not to second-guess. And, as if he'd picked up on my insecurities and Nate-Gate concerns, we took things slow. He held my hand as we walked to his flat – plainly furnished, packed with books, and way tidier than mine had ever been – but that, until later, was our only physical interaction. As the evening unfolded, there was no sense of pressure or urgency, which made the anticipation of what we both knew was inevitable somehow sexier than if we'd fallen through the doorway and bonked in the hallway B-movie style. A bottle of wine for me, lager for him. He cooked, while I acted as sous-chef as if we'd been doing it for years. (<What did he make?> <pasta with parsley, chilli and lemon> <big deal, even I can do THAT >)

We spoke about family, friends, swapped anecdotes, and yes, okay, I cherry picked ones that had made Nick laugh – feeling slightly guilty about exploiting this insider info. (<Don't be – I would have done the same>) No hint of arrogance. The opposite, in fact, confessing that after years of self-doubt and insecurity (<sound familiar, Nick?>) he'd 'jumped on the crime fiction bandwagon' after a publisher had dropped him. (<Oh boo-hoo> <Do you want to know this or not, Nick?> <Sorry. Carry on>)

Then, with that same unhurried ease, he led me by the hand to the bedroom.

I had to think very carefully about how to word what followed.

After my dalliance in the world of one-night-stands, I was well versed in the ups and downs of sleeping with strangers. To misquote *Forrest Gump* (a pop culture reference, incidentally, that Nick didn't get), one-night-stands are like a box of chocolates. Most of the time you get the generic inoffensive ones. Sometimes an orange cream, the ones no one really likes but eats out of desperation. Occasionally, but rarely, a chocolate-covered caramel. (<Nice

analogy, Bee. But where are you going with this? Don't keep me in suspense. Was it one of the good ones, or did you spit it out and put it back in the box? How many did you gobble? Actually, scratch that, don't tell me>)

And I didn't tell Nick that for the first time in years I felt no self-consciousness at all, that I sensed Nicolas saw the *whole* me and not just the outside. I didn't tell him how well we fitted together (and not just physically), that we had the same sense of rhythm, again as if we'd been doing it for years. All right, *maybe* the first time was a little clumsy, but he didn't stop to ask, 'Is this okay?' or 'Do you like this?' because he didn't need to. Reading this back, it sounds lukewarm, but it wasn't. It was . . . *right*.

We didn't leave the flat.

A Sunday morning spent watching a trashy French detective series on Netflix, pausing it every so often to eat, nap, and reach for each other. He had a silly streak as well: at one point we turned down the volume and tried to outdo each other by making up ridiculous dialogue for the characters.

Was this rare ease between us because I felt like I already knew him from the inside (or at least part of him) and he'd picked up on this? Is this how it would have unfolded with Nick?

One of us had to say it, and it was him: 'I feel like I've known you forever.'

You kind of have. Tell him the truth. Tell him, tell him, tell him. I think I knew then that this would be the last chance I'd get before it was too late.

But I didn't, did I?

Chickened out, just like I had with Leila.

Dusk moved into night. I stared at the phone. Looked up, caught my reflection in the darkened train window. I couldn't have gone through with the weekend if the thread between Nick and I had been open. *The phone chaperone.*

I couldn't put it off any longer. The first message I wrote was: <When I was with him, it was YOU who was in my head>

NICK

I loved her for trying to spare my feelings. I loved her for carefully wording everything she said. Emphasising the flaws, glossing over the 'good bits'.

But I hated Nicolas. There. I said it. Which takes the notion of self-loathing to an incredibly literal place. And yes I know that hate is a strong word, but if the adjective fits, wear it.

I hated his life. His relative success as a novelist. His cushy part-time gig teaching creative writing. I hated that he'd confessed to Bee that he felt like a 'sell-out'. *How dare you complain, how DARE you – try walking in my bargain basement ghostwriting shoes for a day, you privileged bastard.* I hated that he'd found the will to give up smoking years ago, went to the gym (fuck him), had a work ethic and a routine, and I LOATHED his flat, which, despite knowing full well I'd regret it, I made Bee describe to me in detail. Three-bedroomed, in a Chapel Allerton 'executive development' (whatever that meant in her world), a communal gym in the basement and a spare room turned into a library. (<Does he have a vanity shelf?> <No. He has three. Two for foreign translations>)

What. An. Arse.

And now he had Bee.

I considered re-reading the reviews, which had soothed the ego burn the last time I was in self-indulgent misanthropic mode, but instead decided to slope my way to the park with Rosie and her beloved Sausage. At least one of us was in a successful relationship. I took along *Crossed Lines* as a distraction. I wasn't going to get any writing done until I'd managed to exorcise those images of Bee and Nicolas having the kind of expensive chocolate sex I knew I wasn't capable of. I wanted to know every detail about that; I didn't want to know a thing. She would have told me if I'd asked. *Get over yourself.*

I made for what I now thought of as 'my bench', and the dogs took a breather on the grass. Gawd bless Patricia Highsmith. I managed to get through a good fifteen pages before I circled back to those semi-pornographic-but-not-in-a-good-way mental images. Rosie yipped, and I looked up to see Scarlett and Rebecca beelining my way.

'Doggy!'

Bad timing. I wasn't in the mood to be my Best Self. If that even existed anymore.

'Do you mind?' Rebecca asked.

'Of course not.'

'Go on then, Scarlett.' Sausage flopped on her back, and this time, Rosie showed some interest – probably because the little girl was holding a rusk.

'The little one's called Rosie,' I said. 'And the other one is Sausage.'

'Sawsage!' Scarlett's voice was sharper and posher than her mum's, which had a soft London burr to it.

'Do you want to hold their leads?'

'Can I, Mumma?'

'We don't want to disturb the nice man, Scarlett.'

'You're not. Go ahead.'

'Thank you, Doggy Man.'

We watched as Scarlett led the dogs away from the bench. 'Don't go too far, Scarlett.' Then, to me: 'I really hope I'm not disturbing you.'

'You're not.' I held up my hand. 'And look, no wipes required today.'

She laughed. *Bee's laugh*. Until I heard it, I hadn't realised how much I'd *longed* to hear it. 'What are you reading?'

'*Crossed Lines*.'

'Oh, I *loved* that book. I remember thinking when I read it that that could never happen nowadays. Sitting in a dining car discussing murder with a stranger without worrying about being overheard.'

'Yeah. Plotting a murder was way more civilised in the olden days.'

She smiled, glanced at the bench.

'Be my guest.'

A hesitation, then she sat next to me. 'Thanks.'

Rosie, the manipulative little shite, was now sitting in her irresistible begging position, paw raised, head cocked. The little girl handed her the rusk.

'Is that okay?' Rebecca asked.

'Sure. If it's okay with you. She'll eat anything.'

'Do you live around here?'

'Just moved into the area.'

'Where from?'

'Leeds.'

'For work?'

'Research.' Well, there was some truth to that. 'I'm a writer. I'm working on a novel set in the area.'

'Oh wow.'

'Not wow. Not even a little bit.'

'Would I have heard of you?'

'If you had, it would be a miracle. I mostly ghostwrite other people's stuff.'

'Why here? And what type of novel?'

Good question. 'It's a love story. Kind of. Enough about me. You?'

Another hesitation. 'I was a designer, but we decided that after Scarlett was born, I'd give her three years of my time.' A tightness to her voice. This hadn't sat well. She seemed to be far more relaxed than she'd been last time we'd run into each other (which wasn't a huge surprise considering it had involved a stressful encounter with one strange man, two strange dogs and an exploding bag of shite), but this hesitancy didn't correlate with my early (and later) impressions of Bee, who rarely came across as if she felt the need to consider so carefully what she was about to say. Right from the start there had been a natural spontaneity to our exchanges, but how much of that was down to the fact that Bee and I had met online, a medium that could mask a multitude of insecurities?

'What kind of designer?'

'Formal wear. Wedding dresses mainly. A big brand – not my own.'

I pinned this mirror-fact to share with Bee later. 'Why that in particular?'

'That's a good question. The romance of it, I suppose.' A self-deprecating smile. 'No. That's crap. I sort of just fell into it, if I'm honest.'

'Well, your wedding day *is* supposed to be the most important day of your life.'

'I know. And how sad is that?'

Interesting. 'Very. Do you miss it? The work, not the wedding day.'

'Yes. Sometimes, I mean. Don't get me wrong, Scarlett's great . . . but . . .' She plucked at her top, fiddled with her hair – nervous tics that I wondered if she shared with Bee. 'I suppose I miss the deadlines more than anything. The rush to get something completed, the adrenaline buzz.'

'Mumma? Can I have another rusk for the doggies?'

I gave Rebecca a 'fine by me' shrug.

'Sure, sweetie.' Rebecca dug in her enormous bag and handed Scarlett a couple of rusks. Rosie trotted after her, eyes glued to her hand.

'I can't believe I just told you all of that,' Rebecca said without looking at me.

'Easier to tell a stranger.' *Ah, here we go*. Mirroring things I'd said to Bee.

On cue, my phone beeped.

'You want to get it?'

Did I? The chances were high it would be Rebecca's other self, and Bee was always going on about feeling discombobulated whenever she was with Nicolas and a message from me came in. But for the first time I got it. The cliché would be that it was like looking into one of those endlessly reflecting mirrors (and as we know by now, I love a cliché). It tipped me a little off-kilter. It also made me feel a little vindictive. *See how you like being ignored.* But I caved in all the same. 'I'll just be a sec. Might be work.'

This lie, for once, turned out to be true. It wasn't Bee, but a missive from Tweedy. Telling me, in his own ungrammatical, halting style that *A Shot in the Dark* was amazingly at the top of the BookPost chart. Not only that, several agents and publishers were sniffing around, enquiring if there might be a sequel. 'Holy. Fuck.' It popped out before I could stop it. I glanced at Scarlett who was still absorbed, thank the little baby Jesus, in Doggy World, then at Rebecca. 'Sorry.'

'Something bad? Or good? You don't have to tell me.'

I didn't, but I did it anyway. She laughed at my descriptions of Tweedy's quirks and country pile and seemed to be genuinely pleased for me. An echo of my and Bee's first interaction – and now she'd lost the hesitancy, a closer correlation to the Bee in my head. *This is what it would have been like if you'd had that conversation in person.* I would have loved to have told her that in a sense, Tweedy had brought us together. That I wouldn't be sitting here, with two elderly dogs and a toddler, and having – it has to be said – a bloody brilliant time, if it weren't for him not paying my invoice.

'What does this mean for you?'

Good question. 'If we do write a sequel, Bernie says this time he'd be willing to go fifty-fifty on the royalty payments.'

'But what about the novel you're working on now? The love story?'

Oh yeah. The cover story. Whoops. 'Hopefully I'll finish it before they finalise any kind of deal. If there even is a deal. It's early days. Nothing may come of it.'

It had been so long since I'd felt like this. Proud. Hopeful. And almost – *almost* – happy.

'We should celebrate. You should enjoy it while you can.'

'There's an off-licence on the high street. Shall I go and get us something?'

She tensed.

'Forget I said that. Drinking with a strange man in a park. I can see why that would be weird.'

'And I should really get Scarlett home for her nap.'

'Sure. Of course.'

She began zipping up her bag. Paused. Then: 'I have some champagne at home. Why don't you come back with me?'

Wow. Where the hell did that come from? 'Really? I wouldn't want to put you out.'

She looked down. 'You wouldn't be.' Hair-tug, top-tug. Signs that she regretted the offer? We both spoke at once.

'You first.'

'I don't usually invite strangers home, just so you know. I just thought . . . seeing as you've just moved into the area and don't know anyone. And . . . in case there's any misunderstanding, I'm married.'

'I really won't take it personally if you renege on the offer.'

She thought for a few seconds. 'No. No. We can sit in the garden with the dogs.' She relaxed. 'I'm Becca, by the way.'

'Nick. See? No longer strangers.'

I offered to wrangle the pushchair and carry the bag, and Scarlett insisted on leading the dogs, which made for a long ramble home as she allowed them to pause and sniff at anything and everything they fancied. I didn't mind. As Scarlett toddled ahead, we fell into step side by side, and I tried to resist sneaking too many sideways glances at her: *It's you.* She was doing the same, though. The air between us seemed to shimmer.

As we neared the entrance to the estate, she hesitated. 'If you turn out to be some kind of mad axe-murderer, I'm going to feel really stupid.'

'You're all right. Left my axe at home. But you don't happen to have any fava beans and Chianti hanging about, do you?'

She huffed a laugh. 'This way.'

She led us through a gate next to the garage and charging point, and into the back garden: a mini wildflower meadow, alive with bees and butterflies, a pond, a section of lawn so manicured it resembled velvet, and an adventure playground for Scarlett that rivalled the one at the park. The rear of the house was a wall of glass – reflective, unfortunately, so other than a few shadowy furniture shapes, the interior remained a mystery. I showed Scarlett how to unclip the dogs' leads, and with a 'I won't be long,' from Becca, the pair of them disappeared inside. The dogs immediately made themselves at home. Sausage conked out in a flowerbed, crushing the tulips, and Rosie padded off to investigate the pond with too much interest. I lay back on the grass and looked up at the sky. *How the other half live*. I considered sending Bee a message: <guess where I am!> but decided against it. I didn't want to spoil the moment.

Becca returned bearing a bottle of what looked like obscenely expensive champagne, a couple of glasses, and a bowl of water for the dogs.

She sat next to me, popped the bottle and poured us both a glass. 'It's a little warm, I'm afraid.'

'Warm is fine. Cheers.'

'Cheers. And congratulations. I've never met a famous writer before.'

'You still haven't.'

A minute of companionable silence. That rare lack of awkwardness you hardly ever get with strangers. Only she *wasn't* a stranger, was she?

'This place is incredible.'

'Thanks. It was . . . one of Ben's friends designed it.'

'Ben's the husband, I'm assuming?'

Top-tug. 'Yes.'

'How did you two meet?'

'He was investing in a company I was designing for.' Flat-toned, a little guarded.

'Love at first sight?'

'No. He was married at the time. And I don't . . .'

'You don't approve of affairs.'

A *whoa, mind-reader* glance. *Cool it with the insider info, Nick.* 'We met again a year or so later, after his marriage broke up. I got pregnant very quickly. Bit of a shocker actually, as Ben was married before and they don't have kids, so I assumed he'd had the snip.' She was knocking the champagne back fast. 'But I don't regret it.'

'I can see that. She's a lovely kid.'

'Do you have children?'

I almost said no. But I did, didn't I? Dylan.

*

From: Bee1984@gmail.com
To: NB26@zone.com

Hang on – why would she assume he had the snip? Would someone as wealthy as Benedict have taken the vasectomy subsidy?

From: NB26@zone.com
To: Bee1984@gmail.com

Here it's the most common form of birth control. In any case, I wasn't going to interrogate her on that point.

From: Bee1984@gmail.com
To: NB26@zone.com

Fair enough. And you just drank champagne? Nothing else happened?

From: NB26@zone.com
To: Bee1984@gmail.com

Nope. Chatted and hung out and then I left.

From: Bee1984@gmail.com
To: NB26@zone.com

But there *must* have been something between you. She invited you back to her house FFS! You don't just invite strange men back to your house for no reason. At least you don't in my world.

From: NB26@zone.com
To: Bee1984@gmail.com

She's married, Bee. You're the one who's always going on about how you'd never cheat.

From: Bee1984@gmail.com
To: NB26@zone.com

Only I kind of am, aren't I? I know, I know, I'm not going to get into all that again.

How different does she seem? From what you know of me, do we match up? I can't think of a better word.

From: NB26@zone.com
To: Bee1984@gmail.com

Quieter maybe. Not as upbeat. More reserved. I think she's a little lonely. It sounds like she's stuck in the house with Scarlett all day. I know you don't want to hear this, but her kid is lovely. You should see her with the dogs.

From: Bee1984@gmail.com
To: NB26@zone.com

It's not that I don't want to hear it. It's more that I don't know where to *put* that stuff – emotionally, I mean.

Do you think maybe she's quieter because she's a full-time mum and is bloody knackered all the time?

From: NB26@zone.com
To: Bee1984@gmail.com

Could be. And I have just met her. We spent weeks getting to know each other from the inside out, Bee. Except for obvious reasons we only have the inside bit.

From: Bee1984@gmail.com
To: NB26@zone.com

Did she mention Leila? Or the infamous Benedict?

From: NB26@zone.com
To: Bee1984@gmail.com

Nowt about Leila. Bit more forthcoming about the husband. I can confirm he's not a 'sexy widower' as you put it. Has an ex-wife but she's still alive and kicking and lives in NY. They met when he invested in a company she was designing for. Oh yeah – she calls him Ben by the way, not Benny as you'd hoped.

From: Bee1984@gmail.com
To: NB26@zone.com

Damn. I was hoping Rebecca had won a Mercer Foundation award, and that's how they met. I applied for it but didn't make the cut.

From: NB26@zone.com
To: Bee1984@gmail.com

Bullet dodged, Bee. Trust me, it sucks when your Other Self over-achieves.

From: Bee1984@gmail.com
To: NB26@zone.com

Is it awful of me to say that I can't help but judge her a little for not working and living off Benny's squillions?

From: NB26@zone.com
To: Bee1984@gmail.com

It's not awful, no, but give her a break, she clearly struggled with the decision and she's doing a champion job with Scarlett. And it's not forever. She said she misses the adrenaline of it and will get back to it when Scarlett starts school.

From: Bee1984@gmail.com
To: NB26@zone.com

You're right. I shouldn't be so harsh on myself ☺

From what you've found out, it sounds like Benny is definitely the alt version of the one living the high life in my world.

From: NB26@zone.com
To: Bee1984@gmail.com

Speaking of your world. Will you do something for me?

From: Bee1984@gmail.com
To: NB26@zone.com

Anything.

From: NB26@zone.com
To: Bee1984@gmail.com

Will you check on Dylan for me? And Poll.

From: Bee1984@gmail.com
To: NB26@zone.com

Of course I will. I've been meaning to ask if you'd do the same re Jonas.

From: NB26@zone.com
To: Bee1984@gmail.com

?

From: Bee1984@gmail.com
To: NB26@zone.com

Magda's husband.

From: NB26@zone.com
To: Bee1984@gmail.com

Oh right. Toy-boy Magda.

From: Bee1984@gmail.com
To: NB26@zone.com

It's strange isn't it, this needing to know about them. It can't be healthy.

From: NB26@zone.com
To: Bee1984@gmail.com

None of this is healthy, Bee. But it's too late to turn back now, isn't it?

BEE

I didn't know how to tell him. I didn't know if I *should* tell him. I put it off for days. It was the closest I came to telling Leila everything. I would have given anything to get her advice.

It had taken seconds to find Poll online: a YouTube clip of her leading a protest outside Westminster, fighting for government funding to raise awareness of male suicide; an interview where she spoke, movingly and with the type of passion that only comes from pain, about the death of her son. About Dylan, who'd taken his own life on his sixteenth birthday. Despite Nick's protestations that Poll wasn't solely to blame for cheating on him, I'd still mentally slotted her into the Bad Person Corner along with my dad and Nate; but watching the clip changed my opinion of her entirely. Donating to her campaign group's JustGiving page was an empty gesture, but I did it anyway, leaving the donation under Nick's name. I wished I could tell her that in another world her son had survived, that he was living a good life, that he was happy and successful. Nick had told me that Dylan was sensitive, took things to heart and had 'dealt with a few issues' when he was a teenager. But this . . . *How do you break this kind of news?*

I mooched around, threw myself into catching up on the side of the business that bored me to tears, but which needed my full attention – filling in courier slips, scheduling orders and fittings, updating Instagram. It helped a little.

Despite my attempts to keep the tone of my messages light, Nick had picked up that something was off. By now we knew each other so intimately that we could gauge each other's mood from something as innocuous as a misplaced comma. We'd sworn to be honest with each other, but this . . . this was different. Thanks to the success of the novel and the fact he was forging a connection with Becca, for the first time in weeks, he was coming across as upbeat, hopeful. This could seriously derail him. *He doesn't need to know*. I could say that I'd tracked down Dylan and he was doing brilliantly.

<What's up? Nicolas hasn't done something has he? With your workload, he'd better not have asked you to read his latest best-selling magnum opus. Insider tip: if he does, when he says he wants your 'honest opinion', he doesn't. Just tell him it's a work of staggering genius>

<Think I'm picking up a bug. Or I'm just worn down. What we're doing . . . it's exhausting. Emotionally and physically>

<Physically for you, you mean after your hard-core Doppelganger sex weekend>

<I told you – it wasn't that hard-core>

<I'm joking. Kind of. Come on, Bee, what can I do to cheer you up? Ok ok. I'll give you another inside track sex tip. Has he asked you to do the thing I like with the mannequin hand and the electric whisk yet?>

Nick wasn't the only one who'd picked up that I wasn't myself. Nicolas and I had made vague plans for him to visit me this weekend, but unlike Nick, he took my lacklustre replies personally. <Hey if this isn't working, just say so, Bee>

It's not you, it's me. I needed to tell someone. Even spilling a modicum of the truth might help. <It's not that. I've just had some bad news>

He called me straightaway, and I answered before I could second-guess myself. The instant I heard his voice, *Nick's voice*, I started crying.

'What is it? Christ, Bee. What is it?'

'I've just heard that . . .' How to phrase it? 'Someone I know . . . they took their own life.'

'Oh shit, Bee. What can I do?'

'There's nothing you can do.'

'I'm on my way.'

'You don't need to do that. Really, I'll be fine.'

'Yes, I bloody do. Text me your address.'

I didn't try and stop him. I wanted him here with me, and not only because I didn't want to be alone. After our weekend, I'd assumed the fissure between the Nick/Nicolas divide was sealed for good, but with every passing day, it had begun to splinter. It was as if I needed his physical presence to smooth it over, keep it together in my head. What we'd shared had been real and rare, and I didn't want to risk damaging that.

It would take him at least three hours to get here. I'd planned to clean the flat before the weekend, but that didn't seem to matter now. He was easy-going; he'd take Clarice and my natural slobbery in his stride. I half-heartedly wiped down the counter, then thought *sod it*. Filled in more courier forms. Responded to more enquiries. Started writing an e-mail to Nick, then stopped. How to word it? There was no way to word it. I was Googling, 'How to break the news about a death,' when, with uncanny timing, Nick messaged to say that he had news about Jonas.

<Do you want to hear it?>

<Depends. Is it bad news or good news?>

<Both, I think>

He'd found a Life Celebration Video online, a clip of Jonas, Magda and their friends having what Nick called 'one hell of a farewell party, live music, dancing, the works'. He said that in his world, these were common for people who chose Elective Euthanasia. <And Bee, I wish with all my heart you could see it. I know I've never met him, but he looked happy at the end. So did she>

This didn't shock me. Nick had told me Elective Euthanasia was standard practice in his world, and I'd half-hoped, half-dreaded that this had been Jonas's choice. What I couldn't figure out – not then, anyway – was how to feel about it.

<Did he have any last words?>

<Kind of. At the end of the clip, he looked at Magda and said,

'I love you. Don't wait'. And from what I saw of her, she took that to heart>

'Don't wait.' Magda had said those words to me when I'd run into Jonas in the hallway. Coincidence? Or something else? I shivered.

If Nicolas hadn't arrived then, I would have been in danger of slipping into a serious funk. It was too much. All of it.

The second he was inside the flat, he wrapped his arms around me, and I listened to his pulse. Real. Flesh and blood.

'Sit. You need a drink. Where's the wine?'

It had been a while since anyone had done this kind of thing for me. Taking charge like Nate used to do, but in a kinder, softer way.

He poured me a glass of wine and sat me on the couch.

'Shall I call someone for you?'

'No. I'm sorry. You didn't need to come all this way.'

'Don't be daft. Who is it?'

'The son of an old friend. I just . . . there are people I need to tell.'

'Do you want me to stay here while you do that?'

'Yes. Yes please.'

Nicolas got out his laptop and sat at the breakfast bar. 'I'm here if you need me.'

'Thank you.' I stared at my phone. 'Can I ask you something?'

'Of course.'

'This is going to sound strange, but say you'd fallen out of touch with someone you'd once loved, would you rather know or not know that something bad had happened to them?'

He thought about it. 'I would rather know.'

'Why?'

'I suppose because if it's someone I loved, I'd like to think they would *want* me to know.'

Don't wait.

*

From: Bee1984@gmail.com
To: NB26@zone.com

I am SO SO sorry, Nick. I would give anything or do anything to make it not so.

From: NB26@zone.com
To: Bee1984@gmail.com

You did the right thing telling me, Bee. I knew, deep down, that it was a possibility. I hoped it wasn't, of course I did, but we all know how much hope likes to fuck me over.

From: Bee1984@gmail.com
To: NB26@zone.com

Why didn't you tell me before about his attempt in your world? It must have taken a huge emotional toll on you. We share everything – the good, the bad, the ugly. It kills me that you were carrying that alone.

From: NB26@zone.com
To: Bee1984@gmail.com

It did take a toll. And I wanted to tell you, Bee, I really did. But it wasn't my story to tell.

NICK

Some of this is going to be hard to express without coming across as a cold-hearted bastard as well as the usual miserable one, but what's the point of reliving this if I'm not going to at least try and be honest?

My first reaction to the news about Dylan was shock. The kind that hits you deep in the pit of your stomach, then bleeds ice water through your body. Then sorrow. The kind that hits you everywhere, but mostly in the heart. Sorrow for Dylan and sorrow for Poll. The *pain* she must have gone through in Bee's world. *Is* going through . . . This brought back the old guilt for not telling my Poll about Dylan's issues. Is this also why I'd held back from telling Bee about it? Because it didn't seem right telling her, when I hadn't told Poll? I'd kept schtum back then because Dylan had asked me to keep it between us and I didn't want to risk breaking our fragile trust before it had a chance to strengthen. It had been a long slow process for both of us – including several months of paranoia where I basically spied on my own stepson, sneaking into his room, delving through his belongings, and (Christ) scouring his Arpanet history for any sign that he was considering trying it again. And, as irrational as it was, the urge to know for sure that he really was fine was overwhelming. My instinct was to hop on a train to Birmingham to see Dylan in person, but that would have been so out of character he'd clock something was up. After I'd calmed myself down, I called him instead.

'Nick? What's happened?'

'Eh?'

'You only ever text unless you have big news. Is Mum okay?'

'Fine as far as I know.' At least in this world she was. 'Thought I'd give you a shout, see how you are.'

'I'm at work, Nick.'

'But everything's okay otherwise?'

'Er, yeah. Course it is. You sound funny. Is everything okay with you? Has the place where you're staying got freakier?'

'That would be impossible. Hey, why don't you come and visit? See the madhouse for yourself? Rosie and I would love to see you.'

'I will when I get time off.'

Then I called Poll, catching her as she was leaving school. I was both devastated for and proud of Alternative World Poll. She would have done much the same here if the worst had happened – channelled her pain into making a change. The conversation was pretty much a re-run of how it had gone with Dylan. 'Nick? Is this about the house? The potential buyers are being tricky, so I can't give you your share yet.'

'It's not about that. Just wanted to see how you are.'

'Has something happened? Are you okay?'

'Everything's cool. I'm really just checking in. All okay with Jez?'

'Fine.'

I'd achieved the opposite of my intention: if anything, they were now worried about me. Mental note: *call more often*.

I'd tried to reassure Bee that she'd done the right thing, but the truth of it was, I didn't know if she had. This doubt was amplified when she confessed that Nicolas was with her, dropping everything to be at her side in what should have been *my* hour of need. I paced around the attic room, managing (as usual) to bang my head on the sloping roof. I eventually dropped off at around three a.m., waking late and missing breakfast (one upside to this tragic mess).

Tiptoeing past the communal areas, I slipped outside for a rollie. I'd just lit up when Erika poked her head around the door. 'Smoking again I see, Nick. And, once again, I see you are being a grump. What is it? Is it the writing that makes you so angry all the time?'

I wanted to lash out at someone, especially someone who had me bang to rights: no one likes to hear the truth about themselves, especially so starkly expressed. She'd do. 'Actually Erika, I've just heard that someone I love has killed themselves.'

No discernible change of expression. 'Come with me.'

'No.'

'*Come*. But put that horrible thing in the bin I have provided first.'

She waited while I mashed the cigarette into the stainless-steel receptacle, which was pointedly placed as far from the door as possible, then I followed her into the lounge. I'd barely been in there before; thought of it as her territory. She opened a cabinet, took out a sticky bottle of schnapps, poured me a glass and barked: 'Drink it.'

'It's only just gone ten!'

'Drink it.' She watched me as I did so. It caught in my throat, but it also warmed me up from the inside. 'Listen to me. Could you have done something to stop this?'

'No.'

'No. We never can. Nor might we ever know why someone makes the choice to do this. And that is something we must learn to live with.'

'You've got personal experience of this?'

'Yes. My father did this when I was a child.'

'Oh shit. I'm so sorry, Erika.'

'Yes, yes. Now. Please do not smoke so near the window again. It blows in. Think of the dogs, Nick.'

Sympathy Erika-style. But she was right. How *could* I have stopped it? And speaking of the dogs, they were waiting by the door for their daily trip to the park. In the days following what Bee called the 'champagne break-through', Becca and I had fallen into an informal routine of meeting by the bench. And today we were running late. *Shake it off, Nick*. But I couldn't. It was more Poll than anything else. I kept circling back to the trial by fire her alternative self had gone through; kept returning to that moment when I'd found Dylan in his room.

I was still lost in Dark Place-ville when I reached the park and Scarlett raced up, yelling, 'Doggy Man!'

I handed her the leads and she led the dogs to their usual spot. Today she had a bag of dog biscuits, which Rosie hadn't missed. Sausage was her usual compliant self, rolling on her back for her tummy tickle.

The day after our impromptu celebration party, Becca had been a little more guarded with me, as if she were holding herself back. Or doing her best not to blast out the wrong signals. But today she greeted me with a warm smile and seemed to be buzzing with energy. 'I thought you weren't coming today.'

'Sorry. Got caught up in something.' We sat on the bench.

'I read your book. Couldn't put it down. It kept me up all night.'

Befuddled by grief, lack of sleep, and the schnapps, I genuinely didn't have a clue what she was talking about. 'What book?'

'*A Shot in the Dark*, of course.'

'Oh. *Really*?'

'I can see why they want a sequel. Do you have any ideas for that?'

I couldn't think about that right then. Not with a head full of Poll and Dylan. A head full of pain.

'Sorry – did I say something wrong?'

'No. It's not you. I'm not myself today.'

'Did something happen? Did they decide they *don't* want a sequel?'

'No. Nothing like that.' I'd spun a version of the truth to Erika; did I want to burden Becca with it too? Yes and no. Bee's words: *We should tell them what we're doing*. A moral grey area. *Quantum Immorality*. If I did come clean, I wouldn't know where to start. As usual, I took the easy option: 'Didn't sleep well.'

'Tell me if I'm overstepping the mark here, because obviously I'm not a writer, but I was wondering . . . what if you flipped it? Made him . . . I don't know. An anti-hero. Like in the Ripley books.'

Highsmith: a shared touchstone. For Becca too, it seemed. And fuck knows I needed something to divert me from mentally stepping into that room, reliving that moment as if through Poll's eyes. 'Go on.'

It helped. The image receded as we bounced ideas back and forth. By the time the dogs and Scarlett had had enough, not only was Dylan's bedroom door firmly shut, I had a basic outline. 'Don't hold your breath though. I'm no Highsmith.'

She rolled her eyes. A mannerism I'd often pictured Imaginary Bee doing whenever I said something self-consciously self-deprecating. 'That's crap and you know it. And comparing yourself to other people is stupid.'

As she turned to go, I took her hand. The first time we'd touched. 'You know, you saved me today. I was in a black hole. And you pulled me out.' Mirroring again what I'd once said to Bee. It was true. She *had* pulled me out of a hole (with a little help from a Scandinavian control freak).

She squeezed my fingers. A moment where the shimmer between us intensified, then she appeared to mentally shake herself and withdraw.

Here's the part where I'm going to sound cold. Or heartless, or selfish. As I walked home, Erika's words and Becca's coalesced into a realisation that would change not only how I felt about myself, but how I felt about Nicolas.

Nicolas may be the one with the success and the swanky pad and the flat stomach and the girl I loved. But *I* was the one who'd saved Dylan. If I'd lived Nicolas's life, that alternative life I envied, then Dylan wouldn't have made it. I may be a chronically miserable, self-loathing failure, but I'd saved him. *Me.* Not Nicolas. And that was worth more than all the success in the world.

PART FOUR

SAY ANYTHING (OR RATHER, DON'T)

From: NB26@zone.com
To: Bee1984@gmail.com

SO: Partly as reparation for the murder he got away with in *A Shot in the Dark*, but mostly because he's a closet sociopath, our posho protagonist turns into a rabid protector of wildlife. Basically a one-man environmental-abuse fighting assassin, wiping out poachers, garrotting rare bird egg thieves, beheading badger baiters. Tweedy loves this of course because his self-insert character basically ends up being a renegade anti-hero. On his trail is a young detective, wily and tenacious of course, but haunted by something that happened in her past, because apparently wily and tenacious detectives ALWAYS have to have some inner conflict bollocks. Fuck knows what though. Becca says I should defy convention and make her a paragon of stability. Happy home life, no nebulous past trauma, then twist it in the end and have her letting Posho get away with his crimes.

From: Bee1984@gmail.com
To: NB26@zone.com

So the detective's actually a secret sociopath too?

From: NB26@zone.com
To: Bee1984@gmail.com

Kind of, yeah. Or maybe she just really, really likes badgers.

From: Bee1984@gmail.com
To: NB26@zone.com

I'm with Becca on this. Sounds like she's good at this brainstorming stuff. Who knew I had that in me? ☺ Go Becca/me!

What's the next step?

From: NB26@zone.com
To: Bee1984@gmail.com

When I've finalised the outline, Tweedy says he'll pass it on to his agent. Set up a meeting.

From: Bee1984@gmail.com
To: NB26@zone.com

Won't you need an agent too?

From: NB26@zone.com
To: Bee1984@gmail.com

I'm hoping she might rep us both. And before you offer, no I don't want you to find out the name of Nicolas the Great's agent. Even if he/she/they exist in my world that would feel too incestuous. Or like cheating. They'd probably turn me down anyway and then I'd be forced to sulk for at least a month.

From: Bee1984@gmail.com
To: NB26@zone.com

I wasn't going to! In any case, I don't think Nicolas likes him that much. I thought you were feeling better about your alter ego?

From: NB26@zone.com
To: Bee1984@gmail.com

I am. I really am. Got over myself. Is he there yet?

From: Bee1984@gmail.com
To: NB26@zone.com

No. Train's running late. It's that odd kind of symmetry again, isn't it? How you only see Becca on weekdays and I only see him on weekends.

From: NB26@zone.com
To: Bee1984@gmail.com

You do a bit more than just 'see' him, Bee.

From: Bee1984@gmail.com
To: NB26@zone.com

I know. I know. I wasn't rubbing it in. It's not a contest. Slowly, slowly catchee monkey.

From: NB26@zone.com
To: Bee1984@gmail.com

Very slowly. But there is something there. Hope is not lost. And yes, before you ask, as you always do, still nowt more about Benny or Leila 2. You/Becca play your cards close to your chest. Loyal.

From: Bee1984@gmail.com
To: NB26@zone.com

There are cracks there. I know there are. I know myself. I wouldn't be flirting with someone in a park if I were in love.

BEE

Slowly, slowly, catchee monkey.

Too slowly for me. Way too slowly.

I wasn't lying to Nick. There must be trouble in paradise if Becca was continuing to meet up with him. Once I'd mentally and emotionally committed to someone, all other options, all other men, seemed to fade into the background, becoming the equivalent of the non-player characters that populated Lev's video games. And sure, I knew she'd be conflicted about this, *massively* conflicted. We shared the same background after all. The thought of treading in our father's footsteps wouldn't sit easy with her. Yet, on some level Becca must know they were meant to be together. Her soulmate of sorts. Like Nicolas was mine. Or *could* be mine. The closest we'd get to it, at any rate.

I didn't just want Becca and Nick to be happy. I *needed* them to be so. The selfish truth of it was, if they didn't close that circle, it would poison what I was building with Nicolas. Because I *was* building something.

That weekend hadn't been a fluke. So far, the ease between us showed no signs of morphing into boredom or turning spiky. As I often had to catch up with work on weekends, Nicolas generously offered to travel to me every Friday (I could hardly schlepp Clarice and my other equipment to him on the train), and since day one, he'd seemed to be totally at home in the flat, carving out a writing space at the breakfast bar, intuiting which side of the couch or bed to take and stocking the fridge without making a show of it.

Whenever he arrived, he didn't seem to care if the flat was a dumping ground of fabric and off-cuts; he didn't make snarky comments about Clarice or whinge when Magda played her music too loud. And so far, no annoying or strange habits had revealed themselves, although he did sleep eerily still (<I do that too. In the early days Poll said she used to shake me awake to make sure I hadn't pegged it in my sleep>). Nor had any incompatible sexual quirks or fetishes surfaced (<What? You mean he hasn't brought out the gimp suit and the spatula yet? You're in for a treat, Bee>). I kept waiting for something to emerge, for a red flag to wave. Nate had waited until he'd reeled me in fully before he'd shrugged off his Best Self suit to reveal the slime monster beneath. But Nicolas wasn't Nate. He was Nick – in a sense.

And he was *kind*. Nick was too – but he cloaked this side of himself in black humour and sardonic comments. Nicolas's kindnesses didn't extend only to me. On our first Saturday together, Magda knocked on the door to ask if I'd sit with Jonas for an hour. I'd stopped avoiding them. Like Nick had been forced to do when he learned the fate of Alternative World Dylan, I'd also come to terms with the other side of the story.

'I have a Skype fitting now, Magda – I can do it after then?'

Nicolas came up behind me. 'I'll do it.'

A glance at me, and then at him. Sizing him up. 'That is very kind.'

After I finished with the client, I crept up to Magda's flat. Nicolas was sitting opposite Jonas, paging through a book, totally at ease. Jonas looked at me and gave me one of his ambiguous smiles. A seal of approval? *Don't wait.*

The only stress came from my side. Occasionally, I'd slip up, forget which in-jokes and anecdotes I'd shared with which doppelganger: 'Hey, I forgot to tell you, Ms Peach's bridesmaid wants me to redo her own wedding dress.'

'Who?'

Cover, cover.

Nick and I didn't repeat our radio silence pact on weekends –

that had been too hard on him – and over time, the phone chaperone aspect faded. The sense that I was cheating didn't. Especially when Nicolas caught me laughing at something Nick had sent through. When he asked who I was talking to, instead of coming clean, I did what cheaters always do when they're caught unawares: lied. 'Just an old friend.'

'The infamous Leila?'

'You don't know him.'

'Him?' Said with a hint of insecurity.

YOU. Tell him. 'You don't know him. He's a same-sexer.'

'What?'

Shit. 'Gay. Same-sexer is a term we use.'

'Weird term. Will I get to meet him?'

'I doubt it. He doesn't live in the country.' *Or the world. And possibly not the universe, either.*

It made me feel dirty. It made me feel like I was following in my father's footsteps, although his behaviour was motivated by the thrill and excitement of doing something illicit and deceitful. This wasn't thrilling; it was exhausting.

But the ease and the kindness outweighed the constant 'think-before-you-speak' stress. He'd passed the Clarice test. The Magda test. There was still the Leila test to come (I'd been stalling her now for weeks, both for Nicolas's sake and mine). The only threats to our relationship were my behaviour and the cracks – the stubborn fissures – between the two Nicks. The cracks that magically disappeared when he arrived on Friday, yet began to re-emerge during the week. The cracks that threatened the foundation of our relationship and which, I hoped, would disappear when Nick and Becca were finally together. And for that to happen we needed to know more about Benedict.

Slowly, slowly catchee monkey.

Whenever Nick brought Benedict up, he said Becca changed the subject or withdrew. This could be loyalty; could be something more insidious (that 'skinny' red flag). It could be because Nick pitching up in her life with his quantum soulmate connection was pushing her off-kilter. It could be because of Scarlett. If I'd met Nick during the Nate days – someone, who, on a gut level, I knew was right for me, maybe even the mythical 'The One' – at the very least I'd feel conflicted that a non-player character had thrust his way into the game. Nick may not be having much luck, but perhaps there was something I could do from my side.

And for that I'd need a cunning plan. Billionaires were like A-list celebrities; they inhabited a whole different sphere to us normal plebs. You can't just friend someone like that on Facebook and invite them for a coffee. But I knew someone who might be a way in. Someone in the industry. Someone who made it his business to network and schmooze the major players. Nate. Aka The Fucker.

Could I? Should I?

I hadn't deleted his number. I should have, because whenever I spotted it in my contacts it gave me a jolt, a nastier version of seeing Mum's name there after she'd died. I had no clue what Nate was up to these days. I hadn't Facebook-stalked him for years.

As I scrolled to the Ns, the only word to describe how I felt was 'squeamish'.

He answered on the second ring. 'Well, *hello*, stranger.' I mock-gagged – a knee-jerk reaction. 'I didn't expect to hear from you again. Not that I'm complaining.'

'How are you, Nate?'

'Good, good. Ticking along. You? I hear your business is booming. Congrats on that by the way.'

'Thanks.' The fact he'd been keeping tabs on me didn't surprise me, but it didn't sit comfortably either. I dredged up the name of the woman he'd been screwing behind my back. I didn't have to dredge too deeply: that wound had healed, but it wasn't forgotten. 'How's Alexa?'

'Who?' Beat. 'Oh. *Alexa*. No idea. That didn't last.'

'Sorry to hear that.' I'd never met Alexa, although yes, *okay*, I did stalk her a little on Facebook back then. I hadn't been her greatest fan at the time for obvious reasons, but now I found myself thinking, *good on you for escaping, too.*

'It's all good. Being happily single has given me time to work on myself.' *Mock-gag, mock-gag*. 'It's funny that you've called actually. I've been thinking about reconnecting with you for a while now.'

Oh, the conceit. As if he was the one who'd ended things. As if I'd jump straight back into his arms. I very nearly hung up on him right then. *Deep breath, Bee*. 'I'd like that, Nate, but I'm in an exclusive relationship.' *Exclusive. Ha!*

Silence. 'Good for you. Good. Anyone I know?'

'I doubt it.' I could have stuck the knife in: *A successful novelist, actually Nate. Not some third-rate fashion buyer*, but I resisted the temptation. To business: 'Do you know Benedict Mercer?'

'Jesus, Bex. *You're* in a relationship with Benedict Mercer?' Shock, awe – disbelief. As if he couldn't believe someone as mundane as me could possibly have landed such a big fish. I would have loved to tell him that in another life, not only was I in a relationship with Benedict, but I was married to him.

'No of course I'm not in a relationship with him. I'm asking if you know him. I need an intro. I'm thinking of expanding the business and I'm casting around for possible investors. And he has a portfolio of sustainable fashion businesses, right?'

'No offence, Bex, but he's a major player, and you're . . . well, you know. Not.'

Offence taken, ass-wipe. Manipulation time. 'You're right, Nate. I suppose I was trying to emulate you and aim high. But if you *don't* know him, that isn't an option anyway. Forget I asked.'

Silence while this ego-stroke and challenge warred in his mind.

'*Do* you know him?'

'I've met him a few times.' Nate usually bigged himself up, name-dropped at every opportunity. This wishy-washy response meant that he'd probably only seen him in passing at a party.

'Can you get me a meeting with him?'

'He's a busy man, Bex.'

'What's he like? What sort of person?'

'What you'd expect. Charming of course, because he can afford to be. Reeks of money. Private too. Although there was a fair bit of buzz when he was dating Kat de Jong.'

'The *designer* Kat de Jong?'

'Obviously.' *Duh, Bex.*

Thinking about it, she'd been in several of the Google Image pics, but I'd assumed they'd just been rubbing shoulders at an industry shindig, because Kat (like me, like Becca) didn't seem to *fit* with him. Her personal style echoed her design aesthetic: dark and edgy and with an androgenous Kronthaler vibe. A million miles away from Benny's conventional yacht-n-country club appearance. 'Are they still together?'

'I doubt it. According to the rumour mill, she got heavily into drugs a few years ago. Hasn't put out a line since 2017 and practically *lives* in rehab.'

'I didn't know that. Poor Kat.'

'Yeah. Happens. Hang on, now I think about it, he's sponsoring one of those dreary stop-the-sweat-shop conference thingies in a couple of weeks. I *was* going to give it a miss, but if you came along to the meet-and-greet, maybe I could introduce you. You'd have to come as my date, though.'

Squirm. Gag. Bleugh. 'Sounds like a plan. Send me the deets.'

I hung up before he had the chance to say anything else.

*

From: NB26@zone.com
To: Bee1984@gmail.com

Blimey, Bee. Talk about being proactive. Can't have been easy asking The Fucker for a favour.

From: Bee1984@gmail.com
To: NB26@zone.com

I had to shower afterwards. But one of us has to meet Benedict, right? Or at least a version of him. I'm so conflicted about it. For Becca's sake I'm hoping that he isn't some Nate 2.0 style arsehole who's making her life a misery. But for all of our sakes I'm also hoping he's a massive, massive dick.

From: NB26@zone.com
To: Bee1984@gmail.com

Who doesn't have a massive, massive dick.

From: Bee1984@gmail.com
To: NB26@zone.com

Classy. Are you this childish with Becca?

From: NB26@zone.com
To: Bee1984@gmail.com

No, but it's my dream to one day share this level of intellectual discourse with her too.

From: Bee1984@gmail.com
To: NB26@zone.com

You'll get there. WE'LL get there.

NICK

I now had a morning weekday routine. Like in the Poll days, but without the self-flagellation.

7 a.m.: Breakfast with the Ealing Three, which mainly involved Erika going off about a minor house rule infraction ('tea bags *must* be squeezed before disposal, how many times am I having to repeat this?'), while I and my fellow lodgers tuned out over the toast crumbs.

8 – 9 a.m.: A check-in with Bee. A call with Lily if I felt up to it, although as time wore on our interactions were becoming increasingly stilted: perhaps we'd always needed Rosie between us to communicate effectively.

9 – 10.30 a.m.: Writing time. I'd started work on the sequel, working title: *Sabotage*. The contract hadn't been negotiated yet, but why not get ahead of the game? And for once the words were pouring out, as if some inner plumber had wrenched open a rusty tap.

11 – 12 p.m.: The highlight of the day: meeting Scarlett and Becca at the park.

An hour a day wasn't much to work with. Compared to Bee, who was super-charging round the track, I was still at the starting blocks. But, as Bee kept reminding me, this wasn't a race: *slowly,*

slowly, catchee monkey. And my approach was working. There was no doubt that Becca was gradually letting her guard down. We hadn't yet reached the say-anything easy banter stage – which Bee and I had had from the start – but we were getting there. We now had our own Park Life in-jokes; making up backstories and nick-names for the other park regulars. The elderly man whose dog pulled him across the park while he yelled, 'Toffee, *no*' was 'The Red-Setter Wrangler'; the depressed-looking mother who let her kids chase the ducks and run riot was 'Mogadon Mom', and the runner who sweated his way past us at the same time every day was 'Regular Roger the Wobbling Jogger'.

Yet, in comparison to the easy rhythm between Bee and I, every so often we stumbled, as if the beat was off, as if our chemistry bass player wasn't quite up to scratch. I put it down to the ever-present but rarely mentioned elephant in the room: the fact that she was married. Because there was no doubt that the physical attraction between us was building. Whenever I saw her, I experi-enced my own internal butterfly effect, and to really mix my shitty metaphors here, the erotic shimmer in the air between us intensified with every meeting. We hadn't been back to her house since the day Tweedy sent through the good news. She hadn't invited me; I hadn't pushed. I think we both knew what would happen if we did: guilty sex on the appliances.

Today I had news about what I thought of as 'our' book, since she'd helped me build the outline. Another threesome of sorts: me, Tweedy and Becca. Tweedy's agent, Nazia, loved the outline and had scheduled a meeting to finalise the details – a solid offer was in the works. Tweedy wouldn't be travelling to London ('still wobbly dear boy, would you mind doing the honours?'), but things were on the up.

After I'd handed the leads to Scarlett, as was customary, I told Becca the news.

'Bloody fantastic!' Becca moved as if to give me a hug, then stopped herself. 'Looks like you'll definitely have to put your love story on hold then.'

'It does, doesn't it?' Art imitating life, yet again.

'Mumma. Biscuits.'

'Biscuits, *please*.'

'*Please*, Mumma.'

Becca dug in the bag and handed over a packet of dog treats. Scarlett never seemed to get bored of asking Rosie to sit and beg for a treat. Rosie didn't get bored of it either.

'Last night Ben asked why I keep buying dog biscuits.'

I held my breath. Thought very carefully what to say next. It was rare for her to let slip a nugget like this. 'What did you tell him?'

'That Scarlett had made friends with some of the dogs we see regularly at the park.'

'Which is true.'

'Yes.'

'I'm guessing you didn't mention that you'd also made a park friend?'

She glanced at me. Tucked her hair behind her ears. 'No.'

'Because that's what we are, right? Friends.'

'Yes.'

Okay. Time to dive in. 'Becca, are things okay at home?'

A long pause. She went to bite a nail, then stopped herself as if she'd been mentally hand-slapped. 'Yes. Why wouldn't they be?'

'You hardly ever talk about him. About your husband.'

'What do you want to know?'

'Are you happy?' Bee had asked me this back in the mists of time. It had unlocked something inside me. *Lanced a boil.*

She snorted. 'Happy. Why does everyone have to be happy all the time? I'm . . . I'm fine. Everything's fine. And Scarlett will start playgroup again soon, so I'll have more time to think about what to do next. Work-wise, I mean.'

As usual, she'd danced away from the subject. 'Have you thought about starting your own business?'

'Not really.'

'I think you'd be good at it.' *I know you'd be good at it.*

'Maybe.'

She was in full withdrawal mode now. I changed the subject. Helpfully, Regular Roger chose that moment to slog his way past us with his usual grimace and wave. We both waved back. We'd decided Roger was in the midst of a mid-life crisis (yes I know, pot, kettle, black), and his attempt to get himself into shape, something he clearly found excruciating, was a stab at reinvention. I admired him ('we should have called him Tenacious Tim'). Quite often when he passed, I had to stop myself from cheering him on: *You can do it, Roger!* 'Do you think the regulars have names for us too? And made-up backstories?'

'They probably think we're having an affair.' Then she froze. Coloured. She rarely blushed.

'Mumma!' Scarlett called, dousing the tension. 'Look!'

A duck was bravely waddling towards the dogs, drawn by the biscuit crumbs, and Rosie was watching it with too much interest. She lunged for it, but Scarlett held strong, pulling her back to heel. 'Rosie, *no*.'

That assertiveness: did she get that from Benedict maybe? Not a question that would have gone down well – being both intrusive and gender-offensive. Not one I really wanted to hear the answer to either.

The colour in her face was back to normal. Clearly the moment had passed, and we eased back onto safer ground with a discussion about the book.

On the way home, I'd got into the habit of indulging myself in a series of 'what if' daydreams. Picturing what life might be like if we did take things further. Where we might live (this was, of course, a clichéd country cottage, a writing shed for me, a studio for Becca). If I'd be a good stepdad and learn from the mistakes I'd made with Dylan. I wouldn't need to bribe Scarlett with a puppy as she'd have Rosie and possibly Sawsage, plus, she and I were already friends, with our own routine of sorts, a high-five greeting, the usual handing over of the dog leads, and I'd taught her to say, 'Adios amigo,' mainly because it amused Becca. The only sticking point was

Benedict. Dylan's dad was well out of the picture when I'd arrived on the scene – had been since before Dylan was born – so I hadn't had to contend with that thorny scenario. Somehow, I doubted we'd end up being buddies, quaffing drinks at the nineteenth hole. I was fairly sure he'd think of me as Becca's 'bit of rough'. I was fairly sure I'd think of him as a privileged arsehole. I *did* think of him as a privileged arsehole.

As I approached the front door, Sausage, who, after the walk there and back and an hour of toddler attention, was usually ready to collapse into her basket, started dancing around my legs like a puppy. 'What is it, girl?'

I was about to find out. Barrelling towards me came the largest man I've ever encountered. Sausage threw herself at him, whining with joy. Then I clocked who he was – Petrus, Erika's semi-mythical other half. The only reason I hadn't recognised him straightaway was because, unlike the dour, terrifying bloke in the photos, he was smiling.

After he finished petting Sausage, he gave Rosie a stroke, looked me up and down, roared, 'So you are the man who has stolen my dog,' and clapped me on the shoulder (it actually really bloody hurt).

In the three days he was home, the whole atmosphere of the house seemed to shift, changing from gloomy and uptight to something approximating party-time. He was a blunderbuss of a person, stomping around, roaring with laughter at the slightest opportunity, chaotic and the exact opposite of his wife. That said, Erika seemed to lighten up when she was around him, as if her brittleness was a carapace that only he could crack. Even the breakfasts improved. Laurel and Hardy kept out of his way. I assumed at first that his larger-than-life personality was too much of a threat to their pathological introversion, but now I reckon it was because they couldn't handle the drinking. Because Petrus loved to drink, and he didn't like to do it alone.

On his first night home he insisted that I help him demolish a bottle of Georgian chacha. He lined up the drinks and lined up the anecdotes. His job, which took him across the globe, seemed to entail everything from acting as a bodyguard for dubious ousted oligarchs to patrolling wildlife reserves. 'You can put me in a book one day, writer man!' He didn't appear to have a moral code about which jobs he took; the only sticking point – which he confessed to me when the bottle was nearly empty, and the room was spinning – was that 'My wife wants me to stay home now. She worries that I put myself in danger.'

I'd be worried too. His stories were hair-raising, a series of Jason Frey thriller-style near-death scenarios. He was certainly useful when it came to researching the novel. He had an encyclopaedic knowledge about weaponry, combat and, troublingly, the numerous methods mercenaries employed to off someone. By the time he left, my liver had taken a beating, but I also felt like I'd made a friend.

The only time he turned serious was on the night before he was due to leave, when he joined me for a smoke in the gulag. 'I am not a jealous man, Nick, but I need to know that you have no lust for my wife.'

'Are you serious?'

'I am.' In an instant he swapped personas, went from jovial and hard-partying to hard-eyed and yes, threatening. His work persona, I assumed. I could see why the good, the bad and the ugly rich would want him watching their backs.

'Fact is, I'm in love with someone and she's all I can think about.'

Back to the friendly persona: another wince-inducing shoulder slap. 'I can see this is true, but I had to be sure, no? Now, another drink, and you must tell me all.'

*

From: NB26@zone.com
To: Bee1984@gmail.com

Worst. Hangover. Of. My. Life. I barely made it to the park today. Becca said she's worried I may need a liver transplant.

From: Bee1984@gmail.com
To: NB26@zone.com

I keep coming back to her 'affair' comment. Means she must be thinking about it. And yeah, I KNOW it's massively conflicting for her because of our background, but when you know you *know,* right? It's not like we're talking about a Nate-style fling here. You and her – me and YOU – it's different. It's meant to be.

From: NB26@zone.com
To: Bee1984@gmail.com

It really doesn't feel weird to you, talking about this? It killed me thinking about you and Nicolas.

From: Bee1984@gmail.com
To: NB26@zone.com

Of course it feels weird. But I want you to be happy, Nick. I want HER to be happy. Symmetry, remember? And if I am envious, it's because your relationship is a proper slow-burn romance.

From: NB26@zone.com
To: Bee1984@gmail.com

Lots of slow, not much romance going on. Anyway, isn't the Boy Wonder supposed to be there? It's Friday.

From: Bee1984@gmail.com
To: NB26@zone.com

He's in the shower. Preparing himself for the Leila Test.

From: NB26@zone.com
To: Bee1984@gmail.com

Oh goody. Well wish him luck. From what I saw of her in this world, he'll need it.

BEE

No luck was needed. He passed it with flying colours. Passed it a little too well, because as Nicolas chatted to Lev about Lev's two greatest passions – his law practice and *Mortal Kombat 11* – over Friday night dinner, Leila kept mouthing 'WOW' at me. And when Leila brought up *her* latest passion, launching into a diatribe about the lack of action 'our useless fucking governments' were taking against the various fossil fuel companies, instead of just nodding along, he actively engaged with her – asking questions about the prospects of lobbyist reform in the US and offering to put her in touch with an old university friend who was an environmental scientist. It was Lev's turn to give me a surreptitious double thumbs-up.

(<Knew he'd nail it, the smooth bastard, whereas I had to create a whole fake persona to get Leila 2 to give me 5 mins of her time> <Well she was comparing him to Nate in her head, not a high bar, TBH>)

Would Nick, who was less obviously charming but funnier, have fared so well if he'd had the chance to meet them? Yes. No. Maybe. As I'd never know the answer, and because thinking too deeply about that opened the door to more guilt and its fuckbuddy, regret, I shoved this inconvenient question out of my head.

As I helped Leila scrape the remains of take-out Thai into the new composting bin, she paused, then said: 'Have you told him yet?'

I went cold. 'Told him what?'

'About the catfish backstory.'

Oh, *that*. Relief, and a mental punch for being paranoid. Leila was the smartest person I knew, but unless she was a mind-reader or had secretly cloned my phone there was no way she could have possibly figured out what was actually going on. 'No.'

'You don't think you should tell him?'

'Do you?'

'Maybe. This one's a real goer. And it's never good to start something on a lie. Or an omission.'

Bit late for that advice. Been there, done that. 'You've only met him for an hour, Leila. He might dump me next week.'

'Nah. The way he looks at you? No chance. He's the one.' Then she hugged me. 'And I am so, so happy for you.'

I should have been delighted that my closest friend, not one to make snap judgements, had given him her seal of approval, but in truth I knew most of this was motivated by relief that for once I hadn't hooked up with someone who would make the UK's Top Ten Arsehole List. That guilt, again, for putting her through so many episodes of the Shitty Bee Dating Show.

As Nicolas and I walked home from the Tube, taking what he called the 'scenic route' through the back streets, and all of this swirling through my head, he stopped and turned me to face him. He was smart – as smart as Nick. Of course his inner radar had picked up that something was off.

'What is it? Did she hate me or something?'

'No. She thinks you're the second coming.'

'Chance would be a fine thing.'

I managed a smile. 'I don't know about that.'

We walked on. As we reached my street he paused again. 'This *is* real, right, Bee? It's not just me.'

'It's not just you.'

And I meant it. I really did. At least, I *wanted* to mean it.

NICK

I'd barely given the Berenstains any headspace since my last run-in with them, automatically deleting Kelvin's occasional i-mails without a second thought. Then, without warning, they crashed back into my life – almost literally. Rambling back from the park, head full of book, heart full of Becca, I didn't see the Mini-Lec until it was too late. It jerked to a stop, wheels up on the pavement, missing Sausage by inches.

Geoffrey's head emerged. 'Get in.'

'No chance.'

'Got to talk to you.'

'Do it here then. How did you find me, anyway?'

'Been watching you for a while. On and off, you know.'

I *didn't* know. How had I missed that? 'You're getting better at it.'

A sniff. 'Went on a course.'

'They have courses for that?'

'Yeah. Now get in.' He ducked back inside, leaned across and opened the passenger side door. Before I could yank her back, Rosie jumped in, and as she scrambled to get at the smorgasbord of half-eaten snacks on the back seat, her lead snagged on the gear stick so I had no choice but to release her. 'Come on. Put the big one in the back as well. You'll want to hear what I got to say.'

The last thing I wanted to do was get up close and personal with Geoffrey and the car's festering interior, but if I didn't, he'd no doubt hold Rosie hostage or drive off with her to spite me. Sausage happily clambered into the back and, after chucking what looked to be half of Geoffrey's wardrobe off the front seat, I slid in next to him.

'Geoffrey, do you live in your car?'

Without answering or checking his mirrors, he pulled out, narrowly missing an Electro-Bus.

'Where are we going? You're not going to stab me, are you? Dump me in a lay-by?' Sausage wouldn't be any help. She was peering between the two front seats, tongue lolling, enjoying the ride.

'Going round the block. In case we're being followed.'

'Who'd be following us?'

He yanked the wheel hard left, cutting across the bicycle lane and almost taking out a tandem.

'Christ, Geoffrey!'

He was a road-rage incident waiting to happen. Scratch that – happening. Without slowing, he stuck his head out of the window to yell 'Fuck you,' at the understandable flurry of abuse we were receiving from the cyclists forced to disperse out of his illegal way. I clung to the door handle as he gunned it down the wrong direction of a one-way street, cut across a pedestrian zone, then stalled to a stop in a disabled bay outside a fruit-n-veg stall.

'Jesus. Was that really necessary?'

He fully wound down the windows, took out a pouch of tobacco and offered me a pre-rolled cigarette. 'Here. You'll need it.'

I took it, rationalising that one rollie's worth of passive smoking wouldn't kill the dogs.

'I know what you're doing, matey-boy,' he said.

'Do you now. And what's that?'

'Meeting up with the . . . the wotsit . . . the *version* of the woman you've been i-mailing.'

His new surveillance skills must be off the chart if he'd found that out. I was seriously impressed and also seriously worried. 'How in the hell did you discover that?'

'It wasn't rocket genius.'

'Rocket science.'

'That either. Found out where you were staying easy enough. Old lady next door to your last place gave me your address. I told her I had a parcel for you.'

'Lily?' I'd given the address to her in case there was any mail that needed forwarding. I couldn't imagine her blithely handing it over to a stranger, though. Nor had she mentioned this during our infrequent awkward catch-up chats.

'That her name? She's a nice old thing, isn't she? Offered me a cuppa.'

Et tu, Lily. Et tu.

'After that, I followed you one day. Then I followed her. Saw where she was living. Took me a bit to put two and two together. Only figured it out when I checked the address against the marriage registry, found your woman's name. Rebecca. Same as the other one. Done all right for herself, hasn't she? Married to a man like that.'

'Get to the bloody point, Geoffrey.'

'What you're doing is proper meddling. They won't like that.'

'The group, you mean.'

'Yeah. And you don't want them to find out. What they said. What Henrietta said, you should take it seriously. They've done stuff before to people who crossed them.'

'What kind of stuff?'

'That journalist who did a story on us. The one what you read that led you to Kelvin. You should see where he ended up.'

Whoa there, Nelly. 'You're not saying . . . what, did they beat him up or something?' I couldn't *quite* picture Isaac and Debbie taking it in turns to bludgeon someone to death with a golf club and an eggplant.

'Nah. Henrietta dug into his past. Found an article he'd . . . wotsitted . . . copied from someone years before and made out was his own. Ruined his career.'

'Christ. What is Henrietta? Ex-MI5 or EU Intelligence or something?'

'Fucked if I know. I'm just saying, take them seriously.'

'Okay. So where are you going with this?'

'I'm saying, they don't need to know what you're doing, do they?'

'You're losing me. I thought you were supposed to be their spy. Or whatever.'

'I'm saying, you help me. I'll help you. You get me what I need, and I'll tell them that you're being a good little boy and behaving yourself.'

'And what do you need?'

'Information. From your woman's world.'

'What info? I thought you lot were dead against this kind of thing in case it messes with the universe blah de blah.'

'Not like that. Info about me.'

And then he told me his story. It took a while. Geoffrey wasn't what you'd call articulate. He'd drift off mid-sentence, he had mild aphasia, and his accent wavered all over the place, lurching from generic Northern to Brummie, with an Irish twang thrown in for good measure. It made him both frustrating and fascinating to listen to.

By the time he was done, even with the windows down, the entire car stank of Sausage's breath.

Geoffrey said that when he was younger, he'd begun to get what he called, 'feelings and memories of another life'. One where he'd been married and had a daughter. Memories that gradually grew stronger and stronger and more detailed, 'like living dreams'. As he wasn't married and didn't have children, he said he'd spent years assuming he had a psychiatric disorder – 'Even got myself sectioned for a few weeks, just in case, like.' Then the Arpanet exploded onto the scene and he'd ended up at the Berenstains' door. He tapped his gut. 'The others in the group, for them it's on the . . . on the surface. But me, I feel it here. Deep down.'

'Don't take this the wrong way, Geoffrey, but could these memories be a side-effect of your accident?'

'Bit rich asking that seeing as you're having an affair with a woman from another . . . you know.' Fair enough. 'And no. They started long before then.'

He wanted Bee to look him up in her world: 'See how I'm doing. See if in her world I do have a daughter, and if so, how *she*'s doing.'

'The group won't like that.'

'Don't need to know, do they? Kelvin's all right, but the others . . . they can get fucked far as I'm concerned.'

A deal was struck. He'd keep an eye on the Berenstains for me, assure them that I was behaving myself and toeing the Non-Butterfly Effect Line; I'd see what Bee could dig up for him.

'But don't get your hopes up. She might not find anything.' Thoughts of alternative-reality Dylan surfaced. 'And if she does, it might be something you'd rather not know.'

'Good or bad, I want to know. I *need* to know. It would mean a lot to me.'

'Fine.'

'Thanks. You're a good'un.'

'I thought you hated me?'

'What made you think that?'

'Oh, I don't know, the number of times you've told me to fuck off?'

'You're all right.'

'I'll need all of your personal details.' I'd been through this before; it would take a while. 'But can we find a beer garden? Either that or I'll need a gas mask.'

*

From: NB26@zone.com
To: Bee1984@gmail.com

Dead? Are you sure it's him?

From: Bee1984@gmail.com
To: NB26@zone.com

We're never going to be 100% are we? But there are too many matches to rule it out.

Mother: Gloria Elizabeth King, Afro-Caribbean. Tick

Father: Donald Alan Gleeson, Irish Catholic. Tick

Born December 31, 1958 in Wolverhampton. Tick.

From: NB26@zone.com
To: Bee1984@gmail.com

How and when did he die?

From: Bee1984@gmail.com
To: NB26@zone.com

March, 85. Motorbike crash. Found the obit in the *Express & Star* archive. Took some doing. I'm turning into a regular Nancy Drew. Or Miss Marple. Or, to get all meta about it, it's the kind of thing retired policeman Kellerman would do in the Sanger books. He's always rooting through archives.

From: NB26@zone.com
To: Bee1984@gmail.com

Sounds riveting.

From: Bee1984@gmail.com
To: NB26@zone.com

Now, now.

BUT Geoffrey did have a daughter. And a granddaughter.

From: NB26@zone.com
To: Bee1984@gmail.com

Christ. Really?

From: Bee1984@gmail.com
To: NB26@zone.com

Yes, Jenny, care worker at a hospice in Wales. BIG social media presence. Doesn't mention Geoffrey on it though.

From: NB26@zone.com
To: Bee1984@gmail.com

Is there any way you could talk to her? Ask her about her dad? It's a big ask, I know. He says he has all these memories of her. I'm thinking: what if hers match with his? Long shot, but worth looking into.

From: Bee1984@gmail.com
To: NB26@zone.com

That's not really something I can do via a DM on Facebook. Let me think on it.

And if they do match, what does that mean? That when he died in my world his memories transferred into the Geoffrey in yours? Like a spin on that Shared Consciousness thingy? Or that Quantum Immortality one? Which is the one where when you die your consciousness or whatever just carries on in another timeline? Hang on, I'll wiki.

From: NB26@zone.com
To: Bee1984@gmail.com

I don't think there is a theory for this, Bee. But it might mean there's something to the Berenstains' displaced persons mesh-crossing gubbins after all.

From: Bee1984@gmail.com
To: NB26@zone.com

What I don't get is this: Say your consciousness or whatever does cross the mesh when you die, why isn't everyone walking around with memories of our alternative lives?

From: NB26@zone.com
To: Bee1984@gmail.com

Kelvin said that for the mesh to be crossed, a glitch had to occur. Whatever that means.

From: Bee1984@gmail.com
To: NB26@zone.com

A glitch in what though? The universe? The multiverse?

From: NB26@zone.com
To: Bee1984@gmail.com

I think the technical term for that is 'fucked if I know.'

BEE

In another life I could have been a PI. Maybe in another life I was. Because I clearly had previously hidden, devious depths.

In the end securing a meeting with Jenny was easy. Under the guise of the business, I friended her on Facebook, then sent through: 'Congratulations! You've been chosen at random for a FREE dress makeover from FOR FROCK'S SAKE!'

Back came: <Is this a scam?>

<Hi! No, it's not a scam, but a promotion> I sent her links to the website (where Gemma's jacket took pride of place) and Instagram. <If you're not interested, no problem! No obligation and there'll be no upselling. All we ask is that you post a pic of yourself wearing the finished garment or accessory on your chosen social media platform>

<First time I've won anything. Does it have to be a wedding dress? Doubt I'd still fit into mine. How does it work?>

If I had any chance of wheedling out the kind of sensitive information Nick and Geoffrey were after, a Skype consultation wouldn't cut it. Best to do it in person and hope she'd emulate the clients who, for whatever reason, chose to confide in me. As she worked full-time, I offered to travel down to her the following Saturday for a fitting. I suggested to Nicolas that we make a weekend of it. Book an Airbnb, hole up in the countryside for a couple of days. He jumped at the chance and offered to drive to me the night before.

He'd passed the Clarice, Magda and Leila tests with flying colours (she was still sending me <WOW don't fuck it up> messages): Going away together was the final frontier. The final test. Nate had been a nightmare to travel with; unfamiliar environments amplified his worst traits, made him extra picky and confrontational. I doubted this would be the case with Nicolas – I *knew* it wouldn't be – but I'd discovered that comparing him to The Fucker rather than Nick was another effective method of plastering over the fissures.

On the drive down, it took me longer than it should have to notice that Nicolas was quieter, more preoccupied than usual. Probably because I was equally as preoccupied.

If he'd asked what was eating me, I would have been forced to trot out another lie or half-truth. They were becoming second nature to me now. Untruths are habit-forming, but they also breed until they're out of control and turn on you (<Like rats. Or nasty gerbils> <Lie Vermin. I like it, Bee> <NOT HELPING, Nick>). Perhaps, out there in Multiverse Land, there's another, braver version of me who'd have had the guts and integrity to tell Nicolas the truth from the beginning. A version of our story where he and Nick became friends of sorts, a version where I could tell him what was on my mind without worrying that he'd think I was crazy or a manipulative monster. A version where he'd ask: 'Hey, what's up, chuck?' And I'd say, 'Oh you know, just the fact I'm about to lie to a woman whose father is dead but not dead if you know what I mean. The fact that quantum immortality might actually be a THING and I may be about to prove it. Also, I really, really want to stop at the next McDonald's for a quarter-pounder.'

Instead, I asked him: 'What's up? You're way quieter than you usually are. And although I've never been in a car with you before, I'm pretty sure it's not because you need all your concentration to keep us from running off the road.'

'That obvious?'

'That obvious. Spill it.' A touch of apprehension: the ever-present dread that he'd caught one of my Lie Vermin in the act of gnawing at the truth. (<Ok that's taking the analogy too far, Bee>)

'My publishers aren't keen on the outline for the next Sanger book. My editor says getting the crusty old bastard to look into a political corruption scandal rather than solving his usual *Midsomer Murders*-style convoluted murdered woman mystery will "alienate my readers".'

'Well tell her that I'm one of your readers, and it wouldn't alienate me. I'm a "fan" remember?'

A rueful smile. 'Still can't believe I said that. Sometimes I forget that's how we met.'

How I made *us meet. Oh, hello, guilt, haven't seen you for at least sixty seconds*. 'Really? Our eyes meeting over the breakfast buffet table meant nothing to you?'

'Nah. It's not that. I guess it's because I'm so used to being in relationships with women who aren't that interested in what I do. In the five years Jodie and I were together, if she read half of one of my drafts, it was a lot. And yeah, I know she had her own career and interests, but I got into the habit of keeping that part of my life separate. I keep forgetting you're the first girlfriend I've ever had who *gets* what I do. Who's interested.'

We'd danced the swap-the-ex story fandango on our first weekend together, but he hadn't mentioned this before. It struck me then that I knew more about *Sabotage* than I did about Nicolas's plans for his next book. 'Can I help? If you ever want to bounce plot ideas, I'm totally up for it.' If Becca had it in her, so did I.

'You'd do that? Haven't you got enough on your plate?'

'I'd love to help. Really.'

He took my hand. 'Thank you. When I've got over myself I'll take you up on that.'

'What would you write if you could? If you had a choice?'

'Not another book about a retired policeman with too much time on his hands, that's for bloody sure. Bloody Kellerman. *Christ* how I'd love to kill off the old arse.'

'How would you do it?'

'As painfully as possible.'

'Death from a thousand paper cuts?'

'Ha! Give him a stroke and shove him in a home.'

'It could be a whole new series: *The Dementia Detective.*'

'*The Care Home Capers.*'

'Just *who* was responsible for the theft of the catheter tubes?'

'If only he could remember where he'd left that last clue.'

It was when we riffed like this that I almost forgot he wasn't Nick. *Almost.* This, if examined too closely, could bring on a feeling that was uncomfortably close to betrayal, as if by growing closer to Nicolas I was gradually erasing Nick – so I did what I always did and locked it into the mental box marked 'Mind Fuck: Do Not Open'.

We checked into the cottage, which, for once, lived up to its staged Airbnb pics, and had the surprise bonus of a hot tub and a complimentary stack of Welsh cakes (which I immediately scoffed for luck), and then Nick drove me to Jenny's two-up-two-down, stone-clad terrace in the nearby village. He'd brought along a book and said he'd wait in the car until I was done.

Okay. Here goes: *Nice dress, now tell me about your dead dad.*

Jenny, thank the little baby Jesus as Nick would say, was a talker. Bubbly, as round as she was tall, and relentlessly and naturally positive, she reminded me of the wonderful hospice nurses who'd helped take care of Mum in her final days.

Her cottage mirrored her personality: cluttered and charming. A tray of tea and more Welsh cakes (sorry, cellulite) were already waiting on the coffee table; the dress, a musty confection of tulle and polyester that she said she'd 'dug out of the attic' was draped over the sofa. 'Good luck doing something with that, my love.' I'd need it. As she said there 'wasn't much call for anything too glamorous in my life,' I suggested an all-purpose jacket, lining it with the underskirt – the only fabric I reckoned was salvageable. We flipped through Instagram until we hit on a design we both thought would suit her (not dissimilar to Gemma's commission – which would mean an expensive trip to the Goldhawk Road emporium for extra fabric and a slew of late nights). But it would be worth it. This was a woman who deserved to be spoiled. She said her divorce had been amicable, but 'turning that old thing into something beautiful would mean the world to me'.

As I took her measurements, I scanned the room, looking for an 'in'. The little baby Jesus was on my side once again, as the room was awash with family photographs, including several of her wedding day.

'Tell me about your wedding day.' I gestured at a pic of Jenny flanked by a pair of older folks. 'Are those your parents? They look so happy. Your dad especially.'

'That's my stepdad. He gave me away. My real dad died when I was six.'

'I'm so sorry.'

''S'all right. My folks had split up by then.'

'I lost my mum when I was in my early twenties. I know how hard it can be. I hope it wasn't a long illness.'

'Motorbike accident. Mum said he could be reckless. On my birthday as well. He didn't go straightaway. Spent weeks in a coma. I didn't understand what was going on at the time. Should have put me off hospitals for life, but look at me now.'

'How awful. But I'm sure you have some good memories too.'

'You know, I haven't thought about him for years. But this one time, he filled the whole room – the whole bloody room, my mum said – with balloons. She said he did things like that all the time.'

I was beginning to feel like an emotional strip-miner. 'What else did he do?'

'Let's see . . . bought a camper van on a whim and drove us up to Scotland. Mum said it broke down on the way and we all got carsick. Mum said he wanted to be a doctor but didn't have the smarts. Became an ambulance driver instead. You'd think, wouldn't you, that he'd be more safety conscious what with all the accidents he must have seen.' She clucked. 'I honestly haven't thought about him for years. How funny!'

'I hope I haven't upset you.'

'Of course, you haven't, my love. The opposite really, because although my mum said he could be a bit of a bugger at times, he was one of life's characters and he isn't someone who should be forgotten. Telling his stories is a small way of keeping him alive, I s'pose. I've others if you want to hear them? They're coming back to me.'

'I'd love to.'

I was on a high as I made my way back to the car, buzzing at the unexpected success of Operation Jenny and itching to fill Nick in. I was midway through an apology for taking so long, when Nicolas handed me my phone, which I hadn't realised I'd left in the car.

'A message came in while you were gone.' Not accusatory, but deadpan, which was somehow more ominous. My stomach dropped. *Shit, shit, shit.* I must have stupidly left our Gmail thread open. *This is it. He's found you out.*

'Nate's your ex, right?'

'What?'

'The phone beeped while you were gone. I don't want you to think I was snooping or anything, but I couldn't help seeing the text.'

I swiped it into life and read the message: <We're on, Bex! Call me. Xx>

The *relief*. And also, regret: if it *had* been a message from Nick, I would have been forced to come clean. Forced to do the right thing.

'There's nothing going on between you, right? Because if there is, just tell me.'

'All that's going on is that I asked him to introduce me to someone who may be interested in investing in the business. And doing that made feel like throwing up. I swear that's it. There's a reason we all call him The Fucker.'

He searched my face for a second, then nodded. 'Okay.'

'You believe me?'

'I believe you. Sorry for being such an insecure arse.'

You've every right to be.

He leaned over and kissed me. 'Now, how about we get shit-faced and try not to drown in the hot tub?'

'Sounds like a plan.' Thinking: *Bee, you coward, you utter, utter coward.*

*

From: NB26@zone.com
To: Bee1984@gmail.com

You're amazing Bee.

From: Bee1984@gmail.com
To: NB26@zone.com

It wasn't that difficult. She really was a talker.

Isn't it weird how the implications of this are incredible, but we've sort of just accepted them? How quickly we accepted *our* situation. How it became the new normal. Well not NORMAL, but you know.

From: NB26@zone.com
To: Bee1984@gmail.com

I know. And now I have to break the news to Geoffrey that his new normal means that in your world he's dead. Something best done in person I reckon. I'll see if he can meet me in town after I've met with Tweedy's agent on Friday.

From: Bee1984@gmail.com
To: NB26@zone.com

How are you feeling about that? Nervous? Excited? So happy for you. Amazing how far you've come since the Tweedy Twat Invoice Avoiding days.

From: Bee1984@gmail.com
To: NB26@zone.com

Sorry – that sounded patronizing . . .

From: NB26@zone.com
To: Bee1984@gmail.com

Not patronizing at all. Wouldn't be in this situation at all if it weren't for you if you think about it.

From: Bee1984@gmail.com
To: NB26@zone.com

And Becca. She was the one who helped you with the outline, after all.

From: NB26@zone.com
To: Bee1984@gmail.com

Speaking of Operation Doppelganger, how's Nicolas the Great? You haven't mentioned him for a while. All ok?

From: Bee1984@gmail.com
To: NB26@zone.com

Sort of. He's taking strain work-wise. His publisher biffed his latest outline.

From: NB26@zone.com
To: Bee1984@gmail.com

My heart bleeds.

From: Bee1984@gmail.com
To: NB26@zone.com

Snark alert. What happened to 'I'm feeling better about myself Bee?' I KNEW I shouldn't have told you.

From: NB26@zone.com
To: Bee1984@gmail.com

I'm just being my usual dick-ish self.

Hey – why not give him the plot of A Shot in the Dark? Could be a cold case his lame detective could look into.

From: Bee1984@gmail.com
To: NB26@zone.com

I can't! It's yours!

From: NB26@zone.com
To: Bee1984@gmail.com

If we're getting pedantic about it, that one is really Tweedy's. Do it, Bee. See what he says.

From: Bee1984@gmail.com
To: NB26@zone.com

Wouldn't that break the Berenstain Omerta code?

From: NB26@zone.com
To: Bee1984@gmail.com

They'll never know. Christ! Just thought – make sure you check that Tweedy didn't hire another ghost and put it out in your world.

From: Bee1984@gmail.com
To: NB26@zone.com

So you really are feeling better about yourself.

From: NB26@zone.com
To: Bee1984@gmail.com

I really am.

From: Bee1984@gmail.com
To: NB26@zone.com

Good. Hey – wear the tweed suit for luck when you meet the agent. I dare you.

NICK

I didn't wear the tweed. And nor did I need luck. Nazia, Tweedy's agent, a woman with a streak of pink in her hair and a streak of ruthlessness to her demeanour (which, I suppose, is what you want in an agent), greeted me with a perfume-scented double air-kiss and swept me into her office. Watched over by the enlarged, framed book covers of the impressive authors she represented, she spent half an hour bombarding me with espressos and ego-boosting compliments ('you have such a *natural* writing voice, Nick, I could really tell you'd fully *immersed* yourself into the character's inner life') – all bumf of course, but who cares? Not me. She not only agreed to represent me, 'for this and other, further projects', but broke the astounding news that an advance had been negotiated with 'a publishing house who I really think will give *Sabotage* the *push* it deserves'. It wasn't silly money, but even after splitting half of it with Tweedy and minus Nazia's commission, it still amounted to more than I'd made in total last year. A rough deadline was agreed, and with a final, 'I'm so *excited* about this, Nick,' she air-kissed me out the door.

If it weren't for the fact that I was en route to Euston to meet Geoffrey to relay Bee's intel, I would have skippety-skipped my way down the street like a character in a musical. The first person I told was Bee of course: <Told you you'd rock it, Nick. I've just shouted YAY so loud a passing dog walker almost shat himself>, then Dylan (secretly hoping he'd pass the news on to Poll and Jez): <SO PROUD of you ex stepdad>), but I'd have to wait until Monday to tell the person I *really* wanted to tell: Becca.

*

Geoffrey was waiting for me outside the Frites outlet where we'd almost come to blows, scowling at random passers-by, shoulders hunched as if he were readying himself for a fight. He might be. The Alternative World Dylan news had floored me. How would he react?

He greeted me with a nod and didn't argue when I suggested we find a table and grab a drink as 'this could take a while'. It certainly took a while for him to decide what to order; the customer-friendly smile on the face of the poor sod behind the counter became more and more like a rictus grin as Geoffrey changed his mind for the umpteenth time.

We sat at a corner table. I tried to make small talk to ease him into it, but he batted me away. 'Just fucking tell me.'

'Do you want the bad news or the good news first?'

'Bad.'

I composed myself. 'The "you" in Bee's world didn't make it, Geoffrey. I'm afraid he – you – died in an accident.'

If this shocked him, he showed no sign of it. 'When?'

'1985.'

He gazed into the distance. 'That's when I started getting the . . . the memories. How?'

'How did you die?'

A *duh* look.

'Motorbike crash.'

He nodded. 'Makes sense. Used to tear it up on my KTM here too.'

'You ready for the rest of it?'

'Go on.'

I was two minutes into unspooling Bee's info about Jenny when he started bawling. Proper bawling. I kept asking him if he wanted me to stop, but he shook his head, couldn't give a toss that the staff and our fellow customers were eyeing us with increasing concern. They probably thought we were in the middle of a bad break up. It was obvious that the memories correlated – the balloon anecdote especially – as this one brought forth something approximating a howl.

Little by little, the bawling turned into sobbing, and the sobbing into snuffles.

'I knew I wasn't mentally wotsit. Knew there was something to it. And she's all right? She's doing well?'

'From what Bee says, she's doing brilliantly. Said it's been a long time since she's met someone so happy.' Overegging it? Absolutely. But so what? 'You've got a granddaughter, too. Megan. Bee says she'll be starting school soon.'

There were napkins to hand, but he wiped his streaming nose on his sleeve. His Adam's apple was still bobbing like a nodding dog, but the worst of it seemed to have passed.

'Worries me though. Them being there. In that world, like. Must worry you too. Can't be a good place if they voted in a total fucking cock-headed arse like that Trump.'

'Eh?' Then: of course. The i-mails I'd stupidly shared with the Berenstains in the early days. 'Bee says things are improving. There's hope.' She hadn't said that. She'd never said that. The only time we'd ever discussed 'real-world' issues was when we'd compared notes and Red Flags. Operation Doppelganger and our own personal dramas sucked up all our time and oxygen; in retrospect, I reckon that on a subconscious level neither of us wanted to delve too deeply into what was going on behind the scenes in our respective worlds. We inhabited our own little universe, and that was enough for us.

Geoffrey toyed with a stevia packet. 'And I was an ambulance driver, you say?'

'Yes.'

'Remember thinking about doing that when I was younger.'

'Why didn't you?'

'Joined the Land-life Corps instead. Specialised in tree grafting and reforestation.'

Once again: *You think you know a person.*

He tapped his forehead. 'Then this happened. Unlicensed logging truck T-boned my Landy. Had to give it up.'

After experiencing his driving, I'd assumed he'd been responsible for the accident. 'I'm sorry that happened to you.'

A shrug. 'Life. Throws shit at you, doesn't it?'

It certainly does.

'I'll keep up my end of the bargain. Tell the others you've moved on and aren't meddling. What you done for me, it . . .' His Adam's apple sprung dangerously back into life.

'I can give you more info if you like. Updates. Ask Bee to keep tabs on Jenny and Megan.' I hadn't planned on making this offer: it popped out, unbidden, partly as an attempt to stem another bout of hysteria.

'You'd do that?'

'Course.'

A sniff, a nod, another silver-sleeved nose-wipe. 'Let's go out for a smoke.'

As we made our way through the concourse, I averted my eyes from the clock. This didn't stop me from mentally reliving the gamut of emotions I'd gone through before, during and after that fateful non-meeting though. The hope, the excitement, the confusion, and then the hollowness. This must have shown on my face, because Geoffrey gave me a quizzical look, then asked: 'How's it going with her? The one here.'

'Becca? It's . . . going.'

'Have you told her? Who you are? Why you want to be with her?'

'No.'

'Worried she'll think you're a crackpot?'

'Yes.'

'Don't blame you.'

'Bee – Other World Bee – says we should. Says it's starting a relationship on a lie.'

'Yeah, well. All relationships start like that. You show your . . . your best side when you first meet someone. That's a bit like lying.'

Wisdom Geoffrey-style. And something Bee and I hadn't felt the need to do when we first 'met'. 'But she isn't doing too badly at her end. With the version of myself in her world, I mean.'

'Go on.'

Oh, why not. As we sat outside and smoked, I told him the lot. The insecurity, the jealousy, the full, unvarnished, Miserable Bastard truth. Who would have thought that Geoffrey of all people would help lance yet another of those tiresome emotional boils?

*

From: Bee1984@gmail.com
To: NB26@zone.com

So he really is a displaced person. You know, all this, it makes me feel a little less sad about Mum, if that makes sense. The thought that maybe, we just carry on when we die.

From: NB26@zone.com
To: Bee1984@gmail.com

Getting deep there, Bee.

From: Bee1984@gmail.com
To: NB26@zone.com

Glitch Life does that to you, I suppose. It's like looking over the edge of a cliff. Look for too long, you'll be tempted to jump.

From: NB26@zone.com
To: Bee1984@gmail.com

Before you do, I need to know something first: Did you give Nicolas the outline?

From: Bee1984@gmail.com
To: NB26@zone.com

Not yet. Waiting till I see him in person. Still can't think of a way to explain where or how I came up with it, although there's always the good old 'a client said something that got me thinking' excuse. He's only arriving tomorrow because tonight is the night that I finally get to see Benny in all his one-percenter glory.

From: NB26@zone.com
To: Bee1984@gmail.com

Christ! I've been so wrapped up in Geoffrey drama + my own agenty goodness that that went out of my head. You should have reminded me!

From: Bee1984@gmail.com
To: NB26@zone.com

Been trying not to think about it too much, TBH. Wish me luck & here's hoping I don't fuck it up.

BEE

The event meet-n-greet was the sort of soulless schmooze-fest that would usually have made me wither inside, but not tonight: tonight I was a woman on a mission. I should have been more nervous than I was. Not only because if things went well, I'd be meeting my alternate-reality husband in the flesh – it would also be the first time I'd seen Nate since the break up.

He was waiting for me outside the venue, scrolling through his phone while keeping half an eye out for anyone worth snagging for a spot of opportunistic networking. Seeing him there, in his Paul Smith suit, fake glasses, and slicked-back hair, I felt . . . nothing. No. That wasn't entirely true. A flash of self-censure: what the hell were you *thinking*, Bee?

'Hello, Nate.'

'Bella-Bex!' *Mwah, mwah*. He looked me up and down with that familiar proprietary gaze. 'You're looking wonderful.' I'd like to think he meant it. But you could never tell with him. I'd certainly put in the effort, splurged on a Westwood suit (secondhand, but good as new), and visited a salon for hair and makeup (I'd asked the stylist to straighten my hair – Nate had loathed it whenever I did that).

'You too.' Not true. Up close, he'd put on a few pounds, and there was a hint of saggy skin beneath his chin. *Been at the Magnums, Nate?*

'Shall we? I saw him go in about ten minutes ago. I've put in a good word for you, by the way.'

'Thanks.'

The room was heaving with fashionistas dressed in their best 'look-at-me' finery, but I picked him out straightaway, as if a literal spotlight were shining down on him. He was shorter and stockier in person, holding court while a gaggle of designer-clad sycophants frittered around him.

'I'll get us some drinks,' Nate said. 'I know how much you hate this kind of thing.' This considerate side, a flashback to the Nate I'd first met, the one I'd fallen for (or thought I'd fallen for), didn't soften how I felt about him. *But nice try, arsehole.*

'Bee!' Wafting towards me came Meru, a fashionista who'd been one of my early high-profile commissionees. Another round of mwah-mwahs. 'So happy to see a friendly face here.'

We caught up on each other's news, Meru doing most of the talking. She'd been a Ms Peach-grade nightmare of a client, but I liked her on a personal level, and it saved me hanging around awkwardly by myself.

Nate returned, handed me a glass of red, and charm-bombed Meru until she was dragged away by a selfie seeker.

'Ready?'

I nodded. This was it. The first threads of anxiety began to knit themselves together.

An arm around my waist (ugh), Nate smarmed his way into Benedict's circle. 'Ben, let me introduce you to Rebecca Davies. She's the designer I was telling you about. The founder of For Frock's Sake?'

Benedict looked me straight in the eye and smiled. 'Of course. How wonderful to meet you.'

'I'll leave you to it,' Nate purred. 'Come and find me afterwards, Bee. We're due for a catch-up.'

Alone at last. *Hey there husband. For richer or poorer, in sickness and in health, till death or quantum fuck-ups us do part.*

'Love the name of your business, Rebecca. What you're doing, it's exactly the sort of sustainable enterprise we support.'

Our interaction couldn't have lasted more than five minutes, and for the entire time he gave me his full attention, as if no one but me existed in the room: a charisma death-ray blast. Charisma. So few people have it that when you meet someone who does, it's hard not to be dragged into their orbit. Is this what had sucked Becca in? He asked question after question (client base, social media reach, process), and I answered by rote, thinking: *I married you. We've shared a bed, had sex, a child. I've seen you naked. You've seen me naked. I've heard you fart in your sleep, seen you floss.* I couldn't see the real person behind the glare. But nor did I pick up any obvious warning signs, other than a moment where he seemed confused that I wasn't crawling up his arse.

'If you have a business plan or ideas on how it could be upscaled, let's talk. But it's been a pleasure, Rebecca.' He handed me his card. '*Please* don't hesitate to contact me.'

He didn't make me cringe inside. Nor did I find him attractive. Charming, certainly. Not lascivious. Not really flirtatious. But on a gut level him and me – him and Becca – felt *wrong*.

And yes, okay, selfish relief: this wasn't some fragile soul who'd be crushed if his wife divorced him.

I left immediately after that. I didn't bother saying goodbye to Nate.

When I returned home, the flat felt emptier than usual. I was about to open the thread to fill Nick in, but instead called Nicolas first.

'Hey.' (I still thought of this as a 'Nick' word: whenever Nicolas said it, in would come a shadowy *it's him, but not him.*)

'Hey.'

'How did it go? Did the investor bite?'

'Nah. Don't know what I was thinking. I'm happy as I am. It'll always be a small business and that's fine with me.'

'What was it like seeing The Fucker again?'

'Gross. But it reminded me how lucky I am to have someone like you in my life.'

The truth: for once.

*

From: NB26@zone.com
To: Bee1984@gmail.com

A charismatic cipher of a bloke. That's it? You can't be more specific than that?

From: Bee1984@gmail.com
To: NB26@zone.com

Only spoke to him for 5 mins. 5 very long and weird mins, granted. But what I do know for sure is that he's not a man I'd ever be happy with. Which means he's not right for Becca either.

From: NB26@zone.com
To: Bee1984@gmail.com

We don't know that for sure, Bee. Nature versus nurture, remember?

From: Bee1984@gmail.com
To: NB26@zone.com

I DO know that for sure. I know it in my gut. Feel it in my genes. Or genetic code. Oh sod it. I just KNOW. AND he's not a sexy widower in her world so she has no excuse.

From: NB26@zone.com
To: Bee1984@gmail.com

He's Scarlett's dad, Bee.

From: Bee1984@gmail.com
To: NB26@zone.com

Yeah. And Becca knows better than anyone that staying in a marriage for the 'sake of the kids' is the worst thing you can do. It fucks you up and it fucks them up.

From: NB26@zone.com
To: Bee1984@gmail.com

I hear you. All we can do for now is play by ear. Subject change: did you give Saint Nicolas the Shot in the Dark idea?

From: Bee1984@gmail.com
To: NB26@zone.com

Yes.

From: NB26@zone.com
To: Bee1984@gmail.com

And?

From: Bee1984@gmail.com
To: NB26@zone.com

He loves it.

From: NB26@zone.com
To: Bee1984@gmail.com

Ha! Good. But he'd better not fuck it up.

NICK

Bee called it serendipitous synchronicity. How events in our worlds would mirror each other, too often to simply be chance. A week after she met the infamous Benedict, I ran into him too.

Weekends had a tendency to drag as Becca and Scarlett were off-limits on Saturday and Sundays. 'Family time', Becca called it without elaborating further, but clearly Benedict brought his charisma home from the office on those days. She rarely said much about what they got up to *en famille*, that part of her life was still ring-fenced, but Scarlett would let slip the occasional behind-the-scenes nugget. A mention of a trip to see 'Gram-gram' (presumably Benedict's mother), who 'smelled funny and made Daddy angry'. A 'We had pizza, but Mumma said she wasn't hungry.' And once, a matter-of-fact: 'Daddy says if I don't clean my room then he'll give my toys away to all the poor children who live in Texas.'

When Monday came around, I bounced out of bed like a child on Christmas morning. I couldn't wait to tell Becca the news about the book, thought about wearing the tweed suit for a laugh as a tribute to Tweedy. And I was still buzzing from the ego-boost of Nicolas taking on *A Shot in the Dark* (all right, there was an edge of anxiety that he'd do a better job of it, but I managed to shelve that). So upbeat was I that even Erika noticed. 'For once you are happy. This is nice to see. But I see also you did not leave your used towels in the designated area. This must not happen again.'

The dogs, too, were perkier as if my energy was contagious. Sausage's hips had been giving her trouble lately, but that day she bounded along like a puppy. We were early, but Scarlett and Becca were already waiting for us. As Scarlett grabbed the leads, joyfully shouting, 'Sawsage! Heel!' Becca took one look at me and said, 'Are we on?'

'Signed and sealed.'

Then, forgetting herself, she threw her arms around me. 'I'm so happy for you.' I responded – of course I did. Drew her in close, pulled her to me, the first time we'd had any substantial physical contact. I stroked her hair, she looked up at me, and there was a moment, more than a moment, when I could see that she wanted this as much as I did. An in-drawn breath, then she stiffened, stepped back, mumbled, 'Sorry.'

'Sorry for what?'

She turned away, did that nervous thing where she adjusted her clothing. 'That . . . that's great news, Nick.'

'Becca . . . shouldn't we talk about what just happened?'

'Nothing happened.' She gestured to where Scarlett was rolling on the grass with the dogs. 'I don't want to spoil this. You get it, right?'

'I get it.'

After a few false starts – that missing beat again – we fell into our usual Park Life routine, bantering, chatting about the book, gossiping about the regulars. Only it felt like play-acting.

I half-expected that she wouldn't show up on Tuesday, but she did. Another play-acting session: pretending everything was normal, pretending the erotic shimmer between us didn't exist.

(<God, Nick. Like a sexual tension elephant in the room? Or the park>; <You need to work on your analogies, Bee. That one rivals 'sex is like a box of chocolates'. But yeah>; <It sounds as sexy as hell>; <It is and isn't. Let's just say when I get home I need some serious alone time>; <You know it's only a matter of time, don't you?>; <Maybe. But we can hardly have a quickie behind the bandstand while Scarlett bribes the dogs with biscuits. We'd need a fuck-ton of biscuits for a start>)

Wednesday and Thursday were a replay of 'Let's pretend'.

It happened on Friday. Later, I'd blame it on the rain. But really, we were just looking for an excuse. If the weather turned, we'd usually decamp to the bandstand, but that day, shortly after we met up, it tipped it down out of the blue, one of those late summer showers where the raindrops are the size of a baby's head.

Within seconds, all of us were soaked, and it was a struggle not to stare at the way Becca's sodden T-shirt clung to her body.

'Mumma!' Scarlett half-laughed, half-screamed.

Becca dug in her bag. 'Bugger. Didn't bring the cagoules.' Then she looked up at me and said: 'Let's go back to my place.'

Whoa. 'Are you sure?'

'I'm sure.' She swallowed, wiped damp hair from her eyes. 'Ben left for New York this morning.'

I wasn't about to argue. We embarked on a damper, more hurried replay of our first expedition to her house, only this time I carried Scarlett, who clung to me like a monkey and kept shouting, 'Faster, Doggy Man!' We arrived at the Wilderville entrance out of breath and laughing, and when I put Scarlett down so that she could walk the dogs herself, Becca caught my eye. A shared look of desire: a terrible, terrible word, but that's what it was. Okay, maybe 'lust' would be more accurate. I felt it zing through my entire body. And I mean my *entire* body.

This was it.

Only it wasn't, because as we reached the driveway, she stopped dead, muttered, 'Oh fuck, no.' Parked in front of the garage was a sleek Tesla-Jag. I was about to suggest that the dogs and I beat a hasty retreat, when the front door opened and out he stepped. A glance at Becca, a glance at me – unreadable – then straight to Scarlett. 'Letty!'

'Daddy!'

'Oh, baby. Look at you. You're soaking.'

Scarlett, oblivious to the tension – thank God – held up the dogs' leads. 'Look, Daddy. This is Sawsage and Rosie.'

'I can see that.' Back to me: 'And I'm guessing you're the "Doggy Man" Scarlett's always talking about?'

'That's me!' Overly jaunty – a crass attempt at radiating innocence.

'But I'm sure you have another name.' He approached and held out his hand. 'Ben.'

I wiped mine on my jeans before we shook. As they were soaked, it didn't help. 'Nick.'

Shorter than me, barrel-chested, confidence blasting out of every pore. 'Good to finally meet you.'

I didn't look over at Becca, but I could sense every fibre of her being was on edge.

'I thought you were going to the States, Ben?' she said.

'Elana cocked-up. Miscalculated my flight allowance.' He gave me a fake-matey grin – as if I, too, regularly encountered these rich-people problems. 'That's quotas for you, am I right?'

'I said Nick could come back here and dry off. We got caught in the storm.'

'I can see that. Come in. You're soaking.'

'I should go. I've got the dogs.' Sausage punctuated this by helpfully shaking herself over his silky suit.

'Don't worry about that. Bring them in!'

'Ben . . .'

'Don't fuss, Rebecca. It'll be fine. Go and get yourself and Scarlett into some dry clothes.'

Studiously avoiding looking at either Ben or me, Becca picked Scarlett up and disappeared into the house.

Benedict waved the dogs and I into the cavernous kitchen-cum-whatever it was. 'Hang tight, and I'll get you a towel.'

'Thanks.'

I'd never been inside a place like it before. A study in grey-toned minimalism, the kitchen counters seemed to organically emerge from the polished floor. At the far end, two austere grey leather couches faced off against each other aggressively. Apart from a huge, splattery abstract painting above a glass-shielded hole that I assumed housed some kind of heating source, there was a disconcerting lack of colour, clutter or comfort. No sign of anywhere to cook, store food, or wash up. No toys, books, or even a stray coffee mug. The space made me feel even more self-consciously scruffy than I had in Leila's offices: this was not my world. I suspected it wasn't Becca's, either – Benedict must have been responsible for commissioning this characterless, insanely expensive cell. Naturally the dogs didn't give a shit about high-end interior design and made themselves at home. Sausage slumped on the mirror-polished floor, where she'd no doubt leave a canine-shaped mat of damp dog hair like a crime scene outline. Rosie half-heartedly snuffled at the base of the counters in the hope of detecting any stray crumbs, then gave it up as a bad job and collapsed next to her girlfriend.

Benedict returned and threw me a towel.

'Cheers.'

'Wish I could lend you some dry clothes, but I doubt we're the same size.' He smiled. I smiled back. 'Coffee?'

'I don't want to put you to any trouble.'

'No trouble. Always great to meet a friend of my wife's. Especially the infamous Doggy Man. Espresso? Or are you a milky man?' He somehow made this sound like a test.

'Espresso would be great.'

He pressed an invisible button on an invisibly seamed surface, and with a mechanical sigh, up popped a machine that wouldn't have looked out of place in a high-end Italian restaurant. Another seemingly random press on another seemingly seamless cupboard revealed a shelf of miniscule crystal espresso cups. It was like watching a rich person's magic show. The scent of freshly ground coffee beans filled the room.

He passed me a cup, then leaned against the counter. I stood where I was. Dripping on the floor. Towel dangling from one hand. Sipping from my teeny doll-sized mug. The coffee was bloody delicious, though.

'Tell me about yourself, Nick. I'm assuming you're part of the home-based workforce seeing as you're able to visit the park with such frequency.'

'I'm a writer.'

'Are you? Impressive. Would I have heard of you? I'm not much of a reader, I'm afraid.'

'You won't have heard of me.'

'I'm sure you're just being modest.' His expression changed. 'Here she is!' I turned to see Becca approaching, tugging at her clothing and obviously, *too* obviously, avoiding looking at me. Benedict held out his hand and she padded over to join him. Shoulders slightly hunched, body language carefully choreographed, directing every movement inwards or towards him – basically anywhere that wasn't me. This was more than the guardedness I'd picked up when we first met. This was someone desperate not to draw attention to themselves.

'Are you married, Nick?' He glanced at my ring finger.

'Separated.'

'Ah.'

Fuck it. It had worked on Leila, and I had to do something to help diffuse the tension. 'My partner . . . he found someone else.'

A brief moue of surprise from Benedict. Becca relaxed her guard a little.

'I'm so sorry to hear that. How long had you and . . . I'm sorry, what was your partner's name?'

Shit. Bugger. Then, out it popped: 'Jez.'

'How long were you and Jez together?'

'Twelve years.'

'Well, that's good going.' A glance at Becca. 'Nine more than Rebecca and I have managed so far, but we'll get there. Isn't that right, my love?'

He drew her to him and kissed her forehead without taking his eyes off mine.

That charm. Bee was right. You could see how it would be easy to be sucked in. And spat out.

*

From: Bee1984@gmail.com
To: NB26@zone.com

And?

From: NB26@zone.com
To: Bee1984@gmail.com

It was as if she was making herself . . . lesser around him.

BEE

Lesser. Did I do that when I was with Nate? Make myself lesser? I even called Leila to ask her about it.

'Not lesser, exactly. But you definitely weren't always yourself around him.'

'Thanks for telling me.'

'I *did*, Bee. You just didn't listen.'

'You're right. I'm sorry.'

I *had* listened. I just hadn't wanted to hear it.

And having met Benedict, I could see how easy it would be to wither in the shadow he cast.

If you want to know the truth about someone, judge them by their friends – or exes. Like Kat de Jong: Benedict's ex-girlfriend.

Time to test the old PI skills again. Offering Kat, a rock-star designer, a free dress makeover wouldn't swing it this time. In any case, I decided there was no need for outright subterfuge as this situation demanded a more direct approach. I'd send her an e-mail, saying that a close friend of mine was about to embark on a relationship with Benedict, and seeing as said friend had a history of hooking up with men who were less than ideal, as a concerned mate I was desperate for reassurance that he was a decent man. There was some truth to it (kind of) – a baby hamster lie rather than a full-on vermin epidemic – and I'd just have to hope that a) he wasn't currently in a relationship that she knew about; and b) she would be prepared to share this kind of information with a stranger.

Tracking down her contact details was a far trickier proposition. Nate was correct: she hadn't put out a line since 2017 and her website was no longer live. I couldn't find her anywhere on social media, including Instagram – unheard of for a designer. I was lost in a Kat-shaped Google hole, when a message from Nicolas came in: <You on the train yet?>

Shit – I'd been so absorbed I'd forgotten I was meant to be on my way to Leeds. Speaking of judging people by their friends, I was due to meet the infamous Jez for the first time.

<Stuck on the Tube! Will keep you updated x>

An hour into the train journey, and fifteen search pages later, I finally found an e-mail address on a cached business list page. It was ten years old, so could well be defunct, but it was worth a shot. I said my piece and sent the message into the ether. It didn't bounce back, so all I could do was hope.

Antsy. Ants in my pants. On the walk to the tapas bar where we were due to meet Jez, Nicolas didn't need an inner radar to pick up that something was off: I kept obsessively checking my phone like a teenage Snapchat addict.

'What's up?'

Unleash the vermin! 'Nothing's up. I've been offered a commission that could be huge. From a big-name designer. Waiting to hear back from her to see if it's confirmed, is all.'

'That's great, Bee. Are you sure you're not nervous about tonight?'

'No. Not at all. Jez sounds . . . great.' Cheating Jez. *Watch your back, Nicolas.*

In my head, I'd built Jez up as an almost cartoonish villain, a suave moustache-twirling Nate-ish figure, cocky and confident and smoothly handsome. Jez was none of these things. Nervy, a tendency to ramble on, and even more of a sloppy eater than I was. I couldn't picture the Poll I'd seen on the clip – that brave, brilliant woman – finding him in the least bit attractive.

I tried to engage, I really did. I put on a happy face, fake-laughed at Jez's attempts at humour, said all the right things. Smiled as

Nicolas regaled Jez with the news that his publishers were 'ecstatic' about the *A Shot in the Dark* chapters he'd sent them.

'Bee gave me the idea.' He kissed my hand. 'My muse.'

I forced a smile to mask what I was thinking: that there was no way Nick would ever say something like this. Not unless he was taking the piss. *Not fair, Bee*. 'I wouldn't say that.'

'It's true.'

Jez launched into a spectacularly boring anecdote about the trials and tribulations Ofsted posed, and when he paused for breath, I made my excuses and slipped into the ladies, reverting to the habits of the Bad Old Days. I had to channel the nervous energy somehow. Covertly messaging Nick behind Nicolas's back was something I tried to avoid, but I decided a quick gossip about Jez didn't count as disloyalty, considering what Jez had done to Nick.

<I've just met the infamous Jez>

<And?>

<It was really, really hard not to punch him in the face>

<Feel free>

<Nothing like I expected. He can go on a bit, can't he?>

<That's him all right, as boring as shite. Nah. Ignore me, he's ok>

<Wow. You have changed your tune!>

<I know. Call me Mr Magnanimous>

<Best get back. They'll think I've fallen in>

I'd just sat back down at the table, when my phone trembled. I almost ignored it – assumed it must be Nick, unable to resist sending through a Jez-themed snark attack after all.

'Get it, Bee,' Nicolas said. 'It might be your client.'

'No. That can wait, I don't want to be rude.'

'We don't mind, right Jez?'

Jez shrugged. 'Knock yourself out.'

So I did, and it took everything I had to hide my reaction to Kat's response: <Tell your friend to STAY THE FUCK AWAY>

NICK

Monday arrived, Becca didn't. I waited until one, me: worried; the dogs: bereft at missing out on their usual hour of tummy tickles and treats.

We didn't have each other's contact details, so for all I knew, she hadn't shown up because Scarlett was sick. Or the darker possibility, that Benedict hadn't bought the same-sexer bullshit, picked up on the chemistry between us, and had locked her away like a princess in a sleekly designed eco minimalist tower.

Despite Bee's best efforts to press Kat for further details, that ominous F-bomb phrase was all she wrote. Praying that showing up wouldn't make things worse, I detoured to Wilderville instead of returning to The Bergs. Double-checking that Benedict's slick-mobile wasn't in the driveway or garage, I knocked on the door. Nothing. I tried the side gate, but that was locked. The cladding on the front of the house gave nothing away: if windows are the eyes of an interior, these were firmly shut.

I doubted it was the type of place where people were neighbourly – the houses were practically sealed off from one another – but on the off-chance, I went over to the mini-mansion opposite (the one I'd been lurking outside when I'd first seen Becca), and rang the bell.

A woman who could have been a wealthy Lily clone peered out at me. 'What religion are you peddling, young man? Because before you start, I'm the chairperson of the Atheists' League.'

'Good for you. I was wondering if you knew if your neighbours across the way had gone away?'

'Why would I know that?'

'Because you're . . . neighbourly?'

'And what business is it of yours if they have or haven't?'

'I'm friends of theirs. Of Becca's. We usually meet at the park, only she didn't show up today.'

She looked as if she were about to say, *Likely story, a scruff like you, friends with* her*?* but then Rosie, picking up on the Lily vibes, went into full cutesy begging mode. On her haunches, paw up.

The woman softened. '*What* a sweetheart.' Good old Rosie.

'Scarlett – Becca's daughter – taught her how to do that.'

'How charming. I can tell you that she's definitely home. I saw her entering the house half an hour ago while I was checking on the azaleas.'

'And beautiful they are too. You've a lovely garden here.'

'Yes, isn't it nice.'

After ten minutes of further chit-chat and a promise to read the Atheists' League pamphlet that she thrust into my hands, I managed to escape and crossed back to the house, where I knocked again. Rosie, doing her bit once more, scrabbled on the door, scratching the reclaimed teak or whatever it was. I ended up shouting, 'Becca!' like a nutjob.

This did the trick, as she finally slipped outside, shutting the door behind her. Physically she looked fine, albeit as tense as hell.

'We waited for you at the park. I was worried about you.'

'I'm fine.'

'And Scarlett?'

'She's fine too.'

'So why didn't you show?'

'I thought it best we not see each other again.' Said in a monotone, without looking me in the eye.

'Did he tell you not to?'

'No.'

'Does he hurt you, Becca?'

'No! And anyway, that's none of your business.'

'You looked scared of him when I was at the house.'

'I'm not scared. He's . . . Scarlett needs her dad. And I like you, Nick. I do. But I can't . . . even if I wanted to . . . I can't.'

'But we can be friends, can't we?'

'No. You know and I know where that will end up.'

And what's wrong with that? 'If he doesn't make you happy, why do you stay?'

Then she shut the door in my face.

BEE

After sending message after message asking for more details, the last one a simple, plaintive <PLEASE>, Kat finally got back to me. <Are you a journalist?>

Thrown by this, I responded that I was a concerned friend and a fellow designer and sent her links to my website. After more back and forth-ing, she eventually agreed to meet me <but you'd better be who you say you are>.

Cancelling my afternoon fittings, I made my way to the address she'd sent through, a coffee bar in Shoreditch that reminded me of Satchel Man's restaurant. I didn't recognise her at first, so different did she look from the photographs I'd seen of her online. A beanie hat and baggy parka instead of the envy-making gender-neutral chic suits and trademark asymmetrical haircut.

'Kat?'

A sharp nod. An assessment. 'Sit.'

I sat.

'What made you reach out to me? Or, to put it another way, what was it about Benedict that set the alarm bells ringing?'

And here I was again, in half-truth bullshit land. There was something of Leila's sharpness about her; I'd need to watch my step. 'As I said in my first e-mail, my friend has a history of bad relationships, of choosing men who aren't what you'd call good for her. I just wanted to check Benedict was kosher, because to be frank, when I met him, he seemed to be too good to be true.'

A snort. 'Yeah. He can be a charming bastard when he wants to be.'

'And when I got your response, I encouraged her to steer clear, but she hasn't. It's not just her either, but her daughter.'

A breathy, 'Oh fucking hell.' Then, 'Your instincts about him are correct.'

'How bad are we talking?'

'Bad.'

She told me that when she met him, it had unfurled like a fairy tale at first. She, the penniless wannabe-designer from a working-class family, he the heartbroken widower, philanthropist, and heir to a fortune: 'Mostly made off the backs of slaves of course, but whoever mentions *that*?'

'I hope you don't mind me saying this, but he doesn't look like your type.'

'He isn't. But like I said, I was trying to get started, and you know how difficult that can be. And here he was, Mr fucking Rochester.'

The other tragic literary hero. Or monster, depending on how you looked at it.

'How *did* you meet?'

'I won a Mercer award. And sure, it's not ethical for the patron to fuck the recipients, but hey, who doesn't like a bit of sneaking around? And then there's the money of course, which blinds you. Holidays, clothes, houses, all that empty crap. It's just . . . it just wrong-foots you at first. Sucks you in. The thing about Ben, he doesn't use a hammer, he uses very fine sandpaper. Takes his time. No physical violence, but a subtle undermining of your confidence. A subtle control. Textbook really. You know the gaslighting score – we all do. Isolates you from your friends and family, so you make him your whole world, and all the while dangling the "I'm going to make you a household name!" carrot. And yeah, like pretty much everyone who goes through this, I was certain it wouldn't happen to me. But it did.' She paused. 'His big thing was trying to get me pregnant.' I went cold. Properly cold. 'That's the ultimate control, right? Barefoot and pregnant in the kitchen. Collateral as well when the kid comes along.'

'What made you finally leave?'

'I was lucky, one of my mates saw through his crap, staged his own intervention. Helped me get away. But that's when it gets really dangerous. When you leave. He tried to destroy my reputation and career, but at least I got away with my life. Alina, his ex, wasn't so lucky.'

The cold turned into ice. 'But that was an accident, wasn't it?'

Long pause. 'If I tell you this, you can't say anything. Not to anyone. Not even to your friend.' She made a nest with her hands and squeezed. 'After I . . . got away, I reached out to Alina's family in the States. The story was that she'd taken a few too many tranquillisers, slipped, banged her head and drowned in the bath. What wasn't put out in the media was that she was about to file for divorce, and according to her family, she wasn't on any medication. They don't believe it was an accident.'

'Oh shit.'

'That's why I asked if you were a journalist. The family have been pushing for Alina's death to be re-investigated, and for another autopsy to be conducted. It was hush-hush at the time because of who he is. And I'm not the only one who got out. There are others like me out there. But if we have any hope of bringing this to light, to prove a pattern of behaviour, he can't know, not yet. He won't get away with this, I promise. But until then, do whatever you can to keep your friend and her daughter away from him.'

Self-realisation. Self-actualisation. Language straight out of those crappy self-help books I used to semi-read. But it turns out they were right: figuring out – no, confronting – who you really are, what you're capable of and not capable of is a game-changer. I'd read the books, I'd seen the campaigns, I thought I understood why someone seemingly intelligent would continue to stay with an abusive partner; and like Kat, I was certain it *wouldn't happen to me*. But it had. It had happened to both of us. It *was* happening.

But never again. Not to me, not to Becca, and absolutely not to Scarlett. My daughter in another world. The daughter who I'd tried and tried not to think about. Tried not to feel anything about, but deep down, did: a fierce protectiveness. She was *my* daughter too.

*

From: NB26@zone.com
To: Bee1984@gmail.com

Shit. SHIT

From: Bee1984@gmail.com
To: NB26@zone.com

Yeah. Shit

From: NB26@zone.com
To: Bee1984@gmail.com

She basically said he's a murderer?

From: Bee1984@gmail.com
To: NB26@zone.com

Possibly. But he's one hundred per cent a dangerous, controlling bastard.

From: NB26@zone.com
To: Bee1984@gmail.com

What if he's different in this world? Nature versus nurture? Look at us. In your world I'm a best-selling author.

From: Bee1984@gmail.com
To: NB26@zone.com

You're a best-selling author in your world too, remember? And you're not that different. Nicolas has the same insecurities as you – if not more.

It's not worth the risk. And even if he isn't the monster he is here, he's bad enough, isn't he? From what you've told me, she's only staying with him because of Scarlett. You have to get Becca and Scarlett away from him – and without him knowing.

From: NB26@zone.com
To: Bee1984@gmail.com

How? I can't kidnap her. She doesn't want to see me, Bee.

From: Bee1984@gmail.com
To: NB26@zone.com

Would she see Leila?

NICK

Bee was right. We'd have a better chance if Leila 2 were on side. We discussed at length the best way to go about this, eventually coming to the conclusion that the only option was to tell her the truth. The whole truth. Seeing as I'd already lied to her twice, and she thought I was Becca's long-lost same-sexer college pal, our chances were slim that she'd give me enough airtime to unspool the whole sorry mess. I tried to mentally rehearse it, even thought about going over it with Laurel or Hardy as a trial run to see if I could convince either of them that '*other worlds do exist, guys, and here's how I know for sure*'.

Oh, for the faith and certainty of a Berenstain.

Rather than calling Leila or attempting to inveigle my way into her office again, I channelled my inner Geoffrey and hung around outside her building. Classy. Not stalkerish at all. And uncomfortable. There was a bite in the air that evening, and her block was a strict no smoking zone.

<I might need you on this, Bee>

<I'm here. Just so you know, Nicolas is here too, but I'll tell him I have a client consultation>

Bloody Nicolas. *We mustn't have* him *inconvenienced, must we?*

At around seven – and just as I was about to head home and write the whole thing off as a bad job – she finally emerged.

Buttoning her coat and walking at a fast clip, I had to jog to catch up with her. 'Buy you a drink?'

She paused and looked me up and down. 'Did Becca send you?'

'In a way. Look, first up you should know that I haven't been entirely truthful with you about my relationship to Becca, but I wouldn't be here if it wasn't really important. Just one drink. That's all I'm asking.'

I was treated to an intense, eye-piercing gaze: what Bee had termed Leila's 'Paddington stare'. 'One. And you're buying.'

We found an old-school pub hidden down a side street and, after ordering our drinks, made for a table at the back.

'Well? This had better be good.'

I'd only have one shot at this: it *had* better be good. 'I'm about to tell you things that are going to be very difficult to believe. You are going to think that I'm crazy. I won't blame you for that. If, at any stage, you feel like telling me to fuck off, I will leave and you will never hear from me again.' Did I sound like I was spouting movie dialogue? Oh yes. Was there any other way of saying it? Nope. And it seemed to work.

'Okay, now I'm intrigued.'

It took two bottles of wine (red, so I wouldn't be getting much sleep that night). She listened. And listened. What I'd envisaged her doing – storming out, chucking wine in my face, calling the mental health association – didn't happen. At one point (while I was telling her about meeting Becca for the first time in the park), we had to stop to order some food. One of those mundane things you never expect to happen in high-stress convoluted situations like this.

'So that's it. Bee – *my* Bee, not your Becca – is convinced that Benedict is dangerous. She's convinced Becca has to get away from him.'

'Because of what she knows about it from her . . . what do you call it? Her world? Reality?'

'Yeah. "World" works. Call it whatever you like. And we can't do that without your help.'

A long silence. 'Can I see the i-mails?'

'You mean . . . mine and Bee's?'

'Obviously.'

I'd been here before with the Berenstains. Who could forget the exquisite awkwardness of making stilted conversation with Kelvin while Henrietta scrolled through my and Bee's private correspondence? But this was somehow worse. Bee and I had moved on from our strangers on the Arpanet days, and just the thought of Leila sifting through the thread made me feel vulnerable and exposed. Then there were the other areas of my life lurking beneath the phone's (embarrassingly grubby) bio-glass shell. No porn (thank Christ), but my search history was a Google nightmare of *Sabotage* research: 'how to make a garrotte'; 'banned substance glyphosate: can it kill you?'; 'Can you resomate a body at home?' etc. But what choice did I have? Leila wouldn't just take my word for it: she'd need proof. As it usually did in times of moral uncertainty, the phrase 'fuck it' came to the fore.

I opened the thread, handed over the phone and went for a piss while she read it (the fastest piss in history, because on top of the other uncertainties, I was hit with the irrational paranoia that she'd run off with the phone while I was gone).

When I returned, she was still there, scrolling through the messages, her expression inscrutable. When I opened my mouth to speak, she held up a hand. 'Wait.'

I waited. And waited. I bought us another bottle of red. One of Bee's catchphrases: *I'll sleep when I'm dead.*

Finally, she handed it back. 'This is . . .'

'Insane? Impossible? Batshit crazy with mind-fuck sprinkles?'

'It really is. I really, really want to tell you to fuck off and that you're crazy.' She sighed, dragged a hand through her hair. 'But I believe you.'

'Really?'

'Why would you construct such an elaborate story? It doesn't make sense. And those i-mails . . . They sound like my Becca. Before . . . you know.' She sat back in her chair. 'Your Bee is always talking about "Leila". That's me, right?'

'Right.'

'So? Go on. Tell me about me.'

'What do you want to know?'

'Everything.'

It was only later, when Bee and I had time to do an autopsy, that she said she wished she'd thought to warn me that there were things that Leila 2 might prefer not to hear. Oblivious to this, I spilled the beans. But it wasn't all on Bee: sensitivity radar blunted by booze, tactful I was not.

'Hang on . . . I have twins? *Twins*?'

'Yes.'

'Twins. Bloody hell.' She breathed in deeply. Exhaled. Flapped a hand in front of her face. 'And a husband.'

'Yes. His name's Lev.'

'Lev. Wait . . . Lev Ali?' I nodded. 'Jesus. I broke up with him years ago. Always wondered if that was the right decision.' She knocked back half a glass. By now, the edges of her mouth and teeth were stained with tannin: mine were too. We resembled booze-raddled vampires.

'Twins. Christ alive.' She reached for the bottle again.

Change the subject. 'Leila – did you fall out with Becca because of Benedict?'

'Partly. I told her not to marry the bastard. She did it anyway. I just couldn't watch.'

'Is he physically abusive?'

'Not that I know of. More controlling. As if he's . . . hoovering up her spark. Thing is, I know what Becca wants. Stability. Someone to love. She doesn't want to fail. Not like her parents did.' She slapped the table. 'I want to talk to her.'

'Great. That's why I came to you. We need you in on this, Leila.'

'No. I mean I want to talk to *your* Becca.'

BEE

Midnight. Nicolas was snoozing stock-still next to me, his left arm draped over my waist. On the nightstand my phone buzzed. Then buzzed again. I opened up the thread. Against all the odds, Nick had managed to get Leila 2 on side, and she wanted to talk to me.

I gently disentangled myself and slipped out of bed.

'Where you going?' Groggy. Mussed hair. His sleep face.

'Leila's having a crisis.'

'Can I help?'

'Nah. It's not that serious. Go back to sleep.'

He flopped back down.

Without bothering to get dressed, I padded through to the work-table and Clarice, tapping as I went.

<How much does she know, Nick?>

<Everything>

<Does she have kids in your world?>

<No>

Then: *oh shit*. <Does she know about her other self? Does she know about the twins?>

<Yes>

Oh Leila. Stupid of me not to have thought of this before. Stupid of me not to have warned Nick to keep this potentially wounding information to himself. My Leila had gone through agonies as round after round of IVF had failed. It had almost broken her: 'I know that this world is a fucked-up place and I shouldn't bring a child into it. I know this, Bee. I know it seems irrational. I just can't stop thinking about it. I can't stop the longing.' Had Leila 2 gone through – or was she going through – the same agonies? Back in our note-comparing days, Nick had told me about the Attenborough Accords – a series of humanitarian and environmental laws designed to protect women's reproductive rights, incentivising vasectomies as a form of birth control and promoting smaller families. And hadn't he also mentioned that IVF was out of reach for those who weren't obscenely rich?

<Handing you over now>

My fingers were trembling. Gooseflesh on my arms. And not just from the chill in the air. A *buzz* as her first message came in: <Tell me something to prove it's really you>

I shook out my fingers. <About me or you? Because we're the same but not the same if you get what I mean>

<Both>

<OK. Me: mashed potato makes me gag. You: you were born with a caul that your mum kept, dried out and once took out to show a boyfriend & he threw up when he realised what it was> Nothing. I counted to thirty. <Did the boyfriend caul thing happen in your world too?>

<Yes. Only he didn't puke, he just ran a mile>

<Acne Face and Fatty Boom Boom ring a bell?>

<God yeah. But Ms Dennis put a stop to it>

<In my world she didn't>

<What a bloody cow!>

<Do you believe it?>

<I do. And I don't. I want to>

<I get it>

<SO>

<So. I asked the Other You what would make you fall out with me>

<And>

<She said if I killed a child>

<Ha! Turns out that you didn't need to do anything near as drastic. I didn't fall out with you exactly. After I gave you my real

opinion about Benedict, you pushed me away. I let myself be pushed>

<Why?>

Nothing again for a while, then: <Because when I found out you were pregnant it hurt. I'd had the tests, knew that wasn't an option for me. I didn't want to be around you for a while. Shitty person, huh?>

<No. Not shitty at all. You went through the same thing here. The same pain. How much do you want me to tell you?>

<I don't know. Oh fuck it. Am I a good mum?>

<The best> Think, think: would it better or worse for her if she thought her alternative self lived a life of fulfilled, kiddified joy? Worse. Definitely. <Giving up work to look after the kids was a real nightmare for you though. And the twins can be a right handful>

<I gave up work?>

<You did. Almost killed you>

<And am I really married to Lev Ali?>

<Yes>

<Happily?>

<Yes> *Kind of*. <Hearing this, are you OK? I'm sorry it's a shock>

<Shock is an understatement. But yeah. I'm okay. Came to terms with it all a while back. It'll always hurt, but it's not fatal>

<Nick says you're killing it professionally. Top of your game>

<Did he? It's so strange thinking of him talking to you about me>

<Strange is an understatement ☺>

<He says you're killing it professionally too>

<Did something happen to the other me, Leila? To make me . . . different?>

<Like what?>

I didn't know how to word it without sounding insensitive. <When I got pregnant in my world, it didn't occur to me to go through with it. She did>

<Yeah, but it was a struggle for her>

<What made her change her mind? Was it him? Did he pressure her into it?>

<To be honest, I think it was me. I think she thought that if I couldn't have my own child, at least I could act as a proxy mum or aunt to hers. Only that backfired on both of us when I couldn't handle it. Which played into Benedict's hands. He must have been delighted when her mouthy mate left the scene>

The *relief* that it was entirely Becca's choice to fall pregnant, albeit partly motivated by concern for her best friend. Would I have done the same for my Leila if there was no chance she could get pregnant? Honestly? I love her, but I don't think I would. <Nothing else? Anything traumatic?>

<Like what?>

The things that had been going through my mind . . . endless, really. The things that had happened to me: going through with sex with a pushy guy in college because it was easier than saying no. Satchel Man. What countless women go through every day. Nate. <Not sure>

<Her mum's death really messed her up>

<Messed me up too>

<And she had a bad break up just before she hooked up with Benedict. Broke her heart>

<It wasn't Nate was it? Nathan Ellis>

<No. One of the designers she worked with. Jackson somebody? I wasn't a fan of him either but compared to Benedict he's a saint>

Click. Nate-Gate had made me relationship-phobic. Becca had gone the opposite route when her heart had been smashed – found someone who, on paper, screamed security and stability. (Oh the irony: who would have thought a dating app and a series of soulless one-night-stands would be safer than hooking up with a philanthropist?)

<Have you told your version of Nick the truth?>

<No. Meant to, but it's gone too far for that>

<Have you told your version of ME what's going on?>

<No>

<Why?>

<You have enough on your plate without dealing with some

insane Quantum Anomaly love triangle shit. And to be honest, I knew you wouldn't approve of what we're doing. You'd think it was manipulative. *I* think it's manipulative, only I don't think I could stop it now if I tried>

<Love. It fucks you up>

That was such a Leila-ism it made me smile. <It really does>

<And I don't approve. I do think it's manipulative and a bit like you're grooming your other selves. But I can see why you're doing it. Nick really loves you, you know. I hardly know him but I can see that>

<I know. Just like I know he should be with Becca>

<Because it's working out with his other self and you?>

A chance to confide in Leila – or a version of Leila. A chance to air the doubts I couldn't share with anyone else. But this wasn't about me. The priority here was Becca and Scarlett. I let it pass. <Yes>

Then, on to business: Operation Becca and Scarlett.

*

From: NB26@zone.com
To: Bee1984@gmail.com

Well she didn't leave immediately when she saw me, which is something. Got the dogs and Scarlett to thank for that. I had my doubts, but an ambush at the park might just work.

From: Bee1984@gmail.com
To: NB26@zone.com

What are they doing now?

From: NB26@zone.com
To: Bee1984@gmail.com

Leila's still doing most of the talking. Becca looks seriously pissed off. Can't hear what they're saying.

From: Bee1984@gmail.com
To: NB26@zone.com

I keep trying to imagine how I'd feel if I was hit up with that story.

From: NB26@zone.com
To: Bee1984@gmail.com

You were. And you handled it. Hang on, Scarlett wants me to make mud pies. BRB.

From: NB26@zone.com
To: Bee1984@gmail.com

Still talking. Wait. Leila's coming over.

From: NB26@zone.com
To: Bee1984@gmail.com

Becca's not buying it. On the verge of leaving. Listen to me, Bee. We might only get one shot at this. You need to have a word with yourself.

BEE

<And make it quick. We don't have long. Write something. Anything you think will help>

A word with myself. Talking to Leila 2 was one thing. Talking to Becca . . . Back in the Nate days, when I was in full denial, what would have made the scales fall from my eyes? *Think, think, think*.

Zapped out of these thoughts by: '*Bastard*.' I'd been so absorbed in the unfolding drama, I'd half-forgotten Nicolas was in the room, sitting at his usual place at the breakfast bar with his laptop (he'd come down a day earlier than usual, which, if it weren't for my current alternative-world concerns, I would have appreciated).

'What?'

'Shitty review on Amazon. Not only a one-star rating, but full of spoilers as well.'

'Is that all?' *Because* I *have to somehow come up with the right thing to say in order to convince a version of myself to leave a toxic and dangerous relationship*. It came out as snappish, dismissive.

'Thanks for the support, Bee. And who are you messaging anyway? You've been at it for hours. It's not Nate again, is it?'

'Of course it's bloody not. I'm not the one who can't stay away from Twitter and Googles himself non-fucking-stop.'

That was so unlike me, Ms Confrontation Avoider, that it shocked both of us. Our first fight. Bad timing.

'I'm going out for a walk.'

'Good idea.'

He slammed the laptop shut and stormed out.

I shrugged off the shame. There wasn't time to do anything other than go for it:

Becca. I know how hard this is for you to believe. I've been there. I promise I'm not messing with you. I'm you. In another world. Living a different life. And a GOOD one. You could have that too.

I don't know how to prove this. What can I say that will make you believe it? There are things that will have happened to me and not to you. But here goes:

You bite your nails but never down to the quick so that no one notices.

You sucked your thumb until you were 12.

If someone strokes your hair it makes you cry because that's how Mum used to soothe me to sleep. I hope she did that for you too. I still have her dress form (I call her Clarice, I don't know why).

One of our breasts is bigger than the other and this used to make us as self-conscious as hell.

I get why you are with Benedict. Like you I had my heart smashed. Only after that I went the opposite route to you. Avoided commitment, avoided relationships, thought I'd cut that part of my life out of me like a tumour. Until I met Nick and everything changed.

But I didn't have a child. You do. I get that you want security for Scarlett after what we went through. After what Dad did to Mum. After the arguments, the constant arguments, hiding in your room and pretending it wasn't happening. The relief when Dad finally left, but the sorrow too.

I get why you let yourself be drawn in by a man who on the surface promised SECURITY, STABILITY, everything we didn't have as kids. I get why you avoid conflict. I do that too.

But in my world he's dangerous. In your world he might be dangerous too. Dangerous to you and dangerous to Scarlett.

And you don't like giving up, Becca. But it's OK to do that. You have it in you, I promise.

You don't need to believe any of this. Tell me and Nick and Leila to fuck off. But for Scarlett's sake at the very least PLEASE just look into what we're saying. Talk to his ex-wife. Talk to his ex-partners. Just do this at least.

And Leila needs you. You need her. You don't need to do any of this alone.

DON'T WAIT

Without reading it back – there wasn't time – I pressed SEND.

And waited.

*

From: Bee1984@gmail.com
To: NB26@zone.com

And? Did she read it?

From: NB26@zone.com
To: Bee1984@gmail.com

She read it. Then she handed the phone back and walked away.

NICK

As the days of radio silence rolled into a week, then another, I had Nicolas to thank for taking the edge off the increasing worry about Becca and Scarlett. He was well into writing *A Shot in the Dark*, (<He's even using the same title>) and Bee had got into the habit of feeding me snippets regarding the direction in which he was planning to take it. I would spend hours raging with righteous anger when she revealed a plot route that diverged from the original (<the saboteur CAN'T be a bastion of morality! Can't he see that makes him one-dimensional? TELL HIM NO>).

Speaking of morality (or amorality – which so often characterised our dealings with quantum fuck-up land), Bee was clearly struggling with the guilt of going behind Nicolas's back, but she'd intuited I needed something other than my own writing to channel my anxiety (in case *Sabotage* turned into self-sabotage, no doubt), and this trumped her feelings of disloyalty. (<And hey, it IS kind of like the two of you are collaborating, Nick>)

Then, Leila 2 finally called with news.

'Did it work?'

'It worked.'

Leila 2 revealed that Becca had reached out to Maria, Benedict's ex-wife, who was working as a costume designer in New York. Maria had refused to talk to her, which raised enough of a red flag for Becca to track down Maria's sister. The sister confirmed our worst fears – that when Maria finally attempted to leave Benedict, he'd gone on the offensive, threatening to destroy her career and worse. Maria had been forced to 'go into virtual hiding' and was genuinely in fear of her life. The inference was that he'd only stopped this campaign when he'd found a new victim – Becca. But because Benedict was smart enough and paranoid enough to cover his tracks, other than hearsay, there was no concrete proof of this behaviour – certainly not enough to bring a criminal case. And it was the age-old story: he was the one with the money and the power.

But it was enough to convince Becca to get out of Dodge.

Leila 2 had contacted Lev, who'd agreed to take on the case. However, they'd have to play it carefully. Especially because in this world Benedict had a daughter. *Daddy's little girl.* Collateral. 'Lev says we'll need time to build a case against him, in case he pushes for custody. Time to dig around for other possible victims.'

To that end, they'd come up with a plan. Becca had reconnected with her estranged father, who, semi-mirroring his Australian ex-pat self in Bee's world, was living in New Zealand. He'd jumped at the chance to reconcile (<I bet he did, the guilt-ridden bastard>) and offered to do anything he could to help. That 'anything' involved him saying that he was seriously ill, possibly terminal, and desperately wanted to mend ties with Becca and his only grandchild before it was too late. (<Smart. Who came up with that, Nick?> <Becca, I think>) Benedict could hardly refuse that request. And it would give Becca the perfect excuse to extend the trip if necessary.

Then: 'She wants to see you, Nick. She says you'll know where.'

When I saw her, waiting at our bench, the usual butterfly effect fluttered in, but it was *lesser*. Fainter. It was clear from her body language, buttoned up, tense, that she felt much the same way.

Scarlett ran up and gave me a hug. 'Doggy Man! I'm going on an airplane.'

'I know.' A lump in my throat: that sad old clichéd daydream of being part of their lives was over, too.

We waited until the trio had decamped to the grass.

A tepid *how are you?* didn't seem like the right thing to say. 'It's good to see you, Becca.'

'You too.' Flat.

'When are you leaving?'

'On Friday.' Top-tug. Hair-pull. 'I feel like a spy. Lying to Ben, leaving all this. And going to Dad's as well. Who thought *that* would ever happen.'

'It's not forever.'

'It feels like it is. Ben won't stop. He'll want to win.'

'Leila and Lev won't let that happen. It'll give you all some breathing room.'

'What a mess. Remember when you asked me if I was happy?'

'Oh yes. The most facile question in the world. Sorry about that.'

'Don't be. I was happy at first. Kept telling myself if I just stuck it out, I'd be happy again. That it would get better. I'm such a bloody idiot. I feel so *stupid*.'

'You're not stupid. You're anything but stupid. You mustn't blame yourself. Hey, I stayed in a marriage for at least five years longer than I should.'

A shadow of a smile: 'I know. Poor you and *Jez*.'

'And really, you have to trust me on this, there's a better life waiting for you out there. There's proof of that. Leila told you that, right? She told you everything. Bee told you that.'

'Proof. *Proof*. There's a big part of me that can't believe I'm actually buying into any of this.' She shivered. Rubbed her arms. 'I . . . I suppose I should thank you, but at first, all I felt was anger. No, fury. I was furious with you. Furious with Leila. Furious with . . . *her*.'

The way she said *her*, stuck with me for a long time afterwards. There was an edge to it that I related to – an echo of the resentment I'd felt towards Nicolas. 'Yeah, well. I don't blame you. It must have felt like the world's most insane intervention. I don't blame you for not believing us. Long as you know, I'm here for you. I'll always be here for you. The dogs, too.'

'I can't see you anymore, Nick.'

'I get that, Bee,' – she winced at that, *shit* – 'Becca, I mean. You must have a ton of stuff to organise.'

'No. I mean, ever. If – when – I come back. This thing . . . this thing that's happening. Whether I believe it or not, it's not right what you're doing. You and . . . *her*. You know that, right? It's manipulative. You must see that. She must too.'

Manipulative. The same word Bee had used right at the start. Only now it was coming from the other side of the mirror. It had the intended effect: one of those sobering, shame-filled wake-up calls. 'I'm sorry.' Lame, but all I could manage.

'It's not just that. I did have feelings for you. You know I did, even if I did try and fight them. Even if we could be together – and I won't lie and say that I haven't thought about that, *imagined* that – I can't. I don't want to think that there may be a world out there in which Scarlett doesn't exist. And you would always remind me of that.' She squeezed my hand, which, like the rest of me, was numb. 'You get that, right?'

'I get it.' And I did. Of course I did. *Dylan*.

'I'm going to say goodbye now.' She wrapped her arms around me, and I pulled her in close. It felt different this time. Like embracing a friend, not a lover. We stayed like that for a long time. 'Thank you for what you did, Nick. And think about what I said.' She stepped back, turned away, let out a shaky sigh, then, with artificial brightness, told Scarlett it was home time. I played along, trilling, 'Adios, Scarlett!' as if it were just another day. As if I'd be seeing her tomorrow.

'Adios amigo! Bye Sawsage. Bye Rosie.'

I watched them go. Mourning them and yet . . . there was no magical strand connecting me to Becca like there was with Bee. An attraction, sure, a chemistry, but not that.

*

From: Bee1984@gmail.com
To: NB26@zone.com

You saved me, Nick. Becca, I mean. And Scarlett. You saved all of us.

From: NB26@zone.com
To: Bee1984@gmail.com

YOU saved you. With help from Leila 2, and your dad. I know you don't have a high opinion of him, but it sounds like he really stepped up.

From: Bee1984@gmail.com
To: NB26@zone.com

Yeah. I know. I really want to believe he's doing it because he genuinely cares, and not just because he likes the thought of playing the hero. But either way, what counts is that he *did* step up and Becca and Scarlett are out of Benedict's clutches. And whatever you say, if it wasn't for you, they'd still be there.

From: NB26@zone.com
To: Bee1984@gmail.com

There's a long road to go yet, Bee. Benedict won't just walk away.

From: Bee1984@gmail.com
To: NB26@zone.com

I know. But there's hope at least. Lev's a good lawyer. The best.

And it means she'll eventually be free. A long wait for you, I know, but Operation Doppelganger lives to fight another day!

From: NB26@zone.com
To: Bee1984@gmail.com

It doesn't, Bee. My side of that has crashed and burned. Becca made that very clear to me.

From: Bee1984@gmail.com
To: NB26@zone.com

She's only saying that because she needs time to regroup.

From: NB26@zone.com
To: Bee1984@gmail.com

No. She meant it. She said what we were doing was manipulative – sound familiar? She said she didn't want to imagine a world in which Scarlett doesn't exist, and I would always remind her of that.

From: Bee1984@gmail.com
To: NB26@zone.com

I know myself, Nick. I can be stubborn, not see things clearly at the time. She'll get there, I promise.

From: NB26@zone.com
To: Bee1984@gmail.com

It's not just from her side, Bee. There was something there at the beginning, but it's run its course.

From: Bee1984@gmail.com
To: NB26@zone.com

What do you mean? You don't find her attractive anymore?

From: NB26@zone.com
To: Bee1984@gmail.com

It's not that. I've let her go, and it's for the best. And I'm fine about it. I really am.

From: Bee1984@gmail.com
To: NB26@zone.com

That's only because you've never had a chance to be together. I had the same struggles with Nicolas. I told you that.

There's still some hope, right?

From: NB26@zone.com
To: Bee1984@gmail.com

No. But hey, one out of two ain't bad.

From: Bee1984@gmail.com
To: NB26@zone.com

I don't get it. How can you let her go so easily? I mean, she's ME. Sort of. And I don't care how insecure and needy that makes me sound.

From: NB26@zone.com
To: Bee1984@gmail.com

It's the 'sort of' that's the clincher though, isn't it? She is you, but not you.

From: Bee1984@gmail.com
To: NB26@zone.com

What are we going to do about this? Me still being with Nicolas, how is that fair?

From: NB26@zone.com
To: Bee1984@gmail.com

If you say that word one more time, I'm going to send you nothing but inspirational quotes for a week.

I'll be fine, Bee. I swear on Rosie's life. I'm going to put my head down and write. I'm ok. I really am.

PART FIVE

LOVE ACTUALLY SUCKS

NICK

It worked – for a while. The writing I mean.

I got lost in it. Absorbed. To the extent that I'd occasionally get irritated if Bee messaged me during what I thought of as 'work time'. *Bet you don't interrupt Nicolas when* he's *writing*. The word count rose steadily, sometimes as if it were doing so of its own accord. Tweedy would check in every so often – I was becoming increasingly fond of the old bugger – and I'd throw him a bone and give him small research tasks to do, which I hoped made him feel like it was his project too.

And I stuck to my routine. Including taking the dogs to the park, although I avoided our bench – seeing it without them still gave me a lurch. The dogs missed Becca and Scarlett, too. It took weeks before they stopped tugging on their leads, attempting to pull me in our usual direction. Leila 2 sent me updates every now and again: they'd managed to extend their trip, giving Lev the lawyer more time to gather ammo for when Benedict clocked what was going on and attacked. Because he *would* attack. Leila 2 also let slip that she and Lev were seeing each other again. *Look at me: Nick the matchmaker*.

Once a week, I sent Geoffrey updates on his daughter and granddaughter. Once a week I checked in with Lily (a chore I had to steel myself for – the old bag was getting crankier by the day). Every so often I traded banter with Dylan, but while it was easy to lie to Lily on the rare occasions she asked about my 'fancy woman' and trot out vagaries in response, I couldn't do that to

Dylan – bad enough I'd been feeding him half-truths for months, painting a picture of a woman who was more Bee in essence than Becca. Plus, Dylan had been there (almost) at the start. Had encouraged me to take the jump and meet Bee in person; donated his holiday allowance to facilitate my makeover and tweed-suit shopping. He was invested in us on some level, and fully expected to meet Becca/Bee at some point. So the whole truth was out, but I stuck as closely to it as I could.

'New Zealand? But she'll be back, right?'

'No. The work placement is permanent and neither of us would be any good at a long-distance relationship.' *Fuck's* sakes *Nick*.

'You didn't think of moving out there with her?'

'I did, but there's Rosie to consider and the spiders out there are fucking huge apparently, so I thought, nah. It was getting close to running its course anyway, if I'm honest.'

'Are you sure you're okay? You know you don't have to put on a front with me, right? If you want to have a cry or whatever, go for it.'

Oh, Dylan . . . 'I'm over the worst of it, but thanks. Now, that's enough shite from me, what happened with that artist you discovered? The dairy activist one who does those creepy cow-human hybrid sculptures. Those pics you sent through still give me nightmares . . .'

Shortly after that, Poll shit-sandwiched me with a message saying that the house sale was going through, to look out for the divorce papers, and that I'd receive my share of the house cash in a matter of weeks.

And every day I resolved to attempt to divorce myself from Bee as her attachment to Nicolas grew. And failed.

Then, within weeks of each other, came two unexpected routine-breaking occurrences.

I came down to breakfast one morning to find the table empty for once. Laurel and Hardy always arrived before I did, at seven on the dot.

'Where are they?'

Erika shrugged. 'Gone. They left last night.'

'Why?'

'Their contract was over.'

In the entire time I'd lived there, other than a 'morning' at breakfast, or a 'hey' if I passed them on the stairs, we'd barely interacted. Occasionally a faint giggle would float from behind Hardy's door, but other than that they were so unobtrusive that I'd come to regard them as little more than background fixtures, like the laminated signs and Petrus's wall of fame. Yet I missed them to a surprising degree.

For a few days, Erika, the dogs and I rattled around by ourselves. This should have added an extra layer of awkwardness, but having fewer people to boss around seemed to loosen her up. We weren't becoming mates as such; we rarely had what you'd call a personal conversation. She'd occasionally ask how the book was coming on; I'd enquire how Petrus was faring, and the breakfast room apart, we tended to keep to our own territories in the house, but she stopped accusing me of house-rule infractions and, every so often, we'd have a drink together. I reckoned the carapace was there to protect her (I'm not a psychologist's arse, but I suspected it began to form after her father's death), and her obsessional need to control her environment was part of that. Then she announced that she'd secured a contract with a local college, and, as the place became a revolving door of visiting professors, students and other weirdos who needed to be corralled and bombarded with passive-aggressive house-rule warnings, she reverted back to her old brittle self.

A week or so after the first new arrival moved in (a student from China, who, to my amusement and Erika's wrath, was in the habit of sneaking down to the fridge in the middle of the night and drinking all the milk) came the second routine-breaker. Erika tapped on my door to inform me, with eloquent surliness, that I had a visitor. Geoffrey was in the lounge, looking as uncomfortable as I'd ever seen him. Erika handed me a large brown envelope ('this came, too'), and with a pointed glance at the 'Visitors must not stay the nite' sign, she left us to it.

'She's a charmer, isn't she?' Geoffrey sniffed within her hearing.

I suggested we take the dogs out for a ramble. As we walked, passers-by giving us a wide berth, I filled him in on the latest intel Bee had gathered from Jenny's social media accounts: a TV show she was watching, a rundown of Megan's first week at school, a new recipe she'd tried. He drank in every detail, however banal. We stopped at a bench for a smoke, and Geoffrey took a couple of cans of cider out of his backpack and handed one over.

'Why have you come here in person, Geoffrey?'

'Thought you might need a drink.'

I hadn't told him that my side of Operation Doppelganger had crashed and burned, but he must have picked up that something was off during our calls. I told him the lot. He listened, drank and smoked, smoked, drank and listened, and when it was over, he said:

'Not surprised the rich fucker turned out to be a wrong'un. Bastard. If I had my way with him his arse would be pigfeed right now.'

'If only.'

'But your lass and her daughter are safe.'

'For now. She doesn't want to see me again though. Or talk to me.'

'Knew something was up with you.' He eyed me. 'You don't look too broke-up about it. Don't sound it, either.'

'Maybe it wasn't meant to be.'

'It was always the other one for you.'

'Yeah. The one I can't have.'

He drained the can, crushed it, lobbed it into a bin, went for another. 'It would help if you came to a meeting.'

'Why? Do they suspect something's up?'

'Just saying it would help is all. Henrietta gave me a right . . . wotsit, grilling about you at the last one.'

'And?'

'I told her you were doing nowt suspicious.'

'That's true enough now, isn't it?'

'Suppose.'

The cider was warm and took the edge off the chill in the air. Sausage let out a sigh and flumped at Geoffrey's feet. He stroked her belly. 'Good girl. Always wanted a dog.'

'So get one.'

'Can't. Move around too much.'

'What do you actually *do*, Geoffrey?' I couldn't believe I hadn't asked him this before.

'What do you mean?'

'Work-wise. Life-wise. You know.'

A shrug. 'Drive around a bit. Sit. Think. Read. I read that book of yours.'

'*A Shot in the Dark*?'

'Eh? Nah. Hang on.' He rooted in his backpack and took out a battered copy of the debut shitpile.

'Where the hell did you find that?'

'Ordered it from one of them . . . specialist bookshops. Didn't cost much, mind. Enjoyed it.'

'You're the only person in the world who did.'

He drained and crushed the second can. At the rate he was knocking them back, he could give Petrus a run for his money. I was still only a third of the way through mine.

'Will you ask your woman something for me?'

'Sure.'

'Can you ask her if I was in a coma before I pegged it?'

'Why do you want to know that?'

He didn't answer immediately. 'Just wondered. Been thinking about death lately, what it means, all that.' Later, I'd weigh this up; it hadn't quite rung true at the time, but I'd let it go.

'You were. Jenny told Bee she remembered visiting you in hospital. I didn't tell you before because I reckoned finding out you were a goner was bad enough without going into all the gory details.'

'Right.' He gazed into the distance. By now I was familiar enough with his idiosyncrasies to know that this sometimes signalled an abrupt mood change. He ditched the cig and gave me one of his clumsy hugs. 'When I said I owed you, I meant it. Hang in there.'

*

From: Bee1984@gmail.com
To: NB26@zone.com

What, ALL the milk?

From: NB26@zone.com
To: Bee1984@gmail.com

Yeah. Erika's already working on a new batch of laminated signs regarding dairy produce.

How's Shot in the Dark shaping up?

From: Bee1984@gmail.com
To: NB26@zone.com

Uh-oh nice try. We decided not to do this anymore, remember?

From: NB26@zone.com
To: Bee1984@gmail.com

Please just tell me he's changed his mind about not letting Posho get away with the murder.

From: Bee1984@gmail.com
To: NB26@zone.com

Not. Going. There.

From: NB26@zone.com
To: Bee1984@gmail.com

He hasn't has he? That's the whole point!! That if you have cash and influence you can get away with shit like that.

From: Bee1984@gmail.com
To: NB26@zone.com

I know.

Subject change alert.

From: NB26@zone.com
To: Bee1984@gmail.com

Well how's this? My divorce came through today.

From: Bee1984@gmail.com
To: NB26@zone.com

Oh Nick. How are you feeling?

From: NB26@zone.com
To: Bee1984@gmail.com

Fine. Totally fine. Really. Relieved that Poll can move on more than anything. Don't worry about me, Bee: Monsieur Miserable Bastard is still firmly in his box, I promise.

BEE

If anything, the divorce news, and what it signified, shook me more than it did Nick. *In another life . . .*

But I wasn't living another life. For all intents and purposes, Nicolas had moved in. I don't remember us discussing it, it just happened, as if by osmosis. Bits and pieces of his clothing and belongings melding with mine in the same effortless way that *we* melded.

Once a week Nicolas returned to Leeds for his teaching gig. Wednesday nights were Nick Nights. Nights where I could message him with zero guilt (or just a little). Where I could let go of the paranoia about leaving the Gmail account open. Date Night if that didn't have such awkward connotations. The three of us, our quantum thruple, rambled on: a routine that – for now – was working (even though a member of our threesome was oblivious).

But. BUT. Because there's always a 'but' with me.

Sometimes, while I was working, I found myself compiling PROS and CONS lists in my head, like Leila and I used to do when we fancied some boy or another (or girl when we went through our teenage bi-curious phase):

PROS:

Our sex drives gelled: two or three times a week. I never felt obliged to have what Leila termed 'Maintenance Sex'. (Nate had wanted sex constantly, to the point where I began to dread it.)

He was a domestic god. Took over the Tesco online shop and

never forgot to order things like tampons or toilet paper. Unpacked the dishwasher, my most hated chore.

Could cook (okay, yeah, he only had a repertoire of seven dishes, but they were all delicious and that was three more than me).

Magda liked him. Plus, he'd solved the mystery of the weird Thursday night noises that would float down from her flat. 'Bizarrely, she crushes all their cans before she puts them out for recycling. I think she takes her frustrations out on them.'

Most importantly Leila (and Lev) liked him.

Never commented on my weight.

Never complained when I left my clothes lying on the floor or remarked that my side of the bed resembled a discarded underwear and tissue war zone.

Always hung towels up in the bathroom. Always put the seat down.

Listened to me when I needed to vent about work. And really listened, didn't just pay lip (or ear) service.

Really did treat me as his muse: we could spend hours discussing and debating character traits or plot twists and he never once told me my ideas were shit, even when they clearly were.

Like me preferred to flump in bed and watch crappy box sets rather than go out (he once sat through a *Project Runway* binge session and didn't whinge once).

Was politically engaged. More so than me, which gave me a much-needed kick up the arse.

Was a caffeine psychic: he'd bring me tea or coffee just when I was thinking of getting up and putting the kettle on.

When he was writing, he'd wave a hand or cock his head, as if he were acting out the way one of his characters might move, which I found endearing.

Nick Nights and covert messaging aside, I never felt like I had to watch what I said around him.

He encouraged me, without being pushy or controlling, to farm out some of my finishing work to a seamstress in Hammersmith, which really helped take the strain off.

Even though whole days would go by where we were both so lost in work we barely said a word to each other, he didn't bore me.

If I had a client coming over, he'd decamp to a café, or offer to sit with Jonas so that Magda could have a few hours to herself (that kindness again).

Our first fight was our only fight. When he returned that day, me still shaken by Becca stress, he apologised first even though I was the one in the wrong.

He always smelled nice.

He wasn't tight with cash. Within a week of moving in, he offered to split the rent, despite still paying the mortgage on his own flat.

He made my life . . . *easier*.

CONS:
He wasn't Nick.

That was it. The only CON. It was as if Nick and Bee worked because we had an extra, mystery ingredient that was lacking in the Nicolas and Bee stew-pot: the equivalent of a sprinkling of parsley. An extra clove of garlic. I'd convinced myself the cracks would fade when Becca and Nick closed the circle, and despite this no longer being an option, they *were* fading. But that had never been the real issue. And it was too late to add in that extra seasoning: the meal had already been served.

One CON. Not enough to throw everything away for. We worked on every other level. In every other way. In any other circumstances, it would have been perfect. It *was* perfect.

So, when it happened, I shouldn't have been surprised.

Thursday night was can-crushing night. Nicolas and I had got into the habit of timing Magda as she rolled and stomped. Whoever guessed to the closest minute how long the task would take, would get to choose that evening's Deliveroo order. It had become a silly tradition. But just as she got underway, Nicolas said: 'Get your coat. We're going out.'

'Eh? But it's timing and take-out night. Oh shit . . . do you have a book event or something I've forgotten about?'

He grinned. 'Nope. It's a surprise.'

'I don't like surprises.'

'Yeah, you do.'

I was in my work clothes, makeup-free, a scarf tied, Magda-esque, around my unwashed hair. 'Do I need to get changed?'

'Nope. You'll do. Come on. The Uber is here.'

As the taxi ferried us along, he refused to tell me where we were going. He was thrumming with tension: excitement, and something else.

The cab pulled up outside what I still thought of as Satchel Man's restaurant. 'What the hell are we doing here?'

'It was where we had our first date.' I should have figured it out then. He swept me inside, and to the booth he'd reserved – 'our' booth, opposite that ridiculous elephant head. Instead of lager, he ordered a bottle of champagne.

'What are we celebrating? Did something happen with the book? Were you shortlisted for that Dagger award thingy?'

He took my hands in both of his. 'Bee. I've never felt like this before. What we have – it's rare. I love you.'

'I love you too.' *Did* I though? A question I'd asked myself countless times. Did I love him on his own terms, and not just as a proxy for Nick? They *were* the same, but also not the same. Nicolas was a touch needier. Less cynical, as if Nick had needed to fail and struggle to form that part of his character. Was this the missing ingredient? One CON. ONE.

'What I'm saying in my convoluted way is: will you marry me?'

I told Leila halfway through a gin-walk, dropping the news while we were admiring the Gnome Home's wisteria, which was reaching the end of its summery bloom.

She let out a semi-scream, then said: 'I cannot *believe* you let me bollock on about the twins when you had this news.'

'So? What do you think?'

'Isn't it obvious what I think?' Forgetting she was holding the can of gin, she threw her arms around me, spattering us both with froth. 'Shit. Sorry, Bee. But hey, think of it as poor woman's champagne. Christ. This is fast, isn't it?'

'Yeah. Too fast?'

'Hey, when you know, you know.' She gave me a Leila look. 'And you *do* know, right?'

Yes. No. Maybe. 'I know.'

She assessed me again. But her happiness for me – and herself – overrode her usual perspicacity. A wedding signified an end to her messy friend's messy life. 'I know we're feminists and shouldn't get excited about this stuff, but any thoughts on the wedding?'

'Not yet. But neither of us are into big affairs. The smaller the better.'

'Don't blame you. Mine was a nightmare, remember? Relatives from three continents creeping out of the woodwork like cockroaches. And who could forget the halal fuck-up? Lev's mum still brings it up.'

'It wasn't a nightmare. It was lovely.'

'Yeah well, we're still paying it off, so it bloody well should have been.' She nabbed my can and took a sip. 'But small or not, can I help plan it? Please?'

'Don't you have enough on your plate with the boys and saving the planet?'

'Yeah, but this'll be fun. Please?'

'We haven't even talked dates yet. Probably won't even start doing that until next year.'

'Can I though?'

'Of course. It's all yours. But no Cinderella carriages, butterflies, or doves.'

'How about a trained swan as a ring bearer? Just the one.'

'Fuck off.'

'Spoilsport. What about the dress?'

'Seriously?'

'Oh, humour me.'

'I've still got Mum's.'

'She would have loved that, Bee. And she would have loved Nicolas.'

And Nick. I drained the can to take my mind off meetings that would never happen, in any worlds.

'And kids?'

'The twins are welcome to come.'

'I didn't mean them! Although seriously, if you decided to choose a destination wedding somewhere non-kid-friendly, you'd have my undying gratitude. God, I need a break.'

'What happened to "never flying again" and shrinking your carbon footprint?'

'I'll off-set it. Or you could choose a venue in the UK that hates kids. Anyway, I meant you and Nicolas. You have had the kid talk right?'

'Not yet.' God knows why not. It's pretty much fundamental, to the extent that it's a question on every dating app. More important than 'Are you a member of a cult?' or 'Have you ever murdered someone?'

'You should let him know you don't want any. Unless you've changed your mind?'

'I haven't.' I hadn't. I now understood Becca's decision – or thought I understood it – and I knew I had it in me to be a good mum. But knowing Scarlett was out there in the universe was more than enough for me.

'Have you told your dad?'

'No. I don't want to risk him flying over and insisting on giving me away. He loves all that patriarchal crap. I'll think about that when the time comes.'

She gave me a sympathetic arm punch. 'So, who else knows?'

'Just you, Magda and Jonas. The people who matter to me.'

Not true of course, because I hadn't yet told the person who mattered the most to me. I was building up to that. Once again, I was facing a moral crossroads. Like the Dylan news, it *was* something I could keep to myself. He would never have to know about it. *What are you doing this weekend, Bee? Oh nothing, just going away with Leila and Lev.* But I couldn't do that to him. He knew when I was hiding something.

*

From: Bee1984@gmail.com
To: NB26@zone.com

I don't how to tell you this, Nick. Written it and deleted it more times than I can count. OK. Here goes: remember when you said if I didn't watch out I'd be married by Christmas?

NICK

Marriages typically symbolise the ending of the story. The happily ever after. There's a reason why no one wants to see *Cinderella 2: The Divorce*. Or *Beauty and the Beast: The Battle for Custody of the Candlestick* or whatever the fuck that thing was. When Bee broke the news, that was the first thing that popped into my head: *so that's it, then: the end of our story.*

Misery loves company. After I got the news, I thought about travelling to Leeds to see Lily or Poll and Jez, hopping on a train to Brum to cry on Dylan's shoulder; I even – God help me – very nearly contacted Geoffrey. In the end I called Leila 2. I needed to talk to someone in person, *confide* in someone who was in on Operation Doppelganger, but was more level-headed than Geoffrey. We met at the pub where I'd truth-bombed her.

'Getting married, huh?'

'Married.'

'Married to you, if you think about it.'

'Yeah. Not really.' Married to perfect Nicolas with his perfect life.

'Well, send my congratulations.'

'You could do that yourself. Use my phone. Send her an i-mail if you like.'

She grimaced. 'No. Talking to her last time . . . afterwards . . . it sort of freaked me out. Too uncanny. You know, since you first dragged me into this situation, I've been doing a lot of reading.'

'Good for you. Everyone needs a hobby.'

She gave me a 'ha bloody ha' look. 'Research reading. Into what's happening here. What's going on with you and Becca – Bee, I mean. Even messaged a woman who specialises in this stuff and posited the scenario, although I reckon she must have thought she was dealing with a conspiracy fanatic or a shitty writer trying to fix a last-minute plot hole. She described it as being 'beyond physics'. I mean, the implications . . . they're endless. This is definitive proof that there *are* other dimensions out there. It could fundamentally change our understanding of the universe. Don't you feel like you have a responsibility to get this out into the world?'

'No. Yes. Maybe. But apart from the Berenstains, who would believe it? All we have are the i-mails. There'd be no way to prove we hadn't faked them.'

We drank in silence for a while.

'Lev and I broke up.'

'What? Why?'

'No real reason. I'm just happier by myself.'

'Really? Because people always say that when they actually aren't.'

'Not the case with me. Maybe one day that'll change. But for now . . .' She shrugged.

'Me too.'

'Me too what?'

'I'm happier on my own.'

'You clearly aren't.'

Another round of pity-drinking.

Leila caught my eye. 'We could always have misery sex.' One of us had to say it.

'I'd kind of feel like I was cheating on Bee. Even if she is getting married.'

'Yeah. Me too.' I could see why she was Bee's best mate. 'So. When's the big day?'

'Bee says they haven't set a date. Next year maybe.'

'I suppose my other self will be the maid of honour. I used to love going to weddings, but now they make me feel kind of empty.'

'Me too.' I didn't want to say it. But out it came anyway. 'And

I'm pretty sure I know who the best man will be.'

'Who?'

'My mate Jeremy. Jez.'

'So?'

'In our world he ran off with my wife.'

Leila bit her lip, looked away, her shoulders shaking. I thought she was crying at first, then realised she was trying not to laugh. 'I'm sorry, Nick. It's just . . .' She couldn't hold it in any longer. I joined in. Because at the end of the day, if you can't laugh, what else can you fucking well do?

*

From: NB26@zone.com
To: Bee1984@gmail.com

Us carrying on being *us* doesn't seem like the right thing to do any more. Not now you're getting married. I know how much you struggle with the guilt of all this.

From: Bee1984@gmail.com
To: NB26@zone.com

It's not just me. It's hurting you too. I know it is. And it's not fair on Nicolas. It's not fair on any of us. But GOD I don't know if I can stop. The thought of you not being there . . . I'm already feeling like I'm about to have a panic attack. And what about Geoffrey? He'd be lost without those updates.

From: NB26@zone.com
To: Bee1984@gmail.com

I feel the same way. But however you spin it, this is an emotional affair. Can you live with that?

From: Bee1984@gmail.com
To: NB26@zone.com

Can you? You should be out there meeting other people. Dating other people. Why aren't you doing that? I WISH I could write to Becca and tell her to change her mind.

From: NB26@zone.com
To: Bee1984@gmail.com

How about this: let's slow things down. See how it goes. Play it by ear like we always do.

BEE

We did try to slow it down. We did try to stop. The longest we lasted was twenty-four hours. Then in would come a <hey> from one of us and we'd be off again.

The 'big day' was a nebulous thing. Set for some time in the future: next year, the year after that. It didn't feel *real.* I suppose that's why I enjoyed, to some extent, discussing it with Nicolas.

We decided we'd continue living here for a while, he'd sell his flat and then we'd think about pooling our resources and relocating. We both worked from home, so there were no geographical restrictions, although I did feel an initial gasp of panic at the thought of moving too far away from London and Leila. Still, I enjoyed scrolling through Rightmove, indulging in property porn and imagining future alternative lives. Unthreatening, *nebulous* future lives. We agreed on everything: neither of us wanted a big wedding. It would be just us, our closest friends (Leila and Jez), at an intimate venue sometime in the *nebulous* future.

The only sticking point came up while I was pressing the sleeve of Jenny's nearly completed jacket (the tailoring of which had been easier this time around), and Nicolas turned from his laptop and blindsided me with: 'How do you feel about kids?'

Uh-oh. Here it was, finally. The Conversation.

I tried to keep it light. 'In general? I think they're fine, as long as you can hand them back.'

'Does that mean you're against us having one?'

'How important is this to you, Nicolas?' A slippery, sneaky voice whispered: *This could be an elegant exit if you wanted to take it.* Most of the time, the exit light above *that* particular door was switched off. But occasionally, mostly late at night, or when I was illicitly messaging Nick, it would blink on and tempt me with its greenish glow. (<Have YOU ever wanted kids, Nick?> <My own you mean? Can't really answer that because Dylan filled that space if it was ever there. Plus, I took the vasectomy subsidy just after I married Poll>)

A shrug. 'It's not a deal-breaker. Never felt the urge before. That was one of the reasons I broke up with Jodie – she wanted kids, I didn't. But now . . .' Another shrug.

'How about we compromise and get a dog?'

He wavered, then said: 'Always wanted a dog.'

Time stretched like elastic into the future, only elastic has a way of snapping back at you. Because then Leila went and spoiled it all by rocking up, unannounced at the flat and saying something stupid like: 'You are *not* going to believe this.'

I don't blame her. How could she have known? And ever since I'd agreed to let her take charge of the plans, she'd been flooding my inbox with venue suggestions, mood boards and 'DIY intimate wedding' Pinterest links.

She got straight into it without even waiting for me to pour her a drink.

'I know you guys were thinking of sometime next year. But that *amazing* venue in Cornwall I told you about – you know the one, Bee, I sent you the pics – they've had a last-minute cancellation.'

My face must have been a picture. Neither noticed, because by then Leila had her MacBook open and Nicolas was looking over her shoulder while she scrolled through the pics. Okay – admittedly it was gorgeous. A series of artfully decorated stone cottages on a cliff top, overlooking the ocean. 'Perfect, isn't it? I'd put it at the top of the list but didn't hold out much hope as they're booked up for two years.'

'How last minute?' Did I sound panicky? Probably.

'Next month.'

'Next *month*?'

'I know, I know. Only, they need us to confirm now. There are a shit-ton of other people interested.'

Nicolas turned to face me: 'I say go for it. Bee?'

My gut screamed NO. But the people-pleasing side, the weak side, the treacherous side that had tricked me into staying with Nate for far too long, the side that had betrayed Becca too, the side I swore I wouldn't let win again, took over. I smiled and heard myself saying: 'Lovely.'

NICK

Just one more message then I'll stop. Like: *just one more rollie then I'll quit*. It wasn't only an addiction. That thread binding us together was still there and, as overly dramatic and selfish as this sounds, I suspected that severing it would cause permanent damage. Pain I wasn't ready to face.

As the days and weeks ticked by, and the crisp air of autumn gradually banished the late summer mugginess, we still spoke every day, and sometimes, occasionally, I managed to forget about the wedding-shaped storm on the horizon (the situation called for a shitty metaphor – so sue me). We avoided the subject – mostly. Spoke about the book (mine, not Nicolas's version – that was now out of bounds), her clients, the everyday nonsense we'd bonded over in the good old days. We were both talented avoiders. The Red Flags were proof of that.

Otherwise, life, for me, was looking better than it had for years. I had career prospects. The house sale money was in, bolstered by the first tranche of the book advance. I could easily afford to rent my own place, even considered moving back to Leeds – or anywhere really. But a) I couldn't be arsed; b) Rosie would kill me if I dragged her away from Sausage.

Leila 2 continued to send me updates. After a brief period of adjustment, Becca and Scarlett were settling into their life of subterfuge, Lev had reached out to Benedict's ex-wife and was following up on a couple of promising leads: two women in the States to whom Benedict had paid settlements, presumably as recompense for some not yet specified malfeasance. There had been a worrying time when Benedict had offered to fly out to join them, but fortunately for everyone, not even someone as wealthy and powerful as him could circumnavigate the long-haul flight quota laws, and that bullet had been dodged.

Petrus came home for a couple of days, filling the house with his usual roaring presence, and terrifying the latest incumbents: a pair of Canadian philosophy students with Laurel and Hardy levels of introversion.

'The writer! How is your woman?'

Petrus wouldn't be my first choice of confidante, but he caught me at a particularly vulnerable moment, and I blurted out: 'She's getting married. To someone else.'

'We are going out. Right now.'

'What about Erika?'

'She won't care.' A shoulder whack. 'Tonight we will find you a woman!'

Erika did care as it happened – 'No, we have many, many things to discuss, Petrus!' – but I let him haul me off to a local dive and get me steaming drunk anyway. The only women in the pub were the elderly bartender and a same-sexer couple who shared three rounds of shots with us, beat us at pool and bounced a joint with me in the charging bay, but even if I had been presented with a smorgasbord of attractive and willing options, I wasn't sure I had it in me to go there. I hadn't turned into a eunuch with no sex drive. It was *her* I wanted. Did I whinge about this to Petrus? Who knows? Any memory of that possible confession is forever lost in a black hole of vodka shots and a two a.m. vomiting session.

As the following day was a literal write-off, I dragged my hangover and the dogs to the park in the vain hope that fresh air would help. It didn't. I was wincing home when a message came in from Geoffrey: <need to meet urgent at the station 2 pm usual place>

<Why>

<just cum>

Not the misspelling you really want to see from anyone, much less Geoffrey.

Thanks to three aspirin and a purloined cup of Erika's secret stash of herbal tea, by the time I reached the Frites outlet I was feeling less like I was going to die and more like I might just have a minor stroke, although the scent of fried food didn't help quell the nausea. I spotted Geoffrey's distinctive head immediately, but he wasn't alone. Sitting opposite him was Kelvin. They made for an odd couple. Geoffrey fidgety and mercurial and scowling at the staff, who no doubt remembered him from his crying jag the last time we were here; Kelvin staring into space and eerily still.

'What's going on here?'

Kelvin jerked into life and got straight into it. 'Geoffrey has told me what you have been attempting to achieve and that due to circumstances beyond your control, it has failed.'

Geoffrey shrugged non-apologetically, as if being around Kelvin had reignited his old rude Berenstain ways. I glared at him. 'I thought we had a deal, Geoffrey?'

'We do.'

'I understand your concern, Nicolas, but let me assure you I have no intention of sharing this with the rest of the group. Geoffrey did not betray you. He and I would like to help you.'

'Help me do what?'

'Achieve what you really want. At the last meeting you attended, you asked if there was any way you could be with the woman you have been i-mailing. The woman with whom you are in love.' He winced a little at this. *Love: icky*. 'And, I am pleased to report, that there is a chance that this may be possible.'

I volley-glanced between them: Geoffrey, now grinning; Kelvin, still expressionless. 'I see. How?'

'We're going to kill you,' Geoffrey said.

'You what?'

Kelvin tutted. 'No, no. What we will do is put you into an induced coma first.'

'Well, that's all right then. What the *fuck*?'

Another wince from Kelvin.

'Like what happened to me,' Geoffrey piped in.

'You see, Nicolas, it is our belief that at the time of expiration, the consciousness crosses the mesh, an occurrence that for the majority of subjects is a seamless and unquantifiable transition.'

My poor fragile head was in no state to digest this typically overdressed word salad. 'Can you repeat that in English?'

'I don't see how I could be any clearer, Nicolas.'

Before I could snap back at Kelvin, Geoffrey jumped in. 'He's saying that what happened to me happens to everyone, only most people aren't aware of it.' He beamed proudly. 'I'm a special case.'

You can say that again.

Surreal. Bizarre. Adjectives that fell short of describing the situation. A normal person would have marched out on the spot. But I'd dumped normality at the door way back when Bee and I had first embarked on this journey. Telling my wannabe murderers to hang tight, I went to the counter for a double espresso, praying that it would help jump-start my booze-addled brain. If anything, it exacerbated the nausea and gut ache. I returned to the table. In my absence, Geoffrey had built a stevia-packet tower.

It was my turn to get straight into it. 'That's why you asked me to double-check if you were in a coma in Bee's world? Because the pair of you were already hatching this . . .' Plan wasn't the right word. 'Insanity?'

'Well, yeah.' Geoffrey said.

'To confirm: you want to put me in a coma. Then kill me. How, by the way?'

'For optimum efficacy, you would need to be induced into a comatose state that would fall below Level Eight of the Glasgow Coma Scale. To achieve this without the need for invasive intervention, such as intubation, from my extensive research I would suggest a high dosage of ketamine.' This from Kelvin, deadpan as per. 'Of course, in order to calculate the dosage, I would need to know your exact body weight.'

'Of course. Right. Then you'd kill me. Any plans for that, Dr Mengele? A pillow over the face? A thump on the head?'

Kelvin pursed his lips. 'Well, clearly, we would simply increase the dosage until your brain and respiratory functions ceased. Please be assured you would not experience any discomfort.'

Hangover aside, I realised I was enjoying myself. It's not every day you get to discuss your own possible murder. 'Why a coma?'

'From the research that I have undertaken, depressing brain functionality for a time before expiration increases the likelihood that the necessary *glitch* will occur. The theory is that because you will be aware, on some level, of what is happening to you, your consciousness will be able to rationalise and accept the mesh-crossing process.'

Glitch. That word again. But rationalise? There was nothing rational about any of this. By now, the caffeine was kicking in, blasting through the booze-murk.

Something Bee had brought up sprung to mind. 'Hang on. Millions of people must fall into comas and die every year. If the consciousness does cross the mesh, why aren't there millions of people like Geoffrey – millions of displaced people knocking about?'

'There might be. Perhaps it manifests itself as déjà vu. Or in dreams. Or panic attacks, or some forms of mental illness. We do not know for sure. But remember, these people would not be equipped with the foreknowledge of what is – of what *has* – happened to them. You will be in the unique position of *knowing* what is occurring, which, we believe, will increase the likelihood of a glitch manifesting.'

'A glitch like me, only with . . . wotchoocallit, ammunition,' Geoffrey said.

'So, after you kill me, you're saying I'd wake up in Nicolas's body?'

'In a sense. If you must express it in such a crude and unscientific manner.'

I somehow managed not to laugh at this typical Kelvin-ism. 'Okay, okay. Say the glitch does occur, and I manage to remain self-aware or whatever, what about Nicolas? How will he feel about all this? Won't it drive him crazy?' I glanced at Geoffrey. 'How did you feel when your other self . . . I dunno, started invading your consciousness?'

'It wasn't like being wotsitted by an alien, Nick.'

'Probed.'

'Yeah. I felt nowt about it at first. It took a while. Crept up on me. Gradual. Like, I didn't wake up one morning going, fuck, where's my kid, know what I mean? Took months. It didn't feel like I was going wotsit . . . schizo or whatever.'

'But you told me you thought you were losing your mind.'

'Yeah, but only because I didn't know what was happening. You will. And honestly, since I joined the group and then you confirmed it for me, I've been . . . I've been *better*.' He tapped his head. 'If it weren't for my . . . wotsit, I'd be hundreds, I reckon.'

Back to Kelvin. 'Let's say I buy this. Let's say I go through with it. There are infinite worlds, infinite realities, right?'

'That is impossible to confirm, Nicolas.'

'But say there are. How do you know I'd end up in *that* Nicolas? In a world with *that* Bee? What if I pitched up in a Nicolas in a reality where, say, Bee hadn't even been born?'

'It is my belief that our two realities are closely linked. That the mesh between them is more porous. There's Geoffrey's experience, which we know, thanks to your investigations, correlate to an extraordinarily degree with his memories – a correlation that one cannot put down to mere chance. Then there is *your* experience of communicating across the mesh.' The thread. A fanciful image, for sure. I could just follow that. Imagined pulling myself along it like a deep-sea diver. *Oh, give over, Nick*. 'I have additional potential evidence too.'

'Like what?'

Kelvin reached into his briefcase, removed a manila envelope that resembled the one in which Poll had sent the divorce papers, and put it on the table.

'Why do you want to do this? I thought you guys were dead set against meddling.'

'I do believe that what we are hoping to achieve here *could* be considered disruptive. But we may never be presented with an opportunity like this again. Think of it, Nicolas. If we achieve an optimum result, you will be in the unique position to communicate directly with us and *prove* the concept of displacement.'

'Via the i-mail thread, you mean.'

'Yes.'

'And you, Geoffrey? Why are you pushing for this? If it doesn't work, then you'll no longer get updates on your family.'

'Yeah, I will. Your woman seems like a decent person, and we'll have your phone.'

Wow. Okay. 'So you'd just i-mail Bee and tell her, soz, we accidentally-on-purpose murdered Nick, but no biggy, how's Jenny doing today?'

An old-school Geoffrey scowl. 'It's not just that, you daft bugger. You're my *mate*. I want you to be happy. And if it does work, Jenny and Megan would have someone in their world who'd watch their backs. You'd do that for me, right?'

Play along, Nick. 'Course I would.' (Well, I would.) Back to Kelvin. 'So why don't you do it, then? Slip into *your* other self in Bee's world. Report back to yourself?'

Another rare reaction: a flinch rather than his usual wince. 'An experiment must have an observer, Nicolas. And I do not have a strong emotional connection to that reality. You do. Geoffrey does.'

'You're saying love is the key.' Rather endearing, if you think about it. I wouldn't have pegged Kelvin as a romantic.

'There is a reason why you forged a connection with Rebecca Davies. It is my belief that it is entirely possible that the Arpanet has opened a rift between our realities and that many misdirected messages from our respective realities may cross the mesh every day. However, it would take a unique and rare series of circumstances for this to come to light. Consider what it took for you and Rebecca Davies to discover the truth of your situation. I believe that this was not just chance or a fluke.'

I couldn't argue with that. Bee and I had discussed it *ad nauseam* back in the day. *It was meant to be*. 'And you're both fine with this, are you? Because what you're actually talking about is murder. That's what you'll be accused of. You can hardly tell the cops the real reason you decided to off me – they'd think you were insane.' Although to be fair, with that story, an insanity defence would be a shoo-in. 'Any plans I should know about concerning the disposal of my body? Landfill? A ditch at the side of the road? Or are you going to go all out and dump me in the allotment?'

Blank looks from both.

'You haven't actually thought this through properly, have you?'

'These are details that we can discuss at length if you wish, Nicolas,' Kelvin said eventually.

No chance. Talking of chance: 'What are the odds of this actually working? A million to one? Two million?'

'Far higher than that. But what are the odds that we will ever have an opportunity like this again?'

I'd come across people like Kelvin before. He'd spent his entire life being disbelieved. Laughed at. Belittled. And now he wanted to use me to prove the impossible.

'But even if it does work, the only proof you'll have are the i-mails. Which, as Henrietta pointed out, would no doubt be seen as fakes.'

'But *we* will know. It will be a start.'

I stood. 'Thank you for your kind offer, but as tempting as experimental murder sounds, you're too late. She's in love with someone else. She's marrying someone else.' A fleeting image of my consciousness pitching up at the wedding like an uninvited guest: 'Surprise!'

'Wait,' Kelvin said. 'Before you dismiss this entirely, Nicolas, please read the material.' He proffered the envelope. Oh, fuck it. I took it.

I left the envelope, unopened, on my desk for a couple of days. It sounds peevish, but I felt *betrayed*. I'd come to see Geoffrey as a friend and confidante, but it seemed my first impression of him had been correct: he was a crazed loon after all. It took a three a.m. bout of insomnia to compel me to open it and examine the contents: two pages of neatly typed notes, intriguingly (and ridiculously) entitled 'Case Study 024: TOP SECRET' and transcribed by Kelvin in his trademark bone-dry and prudish style. After reading it twice, I locked it away in the desk drawer. Easy to hide the pages; far harder to scrub their contents out of my head. And I might have succeeded in convincing myself that Kelvin had fabricated this 'additional potential evidence' in order to help convince me to go along with his ludicrous plan, if it wasn't for the note scrawled on the last page in his prissy handwriting: *Ask Rebecca Davies to look into this from her side.*

I didn't do that (at least, not right away). Instead, I wrote this, not stopping to censor myself, just letting the feelings pour out:

From: NB26@zone.com
To: Bee1984@gmail.com

I wish I could give you and Nicolas my blessing. I wish I was the sort of unselfish person who could not only do that but mean it. Because I know how much you need to hear it. But I can't. You know why I can't. IT SHOULD BE US. Fuck's sake, you'd think the multiverse, with all the alternatives and aeons at its disposal, could have put us together in the same time and space.

I'm trying to comfort myself by imagining that out there in multiverse land, there's an alternate reality in which we did get to meet under the clock at Euston Station that day. And I like to think that this is how things would have played out:

I see you first. Standing under the clock in your red coat, self-consciously toying with your hair. Cue all the clichés: My heart stops. Time stops. Everyone around you disappears. I don't approach you immediately because the first time we see each other will mean everything and I'm terrified that I won't measure up. Then you look over and catch my eye and let out a silent OH.

Then it hits me that the way you're looking at me is the opposite of disappointment and the relief is fucking overwhelming.

I can't feel my feet as I walk over to you. At first, neither of us speaks. We can't stop grinning at each other. Then, both of us talk at once. I say something stupid like, I thought you said you weren't a supermodel. You say, where's the hunch, Quasimodo?

We laugh about the suit. I exaggerate its itchiness. You touch my sleeve to test the material, then blush and apologise. I tell you not to be daft and to please touch it all you like. To never stop touching it if that's your thing, which sounds so dodgy and mad, we both laugh again.

You suggest a coffee. I suggest a drink. We compromise and decide on both.

You insist on paying for takeaway espressos and then you say let's go outside so that you can smoke, Nick. It's the first time you've said my name. I say I don't need to smoke. I have never felt less like I need a hit of nicotine. We clink our tiny paper cups, say cheers and knock back our espressos like shots. Then we head to a pub just outside the station.

You find us a table and I go up to the bar to order our drinks. The warmth inside me must show on my face because the bartender tips me a wink and says good on you mate.

There's no awkwardness, no uncomfortable silences. We chat about Dylan and Rosie and Leila and Lily and riff about work and I can tell you're at ease because you've stopped playing with your hair. The air between us doesn't just shimmer, it's fucking radiant. Then you say, would you like to see the flat? And I say, I thought you'd never ask.

I take your hand as we exit the Tube station. We don't speak because we don't need to.

When we walk in, you apologise for the mess even though there isn't any. I introduce myself to Clarice (she's a bit stand-offish but warms up later) and make a terrible joke about the Ziggy Stardust duvet cover. It feels like home. It is home. It's home because you're there.

You smile and look into my eyes. I smile and do the same. And then I kiss you for the first time and

I didn't finish that i-mail. I couldn't (re-reading it was torture enough). I never sent it either (it's still in my drafts folder).

PART SIX

ONE WEDDING AND A FUNERAL

NICK

Lily died a week before Bee was due to get married.

It was one of her carers – Naomi – who broke the news, said she'd found my number in Lily's old-fashioned telephone book. It was the only number in it that was still in use. Naomi attempted to sugarcoat it, which was kind of her, but reading between the lines it hadn't been an easy death. A fall (no doubt she'd tripped over one of the countless rugs scattered all over the place), a shattered hip, and what sounded like a long wait before she was discovered, too late for the paramedics to revive her. Despite her best efforts, Naomi said she'd been unable to track down any surviving relatives. There was no one but me to arrange a funeral.

I'd promised to visit Lily with Rosie, but I'd never got around to it. And now it was too late.

I couldn't exorcise the guilt with Bee: it wasn't the sort of thing anyone should hear during the run-up to the 'best day of your life'. The day that would signify an end to our connection. I'd be mourning that soon. Fresh off the back of mourning the miserable old cow who'd once been my neighbour: the woman who'd once been in love but who'd spent the last decades of her life alone.

Instead, I called Poll, practical, no-nonsense Poll, even though she and Lily hadn't got on. But when I broke the news, Poll immediately offered to help, and invited me to stay the night with her and Jez in the fixer-upper they'd recently bought. Oh, why the hell not. I was long past the resentment stage, and I could do with a night away from The Bergs.

On my way out, I stuck my head around the door of Erika's lair. She was on the couch, bookended by the dogs, and watching morning telly (my old favourite – *Baby Animal Rescue Squad*), which was highly unusual for her. At this time of the day, she'd usually be spritzing every surface with her lavender spray and mentally compiling house-rule infractions.

'Can you walk the dogs today, Erika?'

'You are unwell?'

'No. Have to go to Leeds. A friend of mine died last night.'

'*Another* one? Suicide also?'

Jesus. Maybe she thought self-harm was par for the course if someone was stupid enough to be my mate. 'No. Old age.' And loneliness, probably.

'I am sorry for your loss, Nick.' Whoa. This wasn't like her.

'Are you okay, Erika? Is our new arrival doing your head in?'

The latest, a garrulous American professor, was in the habit of regaling us over breakfast in stultifying detail about the dreams he'd had the night before. Still, he didn't steal the milk.

'No, no. That is all fine.'

'Is Petrus okay?'

A long pause, as if she were fighting a battle with the carapace. The carapace won. 'Yes, yes. He is doing very well.'

Poll had offered to meet me at the station, but there was something I wanted to do first. Something I needed to do alone. For some reason, I'd assumed my old environment would have changed as much as I had since I'd escaped, but the background to The Dreadnought Years was defiantly stuck in time and hadn't missed my absence one bit. It was both a melancholic and cathartic experience retracing Past Nick's steps, taking the old familiar loop through Dog Shit Meadow, past the Stop n Shop, the orange façades of the estate, and onto Dreadnought Street. It no longer felt like home, although, when I reached Lily's gate, I didn't glance at my old house. I didn't want to know if the new owners had given it a facelift or had taken down my shed.

As Lily had left no will, the council would be dealing with her things. They'd be shuffled off to charity shops, landfill, recycling centres: a life erased. The spare key was still under the mat, and I held my breath as I entered. But I needn't have worried: the house's habitual scent of cooked meat clung on stubbornly. Trying not to look at the cloths still draped over the chair arms and tables, I made straight for the drawer and removed the photograph. In decades to come it would end up in landfill. I just wasn't ready for it to end up in landfill *yet*.

Had Lily's soul – or whatever – slipped seamlessly into another timeline, one where she was younger, perhaps, to continue the never-ending cycle? In another life, would she and Marion have found each other at an earlier stage? Gifting them with the chance of more time together? As I gazed at the portrait of Marion and Lily, forever stuck in the eighties, the temptations of Kelvin's offer pulled me into their gravitational force. Sure, late at night, I'd allow myself to dance down the scenario's ridiculously convoluted alleyways and think, what if, *what if*, but up till now, that was as far as it went. But there, in Lily's lounge, I went so far as to take out my phone to ask Bee to check out the flipside of Kelvin's case study, before snapping back to my senses. No. I might have been in emotional pain, but I wasn't – yet – at the stage where I was desperate enough to put my life in the hands of a couple of loons. Nor was I ready to interrogate why I hadn't told Bee about Kelvin and Geoffrey's delightful plans for me. I'd been tempted after I left the station café that day – the undiluted lunacy of the plot was a black humour gold mine, and we could have riffed about it for days – but had held back. Just like I'd held back on finishing and sending that self-indulgent what-might-have-been i-mail.

I dragged my heels to Poll and Jez's new love palace in Bradford. She'd painted a picture of dereliction and decay, but it was a fairly pleasant re-insulated Victorian villa that only needed a cosmetic overhaul. Poll greeted me with a hug; Jez, after a hesitation, did the same. It felt way less weird than it should have done. *Hey, Jez, in another life you're my best man.* I'd be sleeping in the spare room, which, judging by the superhero wallpaper, had once housed a child. Fitting, really, as that's how Poll treated me at first: as if I were one of her pupils who'd recently gone through a traumatic experience and needed sensitive handling.

A cup of tea, some carefully worded trauma counselling: 'There was nothing you could have done, Nick,' then on to business. Lily hadn't expressed any preference about how her remains should be distributed, so in the end we went for the obvious: resomation. The fact that we dissolved our dead, essentially turning their bodies into fertiliser, had fascinated Bee back in ye olde note-comparing days. They still cremated their dead in her world. But who cared anyway? *There is no death.*

The business side concluded, Jez made dinner while Poll and I shared a bottle of wine. She said she was currently reading *A Shot in the Dark* (to which the film rights were now being negotiated – take *that*, Nicolas) and 'so far, Nick, I think it's pretty good,' which for Poll was the equivalent of a five-star BookPost review. This unexpected ego-stroke yanked me away from the edge of a temptingly deep self-pity chasm, and after dinner, I offered to head to the Stop n Shop for more booze. Jez faded fast, but Poll and I stayed up until three, drinking, reminiscing and giggling, unexpectedly recapturing some of the fun we used to have at the beginning. I wanted her to know that despite Jez, *I* was responsible for letting the relationship grow stale. It was my fault. I'd checked out. Boring as shite or not, Jez made her happy. He was *her* version of Bee.

As we drunkenly stumbled off to bed, she said: 'You *will* be okay, won't you, Nick?'

'Course.' Bullshit, but what she needed to hear. That's what everyone wants to hear: it allows us to get on with our own lives, free from guilt and worry.

I arranged the actual resomation and memorial to take place on the day of Bee's wedding. Why not? It seemed fitting; and if Lily could have known the whole story, I reckoned she'd enjoy the irony of it.

BEE

You're happy. He's happy. Everyone's happy.

And we were, mostly.

If you've never found yourself in this situation (and really, who has?) you won't understand. You'll think I'm an idiot, a selfish monster for letting it get this far.

Was this how Becca had felt the day before she was due to marry Benedict the Bastard? As if she were on a treadmill she couldn't get off? Not fair. Nicolas wasn't Benedict. He was a decent man. *More* than decent.

The exit light blinked on and off; I bounced back and forth between: *this is right this is good*; and *NO*.

It was all in place. Leaving the twins with Leila's mum, Leila and Lev had driven down to the venue the day before to finalise arrangements: 'Oh Bee, it's beyond perfect. You are going to fucking *die* when you see it.' An early morning ceremony conducted by a registrar, a wedding breakfast, the menu of which I'd let Leila and Nicolas quibble over, ditto flowers and decorations. A three-day honeymoon in the venue's bridal cottage. We didn't need to discuss our choice of wedding song. It went without saying that it had to be: 'Life on Mars?' Was this the song Nick and I would have chosen in another life? *Stop it.*

Time's up, Bee.

I'd revamped Mum's wedding dress, feeling, at times, like I was sewing a funeral shroud, then slapping myself out of it: Leila was right. Mum would have loved Nicolas (and Nick). I wrapped it in tissue paper and slid it into the plastic covering: a body bag of sorts. *Stop it, stop it.*

I was zipping it up when Nicolas wrapped his arms around me, resting his head on my shoulder. 'Hey.'

'Hey.'

'This time tomorrow we'll be married.'

Tell him, tell him. 'I'm still not taking your name.'

'Don't blame you. I'm thinking of taking yours.'

And bounce back to: *this is right, this is good.*

Magda and Jonas came down to see us off. A rare smile from Magda, and a rare sign of life from Jonas, who moved his shoulders in time to an imaginary beat in his head. I half-expected her to say, 'Don't wait' – or even for Jonas to say it.

I enjoyed the drive down, Nicolas and I competing with each to pick the most ridiculous or cheesy track to sing along to: Abba, The Prodigy, Oasis, Kylie, TLC. The kind of thing I'd imagine Nick and I would have done. *ENOUGH.*

And the venue was as glorious as the pics had promised. A tiny chapel, funky and artistic. A converted barn with a hot tub. A garden that led down to a private beach. Perfect, really. Just the five of us: Nicolas and me, Lev and Leila, and Cheating Jez, whose date had bailed on him at the last minute (so maybe karma *is* a thing).

I was calm. Not happy. Not worried. Just . . . Christ. Just numb.

That night the five of us went to a local pub. No hen or bachelor parties in Prague for us. I laughed and drank and put on a happy face while my phone burned a hole in my pocket. Nick and I had agreed to keep radio silence until after it was over. Like we had during what he still called the Hardcore Doppelganger Sex Weekend. But I snuck away from the table and went outside to check all the same. Nothing from Nick. What did I expect? That at the last moment he'd find a time portal or whatever, zap through into my world, and stop the wedding in the equivalent of the running-through-the-airport romcom scene?

Not quite ready (or able) to face rejoining the pre-wedding party,

I sat on a damp beer-garden bench and stared out into the nothingness. The moon, like my conscience, had gone into hiding, and with the line between sea and sky cloaked in darkness, there was nothing beyond the pub's low boundary wall but a seamless black void. A breeze carried a faint salty tang. Someone more poetic than me would probably be reminded of the taste of unshed tears. But I'm not that person. If anything, it made me long for a comforting tube of Pringles Original.

Leila crept up on me, making me jump. Thankfully she was too drunk to notice the guilty way I slid the phone back into my pocket. 'Are you okay, Bee? Getting cold feet?'

Tell her. Tell him. 'I'm okay.'

'Hmm.' A boozy Paddington stare. Then she grinned and pulled a spliff out of her bag. 'This'll help.'

I hadn't smoked dope since my early twenties, not since a nightmare of a night at Glastonbury when I'd eaten too many cannabis cookies and thought I was going to die. But I needed something – anything – to drag me out of the swirling immoral morass into which I'd allowed myself to be sucked. Or something to further numb the numbness.

'Remember the night before I married Lev? You and me, pissed on Bacardi in that shitty hotel room?'

'Of course I do.' I took a deep drag. Coughed.

'I had a shed-load of doubts. Everyone feels like that the night before. Which is crazy really, if you think about it. It's not a death sentence. It's not as if you can't just get divorced if it doesn't work out.'

'I know.'

'And he's lovely, Bee. He's good for you.' The joint was making her weepy. 'You're going to be so *happy*.'

This is right, this is good.

After she staggered back inside, I opened up the Gmail thread.

From: Bee1984@gmail.com
To: NB26@zone.com

If you don't want me to marry him, I won't.

NICK

Sex and death: a classic combo. Like surf and turf. Or Laurel and Hardy.

There is no excuse for what I did. None.

There were only six of us at the memorial. Me, Poll, Jez, two of Lily's unfairly maligned carers, Naomi and Beulah, and Dylan, who I hadn't seen in person since Bee had sent through the news about his other self. I gave him a hug and bit the inside of my cheek hard enough to bleed to stop myself from crying.

I'd thought long and hard about what music to play to see Lily off. The theme tune to one of her favourite TV shows would have been the most apposite, but blasting out the soundtrack to *Baby Animal Rescue Squad* or *Bailiff Bail-Outs* while her coffin trundled behind the curtain was probably too inappropriate even for her. In the end I chose a track from the *Silent* album. Bowie would see her on her way whether she liked it or not. At the last moment, I approached the coffin (which really should have been draped with one of the doilies or cloths she favoured) and placed on top the photograph I'd foraged from the house. Off they went together to be broken down. Ashes to ashes. Or in Lily's case, water to fertiliser.

We decamped to Poll and Jez's for the wake. Naomi and Beulah could only stay for one drink, but we had a laugh competing to see who could come up with the most offensive thing Lily had said to us over the years (there were a *lot*), which I think she would have appreciated.

Dylan caught my eye and mimed smoking. We slipped out into the garden for a sneaky joint. After he'd caught me up on his news, and I'd regaled him with Tales of The Bergs and reassured him that I really was over my relatively recent 'break up', I found myself saying: 'Can I ask you something, Dylan? And feel free to tell me to fuck off, but when I found you that day . . . you know when,' – I paused to gauge his reaction, he was wary, but he nodded for me to continue – 'when I found you, what made you do it? How did you feel? You know, just before you . . .' *Shit*. I was making a right pig's ear out of it. 'Sorry. Ignore me. That's the last thing you need to hear.'

''S'all right, Nick. Chill. I'm okay to talk about it. I wanted it to be over. I wanted it to end. I couldn't see any other route out. I didn't think it *would* ever end.'

'But you don't feel like that now.'

'No.' A shrug. 'I have dark days, sure, but everyone does and when they show up, I've got ways of dealing with them. Why are you asking?'

I clapped him on the shoulder, Petrus-style. 'I love you, mate. Just wanted to make sure you really are okay.' True and not true. I did love him and needed to be sure he'd never consider that option again, but the real reason I'd brought it up was because, despite my resolution at Lily's house, the case study and its implications kept invading my thoughts. But any lingering temptations I'd been secretly harbouring about Kelvin's offer were vanquished by this conversation. I'd called it murder, but really, it was suicide. And if I did go through with it, how would Dylan feel if he found out I'd killed myself? I could never risk that.

Comfortably (or uncomfortably) numb, I declined Poll's offer of staying over, and made my way home, topping up with couple of cans of cider on the train. Memorials bring with them a whiff of future decay, a reminder that *hey, this'll be you one day, matey-boy*. My forays into Quantum Anomaly Fuck-Up Land with its 'there is no death' entry clause weren't enough to eradicate that stench. As the train chuntered on, I compiled a possible guest list for my future funeral. It barely reached double figures: it would only hit *that* number if I preceded Tweedy.

And then, of course, there was the elephant in the room at which to have a good old self-pitying stare. The huge stinking elephant that had shat on the rug and stood on the dog and destroyed all the ornaments.

The wedding.

If you don't want me to do it, I won't.

Sending that through had been unfair; we both knew that. It had to be her choice, not mine. I'd be her bit on the side. An emotional affair that would eventually dwindle out. I'd deliberately kept my phone switched off to avoid temptation. But, as I walked through the Euston concourse, I paused beneath the clock and tapped it into life. Typed: <DON'T>, finger hovering over the <send> icon. No. I deleted it. Went to write it again, then took the battery out the phone and pocketed it. I couldn't make that call for her. Not this time.

When I arrived back at The Bergs, breaking one of the house rules by drunkenly letting the door slam behind me, Erika emerged from her lair, took one look at me and instructed me to join her in the lounge. She knew where I'd been. A resomation tends to resonate with everyone who's experienced one, and that night she was clearly in need of company too. When she offered me a drink, I could hardly have refused (she wouldn't have let me). This led to another. Then a third, because all good things come in threes. And bad things.

It just happened.

Nothing just happens.

Thank fuck Laurel and Hardy weren't around to hear us. At it on the coffee table, eyed by the two dogs with varying degrees of disgust.

BEE

Reader, I married him.

NICK

The following morning was a symphony of self-loathing. Ashes in my mouth. My pulse seeming to beat anywhere but my heart. So hungover I once again felt like I was on the verge of a stroke or a coronary. I would have welcomed either. *These things happen*: the trite sentence trotted out to excuse the inexcusable. What I'd done went beyond the inexcusable. Petrus had been good to me, and I'd betrayed him in the worst way possible. I genuinely wanted to punch myself in the face. Or where it would really hurt.

I needed coffee. Needed to clear my head. Needed to clear things up with Erika. I wasn't going to allow myself the easy option of hiding in my room and hoping it would all go away.

When I entered the breakfast room, Erika took me off guard by treating me with her usual level of contempt. The garrulous professor was midway through a detailed breakdown of last night's dream, which for once wasn't as boring as shite, involving, for some reason, his ex and a buffalo (don't ask). I could have hugged him. His patter took the heat off and gave me enough time to cram down some toast and a couple of cups of coffee before facing the inevitable.

When the American finally left, I lingered. Erika was already spritzing, as if it were just another ordinary morning. The photographs of Petrus glared at me from the sideboard. 'Erika . . . If you want me to move out, I will.'

'Why would I want you to do that?'

'Because of what happened last night.'

'Nothing happened.' Straight-faced. Poker-faced. For a few fleeting seconds I (almost) believed that I *had* actually imagined it. *So that was how it was going to be*. Cowardly relief came next. I'd hang on for a while, but I'd have to move out before Petrus visited again.

But fuck it.

I didn't deserve to be let off the hook that easily. I wanted to punish myself. Needed to. I slid the battery back into place.

*

From: NB26@zone.com
To: Bee1984@gmail.com

Did you go through with it, Bee? If you did, we should stop this right now. I love you. I always will, but we both know what we're doing isn't fair. You were right: it isn't fair on anyone.

BEE

I didn't hear the phone beep. I was in the shower, washing sand from between my toes after an early morning ramble on the beach, the water a background percussion to the incessant: *You're happy, you're happy, you're happy. More importantly, HE'S happy. We're all happy. It's done, you've made your decision, now live with it.*

I dried off, padded into the bedroom.

Froze.

One of those gut-twisting, life-changing moments where time really does seem to slow: Nicolas sitting on the edge of the bed, my phone in his hand, an expression of raw betrayal in his eyes.

From: Bee1984@gmail.com
To: NB26@zone.com
Who the FUCK are you and what exactly is your relationship with my wife?

NICK

At first, my dehydrated brain assumed it was joke. One of those stupid, inappropriately humorous lines Bee and I used to trade. Then I re-read it: an icy, sobering wash as its implications hit home.

There was no reply to that other than: *I'm you. I'm a much less successful yet curiously more emotionally stable version of you. I'm you in another world. The version of you who fucked up and gave up when you didn't. And Nicolas, I'm sorry, I'm so fucking sorry, WE NEVER MEANT FOR IT TO GET THIS FAR.*

But we *had* meant for it to get this far, hadn't we? *Folie à deux.*

I didn't respond. Left all that unsaid. Zombie-shuffled up to my room. Sat on the bed for I don't know how long staring at the phone.

Nothing but silence from Bee's side.

I took the dogs to the park. Returned to the house. Locked myself in my room, tried to write – failed. Tried to eat – failed. *Nicolas knows. She must have told him the truth by now.* I tried to put myself in his position – failed.

Then: <It's over>

*

From: NB26@zone.com
To: Bee1984@gmail.com

Oh Jesus Bee. FUCK. I don't know what to say. How are you? WHERE are you? Do you have someone with you at least?

From: Bee1984@gmail.com
To: NB26@zone.com

Still in the (OH GOD) honeymoon cottage, waiting for a taxi to take me to the station. Nicolas left straight away. And who can blame him?

I don't know how I am. Who CARES how am I? I shouldn't have let it get to this stage. What the hell is wrong with me?

From: NB26@zone.com
To: Bee1984@gmail.com

There's nothing wrong with you. Listen to me. This is not your fault.

From: Bee1984@gmail.com
To: NB26@zone.com

It bloody, bloody well is. I'm a stupid selfish idiot. Worse than that.

From: NB26@zone.com
To: Bee1984@gmail.com

This is on both of us. Me especially. Where's Leila? Isn't she with you?

From: Bee1984@gmail.com
To: NB26@zone.com

She's gone too. After Nick left, I told her everything. Well not everything. The gist. She didn't say a word until I finished, then said, 'Is this a joke? Because if it is, it's not fucking funny.' I swore on my life that it wasn't, but all she said to that was, 'I can't deal with this right now, Bee,' and drove off with Lev. The way she said it. It was so cold. And FINAL. And exactly what I deserved.

From: NB26@zone.com
To: Bee1984@gmail.com

Leila will be back, Bee. You know she will. She just needs time to process everything. It's not every day you hear something like that.

From: Bee1984@gmail.com
To: NB26@zone.com

Maybe. But I doubt she will. I've been lying to her for MONTHS. I've been lying to everyone for months. And Nicolas. Jesus. When he left . . . he was broken, Nick. I've never seen a look like that on anyone's face before. Except I have. On Mum's. And I did that to him. ME.

From: NB26@zone.com
To: Bee1984@gmail.com

What did you tell him? The truth?

From: Bee1984@gmail.com
To: NB26@zone.com

Yes and no. I wanted to tell him everything. Almost did, but . . . He asked me if I loved you.

From: NB26@zone.com
To: Bee1984@gmail.com

And?

From: Bee1984@gmail.com
To: NB26@zone.com

I told him the truth. And then he asked me if I loved you more than I loved him.

From: NB26@zone.com
To: Bee1984@gmail.com

And?

From: Bee1984@gmail.com
To: NB26@zone.com

I told him the truth to that, too.

PART SEVEN

CROSSED LINES

BEE

I made sure I was out when Nicolas came to collect his things from the flat, a week after the wedding. Told myself that being absent was the kindest thing to do. I'd tried calling and e-mailing countless times, but all I'd received was a <please just STOP>. I'd contacted Jez, asked him to be there for Nicolas and make sure he was coping. 'He's absolutely crushed, Bee. What the hell happened? He won't say.' I didn't go into the details – this was the man, after all, I still thought of as Cheating Jez – but I did say that I was the one to blame and that Nicolas needed his support.

Leila had called me the morning after it had all blown up. She was worried about me, seriously worried, but no matter how I worded it, she still refused to believe my story. (<Have faith, Bee. Leila 2 bought it, didn't she?> <Yeah, but your Leila, unlike mine, isn't living in a reality swamped by a tsunami of fake news and conspiracy theories>) And my Leila had her own theory: 'Look. Maybe you're telling me what you think is the truth, Bee. But this other guy you're e-mailing, he's fucking with your head. He's conning you. And you're fucking falling for it.'

It had ended in a rare fight, with Leila insisting I needed professional help, and that she wasn't about to enable me by supporting this 'obvious bullshit'.

When she hung up, I stayed up all night crafting an e-mail to her, laying out 'proof' in the hopes of convincing her. I went back and forth over whether or not to mention Leila 2 – childfree, successful, happy, Leila 2. Lev-less Leila 2. I wrote and rewrote it a thousand times, then shoved it in my drafts folder.

And now Leila was gone, and *I* was the Nate in this instance. I was the Poll. I was my dad. I was the arsehole, the manipulative, selfish, monster of a person. I'd conned Nicolas into loving me, let him find out in the cruellest way possible about Nick, and then I let him walk away without at least having the grace to tell him the whole truth. It took a while to root out my real motivation for not doing so – a bumpy, painful journey to good old self-realisation land. So far, everyone Nick had told in his world had believed him. What if Nicolas did too – and not only that, accepted it? That wouldn't have suited my self-flagellation agenda, the deep-down belief that I didn't deserve both him and Nick. I hadn't lied when I told him I loved Nick more than I loved him. I wish I could say that I couldn't imagine how much that must have hurt. But I can. And it bloody well serves me right. I let it go too far.

I was now almost certain that Nicolas had suspected all along that something between us wasn't quite right. (That something, of course, being some*one*.) *Is this real?* That this was why he'd proposed with such alacrity and jumped at the chance of sealing the deal when the cancellation came up. But whether he had or not, so what? There was only one door at which to lay the blame: mine.

So while he was in my flat removing himself from my life, I took a solo gin-walk. Without the gin. And because life likes to kick you in the ribs when you're down, an estate-agent's board had gone up outside the Gnome Home. The gnome's days, and probably the wisteria's too, were numbered. I thought about messaging Leila to tell her about it, with the promise that I'd fish the gnome out of the inevitable skip that would inevitably appear. Instead, I sent her the e-mail.

When I returned to the flat, heart in my throat in case Nicolas and I crossed paths – half-hoping, half-dreading we would – Magda was waiting for me on the stairs.

'Come,' she said. 'We must talk.'

I followed her meekly up to her flat. It had been a while since

I'd been up there, and she'd let things slide. There was an extra layer of dust on the piles of books and manuscripts, and the piano top was littered with dirty mugs and wine-stained glasses. Jonas was in his chair sleeping, his mouth slightly open. He also looked shabbier than usual: unshaven, and his suit crumpled and peppered with crumbs.

While Magda muttered to herself and rooted around for clean glasses, I stood next to the piano, watching as his eyelids fluttered, and hoping he was lost in a dream and not a nightmare. It was barely eleven, but she poured us both a whisky. I didn't decline. I had a consultation at twelve, but as it was via Skype, the client wouldn't be able to smell the alcohol on my breath, and I could use something to blunt the ever-present guilt.

Magda eyed me with her usual perspicacity. 'Why?'

'Why did he leave?'

'Yes. He was a good man. Very helpful. One time he came and helped me with the crushing of the cans for the recycling. Was it him who broke it or you?'

'Me. In love with someone else.'

I waited for some gnostic wise-woman words, or even a muttered, 'stupid girl', trying very hard not to think about Magda and her toy-boy in the other world. None came. She merely huffed, shrugged, and drank. Jonas let out a long sigh. I tried very hard not to think about him and *don't wait*. Failed.

'Magda, ages ago, just after I found Jonas on the stairs, you said something to me: "Don't wait." What did you mean by that?'

She narrowed her eyes into glittery slits. 'I do not remember this.'

'It was very clear. You said it just after we'd got Jonas settled and I was on my way out.'

A humph. A pause. Then: 'It was on a Thursday, yes?'

I thought back. 'Yes.'

She nodded. 'The day before the recycling. If you wait too long to dispose of the waste, then it sits in the tubs for another week.'

Take THAT, *fate*.

From: Bee1984@gmail.com
To: NB26@zone.com

So here we are. Back to where we started. Just us two.

From: NB26@zone.com
To: Bee1984@gmail.com

Guess we'll have to improve our cybersex skills after all.

From: Bee1984@gmail.com
To: NB26@zone.com

Guess we will.

From: NB26@zone.com
To: Bee1984@gmail.com

Will it be enough?

From: Bee1984@gmail.com
To: NB26@zone.com

It will have to be.

NICK

Returning to our former relationship was like shrugging on an old coat. Not the sexiest way of putting it, but in spite of all that had happened in between, we slid effortlessly back into our pre-Operation Doppelganger say-anything comfort ways. Comfort that Bee desperately needed as she wrestled with the crippling guilt.

She wasn't alone in that. I'd loathed Nicolas. Envied him, and now I pitied him. Nicolas was a flesh-and-blood casualty of my and Bee's nature-versus-nurture experiment. Nor could I share any insider knowledge about how he might be coping with a broken heart. That was something only one Belcher had experienced; the closest I'd come to it was during the Doppelganger Sex Weekend and the weeks preceding the wedding. As painful as all that had been, I'd coped because there was still a glimmer of hope. Hope that Nicolas didn't have. If I ever had the chance to say sorry to him, I would.

And yes, okay, there was a touch of triumph that it was me she'd chosen in the end. The failed version rather than the polished one. The *once* failed version, because I was going to make the deadline, for which Nicolas was partly responsible. If it weren't for the pain I'd needed to channel as his relationship with Bee strengthened, I might have dragged my heels, given in to the lure of self-sabotage.

I stayed on at the lodging house. It wasn't just for Rosie's sake. I could have bribed Erika, offered to buy the mangy old Alsatian and moved the three of us into a country cottage. I stayed because I felt superstitious about it: I'd written – successfully – the majority of *Sabotage* here. I'd move on when it was completed. And it now felt more like home than Poll's place ever had. The little Victorian desk. The smell of cheap coffee and lavender. The revolving door of guests and the breakfast table chit-chat roulette. The low ceiling in my attic room on which I'd banged my head a thousand times. The shower cubicle that felt like a space portal. The view from the loo. It'd do for a while. And Petrus wouldn't be home for months – according to Erika, he'd secured a contract in Qatar, bodyguarding one of the few remaining sheikhs. She said she'd be joining him for a few weeks over Christmas, which would give me the run of the place while I finished the draft. 'And he has promised that this will be the last contract that he will take.' That was part of the carapace too: loneliness.

We never discussed what had happened between us. Occasionally she'd ask me to join her for a drink, and occasionally I'd accept, but neither of us let it go beyond that.

And I had Bee back. All of her.

Would it be enough? Would it?

Late at night, I'd occasionally allow myself to wander down the coma-switcheroo alleyways, and think: What if? *What if*?

*

From: Bee1984@gmail.com
To: NB26@zone.com

Merry Christmas! What did you get me?

From: NB26@zone.com
To: Bee1984@gmail.com

Hasn't it arrived yet? Bloody interdimensional couriers.

How's your day going so far? Anything from Leila?

From: Bee1984@gmail.com
To: NB26@zone.com

No. The radio silence continues. But my dad called, which was less awkward than it usually is. I'm working. It's amazing how much you can get done when you don't have a life.

From: NB26@zone.com
To: Bee1984@gmail.com

Tell me about it. I wrote 3000 words this morning.

From: Bee1984@gmail.com
To: NB26@zone.com

Good ones or bad ones?

From: NB26@zone.com
To: Bee1984@gmail.com

Too soon to tell.

From: Bee1984@gmail.com
To: NB26@zone.com

What else is new? Have you corrected the spelling on The Bergs' laminated signs yet?

From: NB26@zone.com
To: Bee1984@gmail.com

Nah. I did move them into different positions though.

Dylan's over at Poll and Jez's and they gave me a group call. Dylan says he's met someone and will bring them for a visit soon. And oh yeah, got a Christmas card. It was signed, 'love Maurice'. It took me hours to figure out who it was: remember Laurel and Hardy?

From: Bee1984@gmail.com
To: NB26@zone.com

Ha!

From: NB26@zone.com
To: Bee1984@gmail.com

What did you have for Xmas lunch? Turkey with all the trimmings?

From: Bee1984@gmail.com
To: NB26@zone.com

A pot noodle and a kiwi fruit. You?

From: NB26@zone.com
To: Bee1984@gmail.com

Emmental cheese toastie. Had to cut the mould off first though.

From: Bee1984@gmail.com
To: NB26@zone.com

Yum! Right. Now that's out of the way, what are you wearing?

BEE

The guilt didn't lessen, it was always there – *would* always be there – but I had no choice but to deal with it. And yes, I missed Nicolas. I missed the touching, the holding, the sex, the cup of coffee he'd leave by the side of the bed every morning without being asked. I missed having him around, the tipper-tap of his fingers on the keyboard. A punch of sorrow whenever I'd find something of his he'd left behind. The first thing I did when I got home was strip the bed. Which smelled of him. Of *us*. I bundled Ziggy Stardust into a bin-bag. It held too many reminders. On our first night together in the flat, echoing something Nick had once said to me, he'd joked that sleeping under Bowie had secretly been one of his ambitions.

There was guilt and sorrow, but no doubt.

I had Nick back and our equivalent of a long-distance relationship. I had all of him back, like he had all of me back. And life was less exhausting. Work and Nick, instead of work, Nick, Nicolas and all the drama.

But the drama wasn't over. And when it came, it came from an unexpected source: Leila.

I hadn't seen or heard from her since our fight. I thought of the hole she'd left in my life as a richly deserved karmic punishment. Then, on New Year's Day, she showed up at my door with a clinking Tesco bag and a look in her eyes that meant I was about to get the rollocking of my life.

I didn't know what else to say other than, 'I'm sorry.' She pushed past me and made straight for the breakfast bar. As she poured us hefty gin and tonics, she instructed me to 'keep my trap shut' while she said her piece. At first, after our fight and the e-mail, she said she couldn't decide if I was a pathological liar, a warped chaos-maker, in denial or delusional ('I even looked into how to get someone involuntarily committed, Bee'). Her fury and confusion at my actions took a long time to fade. But the worst of it was that I'd hidden the truth from her for so long. 'I mean, we tell each other *everything*. It felt like you'd broken our circle of trust.'

'Can I speak now?'

'Yes.'

I told her that I'd wanted to tell her, longed to, almost had on multiple occasions, but I'd let it get too far for that to be an option. 'And of course, I regret that. I hate myself for it. But Leila . . . are you saying that you now believe me?'

'Yes. No. Fuck it. Yes. It's . . . I *know* you, Bee. You can be your own worst enemy sometimes, but you're not cruel. And what you did to Nicolas was cruel. There had to be a reason, and as much as I would like to believe that you were under the spell of some warped psycho, because as shit as that is, it's fixable, I knew in my gut it wasn't that. As crazy as it all is, the pieces fit. Those messages I read at the beginning, things you've said along the way, the stuff you put in your e-mail. It adds up. And no, I can't believe I'm saying this.'

'Have you told Lev?'

'Christ no. He'd think we'd both lost it. He's way too much of a rationalist to handle this, you know that. Now. There are things I need to know.'

As the Tanqueray level dropped, she fired question after question at me.

The first item on the menu was her other self: childless Leila.

There was conflict there: I could see she was proud of Leila 2, yet also sad for her. 'Can I read it, Bee? The convo you had with her?'

I didn't stop to weigh up if this was a good idea or not. I was too desperate to appease her, save the friendship. I scrolled back through the thread and handed her the phone, watching her face as she read it. A dance of emotions: shellshock, surprise, sorrow, confusion.

'Christ, this is weird.' She shuddered. 'Funhouse-mirror weird.'

'That's exactly how Nick and I describe it.'

'But she's right. I *would* have told you what you were doing was manipulative and cruel.'

'It is – was.'

She nodded. Drank. Then said, in a softer tone of voice: 'Why didn't you tell me, Bee?'

'You know why. It's all there.'

'No. Not about that. About the fact you'd ended your pregnancy.'

Oh shit. I'd forgotten that was in there. 'You were going through IVF at the time. I . . . it didn't seem right.'

She thought for a while. 'I get it. The other me couldn't handle it when the other you went through with the pregnancy. That was . . . you did the right thing not telling me. That was kind of you.' She shook herself. 'How did you feel when you found out that the other you was a mum?'

'Beyond shocked. It was *beyond* funhouse-mirror weird. But knowing that I was capable of looking after a kid helped when I babysat the twins.'

'Ha!' She smiled. The first, hopeful sign that there was a chance of salvaging our friendship. 'The other me says she broke up with Lev. Is that why she decided not to pursue IVF? Because she didn't want to sole-parent?'

'I don't know for sure, Leila. It could be because IVF is harder to access in Nick's world because of the Attenborough Accords.'

'The *what* accords?'

I explained the basics, not realising at the time that I was lighting a fuse.

'And there wasn't a major freak-out about incentivising vasectomies?'

'There may have been. He didn't mention it.'

'Jesus. Can you imagine that happening here? It would be a Men's Rights mob waiting to happen. And they did this to limit population?'

'Yes.'

'For environmental purposes?'

'Yes.'

'Bee . . . just how much greener *is* Nick's world?'

I told her what I knew. Not much. We'd only gone into detail about it during the comparison days. 'They moved away from using carbon-based energy sources decades ago. In the eighties, I think.'

'What are they using now?'

'Um . . .' Delve, delve. 'Nuclear primarily, I think. And . . . solar maybe?'

'You don't know?'

'Not in detail.'

Not so much as a Paddington stare as a Paddington glare. The friendship salvaging operation was going south – and fast. This wasn't Friend Leila. This must be what Work Leila was like. Intense, terse, uncompromising. Feeling like a schoolchild trying to appease a strict teacher, I mentioned the No Drive subsidy, that there was a strict cap on flights per year (which had stymied Benedict the Bastard), and that they had Universal Basic Income.

'UBI? Okay . . . so we're talking about a *very* socialist democracy here.'

'Kind of.'

'So, what are the carbon levels in his world now?'

'I don't know. Um . . . they'd be pretty low, I imagine.'

'And politically? Who's the prime minister in his world?'

'I don't know.'

'Christ, Bee. You're like those people you see interviewed on the news who don't know what Brexit is. How can you not know this stuff? What do you two talk about all day?'

'Um . . .'

'You don't see the significance of this? That somehow, this alternative world has found ways to stop, or at least slow the environmental apocalypse coming our way? Get your fucking phone out *now*.'

*

From: NB26@zone.com
To: Bee1984@gmail.com

This is exactly the kind of thing that the Berenstains warned me not to do.

From: Bee1984@gmail.com
To: NB26@zone.com

But how will they know? Can't you just look into it? Please?

NICK

Maybe Leila was right. Maybe Bee and I had been selfish. We hadn't used our 'powers' for good; instead, we'd used the Berenstains' warning as an excuse to throw all our energies into Operation Doppelganger while Bee's world burned. Even Geoffrey had flagged this up at one point: *Aren't you worried?*

The shameful truth was: no. I hadn't given it the headspace it deserved. <That's not on you, Nick, but on me. I'm the conduit, after all. Leila's right, I'm one of those people who goes through life assuming everything will just be OK. BTW when I told her your world achieved the carbon emission levels we hope to reach by 2040 TEN YEARS ago she totally lost her shit>

It became a side project: *Save Bee's World.*

I spent a couple of weeks putting together a layperson's rundown of the policies that were in common practice here, and found several articles and peer-reviewed studies detailing the development of tech and energy sources – domestic and industrial – which I transcribed and Bee passed on to Leila. (<Is this enough for now? I know saving your world should take precedence, but I have a book to finish. Will get back to it when I'm done> <You've done more than enough! Thank you xx>)

At least the *Saboteur* finishing line was in sight. One final chapter to go. Echoing Nicolas, I'd been prevaricating over whether to let Posho get away with it or not. In the end I decided to go with Bee and Becca's twist. One day, I hoped Becca would read it. I'd already decided it should be dedicated to her and Scarlett: I was fairly sure

I could convince Tweedy, tap into his sentimental side – I'd tell him Becca was the name of my dear departed mum and Scarlett was her loyal spaniel.

But no good deed goes unpunished as everyone says everywhere, because about to hit was a curve ball the size of Canada: a curve ball that came in the form of a call from Leila 2, in another of those synchronicity whammies.

'Benedict knows, Nick.'

'Knows what?'

'That the story is bullshit. He must have hired someone to look into it after Becca told him she needed to extend the trip again.'

'Shit.'

'He's filed an application to bring Scarlett back from New Zealand. If Becca doesn't comply, she'll risk a kidnapping charge.'

'Shit. *Shit*.'

'Not only that, he's threatening to go for full custody, push her out of the picture entirely.'

'How can he?'

'Becca had a tough time just after Scarlett was born. Postnatal depression.'

'So? Why's that an issue?'

'Lev says he's lining up experts and witnesses who will swear that Becca has a history of self-harm and risk-taking behaviour that could put Scarlett at risk.'

'That's utter, utter bollocks. What witnesses?'

'Won't know that until it goes to trial.'

'But what about our collateral? *Our* witnesses? The women Lev tracked down, his ex-wife, her family?'

'The sister is still on board, but the ex and the others have withdrawn. Lev says they're no longer even taking his calls. I think Benedict got to them somehow. All we've got is hearsay.'

And proof from another world. That was hardly going to stand up in court, was it? 'So we're fucked, then?'

'As things currently stand. Yeah. Totally.'

From: Bee1984@gmail.com
To: NB26@zone.com

I wish he were dead. I wish we could get your landlady's boyfriend to take him out.

From: NB26@zone.com
To: Bee1984@gmail.com

He'd probably do it as well. Won't be back for months unfortunately.

From: Bee1984@gmail.com
To: NB26@zone.com

Too bad. I never actually hated anyone enough to wish them dead. But I do. I honestly do.

From: Bee1984@gmail.com
To: NB26@zone.com

You still there, Nick?

From: Bee1984@gmail.com
To: NB26@zone.com

Helllllooooo. Is there life on Mars?

From: NB26@zone.com
To: Bee1984@gmail.com

Sorry. Call came in.

This is going to sound a bit left field, but Geoffrey keeps asking if you'd be prepared to investigate something for him. Been bugging me for ages about it.

From: Bee1984@gmail.com
To: NB26@zone.com

I sent him/you an update about Jenny last week, didn't I? The one where their cat brought in a dead field mouse and Jenny passed her NVQ 5 course.

From: NB26@zone.com
To: Bee1984@gmail.com

It's not the usual. A little displaced-person side project he's got going on. A case study thing that he wants you to check out from your side.

Just say if you've got too much on your plate. It's no biggy.

From: Bee1984@gmail.com
To: NB26@zone.com

If it involves using my new mad PI skillz then I'm in. It'll take my mind off fantasizing about murdering Benedict & stressing about Leila.

BEE

It did take my mind off it. Joke's on me, right? But I don't blame myself for not putting the pieces together and believing Nick's 'Geoffrey's little side project' bullshit. The case study, which included a transcription of an interview conducted by one of the Berenstains with an Irish man named Iain O'Sullivan, struck a chord and I became more than a little obsessed with it. Despite the clinical style in which it was written, Iain's story had a pulse. More than a pulse – a heart. (<Wish I'd had time to jazz it up for you, Bee and do more than just copy it out. Also, the transcriber couldn't bring himself to type out swear words, so use your imagination>)

Iain's tale began in 2015, when he suffered a blow to the head during what sounded like a hellish corporate retreat 'team-bonding' activity (<can't believe you have that terrible shit in your world too, Nick>), lapsed into a coma, and came very close to being declared brain-dead. Defying the medical establishment's prognosis, he emerged from it a year later not only with his mental faculties intact, but with the new and surprising ability to converse in Korean. As Iain had never visited Korea or studied the language, the doctors attempted to rationalise this away as something his subconscious had picked up from a previous, mild interest in K-horror movies, but Iain wasn't so sure. While on life support, he said he'd experienced what he'd initially assumed was a vivid coma dream. One where he found himself 'living a similar, but subtly different existence in a similar but different world. And by different I don't mean better, because it was a [expletive]-hole compared to here. The [expletive]-upped thing was, I felt like I'd always been there. That it was my reality. That I'd always been that version of "me", living in that [expletive]-hole.'

<Just so I've got this straight, Nick: what Iain assumed was a coma dream could actually have been his consciousness somehow travelling across the mesh and – I dunno – bonding with his alternative self in another world?>

<Yep. Otherwise known as 'doing a Geoffrey'>

Iain's mesh-crossing escapades were fascinating, but it was the next part of his story that really resonated.

While living an alternative life in this alternative reality, Iain had moved to London, where he'd met and fallen in love with a Korean student, Kyung-Soo Jeung, with whom he'd lived happily for several months ('despite my mam in that place finding it hard to accept. Which was [expletive expletive expletive] because here we've always had a good relationship'.) No amount of rationalisation could stop him from mourning the loss of the relationship when he emerged from the coma. 'It was as if the love of my life had [expletive] died. But try explaining that to a [expletive] therapist. [Expletive] dream or not, I kept thinking, what if my subconscious mind had shown me an image of the man I was supposed to spend my life with? I couldn't let it go. I knew it was a long shot, but I had to see if I could find him in this world.'

Using details from his 'dream reality', Iain had discovered a likely candidate working as a translator for the British Embassy in Seoul (<wow, Nick, the parallels to Operation Doppelganger are giving me the chills>). He'd flown out there with the intention of cautiously investigating further, but when he encountered Jeung in person, that went out the window: 'I couldn't hold back. It was him. I knew it was him. I threw my arms around him and burst into tears. He thought I'd lost my [expletive] mind, of course. He had no idea who I was, but I knew everything about him. I still can't [expletive] believe he didn't run for the [expletive] hills when I told him why I'd flown all this way to see him. It was almost like a part of him *did* know me, too.'

It was while searching online for a possible explanation for his [expletive]-upped experiences that Iain had been sucked into the Berenstains' orbit (<'orbit of lunacy', you mean>), much like Nick had been shortly after Euston-Gate (<only I can pretty much guarantee that Iain was less hungover>).

Of course, what struck me more than anything about it was that at its heart, it was a love story (<like ours in a way, Nick>; <yeah, seems Quantum Anomaly Fuck-up Land has spawned its own romance genre. What shall we call it?>; <Mesh-cute. Obviously>). A love story that had a happy ending, as Iain eventually moved to Seoul to begin a new life with Kyung-Soo. The happy ending Nick and I would never have – couldn't have – and which I didn't comment on because I was too cowardly to go there.

<SO: you want me to see if I can track down Iain and/or Kyung-Soo here in the hopes of verifying the falling-in-love-in-2015-in-my-reality-while-in-a-coma-in-your-world story?>

<Well to be pedantic, it's Geoffrey who wants you to look into it, but the short answer is: yep>

<Will give it my best shot. Chances must be slim though. Seeing as there are supposedly squillions of realities & it's called the multiverse for a reason>

I assumed I'd *really* have to flex the old PI muscles to dig up the info 'Geoffrey' was after.

I was wrong.

*

From: Bee1984@gmail.com
To: NB26@zone.com

I'm not kidding, Nick. It took me less than two minutes to find the most likely Iain Kelly O'Sullivan match on Facebook. Not only is he Irish and living in London but his relationship status says he's married to a Kyung-Soo Jeung! It has to be the case-study's mirror match, right? It can't be a coincidence.

From: NB26@zone.com
To: Bee1984@gmail.com

Fast work there, Bee. Seems an unregulated social media does have its perks after all.

From: Bee1984@gmail.com
To: NB26@zone.com

Well yeah, one perk ☺ Hang tight. I'm going through his pics & vids now to find out when they met – thank God he's lax with his privacy settings.

From: Bee1984@gmail.com
To: NB26@zone.com

OK. So I can confirm they met in 2015 and were married a year later. There's a clip of their wedding vows, funny and sweet and heartfelt & made me tear up a little if I'm honest. And get this: in one of Iain's posts, he talks about how he'd spent years 'hiding who he truly was' because his mam is super-religious, but early in 2015, 'something came over him' and he decided enough was enough & he bloody well deserved to be happy and fulfilled. He says this 'feeling' gave him the strength to come out to his family (who were shitty at first about it but then got over themselves) and after that he moved to London and met his lovely (and gorgeous BTW) future husband.

There's no doubt that the two sides match up. And I STILL can't get over the parallels to our story.

From: NB26@zone.com
To: Bee1984@gmail.com

Yeah. Me neither.

From: Bee1984@gmail.com
To: NB26@zone.com

I can see why Geoffrey asked you to check it out. From what both Iains say, their glitches helped them. A bit like you helped Geoffrey by telling him about Jenny.

From: NB26@zone.com
To: Bee1984@gmail.com

Yeah. Go me. King of the Glitch-makers.

From: Bee1984@gmail.com
To: NB26@zone.com

Is this enough for Geoffrey do you think? I can always see if I can talk to Iain in person.

From: NB26@zone.com
To: Bee1984@gmail.com

It's enough. Thanks, Bee. I'll pass it on.

From: Bee1984@gmail.com
To: NB26@zone.com

Are you OK? You sound . . . not yourself. Is it stress re the Benedict situation?

From: NB26@zone.com
To: Bee1984@gmail.com

Yeah. It's really getting to me.

From: Bee1984@gmail.com
To: NB26@zone.com

We'll find a way, you'll see. There's an answer, we just haven't thought of it yet.

NICK

Bee, of course, was both wrong and right about that. Because there *was* an answer, it just wasn't one anyone in their right mind would consider.

There can be fewer things more surreal than plotting a hypothetical murder-suicide in a Frites franchise with its giant smiley-faced recycling bins and photographs of smug carb-scoffing couples. But that's where I suggested we meet. It was, after all, 'our place'.

They arrived together, Geoffrey marching in with his trademark semi-aggressive attitude, Kelvin looking, as usual, as if he only had one foot in the real world.

I got into it straightaway – or at least as soon as they'd ordered their coffees.

'I'll do it. The experiment. I want to go ahead.'

Geoffrey leaned back in his chair and roared, 'Fuck *me*,' earning him a now familiar round of worried glances from the staff. Kelvin's reaction was more subdued, a jerk as if he'd received a mild electric shock. Which, for him, was probably the equivalent of dancing on the table.

'What made you decide? Was it the case study?' Kelvin leaned across the table. 'Do you have confirmation from the other side of the mesh? I would be most interested in reading the results.'

I let him read Bee's i-mail regarding Coma Guy, then continued before he could bombard me with questions. 'If I do this, I have a very important caveat. There can be no suggestion that I may have taken my own life – overdosed on purpose or whatever.'

As Kelvin couldn't confirm that 'even after a considerable time' traces of the ketamine used to knock me off wouldn't be discovered during an autopsy, it was a near-impossible conundrum to solve. Disposing of my remains entirely wasn't an option. Disappearing without a trace would worry Poll and Dylan, and, probably, Erika. After a lengthy, bizarrely bloodless discussion, it was Geoffrey who came up with a possible solution. He'd sacrifice his Mini-Lec ('thing's on its last wheels anyway'), stage a crash with my body in the driving seat, and start an electrical fire so that my remains would be as compromised as possible. 'I'll say I loaned it to you, cos you wanted to go back to Leeds to visit your family.' Foolproof it was not.

'When do you wish to do this, Nicolas?' Kelvin asked. 'I will need a week at least to make my preparations.'

There were a couple of tasks I needed to complete first. Finish the novel, and then deal with another (hypothetical) matter that I wasn't about to discuss with them. 'February 14th?' *The Valentine's Day massacre*. Why not?

Kelvin stood up. 'I will be in touch.'

I asked Geoffrey to hang back for a private word. He didn't need any encouragement.

'What really made you decide?'

'I love her. Don't want to be without her. If that means dying, then that's what I'm prepared to do.'

He sniffed. A Geoffrey-ism that could mean anything from approval to 'Yeah, right.'

'Can you do something for me? Becca's husband is on the warpath, and it would help her legal team if they knew what he was up to. Could you follow him for a bit? Use your special surveillance skills to see if he has a particular routine or if he's up to anything dodgy? I'll pay you, of course.'

He eyed me enigmatically, then toyed with one of his favourite stevia packets. 'You don't have it in you, Nick.'

'Don't have what in me?'

'You know what. You're planning to off him, aren't you? That's why you changed your mind. Off him, then off yourself, so to speak.'

Fuck. Busted. By now, I should have known better than to underestimate Geoffrey. 'I don't know what you're talking about.'

'Give over. You wouldn't agree to this unless you knew the other lass and her kiddie were safe. Don't have an eppy, I'm not going to go to the cops. Man like that? Deserves what's coming to him. So. How are you planning on doing it?'

The (still hypothetical at this stage) murder shoe was on the other foot. The back foot. Because for someone who'd spent months inhabiting the headspace of a mass murderer who slaughtered his victims using a myriad of convoluted methods, I wasn't so hot when it came to plotting the real thing. Unlike Posho, I wasn't a sociopath. Nor did I possess Petrus's skill set (I'd once asked him to demonstrate a chokehold on me for research: *big* mistake).

'Not sure yet. Ambush him. Make it look like a suicide.'

A sniff and a sneer. The classic Geoffrey twosome. 'It'll take more than one person to pull that off.'

'How do you know that? Did that surveillance course you went on have another side to it?'

'Common sense. And dangerous abusive bastard or not, I'm not topping anyone.'

'I'm not asking you to.'

'I meant what I said. I owe you. And I'll help, up to a point. Best keep it as simple as possible.'

'Right. Make it look like a robbery gone wrong?'

'Maybe. Where?'

'His place? I know it fairly well. It's secluded. Wait in the driveway and ambush him when he gets back from work or something?' I know how all this looks (and sounds). But honestly, at that stage, I really was just testing the waters. It wasn't *real*. There was still a detachment to it – as if Geoffrey and I were simply brainstorming a plotline for *Saboteur*.

A shrug. 'Could work. You thought about what you'd use to do it?'

That I *had* considered. A knife would be too visceral. Even hypothetically the thought of that made me shudder. Writing about it had been bad enough (although describing Posho's poacher-stabbing frenzy had allowed me to indulge in a full gamut of crappy metaphors). Bludgeoning was equally bloody, so equally out. Poison would be my preferred option (Posho had managed to murder a badger-culling farmer by lacing his tea with a dose of ancient weed killer). But even if I could get my hands on something deadly, how would I administer it? Invite myself round on some convoluted pretext and then sprinkle it into Benedict's teeny glass cup when he wasn't watching?

The only choice was the obvious one. 'A gun.'

Sniff-sneer-sniff. 'Got one of them, have you?'

No. But I knew someone who did.

It was the easiest thing in the world to score an invite to Tweedy's mansion. I was days away from finishing the manuscript and said that for the purposes of 'verisimilitude' I wouldn't mind firing a gun. Would he, as my invaluable collaborator, be prepared to facilitate that?

'But of course! I haven't shot for yonks, but we can frighten the crows, can't we? Why not!'

The one and only time I'd visited Tweedy's pile, I'd gone by public transport: train and then an Electro-Bus that reeked of wet dog and puttered its way along miles of overgrown, rural byways. But this time I hired a car. If I did manage to swipe a weapon, I could hardly sling it on the baggage rail, heft it home unnoticed.

Once I'd de-rusted my driving skills and didn't need all my concentration to not crash, I spent the rest of the journey picking over the plan. The *hypothetical* plan.

According to Geoffrey, and luckily for us, Benedict was a man of routine. 'Gets home at seven every evening on the dot. Once he brought a woman back, but he's usually alone.' We'd just have to pray that on the night we decided to do it, he'd be alone (for this reason, Valentine's Day may not have been the smartest option).

Geoffrey would pick me up outside The Bergs. Drive me to Wilderville, where he'd wait on the outskirts while I slipped in, hopefully unseen, and lurked in the shadows cast by the eco-estate's helpful overabundance of foliage until Benedict arrived home. Then: BLAM.

Then: leg it back to the Mini-Lec, hopefully before the neighbours sounded the alarm.

Geoffrey would then drive me to Manchester and the lock-up Kelvin had hired for the purpose ('he lives with his mum, so we can't do it there'). Kelvin would induce the coma. Then: lights out. Then (hopefully): hello new world.

After a couple of days of coma + death, Geoffrey would transport my body in his car, stage a crash (he said he'd found a suitably rural spot) – *et voila*.

Yes, *obviously* set out in black and white like that it looks stupid.

There were more holes in it than a colander. Too many variables that could go wrong. I – and Geoffrey – could get arrested before we reached Kelvin. Becca could be accused of hiring a hit-person if I *did* get away with it (although that would be tough to prove, as she didn't have a clue what we were planning). Benedict might overpower me and turn the weapon against me. If I were using it as a storyline in *Saboteur*, I would have dumped it in the delete pile. Everyone, we're told, is capable of violence, but was I? I'd beaten up David Melling at school once or twice after he'd bullied one of my mates. I'd deflected a punch thrown at me from a guy in a pub years later. That was it.

Did I have it in me? Geoffrey said I didn't. I wouldn't know until it came to it. If it came to it.

And when – IF – my consciousness merged with Nicolas's, what if Geoffrey was wrong? What if Coma Guy's (admittedly touching) story was just a coincidence or total bollocks? What if Nicolas and I ended up driving each other crazy – a split personality stand-off?

Then there was Bee. What the hell was I going to do about that? She could read me like a book, but so far, seemed to accept that I sounded 'weird' because of the Becca and Scarlett stress. It hadn't felt great asking her to check into Iain Sullivan's case study on a false pretext. But even at this hypothetical stage, there was no way I could come clean. It would worry her stupid. The fact that I was even considering this worried *me* stupid.

In any case, it *still* didn't feel real. I didn't need to commit to anything. I didn't need to actually go ahead with any of it. Or at least that's what I told myself as the car crunched along the ridiculously long approach to Tweedy's mansion.

A large woman who introduced herself as Margie, Tweedy's daughter, met me at the entrance. She'd embraced every countryside cliché in the book (not my doing for once): ruddy-faced, no-nonsense, and thronged by a pack of Labradors. 'Daddy's waiting for you in the snug, Nick. He's so excited to see you.' She paused before she heaved open the front door. 'You may want to keep your coat on.'

She was right: I did. The place reeked of damp, which made the interior feel – if anything – colder than the wintry air outside. 'Excuse the state of things, Nick, we've had a few issues with the roof.' And the walls, and the floors, by the looks of it. We traipsed through a gloomy hallway scattered with buckets placed strategically to catch leaks, warped wooden floorboards, and walls shedding wallpaper like peeling skin. Had it been like this when I last visited? Perhaps I hadn't noticed – it had been summer, after all, and it's possible I'd been distracted by the glorious approach to the house and Tweedy's whisky. Or perhaps there'd been another hike in the land tax since then that was biting them hard.

The snug, a book-lined room with a cluster of tatty old chairs, was warmer, thank God – an illegal wood burner doing its best to fend off the draughts. Using a stick, Tweedy hefted himself out of an armchair. He was frailer than the last time we'd met, but he exuded the same bonhomie.

He shook my hand with knotted fingers. 'So good to see you.'

Margie left us to it: 'Don't exert yourself too much, Daddy.'

There was no booze on offer this time – just as well, as I planned on driving back that afternoon, whether I completed my mission or not. Instead, Tweedy invited me to pour myself a cuppa from a pot waiting on the coffee table. It had been stewing for a while, and reminded me, with a pang, of Lily's tannin-rich preferences. We traded pleasantries for a while, Tweedy enthusing about how much joy he'd taken in completing the research tasks I'd set him (all of which would have taken me less than five minutes to check on Google).

'Right,' he said. 'Shall we be off?'

I followed him through a labyrinth of corridors, their discoloured walls displaying the shadows of paintings long gone (sold, probably), ending at a doorway that led into a utility room the size of Erika's ground floor. Stone tiles, horse tack, dog leads, scores of Wellington boots shrouded in spider webbing, and a giant grumbling freezer that hadn't had a clean in what looked like a decade. And there, in the corner of this mess: the gun safe. I'd prepared myself for some sneaky code-remembering action, but there was no need. The safe, which was almost as ancient as Tweedy, wasn't even locked. There were at least a dozen shotguns piled erratically inside it (he wouldn't miss one, surely?). He removed a couple, checked them over, then handed me one. I'd never held a gun before. There was a sliminess to it, and also (Christ): holding it felt . . . *good.*

'They've been cleaned recently, old boy, don't worry. It shouldn't backfire and take your eyes out, ha ha.'

'But this *would* kill someone wouldn't it, Bernie?'

'I hope so, old boy. It certainly did in the first novel. The shot we'll be using is banned these days, of course. Tiresome nanny-state nonsense.'

'To confirm – to kill someone, you'd only have to shoot them once, right?' Picturing of course, Benedict climbing out of his slick-mobile. Me. With the gun. In the driveway. About to play a real-life version of Cluedo and no doubt fuck it up.

'Well, you'd have to be a *terrible* shot not to do some serious damage.'

Let's hope I'm not.

Tweedy slid a box of cartridges into his overcoat, handed me a pair of mangy ear protectors, and then, guns crooked under our arms, off we went to the killing fields, aka the back garden. It took a while to get there. Tweedy favoured his right leg and had a gait like a drunken sailor. The poor old bugger wasn't as fit as he'd been making out in his i-mails, and by the time we'd reached what he called 'our spot', he was out of puff.

Tweedy showed me how to slide the cartridges into the barrel. ('But of course you'll know how to do this from describing it in such super detail in the book.') That had come from a Google search. This was a different matter.

'What should I aim for?'

In front of us was a series of sorrowful, naked trees. The promised crows hadn't come to the party. Tweedy suggested aiming for the 'elm in the middle, as it has to come down in any case'. It felt a bit cruel shooting a tree that was already on death row, but if I couldn't muster up the guts to murder some foliage, how would I feel when faced with a human target?

I aimed, steeled myself for the kick and pulled the trigger. A second later: BLAM. The kick wasn't as strong as I expected, and, against all the odds, I'd hit the poor tree on my first try, knocking off one of its limbs.

'Good work, old boy. Now try for the trunk.'

Blam: A near miss.

'Bad luck.' He passed me the box of cartridges and, while he was taking his shot (he also missed), I pocketed a few.

Reload. Aim. BLAM. A hit: pieces of bark scattered in a splintery shower.

'A natural shot! Is this what you needed to complete the novel, old boy?'

'It certainly is.' Adrenaline up, I now barely felt the bite in the air. *It's just research. It's just research. It's just research.*

'Lunch!' Margie hollered.

We sailor-gaited back into the freezing monolith and ate in the snug, trays on our knees, the Labrador gang watching our every mouthful. Every shaky mouthful in Tweedy's case, as our excursion had clearly exhausted him. He hadn't been exactly what you'd call a collaborator, but I blethered on about how his help had been invaluable.

'Too kind, too kind. It's all you, old boy. Could I ask you a favour?'

'Of course.'

'Would you be so kind as to return the guns?' He rubbed his left leg. 'This old fella is playing up.' Was it really going to be this easy?

Not necessarily. There was Margie to consider. Then she said: 'I'll clean up and then I'll be off, Daddy.'

'You don't live here?'

'No. I'm in a cottage on the other side of the estate. He rattles around here alone.' Tweedy was already dozing in front of the fire. It really *was* going to be this easy. I was both relieved and disappointed that this potential obstacle to my stupid plan had been blasted away.

I helped her carry the plates into the kitchen, a cavernous, poorly lit portrait of further decrepitude: peeling linoleum, pipes that screamed and wobbled as she washed and I dried, a chugging Rayburn that had given up its fight against the damp aeons ago.

Margie gave the sink a cursory wipe, then turned to face me. 'There's something I need to say to you, Nick.'

Paranoia: I was certain that she'd seen into my brain, knew the real reason I was here.

'What you have done for my father has given him a new lease on life. You've put in some real work there. He had a hard time after Mummy passed on. He won't show it. And then his fall . . . This is going to be so lucrative and productive for both of you. *Thank you* for being so patient with him.'

She gave me an arm squeeze, and then she and her gang of Labradors exited.

Great. Not feeling guilty at all.

I still nicked the gun, though.

BEE

In one of life's ironies, it was Nate who first broke the news about Benedict:

<Heads up Bex. Benedict Mercer is in some serious MeToo shit & the news is about to drop. Hope you didn't get into bed with him after all ☺>

It didn't hit the media until the following day. There weren't many details at first: a brief article on the *Guardian*'s website, a glossier, gossipy splash on the *Mail Online*, 'Inquest Reopened into Fashion Mogul's Wife's Death'. But it was clear that Benedict was well on his way to joining the ranks of the Epsteins and the Weinsteins and the other bastards who'd got away with far too much for far too long. Kat had been as good as her word.

I messaged Nick immediately. Hope: *If he could be brought down here, he could be brought down there.*

Lev was on the case in Nick's world, which, while it did have its major differences, had a similar legal set-up. It wouldn't hurt to 'consult' with the Lev in mine. Two law brains could be better than one. Leila had made it clear that coming clean with him wasn't an option, but there was nothing stopping me positing a hypothetical situation. I could always trot out the old 'heard it from a client' chestnut. Thinking about it, I was surprised Leila hadn't suggested it before. She knew the full Becca versus Benedict the Bastard story, but to be fair, she had been in full save-the-planet mode that day.

I texted her to ask if I could come over. The bridge between us was on its way to being mended, but it would take a while before it was safe to cross.

She sent back: <ok yeah> Then: <lev says can you stop at the shop & get milk>

I overcompensated, bought milk, wine, Hobnobs, Pringles, three slabs of Lindt and, as an afterthought, some bananas to counteract the Bad Things.

Lev let me in: 'Thank God you're here, Bee.' There would be no chance of manipulatively picking his brain that evening: he was still in his work suit, eyes livid with stress. In the background, the twins were squalling, and the house, while never spotless, was a chaotic mess of toys, unwashed mugs, and take-out containers.

There was no sign of Leila. 'Where is she?'

'Holed up in the bedroom on her fucking laptop. She's been like this for days. I don't know what's got into her. Keep trying to get her to see the GP in case she's depressed. I know you two have had a thing, but has she mentioned to you what's eating her?'

Well, Lev. She's attempting to save the planet if you must know. 'She hasn't. What can I do to help?'

He checked his watch. 'Could you put the twins to bed? They've had their bath. I've got a call in ten minutes I have to take.'

'On it.'

It wasn't as easy as last time, perhaps because the boys could sense the tension thrumming through the house, perhaps because my Becca Mum connection was fading, but I managed to bribe them upstairs. We played apocalypse blocks for a while and I read them a story (which I quite enjoyed – Leila may have been sick of it, but *The Gruffalo* rocked), then stroked their hair like Mum used to do for me until they dozed off. I tidied the room, then tapped on Leila's bedroom door.

She was on the bed, greasy-haired, MacBook on her knees, surrounded by empty Monster Munch and Twiglet packets. She looked as if she hadn't slept for days: her eyes were red-rimmed, her skin sallow.

'Jesus, Leila . . . is this about the stuff that Nick sent through?'

Stupid question: what else could it be? But I needed an opener.

She glanced at me, then continued scrolling and tapping. 'There's nothing he's sent through that we haven't got or aren't developing here.'

'So? It's early days. He'll send through more when he's finished the novel. I told you that.'

'You don't get it, Bee. We *have* all the tech. We just don't have the political will.'

'We'll be fine.'

'You don't *know* that.' Said with such despair it sounded like she was on the verge of tears. I'd never seen her like this: a crack in her calm, rational façade – a crack *I'd* caused.

Tough love time. She was the one who usually took this role. Time to turn the tables: 'Listen, Leila. The kids need you. Lev needs you. You can't save the world in a week. Now snap the fuck out of it and do what you *can* do.'

She reared back, opened her mouth to retort, then scrubbed her hands over her face. 'Oh *God*.'

I sat next to her. 'Lev is really worried about you. So am I.'

'It's just . . . *fuck*, Bee. It's so frustrating.'

'We'll find a way, I promise. Now go and have a shower. You look like shit, and you don't smell too great, either.'

A snort and an eye-roll. Relief: this was more like her usual self. 'Okay, okay.' She slid out of bed, made for the bathroom, then turned to face me. 'You really think we'll find a way?'

'I really, really do.' Seemed I hadn't managed to exterminate the Lie Vermin after all.

NICK

When I pressed <send>, delivering the final draft of the novel, this time I didn't cry. It was my best work. I knew it was. I had more in me, too. But I wouldn't see it published (at least in this world). Tweedy, or another ghost, would have to handle the edits. One task down, three to go before the Valentine's Day massacre, due to take place that evening. In six hours and thirty-four minutes to be exact.

If it all went pear-shaped, I wouldn't be known as a novelist. I'd be known as a murderer. Or an attempted murderer. That would be my legacy. *How does that feel, Nick?* Which reminded me – I hadn't thought to leave a will. *Idiot.* I opened up a document and wrote a couple of lines saying that if anything happened to me, then everything should go to Dylan. I'd have to hope whoever read it wouldn't check the time stamp. I'd considered embarking on a farewell tour. Taking the train to Brum to meet Dylan's new partner, then popping in on Poll and Jez. But if (and knowing them, probably when) Kelvin and Geoffrey did cock it up, the fact that I'd acted massively out of character shortly before my death would add to any suspicion of suicide, and I couldn't have Dylan going through that. If I did end up melding consciousnesses with Nicolas, in Bee's world I could always befriend my ex-wife who wouldn't know she was my ex-wife and introduce her to 'my' best man. Meddle some more, only with other people's lives this time. Because if Bee and I were meant to be together, maybe they were too. And the Poll in Bee's world deserved every bit of happiness she could get. Not saying a proper farewell to Dylan hurt. Really hurt. It felt like I was betraying him. Because there *was* no Dylan in Bee's world, and I'd be leaving him in this one. I compromised with a call. Trying to sound as normal as possible. Trying not to think about his room. Trying not to say goodbye. It helped that after our talk at Lily's memorial service, I knew he'd be okay. He *had* to be okay.

And now: the most difficult task of all. The task I'd been putting off. The i-mail to Bee. The confessional. The thought of her reading whatever I managed to cobble together made me feel physically sick.

I was ten minutes in (all I'd managed so far was 'Dear Bee'), when, with that eerie mind-reader synchronicity, she sent: <You delivered Sabotage yet?>

<Going to give it one more polish first>

<Don't doubt yourself Nick. You can do this!!! Let me know when it's gone so I can have a drink to celebrate>

You'll need more than a drink, Bee . . .

I wrote and rewrote it until I was down to the wire. It would have to do. Geoffrey would be pulling up in half an hour, and there was one last task to complete.

Leaving the gym bag containing the gun in the hallway and the inadequate i-mail grenade in my draft folder, waiting to be deployed, I tapped on the door of the lounge. Erika and the dogs were snuggled on the couch in their usual positions. Sausage flapped her tail when she saw me; Rosie looked up, sniffed as if to say *oh, it's just you*, then yawned.

'Sorry to spring this on you, Erika, but would you be okay to watch Rosie for a few days?' *Aka forever?*

'You have a problem?'

'Nah. Finished the book, and a couple of mates have invited me to celebrate with them. We're going on a bit of a road trip.'

'With that man who came to the house?'

'He's one of them.'

'He is a strange one.' *You have no idea*. 'You are leaving now?'

'Yeah. Are you sure you're okay to look after Rosie?'

'Of course.'

I went over to the dog and stroked her wiry head. 'Good girl.' A lump in my throat: my Adam's apple on the cusp of doing the Geoffrey Dance. Rosie and I had been through a lot together: despite her grumpy old ways, she really was my best mate. I would never see her again, but I knew she'd be happy with Sausage.

Erika was watching me carefully. 'You are okay, Nick?'

I cleared my throat. 'Yeah. I always get like this when I finish a book.'

'I am happy that you have done this.' *Happy.* That fucking stupid word again. *Why does everyone have to be happy all the time?* 'Congratulations on completing it. We must have a drink when you get back.'

'That would be great. Thank you. See you soon.'

'Yes, yes.'

I shouldered the bag and headed out into the night. It was colder than I expected, and I almost returned to collect a heavier jacket, then thought, *what's the point? You won't be needing one for much longer, will you, Nick?*

Geoffrey was right on time, the Mini-Lec purring and coughing, coughing and purring at the kerb. The Mini-Lec: my future, foetid coffin if all went to plan.

I put the bag on the back seat and slid in next to him. It was too dark to read his expression, but his body language was more tense than usual. Which is saying a lot, because Geoffrey was always tense.

This is it. If you do this, you can't take it back.

As he pulled away, I sent Bee the i-mail, then turned off my phone.

From: NB26@zone.com
To: Bee1984@gmail.com

This is the most difficult thing I've ever had to write. The most difficult thing you'll ever have to read. You'll hate me for a while, I know you well enough to be sure of that. And I wish with all my heart I could have shared this with you before, but I knew what you'd say: don't do it. It's madness. It's crazy. You don't have it in you, Nick.

I couldn't tell you before, but I have to tell you now. I can't bear the thought of leaving you hanging, waiting for a message from me that will never come and never knowing why.

The reason I asked you to look into that case study wasn't for Geoffrey, but for me. Kelvin and Geoffrey believe there is a way we can be together. But for this to happen, I can no longer physically be here. I don't know how to write this without sounding either suicidal or mental, but fuck it: when I die here, there's a chance that my consciousness will cross the mesh and merge with Nicolas's. Yes I KNOW how that sounds. But you've looked into that case study, Bee. You know that it CAN work. You know it can work without harming Nicolas either.

But before I do this, there's something I have to do first. Something that involves Benedict. It all comes back to our first Red Flag: Strangers on a Train. Crossed Lines. If all goes well, Benedict will never harm anyone again.

I'm doing this for Becca and for Scarlett, but I'm also doing this for me and for you.

Bee. I love you. I don't want to live without you. You said there was a piece missing with Nicolas. I am that piece. And maybe he's MY missing piece. If there's a chance, any chance at all, shouldn't we take it?

I don't know how long it will take for me to find you. A week? A month? But I WILL find you.

And then we can meet under the clock at Euston at 12 like we planned. You wear the red coat. I'll wear a tweed suit.

Wait for me.

Have faith.

BEE

Nick and Nicolas were always going on about how frustrating it could be when the word or phrase they needed to bring a character to life eluded them. Nicolas's *A Shot in the Dark* draft had been littered with 'XXX's, which he'd use as placeholders whenever the right adjective didn't immediately spring to mind.

When I read that e-mail, 'shock' didn't cut it. Nor did 'horror'. Nor did any adjective in Word's thesaurus tool. SO: *When Bee read the e-mail, she felt XXX.*

I was finishing up a fitting when it came through. The client, Olivia, was one of Ms Peach's bridesmaids, and I'd let her jump the queue because, despite Ms Peach's pernickety ways, I still thought of her fondly – an early Nick and Bee bonding moment. Olivia would've turned Leila and Nicolas's hair white with her political views, but fussy she was not ('Oh do what you like, sweetheart!'), and she was great company. A right-wing version of Geoffrey's daughter Jenny, irrepressible, the kind of person whose house would be littered with signs reading: Live! Laugh! Love!

And she was a right old gossip, filling me in on Ms Peach's nightmare of an ex-husband. ' . . . and *then* he said he had no idea how they'd got onto his hard-drive. But you don't just do a random Google for those kind of pictures, do you? She's gone right off men now. Says she's going to try her hand at being a lesbian. Well, I said, why not?'

I finished pinning the hem, then we looked in the mirror to

check it was the right length. She sighed. 'You're a miracle worker, sweetheart.'

I unzipped the back of the dress and was about to leave her to get changed in private when I checked the phone. I'd been waiting for an e-mail from Nick telling me he'd delivered the novel – good news for once! – and, as Olivia had her back to me while she launched into another tirade about Mr ex-Peach's tame, but numerous, fetishes, I sneaked a peek at it. *Not* the message I was expecting. As I read it, the room seemed to get smaller and smaller. Olivia's babble faded; I was dimly aware that I'd dropped the phone on the floor.

The next thing I knew, I was sitting on the bed, Olivia's face filling my vision, and she was rubbing my hands between both of hers. 'Hey, there. Hey. You're all right, my sweetheart, you're going to be fine. Have you eaten today? Is it low blood sugar? I always get woozy when I skip a meal.'

Speak. I had to say *something*. Mumbled: 'I'm so sorry. I've just had some bad news.' *Bad news*. Understatement of the multiverse.

Still in her underwear, Olivia took charge. 'Right. Sit there. Don't move.'

I did as I was told – I wasn't sure if I could have moved if I'd wanted to.

I sat there still feeling XXX and stared at the phone on the floor. In the background, I could make out the sounds of Olivia rooting through cupboards, the hiss of the kettle being switched on. I retched: almost did throw up.

Gradually, I allowed myself to examine what I'd just read, approaching each part of it with caution, as if it were a dangerous animal. First: murder. Nick was talking about murdering Benedict. *Strangers on a Train. Crossed Lines*. But he didn't have that in him. I knew him. I *knew* him. *I wouldn't feel this way about him if he were capable of that*. I'd fantasised about offing Benedict, had wished the bastard dead; that, at least, was a concept I could take in. *Doing* it was another matter.

Then . . . the other issue. I poked at it gently, then withdrew. No. Uh-uh.

Olivia bustled back in with a mug of tea. 'Drink this, my darling. Sugar for shock. Not scientific, but in my opinion, sugar helps in every situation.'

I took it with numb hands. Sipped. Winced. She must have used half a pound.

She sat next to me. 'Do you want to talk about it? It's fine if you don't.' Then: 'Was it a death, sweetheart?'

Yes. I started crying. Sobbing. She drew me to her, and I buried my face in her fleshy shoulder while she stroked my hair. Dead. *He's dead. Nick is dead.* Suicide. Or murder. *Nick is dead.*

'Was it someone close?'

A nod.

'Is there anyone I can call for you?'

I wasn't about to call Leila – I'd been planning on going round to hers after the fitting to check she really was back on an even keel.

The sobs began to subside. She handed me a tissue. I wanted to be alone. *Needed* to be alone in order to examine the dangerous animal's underbelly. 'You've been so kind. But I'll be okay. I was kind of expecting it.'

'An elderly relative, was it?'

'Yes.'

'Well, I'm not going anywhere until I'm sure you're on your feet again.'

'I'll be fine, really.'

It took some pretty world-class acting and a plague's worth of Lie Vermin to convince her that I was fine to be left alone. I wasn't fine. But. BUT. Undercutting the XXX, the horror, the fear, the looming hole of future loneliness, was hope. Just a little bit of hope. But hope all the same. *What if it worked? What if it actually worked?*

NICK

As anti-climaxes go, it was up there with the best of them. Or worst. If it was the denouement of a novel, the BookPost reviewers would be apoplectic: 'SO DISAPPOINTED WITH THE ENDING!! What was the writer thinking???'

As he sat in the car, contemplating what he was about to do, delicate tendrils of frost formed across the windscreen, lacing across his vision. This beauty, this reminder of nature in all its complexity, also laced doubt into his heart. And he realised, at that moment, that he actually wanted to live.

Bollocks.

Not only would I never actually write something like that, what actually happened was far more mundane.

Geoffrey and I didn't speak as he drove, my pulse thudding in my ears, my left knee dancing of its own accord, the voice in my head going, *Real enough for you now, Nick?* We cruised past the park, along the roads that were now as familiar to me as Dreadnought Street had been, and then, all too soon, to our rendezvous spot just outside Wilderville. I wish I could say that a twist of fate or something profound made me pause. Or that sending Bee the i-mail was the catalyst (because it *should* have been the catalyst). I was reaching for the door handle when quite simply, I woke the fuck up. The clichéd version would be: *I came to my senses*. I basically stopped acting like I was a character in a fucking novel and gave myself the mental equivalent of the gender-offensive 'stop being so hysterical' slap. That was it. The worst of it was, I couldn't believe I'd let it get this far.

I didn't have it in me. When it came down to the wire: *I simply didn't have it in me*. The murder or the suicide.

Geoffrey didn't comment on my lack of action, merely handed me a rollie, and lit one up for himself.

Neither of us said anything until we'd smoked them down to the filter. With a 'Fuck 'em', he flicked his butt onto the street. Seemed a touch of mild littering was the only punishment Benedict was going to get that night. 'Are we still going to Manchester or am I taking you home, Nick?'

'Home.'

'You sure?'

'I'm sure.'

Once more, we drove in silence back to The Bergs. He only spoke again when we were parked outside. 'Don't beat yourself up about it. You got further with it than I thought you would.'

'Yeah. All the way to the sodding driveway.'

'It's not in you, Nick. Told you that.'

'You were right. Will you tell Kelvin that I'm sorry?'

A nod.

I climbed out.

'Aren't you forgetting something?'

'Eh?'

'The gun.'

'Shit.' I *had* actually forgotten about that.

'Ah fuck it. I'll dump it in the river.'

'You sure?'

'Yeah.'

Then he drove off without saying goodbye.

I slunk into the house, tail between my legs. I knocked on Erika's door, mumbled a sheepish, 'I changed my mind,' then scurried up to my sanctuary before she could question why the road trip was a non-starter or offer me a drink. I'd need a clear head for what was ahead. Geoffrey and Kelvin might not have succeeded in killing me that evening, but I was certain that Bee was bloody well going to try.

*

From: NB26@zone.com
To: Bee1984@gmail.com

Have you forgiven me yet?

From: Bee1984@gmail.com
To: NB26@zone.com

No I bloody well haven't. You scared the shit out of me. I thought I'd lost you. If you were here in person I wouldn't know whether to hug you or punch you.

From: NB26@zone.com
To: Bee1984@gmail.com

Punch. Definitely. Or a full-on head-butting, followed by a knee to the groin. And don't forget the chokehold.

From: Bee1984@gmail.com
To: NB26@zone.com

Planning to shoot Benedict the Bastard is one thing, but even considering letting a pair of loons experiment on you like that? Did you REALLY think you could just jump into Nicolas's body like that guy out of Quantum Leap?

From: NB26@zone.com
To: Bee1984@gmail.com

That guy out of what?

From: Bee1984@gmail.com
To: NB26@zone.com

Never mind.

From: NB26@zone.com
To: Bee1984@gmail.com

It isn't as if I actually went through with it, is it?

And if you think about it, if it had worked, then Nicolas and I would literally have become writing collaborators.

From: Bee1984@gmail.com
To: NB26@zone.com

Or soulmates.

From: NB26@zone.com
To: Bee1984@gmail.com

Ha! Brothers in arms. Or brothers with arms. No that one's crap.

From: Bee1984@gmail.com
To: NB26@zone.com

The Man with Two Brains.

From: NB26@zone.com
To: Bee1984@gmail.com

Mind readers. Or writers. No that's shite too.

And yeah, I know the whole thing was stupid. I know it would never have worked. But I still can't help feeling like I've let Becca and Scarlett down. That I've let YOU down.

From: Bee1984@gmail.com
To: NB26@zone.com

They got him in my world, Nick. Lev will find a way. Leila 2 will find a way. WE'LL find a way.

I'm going to get hold of Kat again, see if there's any insider info that didn't make it into the press that we could possibly use. Info that may mirror some nefariousness he got up to in your world. Hang tight.

BEE

And I was doing just that, midway through penning an e-mail to Kat in fact, when Leila rocked up and everything went to shit again.

From: Bee1984@gmail.com
To: NB26@zone.com

I've NEVER seen her like this, Nick. Way worse than before. She says the only way to get the world to change is to PROVE that we can do it. Says if we can prove there's a better world – i.e., yours – that maybe it'll be the push people need to do something.

From: NB26@zone.com
To: Bee1984@gmail.com

And how is she planning on doing that?

From: Bee1984@gmail.com
To: NB26@zone.com

Wants to go to the authorities.

From: NB26@zone.com
To: Bee1984@gmail.com

What authorities?

From: Bee1984@gmail.com
To: NB26@zone.com

I dunno. MI5 or whoever.

From: NB26@zone.com
To: Bee1984@gmail.com

She'll be branded a conspiracy nut.

From: Bee1984@gmail.com
To: NB26@zone.com

You don't know her, Nick. Well, you know the OTHER her. Once she's set her mind to something, she won't stop.

From: NB26@zone.com
To: Bee1984@gmail.com

There's nowt she can do unless you give her your phone. The only proof is the i-mail thread and who'd believe that anyway?

From: Bee1984@gmail.com
To: NB26@zone.com

I hope you're right, Nick. I really hope you're right.

NICK

It was fitting, I suppose, that Erika was the one who sounded the death knell. I was sitting at the desk when it came, a new document open on the laptop, trying to divert myself from stressing about Operation Benedict. This time I was going to write for me. Not for Tweedy, not for anyone else. I was going to tell OUR story. Mine and Bee's. I even had a title: *Impossible: A Fucked-up Love Story.* Life imitating art this time: a version of the lie I'd once told Becca.

Then: tap-tap. 'You have visitors, Nick. They are waiting for you in the lounge.' Said without her usual irritation, as if she knew something serious was in the offing. Paranoia came first: had Tweedy discovered I'd nicked the gun? No – if the cops were here, Erika would have mentioned that, surely. It was probably just Geoffrey and Kelvin, girding their loins to have another go at convincing me to let them kill me.

And Geoffrey and Kelvin *were* there, but they weren't alone. Standing straight-backed in front of the fireplace was Henrietta. No warm(ish) greeting today. Deadly serious: a conspiracy-loon assassin.

Out popped: '*Fuck.*'

An icy smile from Henrietta: 'That is not an elegant greeting, Nicolas, but I understand your reaction.'

I glanced at Geoffrey, who was looking anywhere but at me. Kelvin was similarly dodging eye-contact.

'I am sure you can guess why we are here, Nicolas.'

'But we didn't go through with it!' I blurted.

'Excuse me?'

'The . . .' *Oh just say it.* 'The . . . *meddling* we were planning.'

'You are speaking of the murder?' Said matter-of-factly. 'Yes, I am aware of that. As I am aware of Kelvin's proposal. But do not worry, Geoffrey and Kelvin have been disciplined for their involvement and have assured me that they are penitent.'

'Was it you who told her, Geoffrey?'

He stared at his feet and shook his head.

I turned to Kelvin. 'Did you? Because I backed out?'

'No.' They really did have the look of schoolboys who'd been shat on from a dizzy height by the head teacher.

'There is something you should know, Nicolas,' Henrietta continued. 'Do you remember when we first met, and you graciously allowed me to access your i-mail chain?'

'Obviously.'

'I took the opportunity then to clone your zone account.'

I couldn't find my voice straightaway. Shock, I suppose. 'But that's illegal!' Whiny. *No fair*.

'You are correct.'

'Does this mean . . . have you been reading *all* of my i-mails? All this time?'

'Yes.'

Intrusive – and embarrassing. Very. Especially considering that Bee and I had managed to improve our cybersex skills.

'I needed to be sure you were keeping your side of the bargain.'

'So you know everything?'

'Yes. In fact, the other members, Isaac especially, were rooting for you.'

'You what?'

'Regarding your romance with Rebecca Mercer. He was most distressed when it did not work out.'

Bloody hell. Had they been following my life like soap-opera addicts? 'Did you know about this, Geoffrey?'

'No.'

'Neither Geoffrey nor Kelvin were party to the i-mails,' Henrietta said. 'Only the inner circle.'

'But Kelvin *is* the inner circle. Isn't he?'

'Yes, but he also has a troubled history. I suspected early on when we confirmed your story that he might attempt one of his displaced person's experiments again.'

'What do you mean, *again*?' It was like a non-stop shock-bomb attack. Just as I'd crawled out of the rubble caused by the last one, in came another. 'On who?'

'Himself. Fortunately, he was resuscitated in time.'

That was why he'd been so cagey when I'd asked him why he didn't try it on himself. *Okay, okay. Regroup the defences.* 'If you knew what I was up to right from the start, why didn't you shut it down then?'

'We considered this. In fact, we took a vote on whether or not to do so at every troubling stage. You came close several times.'

'The Benedict situation, you mean.'

'Oh no. Not that one. Allowing you to attempt to murder him was a unanimous decision.' *Jesus*. 'The giving of the book idea was the most contentious.'

'More so than *murder*?'

'Yes. We're not *monsters*, Nicolas. We concluded that he was someone who would do more harm than good in the long term.'

'Okay. So what's this all about then?'

'The threat, of course. From Rebecca Davies's friend Leila. We were concerned when you began sending information through to her, but not *too* concerned, as it was only going outwards.'

'We were only trying to help Bee's world. Don't we have a responsibility to do that?'

'Perhaps we do. But we cannot risk opening the channels both ways, and for her reality to infect or influence *ours*. I am sure I do not need to tell you that there are people out there who would see this as the perfect opportunity to unleash the populism and destruction that has occurred and is occurring in her reality. Just because these people are not in power here, doesn't mean they don't *exist*. This is why we must sever the thread.'

'But you said yourself that no one would believe it.' Desperation laced my voice: who could blame me? Because as cuckoo as the Berenstains were as a group – as much as I wanted to believe that mine and Bee's connection went beyond the technical, that nothing and no one could sever the thread – I was sure that Henrietta was capable of doing exactly that. She'd certainly had the skills to stealthily clone my phone and spy on us for all this time, and according to Geoffrey, she'd had no trouble destroying the career of that journo who'd defamed the society.

'It is a risk we are not prepared to take. We have voted. The decision is final.'

I turned to Geoffrey, my former ally and wild card. 'But you can't want this, Geoffrey. What about your daughter?'

He finally looked me in the eye. 'I can't stop her, Nick. I wish I could.' Did she have something on him? Possibly. 'I really am sorry, mate.'

Here's where I wish I could say that I dug deep and found the words, the eloquence to convince this emotional robot of a person that severing the thread would sever something inside me too. That she didn't need to do this, that there was another way, that Bee and I would swear on our lives that we'd never share any 'real world' details with each other ever again, that I would do literally *anything* if she changed her mind. But I can't say I did that, because I didn't. Couldn't. Too shellshocked. Too numb.

Henrietta held up a hand. 'There is some good news. We have taken a vote and I have ensured that Benedict Mercer will not go unpunished. You will not need to worry about him harming Rebecca or her daughter Scarlett. All powerful men have secrets, financial and personal, hidden in places they believe to be secure and unbreachable. But nothing is unbreachable, and some of these secrets carry with them a mandatory ten-year sentence.'

I barely took this in. Heard myself saying: 'Who *are* you, Henrietta?'

Henrietta stood up and smoothed her skirt. 'And we will give you a chance to say goodbye. We will give you that, at least.'

From: Bee1984@gmail.com
To: NB26@zone.com

Oh God no. I can't . . . How long do we have?

From: NB26@zone.com
To: Bee1984@gmail.com

24 hours.

BEE

What do you do when you're told you only have one day left to live? That's the philosophy we're all supposed to live by. *Live each day as if it's your last*. It felt like that.

We did what people who know they're dying do, what Mum and I had done in her final days: we reminisced. Ran through our greatest hits and touchstones: Tweedy. Ms Peach. Bowie. *Crossed Lines*. And discussed the notion that fate might have had something to do with it after all. Perhaps saving Becca and Scarlett was the real reason we were glitches, the real reason why we were fated to meet. (<If so, then Fate is one fucked-up convoluted bastard of a thing, Bee>)

One day left to live.

A death sentence ironically handed down because of Leila's desire to make things better for everyone on the planet, rather than the selfish catalogue of manipulation in which Nick and I had engaged. I don't hate her for it now, although I did for a while. I couldn't blame her. Because it really did feel like everything in our world was collapsing, as if the Redditors who believed we'd slipped into a mad alternative reality in 2016 where pandemics, populism and pollution ruled were right. I got it. I understood. She had the twins fuelling her concern and panic. I'd felt much the same about Scarlett.

As we laughed and cried and reminisced, I tried not to look at the clock. Time speeds up when you're on death row.

NICK

So that's it. *All she wrote.*

This is my side of the story. Bee will have hers. Maybe.

It's been three weeks since we last had contact. I'll find the courage to re-read our last exchange one day.

Henrietta was as good as her word. Benedict was no longer a threat. Maybe the evidence was there all along, maybe she planted some of it, but either way it was justice of sorts. It's difficult to chase your soon-to-be ex and her daughter halfway around the world when you're locked up for severe tax infringement and are under investigation for criminal negligence, fraudulent business practices, ecocide and more. And maybe Bee's right. Maybe saving Becca and Scarlett *was* what it was all about. If so, I can live with that.

I want you to know – the *you* who may one day read this (and who knows? I may just put it up on BookPost to fuck with the Berenstains) – that the other hoary old cliché: *It's better to have loved and lost than to never have loved at all* is a hoary old cliché for a reason. Because it's true. Sometimes love doesn't come in the form you think it will. It races up like a Jason Frey character and roundhouse kicks you in the heart when you least expect it. (I couldn't end this *without* a tortured metaphor, could I?) I'd had her for a while. And that was enough for me. It had to be enough.

The i-mail thread has been severed, but the one connecting us is still there. I can feel it. I think I always will.

From: NB26@zone.com
To: Bee1984@gmail.com

Maybe we'll find each other again somehow. If it was meant to be, why not?

From: Bee1984@gmail.com
To: NB26@zone.com

Maybe we will.

From: NB26@zone.com
To: Bee1984@gmail.com

Maybe I'll send out another random message and you'll find it. Maybe this has happened in a trillion different ways.

From: Bee1984@gmail.com
To: NB26@zone.com

Maybe I'm the one writing the misdirected e-mail to an arsehole client.

From: NB26@zone.com
To: Bee1984@gmail.com

In another world, maybe we're even together. And happy.

From: Bee1984@gmail.com
To: NB26@zone.com

Or bickering over whose turn it is to take out the recycling.

From: NB26@zone.com
To: Bee1984@gmail.com

It was good while it lasted.

From: Bee1984@gmail.com
To: NB26@zone.com

It was better than good. It was all there was.

From: NB26@zone.com
To: Bee1984@gmail.com

I love you.

From: Bee1984@gmail.com
To: NB26@zone.com

I love you.

Say it. Say goodbye. I can't bear to.

Mail Delivery Subsystem <mailer-daemon@googlemail.com>
[Your message to NB26@zone.com has been blocked. Recipient address rejected: Access denied.]

EPILOGUE

AN AFFAIR TO REMEMBER

From: Bee1984@gmail.com
To: NB26@zone.com
Subject: Is There Life on Mars?

Hey. It's me again. Surprise!

This pandemic beats the one you said your reality experienced in the 90s hands down: my world wins for once!

If you were here, we would have *killed* this shit: our whole relationship was one long virtual lockdown.

I think of these e-mails as messages in bottles thrown from a ship into the multiverse ocean. Like you would say, 'pretentious, moi?' But writing to you helps. I'm addicted to the hope that THIS time the bottle will reach you.

Here goes . . .

[Your message to NB26@zone.com has been blocked. Recipient address rejected: Access denied]

From: Bee1984@gmail.com
To: NB26@zone.com
Subject: Is There Life on Mars?

I re-read the messages today. Have you done that yet? Laughed and cried and cringed. We'll have them for as long as they last.

[Your message to NB26@zone.com has been blocked. Recipient address rejected: Access denied]

From: Bee1984@gmail.com
To: NB26@zone.com
Subject: Is There Life on Mars?

Dad said something funny the last time he called: in the pre-virus days you'd cough to hide a fart; now you fart to hide a cough.

Ventured out to the corner shop to get milk for Magda and Jonas feeling like some kind of brave apocalypse forager. Hunched and scurrying and dodging joggers and cyclists like they were contagious. Which they might be. Yeah, I know. Not funny. You would have done better.

[Your message to NB26@zone.com has been blocked. Recipient address rejected: Access denied]

From: Bee1984@gmail.com
To: NB26@zone.com
Subject: Is There Life on Mars?

Jonas died this morning. Not from the virus. He went in his sleep. His body was collected by paramedics in hazmat suits which was . . . XXX. Sod the regulations, I went and sat with Magda. She seemed to crumple. Not from the grief, although there was that, but as if she could now allow herself to collapse. Sleep.

When she woke up, we cleaned the flat. She kept finding things of his that made her weep. Her equivalent of reading our e-mails I suppose. I wept too.

When she heard that Jonas would have to have a virtual funeral she went: 'Pah! Ridiculous.' I knew then that she'd be OK.

[Your message to NB26@zone.com has been blocked. Recipient address rejected: Access denied]

From: Bee1984@gmail.com
To: NB26@zone.com
Subject: Is There Life on Mars?

Zoom call with Leila today, the twins causing chaos in the background. She and Lev already look like they have PTSD. She's stopped apologising now. There are some things that are beyond an apology. Like how I treated Nicolas.

But she says she has hope that this pandemic could be the catalyst we need to become more like your world. Me? I think it'll take more than that, but hope floats.

[Your message to NB26@zone.com has been blocked. Recipient address rejected: Access denied]

From: Bee1984@gmail.com
To: NB26@zone.com
Subject: Is There Life on Mars?

Here's a biggy.

An e-mail from Nicolas came today.

He wants to talk. I don't know why. Leila swears she hasn't told him that you (the other man) are out of the picture, but she's way better at lying than I am, so who knows?

He says that when this is over there are things he needs to say to me in person. Probably things I don't want to hear, but I deserve to. Things we need to discuss.

Like the fact we're still legally married?

[Your message to NB26@zone.com has been blocked. Recipient address rejected: Access denied]

From: Bee1984@gmail.com
To: NB26@zone.com
Subject: Is There Life on Mars?

I would definitely rather be a reverse mermaid. I realised this morning I'd never actually answered that question.

[Your message to NB26@zone.com has been blocked. Recipient address rejected: Access denied]

From: Bee1984@gmail.com
To: NB26@zone.com
Subject: Is There Life on Mars?

You should see us, Magda and me, sitting at the worktable and sewing masks together like two babushka widows. I've often thought of telling her about Jonas's choice in his other life. I won't. There are some things it's better not to hear.

I can no longer listen to Bowie. How shit is that? I blame both you and Nicolas.

[Your message to NB26@zone.com has been blocked. Recipient address rejected: Access denied]

From: Bee1984@gmail.com
To: NB26@zone.com
Subject: Is There Life on Mars?

The world has opened up. For now, anyway.

Nicolas and I are meeting next week at the train station. King's Cross, not Euston. I don't know how it will go. I wonder if I'll ever see him properly without your shadow behind him.

Whatever happens, I'm going to give him my side of the story. He deserves to know everything. The truth for once. I hope I get the chance to do that, at least.

[Your message to NB26@zone.com has been blocked. Recipient address rejected: Access denied]

Transcript of the minutes of the Berenstain Society, Livestock Road, Manchester, 01/07/2020

Secretary: Kelvin Oduah.
Chairperson: Henrietta Mueck.
Also present: Geoffrey Gleeson, Debbie Gough, Isaac French, and Adil Singh.

Henrietta Mueck suggested we dispense with the usual reading of the mission statement in favour of discussing the reason why I (Kelvin Oduah) had called this emergency meeting.

I suggested that Geoffrey Gleeson take the floor, considering that it was he who had obtained the information that both he and I had agreed was imperative to share.

Isaac French expressed some consternation about this suggestion. Geoffrey responded by telling Isaac to 'Shut the [expletive] up you inner-circle [expletive] and listen for once in your [expletive] life.'

Isaac complied.

Geoffrey said he had information regarding Nicolas Belcher and had obtained a police report concerning the matter which he offered to read to the group and which I have included below:

> At 19.29 hours 30 June, after receiving a report of a serious assault in progress at The Bergs, Syndol Lane, Orpington, officers PC Shawna Ellis and PC Sindiwe Lem responded to the scene. The owner of the property, Ms Erika Berg, who was in some distress, relayed to the officers that her husband, Mr Petrus Humar, had assaulted one of her lodgers, Mr Nicolas Belcher, in the room Mr Belcher occupied on the third floor of the premises. Ms Berg also informed the officers that Mr Humar was currently in the lounge and

> assured officers that there were no weapons on the premises and, in her opinion, that Mr Humar would not pose a risk to the officers' safety as he 'has got it out of his system and is crying his eyes out'. Ms Berg said she did not know the condition of Mr Belcher. While PC Ellis went to ascertain Mr Belcher's whereabouts and condition, PC Lem, who is Level 4 Mental Health Assessment Trained, approached Mr Humar, with the intent to arrest him for possible grievous bodily harm and to assess if he required medical attention. Mr Humar, who is employed in the private security sector, complied with PC Lem's instructions and expressed remorse for assaulting Mr Belcher. He informed PC Lem that after a verbal altercation with his wife regarding his intention to extend a work contract for another year, she had revealed that on one occasion, she and Mr Belcher had engaged in sexual intercourse. This had enraged him, and he had subsequently confronted Mr Belcher. Having ascertained that the injuries Mr Belcher had suffered were serious and life-threatening, PC Ellis requested that paramedics respond to the scene and performed CPR on the victim.

Geoffrey concluded by saying that Nicolas Belcher was currently in ICU and that his ex-wife and stepson, who are listed as his next of kin, are under pressure to turn off his life support.

Henrietta suggested we take a brief break as Debbie Gough and Adil Singh were both visibly upset by this news.

When we reconvened, Henrietta suggested that we vote on how best to commemorate Nicolas Belcher seeing as although he was not an active member of the society, he was aligned with us. Geoffrey responded by saying 'he's not [expletive] dead yet you heartless [expletive]'.

Isaac suggested we 'have a whip-around' in order to purchase flowers for Nicolas Belcher's hospital room to show our support. Geoffrey and I offered to visit Nicolas in order to deliver them. The meeting was then concluded.

messages **NicolasB** ✆

Hey Nicolas. I'm here. At the station.
Standing outside the WHSmith.
You running late?

12.05PM

Or maybe you've changed your mind. If you have, I don't blame you. Just let me know. And feel free to be as brutal as you like about it.

12.07PM

Train a bit delayed. Just getting in now. On my way.

12.07PM

I'm in a red coat. I cut my hair BTW. Did it myself with the nail scissors. It looks really shit. 😱

12.08PM

I'm pretty sure I'll recognize you, Bee. It hasn't been THAT long.

12.08PM

I know. Sorry. Nervous.

12.09PM

ETA + - 2 minutes.

12.09PM

Thanks. Will look out for you

12.09PM

Still can't see you. It's face-mask central here.

12.15PM

Well, I can see you. I'm heading your way. See me now? Tall guy? On his phone? Rainbow face-mask? Tweed suit?

12.15PM

ACKNOWLEDGEMENTS

This book would not exist without the kindness, feedback, and support of the following people, all of whom have my undying gratitude and deserve more than just a name-check on an acknowledgements page (I like to think there's an alternative reality out there where I thank you all properly by buying you each a robot butler): Nigel Walters, Gemma King, Si Walters, Paul Meloy, Carol Walters, Alan Walters, Jason Arnopp, Mack Lundy, Sarah Holtshausen, Paige Nick, Lauren Beukes, Kate Sinclair, Pagy Wicks, Naomi Wicks, Nic Carlean, Suzette Carlean, Tom C. Stein, Tiah Beautement and Alan Kelly.

Huge thanks and hypothetical robot butlers are also due to agent extraordinaire Oli Munson and all at A.M. Heath; Conrad Williams and all at Blake Friedmann; Steve Fisher and all at APA; and to the insanely cool and creative team at HarperCollins: Ellie Game, Jaime Witcomb, Fleur Clarke, Grace Dent, Isabel Coburn, Sarah Munro and Alice Gomer.

Charlotte Brabbin, Miranda Hill and Helen Moffett caught me when I fell, kicked me into touch, hauled me out of plot holes, and helped keep the cliches to a minimum (except – clearly – on this page, where they left me up to my own devices). Thank you for your multiple kindnesses, all round editorial brilliance, and boundless patience (for that you're getting robot butlers and kittens that can talk).

And last but not least, to Savannah Lotz and Charlie Martins, who, as always, beta read ad nauseum and endured countless nocturnal brainstorming sessions (the best bits are all yours, Sav). Thank you for being there. In this world and others, it's impossible to imagine a life without you.

ABOUT THE AUTHOR

Sarah Lotz is a screenwriter and award-winning novelist whose previous work has been translated into over twenty languages. She lives on the Welsh borders with her family and far too many rescue dogs.